D0594831

NANCY DREW FILES VOL. II

Don't miss more mystery:

Nancy Drew Files Vol. 1

NANCY DREW FILES

VOL. II

Smile and Say Murder
Hit and Run Holiday
White Water Terror

CAROLYN KEENE

SIMON PULSE

NEW YORK LONDON TORONTO SYDNEY NEW DELHI

This book is a work of fiction. Any references to historical events, real people, or real places are used fictitiously. Other names, characters, places, and events are products of the author's imagination, and any resemblance to actual events or places or persons, living or dead, is entirely coincidental.

SIMON PULSE
An imprint of Simon & Schuster Children's Publishing Division
1230 Avenue of the Americas, New York, New York 10020
This Simon Pulse paperback edition September 2019
Smile and Say Murder copyright © 1986 by Simon & Schuster, Inc.
Hit and Run Holiday copyright © 1986 by Simon & Schuster, Inc.
White Water Terror copyright © 1986 by Simon & Schuster, Inc.
Produced individually in 1986 by Mega-Books of New York, Inc.
Published separately in 1986 by Pocket, an imprint of Simon & Schuster, Inc.
Cover illustration copyright © 2019 by Fernanda Suarez
All rights reserved, including the right of reproduction in whole or in part in any form.
SIMON PULSE and colophon are registered trademarks of Simon & Schuster, Inc.
NANCY DREW, AN ARCHWAY PAPERBACK and colophon are registered trademarks of Simon & Schuster, Inc.
THE NANCY DREW FILES is a trademark of Simon & Schuster, Inc.
For information about special discounts for bulk purchases, please contact Simon & Schuster Special Sales at 1-866-506-1949 or business@simonandschuster.com.
The Simon & Schuster Speakers Bureau can bring authors to your live event. For more information or to book an event contact the Simon & Schuster Speakers Bureau at 1-866-248-3049 or visit our website at www.simonspeakers.com.
Cover designed by Sarah Creech
Interior designed by Hilary Zarycky
The text of this book was set in Electra LT Std.
Manufactured in the United States of America
2 4 6 8 10 9 7 5 3 1
Library of Congress Control Number 2019944224
ISBN 9781534463158 (pbk)
ISBN 9781481414487 (*Smile and Say Murder* eBook)
ISBN 9781481414494 (*Hit and Run Holiday* eBook)
ISBN 9781481414500 (*White Water Terror* eBook)
These titles were previously published individually.

CONTENTS

SMILE AND
SAY MURDER

CHAPTER ONE

Nancy Drew sank back into the cushioned seat of the commuter train that traveled between River Heights and Chicago and pulled a glossy new magazine out of her shoulder bag. The star of the hottest new TV show smiled sexily at her from the cover. Above his head, in bold pink letters, was the word *FLASH*.

Nancy opened the magazine and skimmed articles about a sixteen-year-old ballet star in Atlanta, a fashion show fundraiser at glitzy Hollywood High School, and a college freshman in Nevada who'd discovered a cure for acne. Without a doubt, Nancy told herself, *Flash* magazine is a winner. No wonder kids all over the country were snatching it up the second it was out on the newsstands.

Nancy had been meaning to pick up a copy for a few weeks, ever since one of her best friends, Bess Marvin, had started raving about it. At the moment, though, Nancy wasn't just trying to pass a boring ride from the suburbs into the city. She was doing research on a new mystery, a mystery that was bound to take her on a flashy adventure.

Urgent—that was how *Flash* magazine's publisher and

coowner had described the situation to Nancy on the phone the other night. And it wasn't slipping sales figures that had Yvonne Verdi worried. Someone had been sending her threatening letters—ugly ones.

Nancy closed the magazine and stared out the train window as suburb melted into suburb. It would have been nicer to drive into the city, but she knew finding a parking space would be completely hopeless. If I decide to take the case, she told herself, I'd better get used to being a commuter. I'm going to have to make the trip every morning, and Dad is against the idea of my driving in all that city traffic.

Nancy's mother had died when Nancy was just a child. So for most of her eighteen years it had been just her and her father, Carson Drew, a highly successful lawyer. Nancy figured she and her father had to take care of each other—with a little help from Hannah Gruen, the Drews' loving housekeeper. Nancy hated to hassle with her father. She figured the best way to avoid that was to leave her blue Mustang at home for the time being.

Nancy's thoughts returned to the new case. It made her heart pound with excitement. Even if the letters turned out to be just some creep's idea of a prank, she'd get a chance to see the inner workings of the number-one teen magazine. Of course, there was always the chance that the threats were serious.

Either way, Nancy felt sure she was prepared. With dozens of difficult and successfully solved mysteries behind her, she'd seen through the most carefully constructed criminal plots, and she was ready to do it all over again.

Nancy crossed her legs and ran her hand through her red-dish blond, shoulder-length hair. Starting a case was like running a cross-country race. You knew that once the gun went off, you had to reach the finish line before the other guy, but you weren't quite sure how you were going to get there. That meant you had to be especially alert and observant, or you'd end up following a lot of dead-end trails.

Nancy's keen blue eyes gazed resolutely at the handsome face of the star on the *Flash* cover. "Whatever secrets you're trying to hide," she said to the magazine, "they're not going to stay secret for long."

As the train pulled into Chicago's main terminal, Nancy stood up, straightened her blue angora sweater dress, and grabbed her gray jacket and shoulder bag from the seat. She hurried outside and found a taxi. Twenty minutes later, she was standing in front of the *Flash* offices on Michigan Avenue. Here goes, she thought. She took a deep breath and stepped into the building.

Nancy waited for the elevator with a businessman and two bicycle messengers. When the doors opened, two casually dressed women walked out.

"Really, Yvonne is pushing me too far," one of the women was saying. "I don't care if she *is* the coowner of the magazine. If she makes one more comment to me about 'proper office clothes' I'm going to . . . well, I don't know what, but I'm going to do something."

"She's definitely annoying," the other woman replied. "But

don't take it personally. She bugs everyone, not just you."

Nancy listened with interest. Clearly, the women were discussing *Flash*'s coowner—and they weren't too fond of her.

Nancy stepped into the elevator and pressed the button for the sixteenth floor. The doors opened onto *Flash*'s reception area, a large, spacious room decorated in a style Nancy liked to call super-tech. Sparse but tasteful, and very, very expensive. Huge glass windows gave a perfect view of Lake Michigan, and a brightly colored painting hung on one wall. Two long hallways, one pale blue, the other cream, led in opposite directions.

Nancy walked up to the young man behind the reception desk. He was playing a game on the computer. "Hold on," he said without looking up. "I just have to get this last clone." He played intently for another thirty seconds. "Got him!" he cried. "Okay, who are you and what can I do for you?" he asked, finally paying attention to Nancy.

"My name's Nancy Drew. I'm here to see Yvonne Verdi."

"Ah, the queen clone herself. If only it were as easy as a game." The receptionist sighed. "She's expecting you. Her office is down that hall and on the left." He pointed to the cream-colored hallway.

Nancy smiled and headed in the direction he had pointed, filing away another bit of information. Already she had the feeling that Yvonne wasn't too well liked around *Flash*.

Nancy found Yvonne's office and knocked. "Come in," called a voice. Nancy opened the door and stepped in. "Nancy

Drew," the woman behind the desk said as she got to her feet. "Welcome to *Flash!*" She extended her hand to Nancy.

At five feet eight inches, Yvonne Verdi was only slightly taller than Nancy, but her imposing presence made Nancy feel almost small. She was one of those young business people who obviously had it all. Nancy decided she couldn't be more than twenty-seven years old. In her stylish skirt and jacket, with her black hair swept into a French knot and her dark eyes flashing, she didn't seem like a woman anyone would want to mess around with. The writer of the letters was either very tough or very bold to be threatening Yvonne Verdi.

"Glad to meet you, Ms. Verdi," Nancy said, shaking the publisher's hand.

"Call me Yvonne," the publisher replied. "We go by first names around here. Please, have a seat." She gestured to a cushy black leather couch, and Nancy sank comfortably into it. "Okay, let's get down to business." Yvonne pulled two envelopes out of a desk drawer and sat down herself. "These are the reasons I called you here today."

Nancy smiled sympathetically. "Threatening letters can be very upsetting," she said, "but they're not always serious. Sometimes the writers only mean to scare their—"

"Oh, but these particular letters *are* serious," Yvonne cut in. "Nancy, someone's trying to kill me!"

Nancy studied Yvonne's face. It was hard to tell what she was feeling. "Why are you so sure of that?" she asked.

"Because I know who's trying to do it!" Yvonne threw the

letters down on her desk for emphasis. "It's Mick, Mick Swanson. He's the other owner of *Flash*—our art director and main photographer!"

"Your partner!" Nancy exclaimed.

"Yes." Yvonne patted a stray black hair calmly into place. "But," she hastened to add, "it's not his fault. He can't help himself. You see, I think Mick is under too much pressure. He's never been very stable, and right now, the pressure of *Flash*'s success is getting to him."

"How do you know he's going over the edge?" Nancy asked.

"Mick and I are old friends," Yvonne explained. "I can tell when he's starting to flip out. In fact, our friendship is the very reason I called you instead of the police. I care about Mick a lot, and I want this thing handled delicately. I don't want any embarrassments—not for Mick and not for *Flash*."

"But why is he threatening you?" Nancy asked.

Yvonne sighed. "To tell the truth, Mick and I have been . . . disagreeing a lot lately. Actually, we've been fighting," she admitted. "It hasn't quite come to out-and-out punching, but almost."

"I see," Nancy said. "Well, then, why now? I mean, why is Mick getting vicious all of a sudden? Has something changed for him recently?"

"Yes!" Yvonne answered, her dark eyes gleaming. "Not just for Mick but for all of us here at *Flash*. Our sales figures are skyrocketing, and that's attracted quite a bit of attention, primarily from MediaCorp, the international news syndicate."

"They want to buy you out?" Nancy asked.

"They've offered us ten million dollars."

"Are you going to accept it?" Nancy leaned forward in her seat, waiting for the answer.

Yvonne's expression remained impassive. "No way," she said. "*Flash* is my baby. I gave up a writing career for this magazine. I'm not ready to get rid of it yet, not even for a whole lot of money."

Nancy was surprised. This was an emotional side of Yvonne she hadn't figured on. "Then it's Mick who wants to sell," Nancy surmised. "That's why he's been threatening you."

"Not threatening, *trying* to kill me," Yvonne insisted. "But no, Detective Drew," she said with a smile, "I'm afraid you've deduced wrong this time. Mick doesn't want to sell either. But somehow, he's gotten the idea that I do! That's the wild part. Now he's willing to do anything to stop me from selling—even though I don't intend to!"

Nancy felt uncomfortable. She didn't like the way Yvonne seemed to be getting a kick out of her wrong deduction. But good detectives never let emotions distract them when they were looking for clues. Keeping her feelings to herself, Nancy said simply, "That's pretty complicated." She reached across Yvonne's desk to take the letters. "May I—"

"Oh, please, go ahead," Yvonne said, interrupting Nancy.

Nancy picked up the two envelopes. She slipped the first letter out and looked it over carefully. There was no doubt about it—it was frightening.

The letter included a photo. The picture was a still from a horror movie. It showed a brutal-looking man with an ax about to attack some poor woman. But the sender of the letter had replaced the face of the movie actress with Yvonne's own picture. There was a note, too.

> *Yvonne,*
> *You're mistaken if you think I'm joking. Unless*
> *you change your mind about the deal, you're*
> *not going to have one to change. There won't*
> *be anything you can do to stop me. So just sit*
> *back and wait for the pain. It's only a matter*
> *of time. . . .*
> *The Grim Reaper*

CHAPTER TWO

Nancy reread the chilling note. "Pretty gruesome stuff," she said. No wonder Yvonne was so upset.

She turned her attention to the second letter. Immediately, she recognized the words from a song that's been playing everywhere for the past few months.

> *So you think the evening's pretty*
> *Hey, but you don't know this city*
> *There's always someone hiding in the night*
> *Looking for a victim or a fight*
> *Hiding round the corner out of sight*
>
> *And that guy will getcha*
> *He'll getcha, he'll getcha*
> *Don't you know he'll getcha . . . soon?*

A letter was attached to the lyrics.

> *Yvonne,*
> *You've made a bad choice, one you're going*

to regret. Tell the people you've been doing
business with that you won't sell—or else pay
the consequences!
    Your mystery friend, The Grim Reaper

Nancy took another careful look at the two letters, which, by the looks of it, had come from a printer running low on ink. The words were faint in places, and smudged. She made a mental note to check some of the printers in the office. Still, if someone had changed the ink cartridge, it would be impossible to trace them to one particular machine or another. The notes could also have been printed elsewhere. There was a good chance that checking the printers would lead nowhere.

"Now do you see why I think Mick's serious about these threats?" Yvonne said earnestly, her dark eyes catching Nancy's blue ones urgently. "I mean, you have to be pretty crazy just to think up stuff that sick. I need help, Nancy, and I hope you're the person to give it to me!" Suddenly Yvonne looked very tired.

Nancy smiled supportively. Obviously, Yvonne was in a terrible situation. Nancy handed the letters back. "I'd like to get these copied," she said.

As she dropped the envelopes onto the desk, she knocked a thin paperback novel to the floor. Leaning down to pick it up, she recognized the title. It was a recent detective novel Nancy herself had enjoyed reading. "Hey," she said, "this is a great book. Are you a mystery fan, too?"

"Oh, *that*," Yvonne said with disdain. "Someone gave it to

me the other day, but I can't stand detective stories. They're so predictable."

It was an innocent enough comment, but Nancy picked up a valuable clue from it. She realized that Yvonne liked to make herself seem more mature, more sophisticated, and more intelligent than the people she was around. She was a woman who liked to have the upper hand in her relationships.

Yvonne returned the letters to her desk drawer. "Well, how about it, Nancy?" she asked. "Will you take the case?"

Nancy paused for a moment, thinking. "If I do," she said at last, "I'll need a cov—"

"Of course, you'll need a cover," the publisher broke in. "And I've thought of the perfect one. I'll set you up as an intern. We always need an extra hand around here."

"That might work," Nancy said.

"Sure it will. Do you know anything about photography and camera equipment?"

"Yes," Nancy replied, "I took a summer course last—"

"Great! Then you'll do it?" Yvonne interrupted.

Nancy gave Yvonne a long, appraising look. Throughout their conversation, the publisher had been perfectly polite, but she was always interrupting, as if what she had to say were more important than anything Nancy had to say. And she masked her feelings. Somehow, Nancy didn't trust her.

Still, Nancy told herself, if she really is in danger, she needs me. She flashed the publisher a brilliant smile. "Yes, I'll do it," she said.

"Great!" Yvonne replied.

Nancy leaned back against the black leather couch. "There are still some things I need to know," she told Yvonne. "Background information about you, the magazine, Mick, anyone else who might be involved, too."

"Ask anything you want," Yvonne said.

"Well, can you give me some idea of your past? What have you been doing for the last few years? Who have you been spending your time with?"

Yvonne told Nancy that she'd graduated five years earlier from a small private college. She'd majored in creative writing and, as she'd mentioned before, she'd spent a few years as a novelist before coming up with the idea for *Flash*. She'd given up everything to get the magazine started, and it was finally paying off in record sales figures.

"What about Mick?" Nancy asked. "How did he get involved with *Flash*?"

"I'd met Mick when he was still in art school," Yvonne explained. "I was friends with his roommate at the time. Anyway, he was studying painting—you know, symbolic impressionism and all that. He hadn't gotten into commercial art yet. He was just an idealistic kid. I had to teach him everything," Yvonne went on condescendingly.

"I see," Nancy said drily.

"After Mick got out of college, he went through a hard time. He was emotionally unstable, didn't know what he wanted to do with his life other than paint. Since he was enormously talented, I asked him to join me when I started *Flash*. I thought the work would straighten him out a little," she told Nancy. "I guess I was wrong."

Yvonne gave Nancy a brief history of *Flash* magazine and a rundown on a few of the people who worked there. She said she'd met the current editor in chief, David Bowers, at a party. She'd stolen him away from the prestigious publication he'd been working for at the time. And she'd been dating him since he'd come to work at *Flash* four months ago.

Yvonne said many of the others who worked on the magazine were talented young people on their way up or college students hired as interns. "We like to give new talent a chance," she explained, adding that many of the key positions at the magazine were held by people who had little practical experience but a great commitment to trying out daring creative ideas. Yvonne claimed this was what made *Flash* so successful.

Nancy didn't learn anything more that seemed important, but she'd already found out a lot. She had the feeling that whatever happened, the case was not going to be boring.

"Well," Yvonne said, "how about if I introduce you to your number-one suspect? Mick needs to meet you, too, if I'm going to hire you as an intern."

"I'm ready," Nancy replied, smiling and stretching her legs for a moment.

Yvonne picked up the telephone and pushed a button on the intercom that buzzed Mick's office. "Could you come in here," she said brusquely. There was a pause. "No, it can't wait." She hung up the phone abruptly.

In a few moments, there was a knock on the door, and Mick walked into Yvonne's office. He was tall, blond, good-looking, about twenty-six years old, and very wild. He was wearing a leopard-print jacket, tight black jeans, and black cowboy boots. And I wondered if this sweater dress would be too casual, Nancy thought, hiding a smile.

Mick had finely chiseled features and high cheekbones. In fact, his face would have been perfect if not for his sullen, angry expression.

"All right, Verdi. What's so urgent?" Mick demanded, glaring at Yvonne. "You interrupted me in the middle of something important."

Yvonne glared right back. "Well, this is important, too, Mick," she said.

"I hope so," Mick retorted, "because I don't like being ordered away from my work for nothing."

Yvonne gave a little laugh, as if she could brush off the seriousness of Mick's comments with it. "I asked you in here because I'd like you to meet Nancy Drew, *Flash*'s newest intern — and your new assistant."

Nancy stared at Yvonne in surprise. Yvonne hadn't said anything about being Mick's assistant. Why had she chosen that moment to spring the development on Nancy? Or, for that matter, on Mick? Nancy had never heard of one partner hiring an assistant for another. But the important thing was how Mick was going to react to it. Nancy turned her attention to the art director.

Mick swiveled his cold blue gaze toward Nancy. Suddenly she felt like a lobster in a restaurant fish tank. The art director looked as if he were about to eat her and spit out the shell. There was a moment of deadly silence. Then Mick exploded. "*You hired an assistant for me?* Yvonne, what kind of game are you playing? If I *need* an assistant, I'll hire one myself!"

"Mick," Yvonne cut in smoothly, "you work awfully hard. I was just trying to do something nice for you."

Nancy sucked in her breath. It looked as if Yvonne and Mick were really into fighting dirty. She could tell that a lot of insults were about to get thrown around.

"Your concern is less than touching," Mick said coldly.

"So is your appreciation, dear. Why don't you just say thank you instead of acting like a spoiled adolescent on an ego trip?"

Nancy glanced at Mick. His handsome face was undergoing an odd transformation, as if he'd lost some kind of inner control. "Yvonne," he said tightly, "you're begging for a fight. And how could I let my dear old partner down? You asked for it. Well, *you're going to get it!*"

Looking Yvonne straight in the eyes, he reached over and picked up a vase on her desk. In one convulsive movement, he crashed the heavy crystal down in front of her, shattering it.

"If you're gonna play games with me," he growled, "get ready to lose—to lose *everything*."

CHAPTER THREE

Nancy stared down at the broken glass which littered Yvonne's carpet, then rested her gaze on the red-faced, trembling Mick. Wow, she thought, he really *is* dangerous! His anger was truly frightening. Without another word, Mick turned on his heel and strode out of Yvonne's office.

For a moment, the publisher stared blankly at the smashed crystal. Nancy almost thought she was going to break down and cry. But then a look of gloating satisfaction stole across Yvonne's face. "You see?" she said. "He doesn't have a hold on himself. Half the time I have the feeling he's about to throw *me* across the room like that."

"That was quite a display of anger," Nancy agreed cautiously. She picked up a piece of glass and studied it, thinking. It certainly looked as though Yvonne were in danger. But what about Nancy herself? It seemed to her that Mick could easily turn his fury on anybody who was near him. And since Yvonne had so thoughtfully made Nancy his assistant, she was going to be near him quite a bit.

But there was something else. Mick's anger hadn't been unprovoked. Yvonne had goaded him into it. And the nasty comments had come as much from Yvonne as from Mick. The case was complicated, more complicated than Yvonne was making it seem.

"I'd like to make a phone call," Nancy finally said.

"Oh, please, use my telephone," Yvonne offered.

"Uh, no," Nancy replied, trying to think up an excuse quickly. It was never a good idea to talk about a case in front of anyone who was involved—even the person who'd hired you. "You need to clean up here," she said. "I'll use another phone." Nancy got to her feet and scooped her bag off the couch.

"Okay," Yvonne answered. "Mick's going to be starting a photo session pretty soon. We're doing an article on Danielle Artman—you know, the lead singer from that new all-girl rock band, Spiders of Power?"

"Hey, great!" Nancy said enthusiastically, suddenly remembering that *Flash* had a lot more to offer than just the promise of an interesting mystery. "Their single's terrific."

"Well, as Mick's assistant, and as a detective gathering information about a man set on murder, you should be there. So why don't you wait for Mick in the photo studio when you're done with your call?"

"Okay," Nancy agreed.

"And make sure you check in with me often so we can talk about the case." Yvonne began picking up the larger pieces of broken glass.

Nancy hurried out of the office. She rushed past the receptionist and caught the elevator to the ground floor. She found a pay phone and dialed Ned Nickerson's number.

Ned's going to be really upset, she told herself. Still, she couldn't help smiling at the thought of her handsome, long-time boyfriend. Ned was too much in love with her to stay mad for more than a few minutes. No doubt about it, she was lucky to have such an understanding guy.

The phone rang twice before Nancy heard Ned say, "Hello."

"Ned, it's me. And you'll never guess what's up," Nancy said excitedly into the receiver.

"Wait, don't tell me. You're on to another mystery."

"Yes! How did you guess? This time, it looks really serious—maybe even dangerous. I might need your help." Quickly she recapped the scene in Yvonne's office.

"Nancy," Ned said testily once she had finished, "what about our trip with my parents up to the cabin at the lake? Did you forget all about that?"

"No, of course not," Nancy answered quickly, toying nervously with the cord of the telephone, "but we've got to call that off. We'll go some other time, Ned, I promise."

"Nancy!" Ned sighed with exasperation. "If I had a nickel for every time you've said something like that to me, I could retire right now, a wealthy man."

Nancy was quiet for a moment. It was true, she'd disappointed Ned before. But could she help that she'd rather be working on a mystery than doing just about anything else?

Ned broke the silence. "How important is this, Nancy?"

Nancy sighed. "It's very important. I don't think I could pass it up, Ned. Yvonne's life might be on the line."

"I think I'm having déjà vu," Ned moaned. "Last time we were supposed to go up to the cabin, you had to cancel because of some mystery. Now it's happening all over again!"

Nancy tapped her fingers impatiently on the telephone. "But, Ned," she said, "you weren't with me in that office. This guy Mick practically turned green with anger. He's *definitely* violent. If I don't deal with the situation, Yvonne might end up dead!"

But Ned wasn't buying Nancy's argument. "Tell me the truth," he said. "Didn't you tell Yvonne you'd take the case *before* Mick flipped out? When it looked as if it was just a matter of a few nasty letters — nothing too serious?"

Nancy coughed, embarrassed. Ned's been hanging around me too long, she decided. He's becoming a pretty good detective himself. "Okay, you're right," she muttered. "But," she rushed on, "that doesn't change the fact that Yvonne needs me badly."

Ned sighed again. "Right, Nancy. Everybody needs you. I just wish you'd realize that I do, too."

"I know that, silly," Nancy said lightly. "And I hope you know how much I love you. And need you, too. Like right now, with this mystery."

"Well," said Ned, hedging, "what have you got in mind?"

"If Mick is going to continue to get violent, I might need some physical protection. A strong, handsome quarterback would be just perfect." Nancy smiled. A little flattery couldn't hurt.

"I don't know. It's not exactly what I had planned for spring break. When I leave Emerson College I really like to get away. I mean, given the choice between hanging around at some magazine office or swimming and sunning with you—"

Nancy frowned. Ned was really holding out. She knew he'd give in in the end (he loved her too much not to), but she hadn't expected to have to work so hard for a simple yes.

"Oh, Ned, say you'll do it." Nancy had run out of arguments. "You're always an incredible help on these cases. I really mean that."

"I don't know why I let you drag me into these things," Ned muttered.

"I love you, Ned. And thanks a lot!" Nancy cried. "You're the best." She threw her boyfriend an over-the-phone kiss and hung up. Good old Ned. He never let her down.

Nancy took the elevator back to the sixteenth floor. The same guy was sitting at the reception desk, still playing a game. "Hi," Nancy said.

"Hi. How's it going? I heard a big crash in Yvonne's office."

"Why didn't you go find out what happened?" Nancy asked curiously. "Someone could have been in trouble."

"Lately," the young man explained, "there's been a lot of yelling coming from Yvonne's and Mick's offices. Mostly when they're alone together. We try not to notice it anymore. As long as they keep their fighting between themselves, none of us really cares."

"I see," Nancy answered.

"So who are you?" the receptionist asked.

Nancy smiled and rolled her eyes, having just introduced herself when she first arrived. "I'm Nancy Drew. Yvonne just hired me as an intern. I'm going to be helping Mick out."

"I'm an intern, too," the young man said, shaking Nancy's hand. "Yvonne likes to hire us because she can give us Mickey Mouse-sized paychecks and make us work like dogs."

Hmmm, Nancy thought. That sure wasn't the way Yvonne had described it. "By the way," the receptionist said, "my name's Scott."

"Nice to meet you. Listen, Yvonne told me to wait for Mick in the studio. Which way is it?"

"All the way at the end of the blue hall. Most of the offices are in that direction. Only Yvonne's and Mick's offices are down the other one."

"Okay. Thanks." Nancy turned down the blue hallway. Ahead of her, she noticed a woman in a tight red dress, walking with a slight swing to her hips. Somehow, she looked familiar to Nancy. The long black hair. And the way she strutted along . . . Oh no, Nancy realized in a flash. It's Brenda Carlton.

Brenda was an amateur reporter who'd gotten in Nancy's way before, practically ruining cases for her on a few occasions. And she was always turning up in the worst places. What's *she* doing here? Nancy wondered. All she needed was blabbermouth Brenda hanging around, blowing her cover and messing with her mystery. What a headache! Impulsively Nancy made a face at Brenda's retreating back.

At least Brenda hadn't seen her—yet. Nancy planned to do her best to keep it that way. She didn't want Brenda ruining things for her before they even got off the ground.

"Hey," Nancy heard someone call from behind her. "Hey, Brenda." Uh-oh, Nancy thought. She's going to turn around. I've got to get out of here!

Nancy looked desperately for a hiding place, but saw only long blue walls and closed office doors. Great. Terrific. Brenda's going to see me—and then I might as well kiss this case goodbye.

CHAPTER FOUR

Nancy did the only possible thing. She dashed through the nearest door, went flying into the room beyond, and slammed the door closed behind her. Panting heavily, she raised her eyes to see whom she'd just barged in on. A dark-haired man, about thirty years old, with steely gray eyes, was staring at her angrily.

"All right, who are you and what are you doing in my office?"

"Um, I . . ." Nancy tried desperately to come up with a believable excuse. "I was looking for the studio," she said lamely.

"Well, my dear," the man said sarcastically, "that would be through the double doors at the end of the hall, the ones under the big sign that says Studio."

"Oh," Nancy said.

"What's your name?" the man demanded.

Nancy bit her lip. This was a great way to get a reputation as the bumbling intern around the office. "I'm the new intern, Nancy Drew," she mumbled, trying to smile.

"And *I* am David Bowers," said the man. "I'm the editor in chief of *Flash*. This is my office. And if I catch you coming in here again without knocking first, you're going to be very sorry. Understand?"

Nancy nodded.

"Good." David Bowers turned back to the stack of papers on his desk.

Nancy ducked out of the office quickly. Luckily, Brenda was nowhere in sight.

"Whew," Nancy breathed. So that was Yvonne's boyfriend! What a creep! Of course, she'd acted like a real space cadet, and that wasn't his fault. Still, he could have been a *little* nicer.

It was funny, but David Bowers looked oddly familiar to Nancy. She shook her head. He probably just reminded her of someone she'd met before. However, one thing was becoming painfully obvious to Nancy. With all the bad-tempered people who worked at *Flash*, the case, although exciting, was not going to be pleasant.

Nancy hurried down the hall and pushed open the double doors. The studio was a huge, windowless room. Seamless white paper hung from the ceiling as a backdrop for the photos. Several people were busy setting up cameras, lights, and props for the session. Nancy recognized Scott, the receptionist, struggling with some lighting filters.

A pretty blond girl with delicate features was hanging red and black rubber spiders from strings attached to the backdrop. She looked about eighteen.

Turning, the girl saw Nancy and smiled warmly. "Gross, aren't they?" she said with a laugh. "They're in honor of Danielle Artman's band, the Spiders of Power."

"I don't know, they're kind of cute," Nancy joked. "By the

way, I'm the new intern, Nancy Drew. I'm supposed to wait here for Mick."

The girl's smile faded. "Oh," she said shortly. "Well, he'll be here soon enough. Why don't you go sit over there"—the girl motioned vaguely—"and wait."

"Can't I help you hang your crawly friends?" Nancy asked.

"I'm doing just fine by myself," the girl replied.

Wow, Nancy thought, do I suddenly have leprosy or something? She moved away from the girl and settled herself cross-legged on the floor. Nancy was beginning to be thankful the job was only temporary.

After a little while, Scott noticed Nancy sitting alone and came over. "Hey, what's happening?"

"Not much. Scott, who's that?" She indicated the yellow-haired girl.

"That's Sondra Swanson, Mick's sister. She's *Flash*'s stylist. You know, gets celebs ready for shoots, coordinates clothes and prop colors, stuff like that. She does a pretty good job, too. Why?"

"I don't know," Nancy said. "She seemed really friendly when I came in, but as soon as I told her my name, she clammed up."

"That's because she thinks you're a spy," Scott said matter-of-factly.

"A spy!" Nancy cried.

"Yeah. She was just complaining about you. She says she knows exactly how long the waiting list for interns is and that Nancy Drew wasn't next up for a job at *Flash*. In fact, she feels the magazine doesn't even need a new intern right now. So she's decided that Yvonne set you up to spy on her brother. It's really the only logical conclusion."

"Oh, great," Nancy said with a groan. "And what do you think?"

Scott smiled sheepishly. "I think it's a distinct possibility. But," he added quickly, "I don't care. You seem nice, and I'm not getting involved in *Flash* Wars."

Nancy sighed. In a way, it was true. Yvonne really had hired her to spy on Mick. "Thanks for the vote of confidence, Scott. Tell me something else. Do you know who Brenda Carlton is?"

"Sure. She's a freelance reporter."

"What's she doing at *Flash*?"

"Writing an article on some swimmer who's been tearing it up at high-school meets around the country lately. I think he's a cousin of hers or something."

Nancy scowled. It figured. As usual, Brenda was getting work because of who she knew, not how good a reporter she was. And also as usual, she was sure to get in Nancy's way, probably at the most crucial point in the case.

At that moment, Mick came in. He was talking to a short, curvy girl with shiny brown hair and laughing hazel eyes. Nancy recognized Danielle Artman. She was wearing skintight red pants with a pattern of black spiders on them. "Hey, cool!" she exclaimed. "Your spiders match mine!"

"Sure, that's how I planned it," Sondra said, approaching Danielle with a charming smile.

"Yuck," Mick shuddered. "Sondra, this is by far the most disgusting idea you've ever had for a shoot."

"Don't be scared, brother dear," Sondra teased. "They won't bite." Playfully, she threw a rubber spider at Mick. "He's the world's biggest practical joker," she told Danielle, "but he freaks out over spiders, even fake ones."

Mick batted the bug away. "Disgusting," he repeated with another shudder. He noticed Nancy sitting on the sidelines. "Excuse me, but just because you're Yvonne's latest flunky doesn't mean you can hang around doing nothing," he said. "Help Sondra hang the rest of these spiders so we can start shooting."

Nancy stood up and smiled tentatively, but Sondra just turned her back. Nancy shrugged and got to work.

Behind her, Mick was checking some camera equipment, singing tunelessly as he worked. "I'll getcha, I'll getcha, you know I'm gonna getcha . . . soon."

That's the song used in the threat letter. Nancy thought. So Mick had two strikes against him. First, he was a photographer and could easily have doctored the picture of Yvonne from a still from the horror movie, and second, he was singing the weird song from Yvonne's letter.

Nancy continued hanging spiders. Soon everything was set for the session, and Mick was ready to begin shooting. "Hey," he shouted at Nancy, "get off the seamless."

"Sure," Nancy said, trying to stay calm and collected as she walked over to where the photo equipment had been set up.

She was determined not to show how much Mick's rudeness was getting to her.

"Okay, 'assistant,' I'm going to need you to keep my coffee cup filled and the set pristine," Mick told Nancy. "You *do* know how to do that, don't you? Or did Yvonne just happen to forget to ask you about those particular skills during your 'interview'?"

Mick was glaring at Nancy. "Great. The least I can get out of you is some decent work."

Mick flicked on a speaker and put on music as Danielle took her place against the white backdrop. An old Rolling Stones song came blasting out of the speakers. "Okay, Danielle," Mick cried. "Let's see some spider action!"

He started shooting as Danielle began moving to the pounding bass beat. She jumped, she wiggled.

"More to the left," Mick called, still shooting. "Beautiful, beautiful. Another jump . . ."

Nancy had to admit Mick knew his stuff. It looked as if he were getting some fantastic shots. Danielle was a great subject to photograph, too. She was very energetic and seemed to have no inhibitions in front of the camera.

With so much action, Nancy barely had time to do any detective work, but she did get a chance to talk to one of the other interns during a five-minute break.

Leslie was a tall black girl about Nancy's age. She said that she'd been an intern at *Flash* for almost six months. "It's a great job," Leslie said, "if you can get past the cattiness, backstabbing, and general complaining." She laughed. "Actually, it's not so bad as long as Yvonne stays in her office. She's really awful! Stay clear of her if you can."

"Why is she so terrible?" Nancy asked.

"I think she loves screaming more than anything else in the world. She'll make you do perfectly good work over again for some petty reason. And she's not above nasty personal comments." Leslie made a face. "I mean, I'm willing to put a lot into my job, but my bosses definitely cannot buy me body and soul—not for *this* lousy pay."

Nancy laughed. "How do the other people here feel about her?"

"Oh, about the same, I guess," Leslie answered. "She makes working here real hell. To tell you the truth, I think any one of us would gladly kill that woman if we had the chance."

Nancy caught her breath sharply. You might be more accurate than you know, Leslie, she thought. But she let the comment pass. "I'll try not to let her bother me," she said. "Hey," she added, "I met the editor in chief today."

"Oh, David Bowers. He's another nasty one. He likes pushing people around. He and Yvonne are a perfect pair."

"I thought I'd met him somewhere before," Nancy told the intern. "Do you know anything about him?"

"Yeah—I know he's a big bore. He just came back from two weeks in Rio. And if I hear one more South America story, I'm going to barf." Leslie sighed. "I don't believe that guy. He started working here a few months ago and immediately began trying to impress Yvonne. He had some hot job before he came to *Flash*, but no one knows what it was. He's a mystery man. Where do you think you saw him?"

"I don't know," Nancy said slowly. "I wish I could remember."

"Let me know if you do. I'm dying of curiosity," Leslie said with a smile.

After another hour of nonstop shooting, Mick hit the power button on the speaker. The studio suddenly went silent. "Okay, Danielle, take a break. Everyone else, get those creepy rubber web-makers off the set as fast as possible. I want to photograph Danielle while she's singing, and I've had just about enough of those things."

Nancy, Sondra, Scott, and a few others got to work cutting down the spiders. Meanwhile, Nancy listened in as Mick talked quietly to the young singer. "Tired?" he asked gently.

"Pooped," Danielle admitted.

"You worked hard and well! You're a natural, Danielle. You've got talent—and not only as a musician. Anyway, we're almost done. Push yourself for just a little longer and then you can rest. You deserve it."

Nancy was surprised to see this considerate side of Mick. Until then, he'd been nothing but awful. Well, you never know about people, Nancy told herself.

Once the spiders were down, Mick asked Nancy to bring over Danielle's red guitar. Danielle decided to sing a song she'd written called "Give Me Freedom to Speak and a Nice Warm Bed." Nancy thought she really rocked it, too.

When the final strains of Danielle's guitar had faded, Mick

ordered the others to take down the seamless. "And you, Nancy," he said, "I want you to stash these spiders in the props closet—way in the back, where I won't have to look at them again."

Nancy dutifully picked up the box of spiders. This time she didn't even notice Mick's rude tone. She was too busy trying to figure out where she'd seen David Bowers before. Suddenly it came to her. Her father, being a famous lawyer, was a regular contributor to the *Midwest Law Review*. About five months earlier, Nancy had gone into the magazine's offices with her father. She'd met David there briefly. He'd been editor in chief at the time. No big deal. Except that, if Nancy remembered correctly, the *Midwest Law Review* was owned by none other than MediaCorp!

That seemed like a very important link to Nancy, since the company was presently trying to buy out *Flash* and was causing big problems between Yvonne and Mick because of it. Was David's last job common knowledge? Was he still connected with MediaCorp? This could be a key to the case.

Suddenly Nancy was no longer so sure that Mick was behind the letters. The evidence against him was purely circumstantial. Since the threatening song was on the radio a couple of times every day, it wasn't so strange that Mick should sing it. And Mick wasn't the only photographer on the *Flash* staff. Lots of people could have doctored the movie still. Nancy herself was capable of it. Furthermore, from the way Leslie had talked, just about everyone in the office had a motive.

Nancy headed for the props closet. "Make sure you put those

things *all* the way in the back," Mick called after her.

Nancy opened the closet door and pushed past wacky costumes, designer clothes, and a strange collection of miscellaneous objects that had been used as props for other shoots. But what was that on the floor? Drops of blood?

Nancy moved aside a few dresses—and saw something that made her skin crawl. Sitting on top of an old chest of drawers was a severed head. A finely honed ax was suspended in the air next to it.

As Nancy looked up, the ax began to fall—right toward her face.

CHAPTER FIVE

Nancy stared in horror as the ax fell toward her head. At the very last moment, she jumped out of the way like a race-car driver bailing out before a crash.

The ax hurtled to the floor—and bounced. It was made out of rubber.

Nancy gasped. A queasy mixture of anger, fear, and relief washed over her. She bent down and examined the toy ax. The blade was rubber, but the handle was hard wood. Some practical joke, Nancy thought. If that thing had hit her, the handle could have knocked her out, rubber blade or no rubber blade. She reached up to touch the "severed head" and found that it was an incredibly convincing mask. She picked up the ax and quietly walked out to the studio.

When she appeared, Mick started laughing wildly. "Mick, the remote control whiz kid, strikes again," he joked, oblivious to Nancy's distress. "Simple but brilliant," he bragged. "I rigged a remote control device to the handle of that ax. Then all I had to do was push a button to make it fall." He laughed again and pulled a small control box out of a jacket pocket.

"Hey, Mick," Sondra called to her brother, "what'd you do?

Pull another one of your sick practical jokes? Why don't you cut that junk out already? People get upset by it."

Mick snickered. "Oh, Nancy didn't mind too much, did you, Nancy?" Not waiting for an answer, he continued, "This one was really great, if I may say so myself." He turned to Nancy and gave her a twisted smile.

Self-possessed as always, Nancy didn't show how much Mick's joke had bothered her. But she wondered whether it was a gruesome warning to stay off his tail, or just his way of asserting his power. After all, Nancy told herself, he *is* coowner. Maybe he likes letting the staff know he can do anything he wants around here, anything at all. If so, Mick was treating *Flash* like his personal playroom.

One thing was for sure. Mick's violent side was becoming more and more obvious.

Mick threw Nancy another sharkish grin. Then he turned to the rest of the staff. "Good shoot," he told them. "You all worked hard." He motioned to Danielle to come with him, and together they left the studio.

As soon as her brother was gone, Sondra hurried over to Nancy. "I'm really sorry about that," she said. She seemed sincere, but still a little wary of Nancy. "What did he pull this time?"

Nancy described what she'd seen in the closet. "I don't scare easily," she said, "but I have to admit, I was pretty flipped out just now."

"Wow, that sounds awful!" Sondra murmured apologetically, her blue eyes opening wide. "I wish that hadn't happened."

"Me too!" Nancy exclaimed.

"Mick's into sick jokes," Sondra explained. "I know it's a drag, but don't take it personally. He does stuff like that to all the new interns." She sighed. "The trouble is, lately, he's been taking his jokes too far." She looked at Nancy with embarrassment. "I . . . I'm sorry."

Nancy smiled graciously. "I'm okay, Sondra. And, by the way, I appreciate the apology."

By that time, the backdrop had been removed and all the equipment put away. Nancy and Sondra left the studio together. "Mick asked me to take you to look at the shots from today's shoot," Sondra told Nancy.

"Okay," Nancy replied. "That sounds like fun. I'm sure I'm going to learn a lot working here."

"Yeah, that's one of the best things about this company," Sondra agreed. "Anyway, I'll show you where we keep everything and how we organize the files. And if you do a good job, I'll let you pick some shots—alone. I've got a lot of other work to do."

Nancy looked through shots on the computer all afternoon, following the written instructions Mick had given Yvonne. He wanted certain photos edited differently, colors brightened or changed. At the end of his letter, he'd added a note to Nancy.

Make sure your taking breaks from looking at the screen. These computers—their dangerous, I'm telling you!

Nancy was once again surprised at the more considerate side of Mick. What did it all mean? Had the incident in the studio really been just a joke? Was the violence in Yvonne's office only a reaction to Yvonne's own rudeness? Or was Nancy dealing with a psycho? Everyone had heard about cases of split personality, people who could switch from being kind and calm to maniacs in just a moment. Suddenly, she wasn't sure *what* to think of Mick.

Nancy read Mick's note over and started to laugh. "Wow," she couldn't help saying out loud. "This guy has the worst spelling in the whole world!" He didn't know the difference between *your* and *you're* or *their* and *they're*.

Nancy rolled up the sleeves of her sweater dress and continued to work on the pictures. She had to admit that Mick was a great photographer. He'd really captured Danielle's spirit—her energy and personality.

It was almost five o'clock by the time Nancy finished her work. As she passed the door to the publisher's office, Yvonne appeared. "Come in for a minute," she said with a smile. "I want to know how your first day went."

"Pretty well," Nancy replied. She closed the door behind her. "I think my cover works. But one of your reporters, Brenda Carlton, knows who I am."

Yvonne shrugged. "No problem. She's hardly ever around the office."

"One more thing," said Nancy. "Do you think there might be an extra intern's job for a guy named Ned Nickerson? He's my assistant."

Surprisingly, Yvonne wasn't keen on the idea. Nancy had figured she'd be thrilled to have an extra pair of detective's eyes searching for the killer, but she wasn't. Still, after a little hard selling from Nancy, she agreed.

Nancy also copied the threat letters and checked a few of the computer printers in the offices for their ink levels. Sure enough, they were all full. And that meant that, if they had been written at the *Flash* offices, it would be impossible to narrow it down to one printer.

With nothing else to be done that day, she said goodbye to several people and got ready for the train ride back to River Heights.

But when Nancy stepped out of the building into the fading afternoon sunlight, she noticed a familiar figure waiting for her. Tall, toned, and terrific-looking, it was Ned Nickerson. "Hey!" he called.

"Ned!" Nancy cried, melting happily into her boyfriend's arms.

"Mmm," Ned said, giving Nancy a long, lingering kiss.

"Mmm," Nancy replied, kissing Ned back and staring blissfully into his soft, dark eyes as she ran her fingers through his fine, light brown hair.

At last the couple broke apart. "What are you doing here?" Nancy asked.

"What do you mean?" Ned teased. "We haven't seen each other since yesterday. The loneliness was killing me! And what else do I have to do on a beautiful Wednesday afternoon besides drive into Chicago and pick up my gorgeous girlfriend?"

Then Ned's handsome face became serious. "Actually, Nancy, I was a little worried about you. After our phone conversation this afternoon, I started having horrible thoughts about that guy you told me about." Ned flashed Nancy a tender smile. "And I'm sorry we argued."

"It was nothing compared to what I went through at the office!" Nancy exclaimed. As they climbed into Ned's car and headed for the suburbs, she told him what had happened, from Brenda Carlton and David Bowers to Mick and his sick sense of humor and Sondra's apology.

"Sondra sounds nice," Ned commented when Nancy had finished.

"I guess she is," Nancy admitted, "but I have a feeling she doesn't want to make things any easier for me. She seems to think I'm Yvonne's latest pet." Nancy rolled down the car window and let the spring air blow through her hair.

"You can't really blame her for that," Ned said.

"No," Nancy agreed. "Anyway, this case is a little frightening—but very intriguing."

"I don't know, Nancy." Ned was doubtful. "I'd say the accent is on dangerous. I mean, Mick may already be on to your true identity. Maybe we should just go to the police and let them handle it."

"No," Nancy argued. "Right now, a crime hasn't even been committed. There've been a few nasty letters, a few ugly fights, a practical joke. None of that's very out of the ordinary for a high-pressure office like *Flash*."

"Right," Ned said sarcastically. "People leave severed heads in office closets all over Chicago."

"Come on, Ned, you can't expect me to give up the case before I've found even one concrete clue, can you?"

"But, Nancy," Ned protested, "this Mick character might be really unpredictable. You could be putting your life on the line."

"If I thought that," Nancy answered, "I'd have you pull over at the next roadside diner and I'd call the police immediately. You know, you're making the most simple mistake a detective possibly can—you're assuming the obvious. Mick *might* be the person behind the threats, but it could be just about anyone at *Flash.*"

"Great! So there are a *bunch* of violent people over there, not just one," Ned muttered.

"By the way," Nancy said, "I asked Yvonne about hiring you as another intern. It was funny, but she was pretty hesitant at first. Anyway, I convinced her that I really needed you, and she said okay."

Ned sighed, keeping his eyes on the road. "I still think we'd be better off at my parents' cabin."

Nancy caught her breath. "So that's what all this is about. You're just upset about missing our trip."

"Hey," Ned said, getting annoyed, "I happen to want to spend a little time with the girl I love. What's wrong with that?"

"I don't know," Nancy replied, her temper beginning to flare. "It seems as if you're being selfish. I mean, who cares about some vacation when a person's life might be in danger?"

Ned took his eyes off the road just long enough to give Nancy a look of disbelief. "And who cares about some boyfriend," he said, returning his eyes miserably to the highway, "when you could be running around, getting yourself killed by an art director with an ax to grind? You know, Nancy, I don't think you appreciate me very much."

"Look, I need to do this, Ned. Okay?" Nancy said shortly.

Ned frowned. "No other guy in the world would put up with this, Nancy. And sometimes, I wonder why *I* do."

CHAPTER SIX

Nancy stared at the floor numbers over the elevator door as they lit up, one after another. It was a gray Thursday morning, and she was about to begin her second day of work at *Flash*. The weather suited her state of mind—dark and cool.

Her fight with Ned had upset her, and she hadn't slept well. She was in no mood for the fighting and nastiness that had gone on at the magazine the day before.

Luckily, Ned would be there now to help handle any really sticky situations. In spite of their argument, he was going to work at the magazine, just as he'd promised.

Or maybe that wasn't luck. Ned hadn't been the greatest conversationalist on the train ride into the city that morning. Obviously, he was still mad about the canceled trip. But Nancy knew she had to push her problems with Ned out of her mind. She couldn't let them interfere with the case.

Nancy had left Ned a few blocks away from the building where *Flash*'s offices were housed. She'd decided that they'd get a lot more information if they pretended they didn't know each other. That way, they could search for clues separately. And with luck, Mick and Sondra wouldn't think Ned was a spy. Because of their feelings for Nancy, they definitely weren't going to open up with her. Maybe Ned could get closer to them.

The elevator reached the sixteenth floor, and the doors slid open. Nancy stepped out. Okay, *Flash*, she thought. I'm ready for whatever you've got in store for me today. She walked over to the reception desk. "Hi, Scott," she said.

"Hey, Nancy, how's it going today?"

"Okay, I suppose," Nancy replied noncommittally.

"Well, I hate to be the bearer of bad news, especially so early in the morning, but Mick wants to see you in his office right away."

"Oh." Nancy frowned. She was sure it wasn't going to be very much fun. On the other hand, it was her first real chance to talk to her prime suspect. If she were lucky, she'd pick up a clue or two.

Scott flashed Nancy a sympathetic smile. "I'm really sorry about what Mick put you through yesterday. It's too bad, because actually Mick can be a pretty nice guy at times. Anyway, he said to send you in to him as soon as you got here."

"Thanks." Nancy hung her coat in the closet behind Scott's desk. She'd been a little nervous about what to wear that day. *Flash* was a fashion magazine, after all. Finally she'd chosen a favorite rose-colored sweater that brought out the red highlights in her hair and some classic, tailored black pants with low-heeled pumps.

Nancy headed for Mick's office. She soon found out that it was just as wild as Mick himself. It was decorated with dozens of remote control toys and tacky plastic things, a complete contrast to Yvonne's high-class image. Mick had everything from toy airplanes that really flew to barking dogs and marching soldiers.

Mick was reclining in a big orange armchair when Nancy came in. His feet were on his desk, displaying a pair of zebra-striped shoes. He was wearing an oversized white suit and a zebra ascot around his neck.

"Hi," Mick said. "Have a seat."

"Thanks," Nancy answered. She walked across the room, almost slipping on the highly polished wooden floors.

"Careful," Mick said.

Nancy smiled cautiously, settling into an orange chair identical to Mick's. Obviously Mick was trying to be pleasant and considerate. But why?

"Nancy," he began. He coughed, embarrassed, and swung his feet off the desk. "I've got something to say to you. It's not easy for me but—well, I've got to apologize to you for yesterday. I'm really sorry."

Nancy stared at Mick in surprise. Was this the same guy who'd humiliated her in the studio? The same guy who'd angrily smashed Yvonne's vase to bits?

"My sister was on my case about that joke all night," he continued. "She told me it was completely sick and creepy and that you could have been really scared. Well, I didn't mean it that way. Who'd leave a real severed head in a props closet? I figured you'd realize it was a joke as soon as you saw the head."

Nancy wasn't sure what to make of Mick's apology. He

certainly seemed to mean it. But where had the nice Mick been hiding the day before? Was he trying to gain Nancy's trust so he could throw her off his trail?

Actually, Nancy thought, Mick had been considerate with Danielle Artman yesterday. Still, that didn't mean the vicious Mick didn't exist, too.

Nancy smiled slowly. "Thanks for the apology," she said simply. "I appreciate it. I *was* pretty worried about all the fighting that went on yesterday."

Mick pressed his lips together. "That's another thing I want to apologize for—my outburst in Yvonne's office. I shouldn't have stuck you in the middle of my fight with Yvonne. And I shouldn't have taken my frustrations with her out on you yesterday in the studio."

"I won't argue with that," Nancy joked. She smiled at Mick sincerely for the first time, realizing that her feelings about the art director were changing. Sure, he was more than a little thoughtless, but he no longer seemed like the malicious person Nancy had first taken him for. He'd behaved badly, and he was apologizing for it. Nancy thought that was honorable. Mick would probably be a really nice guy, Nancy decided, if he hadn't gotten successful so young.

"Well," said Mick, "you've just got to understand that I never asked for an assistant." The bitterness was clear in his tone. "Yvonne is seriously irritating me. She hired you just because it suits some weird plan of her own."

"It *was* kind of bizarre that she made me your assistant without telling you about it first," Nancy admitted.

"Anyway," Mick continued, "as long as you and I are going to be working together, we've got to try to get along. I mean, my problems with Yvonne and MediaCorp aren't your fault."

"MediaCorp," Nancy said, playing innocent. "Isn't that the international news syndicate? They own just about every newspaper and magazine on the East Coast."

"Right, and if I don't watch out, they're going to own *mine*, too," Mick told her. "But I'm not going to let that happen."

Nancy decided to ask Mick a few more questions about MediaCorp. A master at getting information from people without their even knowing it, she set to work. She stretched her long legs and leaned back in her chair, hoping to make Mick feel less formal.

"I used to know someone," the sleuth said easily, "who worked for MediaCorp. Editor in chief at the *Law Review*, I think."

"I hope he wasn't a good friend," Mick said with the hint of a smile. "I wouldn't trust anyone connected with that place."

"Then you wouldn't hire anyone who'd once worked for MediaCorp?" Nancy asked.

"No way," Mick told her. "I hope your friend doesn't want a job here."

"Oh no," Nancy said quickly. Her mind was racing.

So Mick doesn't know about David's old job, she realized.

But Yvonne probably did. There was no way she'd hire an editor in chief without knowing his background. Yvonne was that kind of person. And she must have hidden David's background from Mick.

Nancy pursed her lips pensively. She wondered if anyone else around *Flash* knew about David—and if not, why not? She let her eyes wander around the office as if they could somehow discover a clue.

Suddenly she noticed something that made her break into a huge grin. Mick had a whole library of mystery novels displayed on shelves near his desk. "You must be a fellow mystery lover," she said with a laugh, pointing to the books.

"Definitely," Mick said enthusiastically. "I've been reading thrillers ever since I discovered the Hardy Boys back in grade school."

"Yeah, I always loved them, too," Nancy smiled. "I've been reading a lot of Raymond Chandler lately."

"I guess Agatha Christie is still the great master for me," Mick confided. "There's always some bizarre twist in her stories that no one else would ever come up with."

Nancy had to smile. Who would have guessed that Mick was a mystery fanatic just the way she was? If I don't watch it, she warned herself, I may end up actually getting friendly with Mick.

Mick stood up and extended his hand to Nancy. "You know, you're okay," he said.

Nancy smiled and shook Mick's outstretched hand. Mick

had become human to her that morning—which would help her predict his next move if he really were the culprit.

"You did a good job narrowing down the shots yesterday, Nancy. This afternoon I'd like you to help Leslie do a preliminary layout for the next issue. Think you can handle it?"

"I'll do my best," Nancy said. "See you later."

Nancy left Mick's office and walked toward the reception desk. She felt that she'd made some important discoveries about the case. Now if she could just figure out what it all meant.

Nancy entered the reception area. Scott was nowhere in sight, but Ned was there, talking to Sondra and acting very interested in what she was saying. They were standing close. In fact, it looked to Nancy as though her dependable boyfriend were flirting. At that moment, Sondra let out a peal of laughter and Ned broke into a charming smile.

How could Sondra make a play for Ned? Nancy wondered indignantly. Then she remembered Sondra had absolutely no way of knowing she was going after Nancy's boyfriend. But *Ned* should know better.

Still, Nancy had to give Ned the benefit of the doubt. Maybe he was just trying to get information and pick up clues from Sondra. But there was no reason for him to stand so close to her in order to do it. No way was she going to stand around and watch her boyfriend flirt with another girl.

Nancy took two steps forward. And at that moment, two piercing screams cut through the morning calm.

CHAPTER SEVEN

That was Yvonne!" Nancy cried. She made a dash for the publisher's office, Ned and Sondra momentarily forgotten. What could have happened?

Nancy threw open the door. Yvonne was standing by her desk, staring horrified into one of its drawers.

"Yvonne!" Nancy exclaimed. "Are you all right?"

"I—I thought it was just a toy until it moved," Yvonne gasped.

Nancy glanced around. Most of the *Flash* staff had followed her into Yvonne's office. Ned and Sondra were right behind her. Mick looked on uncertainly and David's steel-gray eyes surveyed the commotion impassively.

Nancy crossed the room and peered into Yvonne's desk. At first she didn't see what had scared the publisher. Then something started to crawl. It was a huge, hairy black spider with pinkish legs—a tarantula!

"Where did this come from?" Nancy asked softly, leaning closer to examine the spider.

"I d-don't know," Yvonne sputtered. "I just opened the drawer and there it was!"

Nancy picked up an empty coffee mug and laid it in the desk

drawer, its rim facing the spider. She prodded the creature with the end of a pencil until it began crawling into the cup. "We'd better save this for evidence."

But Yvonne pushed by, a paperweight in her hand. "No way am I going to leave that thing hanging around here!" She brought the weight down on the spider.

Nancy stared for a second. But by that time Sondra had already begun yelling at her brother. Of course, Nancy thought with a little mental shrug. This is *Flash*. Why did I expect to get through the morning without at least one major fight?

"Mick, how *could* you?" Sondra was crying. "Yvonne might have been bitten! You are taking these practical jokes way too far. They're not funny anymore!"

A look of confusion, fear, and hurt crossed Mick's face. "Wait a minute, Sondra. Are you saying *I'm* responsible for this? You think I would do this?"

"Well, who else could it be? No one else around here pulls creepy jokes."

"I'd never get *near* that miserable spider." Mick shuddered. "The rubber ones you brought in for Danielle Artman were bad enough. Besides, I'm not into dangerous jokes. You know that!"

Nancy watched the exchange closely. Mick really did seem shocked that his sister would assume he was responsible. Then again, maybe he was just a very good actor.

Suddenly Nancy remembered that David had just come back from South America. Isn't it interesting, Nancy thought. That's one of the areas where you can find tarantulas. With his connection to MediaCorp, the editor in chief was beginning to look more than a little suspicious.

In ones and twos, the others left the office. Nancy was by no means too wrapped up in the case to miss Ned and Sondra walking out together, but right then there wasn't a thing she could do about it. Last to leave were Mick, still clearly upset by his sister's accusation, and David, who gave Yvonne a kiss on the cheek first.

"How are you feeling?" Nancy asked Yvonne as soon as everyone had cleared out of the office.

"A little shaken," the publisher replied, dropping heavily into her chair. "But okay, I guess."

"This is something I think the police should know about immediately," Nancy said, taking a seat on the leather couch. "I don't have a single concrete clue, so I have no way of judging the situation, but I do know one thing—this case has gone far beyond practical jokes."

Yvonne caught her breath sharply. "No," she said with a fierceness that surprised Nancy. "The reason I hired you was to keep the police out of this. I told you, I'm worried about Mick. I want to keep him out of any serious trouble."

"It looks as if you're getting yourself into some, though," said Nancy.

"But, Nancy, maybe Mick just wanted to scare me."

Nancy sighed. Yvonne was so sure Mick was behind the things that had happened at *Flash*. But until that was proven, Nancy was going to keep her eyes open for any and all possible suspects.

"Whoever planted that spider may or may not have known that it wouldn't kill you," Nancy replied. "Most people think tarantulas are deadly, like black widow spiders, but they're not. In fact, a lot of people keep tarantulas as exotic pets without any problems. This one probably came from a pet store. But the thing is, we still don't know if the person we're looking for is just trying to scare you or if we're up against a murder attempt. That's exactly why I think we should call in the police. We don't have enough information."

"My point exactly. The police aren't interested in suspicions and possibilities. They want facts, crime victims, switchblade knives. They'll come in here, look around, and do nothing at all. Meanwhile, Mick and *Flash* will have to bear the media coverage that would follow."

Nancy sighed. Yvonne was right. Still, she was a detective, not a bodyguard. She didn't want to feel responsible if another murder attempt occurred and Yvonne got hurt.

Suddenly Yvonne's face softened. "Please," she said, almost pleading, "I want you to handle this yourself. For me, for Mick, and for *Flash*. The next time Mick does something dangerous, we'll call the police, okay?"

"If you're still alive," Nancy replied wryly.

Yvonne broke into a smile. "Great. I knew you'd understand, Nancy. Now I'm going home for a while. I need to cool out after all this."

"Okay," Nancy said, getting to her feet. "Do you mind if I have a look around your office? Maybe the culprit left a clue."

"Go right ahead." Yvonne stood up and got her coat from the closet. "I'll lock the door. Then just close it behind you when you leave." Yvonne slipped into her coat, gathered together a few papers, pushed them into her briefcase and, saying goodbye to Nancy, hurried out.

Nancy got right to work, checking Yvonne's desk drawers first. When she found nothing, she searched the closet and Yvonne's private bathroom. She even looked beneath the cushions of the couch. It was only when she got down on her hands and knees on the floor, peering into every corner, that she found something. One of the large white buttons from Mick's suit was lying underneath the desk.

Nancy picked it up. Then, brushing off her pants, she stood up.

It was a small clue. It didn't prove anything. Mick was in and out of Yvonne's office a few times a day. He may not have lost the button while planting the spider, but it was a possibility.

Nancy decided she needed more definite clues, clues she just might find in Mick's office. She knocked on his door. "It's Nancy," she called.

"Come on in," Mick called back.

Nancy opened the door. "Hi," she said.

"Strange happenings at *Flash*, huh?" Mick said. "I bet you never had a job like this before, did you?" He was joking, but there was a nervous edge to his voice.

"No," Nancy said honestly, "I never have." Now that she was in his office, she had no idea how to get Mick out in order to search it. Well, she told herself, I'll just have to wing it.

"So what can I do for you?" Mick asked.

"Um," Nancy stalled, "I wanted to—to ask you if there was anything I can do for you since Yvonne has gone home."

"No," Mick said, "just go help Leslie with those layouts."

"Okay," Nancy answered. She turned to leave. All at once she slipped on the shiny wood floor and fell flat on her rear. "Ow!" she cried.

"Nancy!" exclaimed Mick. "Here, let me help you. Are you hurt?"

"I think I twisted my ankle," Nancy replied. She allowed Mick to help her limp to the orange armchair. "I don't think it's too bad, but do you think you could get me some ice to put on it? A dancer friend of mine swears it's the best thing for this kind of injury."

"Sure," Mick said, concerned. "There's some in the refrigerator. It's just down the hall. I'll be right back." He dashed out of the room, slamming the door behind him.

As soon as he had gone, Nancy jumped out of the chair. Mick would be gone for just a few minutes. She'd probably only have time to search his desk.

Nancy looked carefully through a few drawers. Nothing. But then she noticed something on top of the desk that was very interesting indeed.

It was a paperback mystery called *Deadly Potion, Deadly*

Bite by an author named Ivan Green. Nancy had read it herself, and the story stuck in her mind because of the bizarre way the murderer had killed his victims. He'd used poisons—all different types, including poison from insects!

Wow, Nancy thought. Yvonne finds a tarantula in her desk while Mick's reading a fictional account of the same kind of crime. Was it just a coincidence?

She heard a noise in the hall and glanced at the door. There was Mick's jacket, hanging from a hook. Nancy grabbed the lapel to check the front of the jacket. A button *was* missing!

Dashing back to the armchair, she dropped into it just as Mick returned.

"I brought you a whole bag full of ice," Mick announced.

"Thanks," Nancy said. She spent a few minutes holding the ice to her perfectly normal ankle, her mind speeding from clue to clue all the while. Once again, things were looking bad for Mick. But what about David? Nancy knew she would have to search his office, too, before she completely condemned Mick. She'd need Ned's help for that.

Nancy lost precious time getting Mick to believe she was all right, but at last she made her getaway. She found Ned alone in the photocopy room, duplicating some articles. "Glad to see you've separated yourself from Sondra Swanson long enough to get a little work done," she said sarcastically.

"Nancy—" Ned cried.

But Nancy wouldn't let Ned get another word out of his

mouth. "I need your help. Do you think you can keep David Bowers busy for fifteen minutes or so? I've got to search his office."

"Piece of cake," Ned said, pulling his copies out of the machine. "But listen. Sondra—"

"Forget it," Nancy said. "We don't have time to talk now. See you in a bit." And with that, she hurried out of the room.

Nancy gave Ned five minutes to get David out of his office. Then she snuck in herself. If David catches me here, she thought, I'm dead. She went straight to his desk. The top drawer held pencils, pens, typing paper, and other standard office supplies.

In the second drawer Nancy found a few old greeting cards and a couple of low-quality novels. Obviously, the big-shot editor didn't want anyone to know he liked to read junk, since he hadn't put the books on his shelf next to the leatherbound classics. Nancy couldn't help but giggle to herself about that.

But it was in the bottom drawer that Nancy found something really interesting. It was a note from a top officer at MediaCorp! "Here's the check for that last freelance job," it said. "Let me know how the new job is going."

Nancy pawed through the papers in the drawer, but she couldn't find the check. David had probably already cashed it. Anyway, she didn't really need it. She had the most important information. She knew that David was still working for MediaCorp. But as a freelance editor—or as a hired assassin? Nancy's mind reeled with new possibilities.

Nancy knew MediaCorp wanted *Flash*. But how badly? Could they really be as unscrupulous as Nancy was beginning to suspect? How far would a major corporation go to acquire a magazine they wanted?

As far as murder?

CHAPTER EIGHT

The question of MediaCorp's possible involvement in the trouble at *Flash* stayed with Nancy all Thursday afternoon and into the next morning. The thought scared her. In her many cases, she'd never come up against such a powerful criminal. MediaCorp wasn't a human being—it was an institution. And how did you fight an institution?

Worse than that, Nancy still wasn't sure the news syndicate *was* behind the threats. Then there was Mick. Slowly she was beginning to think he might be a pretty nice guy. But there was also plenty of evidence against him. He had such a complicated personality that Nancy had no idea how far she could trust him.

Nancy did know one thing for certain. The plan to have Ned help her on the case had really backfired. All he seemed to do was hang around with Sondra. He hadn't brought in a single clue yet.

So, after a long Friday morning of hard work, worrying, and not much detective work, Nancy knew she'd be glad to get out of *Flash* at lunchtime—and even gladder that her two best friends, George Fayne and Bess Marvin, were coming into the city from River Heights for a lunch date with her. Nothing soothed troubles like complaining to your best friends.

Just before noon, Scott buzzed Nancy on the office intercom and told her that George and Bess had arrived. Nancy carefully put away her work and headed for the reception area. She bumped into Ned as she was stepping out of the interns' office.

"Nancy," he said, catching her arm, "we've got to talk. You've been avoiding me, and I want to know why."

Ned's eyes caught Nancy's for a moment, but she quickly looked away. It was true, she *was* avoiding him. She'd purposely stayed late at *Flash* the night before just so she wouldn't have to take the train back to River Heights with him. She'd felt horrible about it, but she just hadn't been able to face a heavy discussion about Sondra or their relationship when she had the case on her mind.

"I know we have to talk," Nancy told Ned, "but not right now. George and Bess are waiting for me." She tried to shake off his hand.

"Okay," Ned said calmly, not letting go. "Then when? This is important, you know."

"I'm not sure," Nancy replied, beginning to feel annoyed. "I've got a lot of work to do. I don't have the time to sit around talking—and flirting." She looked up suddenly, her gaze angry and challenging.

But Ned was getting angry, too. "Why don't you stop being so jealous and *think* a little, Nancy? You're supposed to be a detective. Did it ever cross your mind that I might be hanging out with Sondra because the girl I really want to spend time with is too busy?"

"And did it ever cross your mind that I asked you to be an intern to do more than just socialize? Where's all the help you promised me?"

"Oh, come on, Nancy. You've got a free hour or two to have lunch with George and Bess. But when was the last time we had any fun together? I mean, who am I supposed to have lunch with today?"

Nancy felt defensive and guilty and angry all at once. She knew she'd been taking Ned for granted lately. She'd canceled out on the lake trip and she hadn't tried to make up for it in any way. Still, *he* was the one who was spending time with somebody else, so who was he to complain?

"Look, Bess and George are waiting for me," Nancy said, shrugging off the issue. "We'll have to talk some other time."

Ned pressed his lips into a thin, angry line. "Okay, Nancy. If that's the way you want it." Resignedly, he dropped his hand from Nancy's arm and turned to walk away.

Suddenly Nancy felt as if she were losing Ned. And no matter what was going on between them, he was very precious to her. "Ned," she called, "we'll talk this afternoon, all right?"

But Ned didn't answer. He just stalked off. Nancy heaved a huge sigh and went to meet George and Bess at the reception desk. She knew that if she had to be alone for more than five minutes, she'd probably start to cry.

Nancy found her friends talking to Scott. It looked suspiciously as though Bess were flirting with him. "Bess, George," Nancy said, putting up a happy front. "You two look great!"

Bess's straw-blond hair was fixed in braids, which she'd gathered together in a ponytail. She was wearing a pink skirt and pink high heels—Bess was self-conscious about being shorter than her two friends.

George was her usual down-to-earth self, wearing gray corduroy pants and a matching V-necked sweater that showed off her toned athlete's body. Her short dark hair fell in soft curls.

"You're not doing too badly yourself," George said. "Especially with this neat job. Really, Nancy, I'm jealous," she said with a smile.

"So where do you want to eat?" Bess asked. "I'm starved!"

Nancy suggested a little restaurant not far from *Flash*. It was decorated with big colorful posters and had sunny windows that looked out onto the street.

"So," George said after they had been seated at a corner table and had ordered their lunches. "*Flash* seems like a wild place. The receptionist was playing games during work hours, and some guy walked by wearing the weirdest hat I've ever seen."

"That was probably Mick Swanson," said Nancy. "He's one of my prime suspects."

"Totally gorgeous, too," Bess giggled. "Maybe I could help rehabilitate him from a life of crime."

"He's too old for you, Bess," Nancy said with a laugh.

At that moment the waiter brought over the food. Nancy and George had ordered lasagna, Bess had ordered a salad with steak.

George cut into her lasagna. Then she turned to Nancy and said, "All right, what's going on?"

"What do you mean?" Nancy asked, a little taken aback by the suddenness of her friend's question.

"You've barely said a word today—and when you have, it's been with all the joy of a beauty queen with chicken pox. Now what gives?"

Nancy sighed, pushing her lasagna around her plate. "I guess this case has me a bit down. Someone's doing nasty things to Yvonne so she won't sell the magazine—which she doesn't intend to do anyway. And I'm up against a murderous corporation, an unpredictable photographer, or a malicious practical joker, but I have no idea which one."

"Don't give me that," George said. "No matter how confusing a case is, it never gets you as down as you are now."

Nancy smiled. "You know me too well. Okay, it's Ned."

"What's going on with My Reliable now?" Bess asked sharply.

A little giggle escaped from Nancy's throat. "Yeah, that's how I always thought of him, too. He'd be around for me no matter what I did. But believe it or not, Ned Nickerson might be cheating on me!"

"Who is she?" Bess wanted to know.

"Her name's Sondra Swanson. Blond, gorgeous, and, to be

honest, kind of nice. She doesn't know Ned and I are involved with each other, so I can't even blame her for going after him. All I can say is that she has good taste in guys."

"Wait a sec," George said, swallowing a bite of food. "Swanson. Isn't that the name of the man with the funny hat? The person you say is your prime suspect?"

"She's his sister," Nancy explained.

"You're kidding," Bess said. She munched on a cherry tomato. "Hey," she teased. "Maybe you've got this whole mystery figured out wrong. Maybe Mick's not behind it. Maybe it's Sondra, trying to help her brother take over the magazine."

"Yeah," George added. "Then all you'd have to do is find some evidence, get her thrown in jail, and Ned would be yours all over again. And after a bad experience like that, you can bet he'd never look at anyone else again!"

"It's a great fantasy," Nancy said, laughing. "I'll keep it in mind next time I see them flirting by the water fountain." Then her expression grew serious again. "The thing is, Ned has every reason to be sick of me. I have to admit, I haven't been too nice to him these days. He says I'm more interested in my mystery than in him. And he's right."

"Nancy, don't say that," Bess scolded. "Ned has to understand that your work is your passion, your life!"

"Right," George agreed. "You put up with him during football season, when he has to be in bed by ten o'clock every night.

That's not a great time for you, but you don't complain."

"It's true," Nancy said, beginning to feel better. "I mean, I *do* complain when Ned's in training, but I don't go out and pick up some cute English major who doesn't have to get up at five in the morning to do push-ups. Of course there was Daryl Grey . . ."

"He's gone and forgotten," Bess insisted. "It doesn't make what Ned's doing right."

"Yeah," George agreed. "Dating the prime suspect's sister is simply bad taste."

Nancy had to laugh. It was great having such supportive friends. No matter what she did, George and Bess were always on her side.

The three girls finished their lunches and shared a piece of chocolate cheesecake, amid a lot of joking and laughing.

"So, Bess," said Nancy, "have you heard from Alan Wales lately?"

"My rock star is still on the road," Bess replied, thinking wistfully of the guitarist she'd been dating. "I still don't know what to think of our relationship. It's not over, it's just sort of on hold. Now George, on the other hand . . ."

George blushed.

"What?" asked Nancy.

"She's too embarrassed to say anything, but she's going to see Jon this weekend."

George Fayne didn't fall in love nearly as often as Bess did, but her new boyfriend, a skier, seemed to be very special to her.

Nancy smiled.

She appreciated her friends' company so much that she treated them to lunch. Afterward, George and Bess went off to do some shopping and see an art exhibit before returning to River Heights. Nancy hurried back to *Flash*.

She felt much better. The lunch with George and Bess hadn't solved anything, but the jokes and the gossip had worked wonders for a troubled heart.

Nancy waved hello to Scott and returned to the interns' office. She pulled out the photographs she'd been working on that morning and spread them across the big plank desk.

Mick had asked Nancy to pick out the best pictures from the Danielle Artman shoot. It was harder work than she'd expected because so many of the photos were excellent. Nancy particularly liked one of Danielle kissing a rubber spider.

The work was interesting, and it felt nice to be sitting alone in the quiet office. It almost seemed to Nancy as if everyone else at *Flash* had taken the day off. No problems with Ned. No Sondra Swanson. No potential murderer lurking in the shadows.

Then the sound of a shot rang through the afternoon.

Nancy dashed into the hallway, glancing at her digital watch as she did. It was exactly ten after two. She saw people rushing to the publisher's office and raced after them. Someone threw open the door, and the staff peered into the room, terrified of what they'd find.

Yvonne was standing behind her desk, her ashen face wearing an expression of sheer horror. Then, slowly, her body weakened and she sank to the floor.

CHAPTER NINE

Nancy stared aghast at Yvonne's prone body. Oh no, she thought. Yvonne is dead! If only I'd called the police after the murder attempt with the spider.

Nancy rushed over to Yvonne, bent down, and gently took her limp wrist to check her pulse. To her intense relief, the publisher's heart was pumping like mad.

"She's alive!" Nancy announced. The staff of *Flash* let out a collective sigh of relief.

Nancy took the publisher's pulse a second time, feeling confused. It was funny that Yvonne's heart was beating so fast. The pulse was supposed to slow down when someone passed out. Nancy shrugged and started massaging Yvonne's shoulders, trying to wake her.

After a minute, Yvonne sat up groggily.

"Yvonne, what happened?" Nancy asked gently. "We heard a gunshot."

Yvonne took a deep breath and pointed to the wall above her desk. A bullet was embedded in the wooden paneling. "I guess I fainted," she mumbled.

"You're okay now, though," Nancy told her. "I'll be right back. I just want to check the fire exit."

Nancy jumped to her feet and ran to the back staircase. The gunman had to have escaped that way because the whole staff had come barreling down the hall in the opposite direction just after the shot was fired. But no one was in the stairway.

Nancy rushed back to the office and found Yvonne starting to explain what had happened. She was lying on the black leather couch, and someone had rolled up a sweater to use as a pillow.

"I was sitting at my desk working," Yvonne began, "when I heard my door being pushed open quietly. I looked up and saw a figure—it looked like a man—wearing dark clothes and a ski mask point a gun at my head. I screamed and the man fired. Then he ran away. That's all," the publisher concluded wearily.

"I think it's time to call the police," Nancy said, looking meaningfully at Yvonne.

"Yes, I guess so," the publisher replied, avoiding Nancy's eyes. "Would you call them, please?"

Nancy picked up the phone on Yvonne's desk and dialed 911, the police emergency number. "Hello," she said, "there's been a murder attempt at the offices of *Flash* magazine. No one's been hurt, but we need some help."

Nancy gave the police operator her name and *Flash*'s address and hung up. Then she let her eyes wander around the office, trying to discover a clue to the mysterious shooting.

She gazed again at the bullet buried deep in the wall. It was high up, only about two and a half feet from the ceiling. The gunman had missed by a long shot, Nancy thought. The bullet in the paneling was much higher than Yvonne's head would be if she were sitting at her desk. By the look of the hole, Nancy figured the weapon used was probably nothing too powerful. That was surprising, too. Hitmen didn't usually take chances.

Nancy glanced around at the people in the office. David was kneeling by the couch next to Yvonne, holding her hand. Sondra was standing in the back, looking terrified. Ned was there, too, with Scott, Leslie, and a few other interns and staff members. But where was Mick? The art director was nowhere in sight.

The prime suspect was looking more guilty every minute. And if Mick really had shot at Yvonne, that would explain the bad aim and the bad choice of a weapon. As far as Nancy knew, Mick was just an amateur with a grudge.

All at once Nancy realized she could no longer point the finger at anyone other than Mick. The funny thing was, she didn't want him to be the murderer. She would have much preferred that creepy, bad-tempered David be the guilty one. But there was David, with a perfect alibi, while Mick wasn't even around to defend himself.

Nancy dropped into a hardbacked chair by the door to Yvonne's office. She felt overwhelmed. She'd never completely believed Mick was capable of masterminding the threats until just that moment. The art director had only one chance left at that point—to come into the *Flash* offices with an airtight alibi.

Slowly people began drifting out of Yvonne's office. Nancy stayed and talked to Yvonne, trying to get a better description of the masked intruder. How tall was he? Thin or heavyset? Was there anything distinctive about him? But Yvonne's responses were too vague to help.

However, very shortly three police officers showed up—a tall man who introduced himself as Detective Graham, a tough red-haired woman called Officer Bellows, and a refrigerator-sized man named Officer O'Hara who didn't say much, but was very intimidating nonetheless.

Detective Graham and Officer Bellows questioned several staff members. Yvonne had to describe the incident again.

Then Detective Graham took some pictures of Yvonne's office and dug the bullet out of her wall to keep as evidence. After that he went back to the precinct, leaving Officers Bellows and O'Hara behind to keep an eye out for any suspicious activity. Yvonne got ready to leave, too, and David offered to take her home in a taxi. No one in the office seemed ready to do much work. The incident was too bizarre to brush off.

An hour later, Mick sauntered into the office, a camera slung around his neck. "Hey, where've you been?" Leslie called to him. "You missed all the excitement here."

"What's going on?" Mick asked.

"Just a little murder attempt," Scott replied. "Someone tried to shoot Yvonne! We've got no idea who."

Nancy said nothing. *She* had a couple of ideas who, she

thought, scrutinizing Mick's face. He was certainly an amazing actor. He really did seem shocked as Leslie described the whole incident.

"You've got to be out of your minds," Mick exclaimed. "All this happened while I was out?" He looked completely amazed.

"What have you been doing?" Nancy asked casually.

"Shooting photographs on the street."

Shooting photographs on the street? Nancy thought. Then he probably has no alibi. No one could vouch for his exact whereabouts at the time of the shooting.

All at once, Mick's serious expression softened into a grin. "Okay, guys, it was a good joke. I admit, I almost believed this ridiculous story. Which one of you geniuses thought it up? You actually fooled the Practical Joke King!" Mick looked from face to face, but he was the only one laughing. Finally he said, "You're *serious*, aren't you?"

"You can see the bullet hole in the wall if you want proof," Scott said. He stepped out from behind the reception desk. Mick followed him to Yvonne's office.

Nancy definitely didn't want to miss Mick's reaction to the sight of the bullet hole, so *she* followed Scott and Mick. It was a good thing, too, because as she stepped into the hall she heard someone walk into the reception area. "Hi, Brenda. Has anyone told you the big news?" Leslie said.

Great, Nancy thought. Brenda Carlton was not exactly what she needed just then! At least Nancy managed to avoid her again.

Scott opened the door to Yvonne's office. "There it is," he said, motioning to the hole above the desk.

Mick's eyes widened. He was speechless.

Nancy had to admit Mick was doing a great job of seeming flabbergasted. But it had to be an act . . . didn't it? A tiny sliver of doubt crept into Nancy's mind.

"So Yvonne's all right?" Mick asked.

"Luckily," Scott replied.

"And she went home to calm down?"

"Yup."

"Wow, this is so strange," Mick said, his tone incredulous. "I've got to talk to Yvonne. She must be too flipped out for words."

Nancy watched Mick in amazement. He seemed so sincere. One side of him was wild and funny and concerned with people's feelings. What if the other side was a killer who could set up the severed head and rubber ax to scare Nancy—or try to shoot his partner and longtime friend in cold blood?

Nancy, Mick, and Scott left Yvonne's office, closing the door behind them. Mick disappeared into his office, while Scott headed toward the reception area.

Nancy started to follow him, then said, "Scott, I'm going to work on touching up some photos for a while."

"Okay," Scott answered.

When Scott was out of sight, Nancy tiptoed to Mick's office. As quietly as possible, she turned the doorknob. She pushed open the door without the slightest creak and peeked in, praying to be invisible.

Mick was opening his bottom desk drawer. Nancy had seen him stash his camera there before. All at once a look of utter confusion swept across his handsome face. He reached into the drawer and pulled out a small silver revolver.

Before the rational side of her brain could stop her, Nancy had thrown open the door and was dashing across the room. She threw herself across Mick's desk and tackled the art director.

"Hey!" Mick cried, struggling.

"Drop it, Mick," Nancy advised. "Make it easy on yourself." She grabbed Mick's arm and twisted with all her might.

"Ow!" Mick yelled, but he kept an iron grip on the revolver, hugging it to his chest.

"I'm sorry to have to do this to you, Mick," Nancy panted. Then she socked the art director as hard as she could in the stomach.

Mick doubled over at the same moment that the gun went off. He fell to the ground, and the gun tumbled out of his hand and onto the shiny wooden floor.

Nancy stared in horror at Mick's prone figure. "Oh no," she whispered. "What have I done?"

"All right," came a shout from the doorway. "Freeze!" Nancy looked up—and into the cocked gun of Officer Bellows. "Nancy Drew," she cried, "you're under arrest!"

CHAPTER TEN

Get your hands in the air," Officer Bellows ordered Nancy. "And don't touch that body," she said, indicating Mick, who was immobile on the floor.

Slowly Nancy raised her hands and stepped back from Mick and the gun. She felt helpless and terrified and confused. It had all been an accident, but would that matter to a court of law? She'd been caught red-handed in what looked like murder!

Nancy heard the pounding of feet in the hallway. Officer O'Hara burst into Mick's office, gun in hand. To make things worse, most of the *Flash* staff arrived, too. Ned was there, standing protectively close to Sondra. Suddenly Nancy caught her breath. Brenda Carlton had appeared and was looking at her with a disturbingly triumphant smile on her face. Oh no, Nancy thought, can anything else possibly go wrong?

"Well," Brenda said smugly, "if *this* isn't the scoop of the year! I can just see the headlines. 'Amateur Detective Nancy Drew Murders Top Exec.'"

Nancy felt sick. Brenda had just blown her cover in front of the entire *Flash* staff.

"She's a detective?" Sondra cried. "Then Yvonne *did* hire

you to spy on my brother—*and now you've killed him!*" Sondra burst into tears, crying as if she'd never be able to stop.

To Nancy's amazement, Ned put his arm around her, trying to comfort her.

"Sondra, it's not like that," Ned said. "Nancy's a good person! This is all a mistake." But his arm stayed around her shoulders. Nancy felt betrayed and wounded. There she was, being arrested for murder, and her boyfriend was worried about another woman.

Ned's words didn't make any difference to Sondra, who kept crying, or to the rest of the staff, either. They stared at Nancy in stunned and disgusted silence. She felt like a traitor. Brenda's beady eyes glittered happily. She was thoroughly enjoying Nancy's misfortune.

"Okay, Drew," Officer Bellows ordered, "O'Hara's got you covered. Don't try anything funny." Bellows whipped out her handcuffs and snapped them neatly onto Nancy's wrists. Nancy forced back tears. No way was she going to cry in front of all those people.

Suddenly Nancy found her voice. "You've got it all wrong," she cried, struggling against the handcuffs. "*Mick* was the one who tried to kill Yvonne. When I walked into this office, he was pulling that silver revolver out of his bottom desk drawer."

"*Liar!*" Sondra exclaimed, still sobbing.

"I swear it's true. We were struggling for the gun when it went off. *It wasn't my fault!*" Nancy could feel the tears building up uncontrollably within her.

"Mick's no murderer!" Sondra screamed.

"I saw the proof with my own eyes," Nancy replied vehemently.

"Hey, could you hold it down?" came a voice from the floor. "I've got a horrible headache."

"*Mick!*" cried Sondra. "You're alive!" She burst into a fresh storm of tears. "Thank heavens!"

Nancy breathed a giant sigh of relief.

"My head's killing me," Mick said. "I think I must have hit it on the edge of the desk when I fell."

"All right, Swanson," Officer Bellows said to Mick. "Off the floor. Why don't you tell me *your* side of the story? Drew here's just accused you of trying to kill Yvonne Verdi."

Mick stared at Nancy, a look of hurt betrayal in his blue eyes. "How can you possibly think that?" he asked.

Nancy rolled her eyes. "The gun, Mick, the gun! Don't you remember? You were pulling it out of your desk when I walked in here."

"But it's not mine!" Mick said, turning from Nancy to Officer Bellows. "I've never seen it before in my life. I don't own a gun. The only kind of shooting I know about is photography!"

Officer Bellows stared suspiciously at Mick and Nancy. At last she said, "Looks as though you're *both* going to have to come down to the station." She turned to the others in the room. "The rest of you clear out of here. Detective Graham will be back to question you all."

Slowly, the staff filed out. Brenda threw Nancy a sleazy smile before she left. Soon only Ned and Sondra were left. "Uh, Officer Bellows," Ned said tentatively, "do you think you could take those handcuffs off Nancy? I'll vouch that she's not dangerous, and I think she's pretty uncomfortable with them on."

"Sorry," said Officer Bellows. "Cuffs are standard procedure for bringing in a murder suspect."

"But, Officer, nobody's been murdered," Ned pointed out. "So how about it?"

Officer Bellows blushed, embarrassed. Then, without a word, she set Nancy free. Nancy was filled with grateful relief. For a moment she wanted to throw her arms around Ned and kiss him. But the fact that he had his own arm around Sondra killed the urge right away.

"Let's get moving, you two," Officer Bellows said. Still holding her pistol, she and the silent O'Hara ushered Nancy and Mick down the hallway, past the gawking staff members and into the elevator. The doors opened and Mick turned to Nancy. "After you, Miss Detective," he said wryly. Ned and Sondra followed, like mourners at a funeral.

Nancy was beginning to have compassion for all the criminals she'd helped to arrest over the years. The public embarrassment of being led off by the cops was horrible! Ned and Sondra hailed a cab and headed toward the police station. Nancy and Mick got into the back of the patrol car while Bellows and O'Hara settled into the front. After a short, miserable ride, they arrived at the precinct.

Officer Bellows had confiscated the revolver as evidence

before she'd left *Flash*. As soon as Nancy and Mick had been fingerprinted, she sent the gun to the police lab to be tested against the bullet that Detective Graham had taken out of Yvonne's office wall. Then she let Nancy and Mick make one phone call each.

Luckily, Nancy's father and her attorney were one and the same. It just so happened that Carson Drew was one of the state's finest criminal lawyers. When he heard that Nancy was being held at the police precinct, he promised to be there as fast as he could.

Once Mick had called his lawyer, Officer Bellows and Detective Graham sat down to interrogate their two suspects. The questioning was grueling. The police went over every aspect of the afternoon repeatedly.

The ordeal was made even worse by Ned and Sondra standing around watching the whole thing. Since neither Nancy nor Mick had been accused of a crime yet, they weren't interrogated in private. That meant that Nancy had to watch Ned consoling Sondra, comforting her, trying to calm her fears.

Nancy struggled to keep her mind on Detective Graham's and Officer Bellows's questions, in spite of Ned and Sondra. She had to. If she seemed unsure of her answers, the police would be less likely to believe her side of the story.

When the two officers had finished questioning Nancy, they turned to Mick. To her surprise, he didn't deny anything that had happened. He admitted that the gun had been in his desk, that Nancy hadn't been trying to kill him, that it had all been a mistake. But over and over again he repeated adamantly that the gun had been planted in his desk. "For once," he said, "the joke's on me. And it's not very funny."

Nancy actually felt sorry for Mick. How could he expect the police to accept his silly story when all the evidence was against him? He had no alibi for the afternoon, and any number of motives for wanting to knock off Yvonne.

Nancy wasn't too worried about herself. What could the police accuse her of? Nothing illegal. However, she greeted her father with great relief. He looked so sure of himself and so in control. "Nancy," he said, coming over to kiss his daughter. "Honey, are you all right? I know this isn't pleasant, but just hang on for a little while longer. We'll have you out of here in no time."

Nancy gave her father a huge hug. He'd made it from River Heights in under forty-five minutes. He must have sped all the way here, Nancy thought to herself. Probably the only time he's ever gone above the speed limit in his entire life!

Moments later, the results came back from the lab. The gun and bullet matched.

Officer Bellows turned to Nancy. "Ms. Drew, you're free to leave." Then she faced Mick. "Mr. Swanson," she said solemnly, "you're under arrest for the attempted murder of Yvonne Verdi." Quickly she read him his rights. "Would you come with me? We're going to have to put you in a cell." For the second time that day, the policewoman pulled out her handcuffs.

At first Mick didn't move from his seat. He just blinked

uncomprehendingly. Then he jumped up, knocking over his chair. "You think I'm a murderer? Me?" he cried. "But I didn't do it, I swear. That gun isn't mine! *Someone planted it!*"

"You'll have to explain that to the judge and jury," Officer Bellows said calmly.

"And how long will that take?" Mick asked. "A month? Two months? More?"

Suddenly Mick's face turned bright red. Nancy had seen his expression change in the same way on the first day she'd met him—just before he'd smashed Yvonne's vase. He seemed to be losing control of himself.

Grabbing Officer O'Hara's gun out of his holster, Mick shrieked, "You are not going to lock me up for a crime I didn't commit!" He kicked the overturned chair out of his way and made a desperate dash across the room, straight for the precinct door.

CHAPTER ELEVEN

Mick was halfway across the room before anyone reacted to his desperate dash toward freedom. And because of his head start, it looked as though he might just make it out of the police station untouched. Then Detective Graham pulled out his pistol. "Stop or I'll shoot!" he cried. But there was no way he could fire with so many people in the room.

Nancy thought fast. She picked up the chair and slid it across the floor, hitting Mick hard in the legs. Mick went down, sprawling just out of reach of the precinct door.

Officer Bellows pounced on the now-prone Mick and snapped her handcuffs on him. "It's a good thing this young woman stopped you," she said. "If you'd escaped, we'd only have tracked you down, and the jury would have been much tougher on you. Now let's go." She pulled Mick to his feet.

"No!" Mick screamed. "I didn't do it!" But Officer Bellows pushed him toward the hallway that held the temporary cells. Soon Mick had disappeared and his cries had died away.

It was then that Nancy noticed Sondra quietly weeping in the corner. But Mick's sister wasn't alone in her misery. Ned was right there with her. Nancy almost swallowed her teeth when she saw him take her in his arms and gently stroke her hair.

"It's all right, Sondra. Don't cry."

"Mick," Sondra sobbed.

Ned continued stroking Sondra. "Don't worry," he told her softly. "If your brother's innocent, we'll get him cleared. Nancy will help us. She's the best detective around." Ned glanced pleadingly at Nancy.

But Nancy was seething. "I can't believe what I'm hearing," she said through clenched teeth. "Look at you. You're hugging her, and I'm standing right here! You're supposed to care about *me*, Ned. I've been through a lot today. But you don't so much as say a comforting word."

"Nancy," Ned said, letting go of Sondra and walking hesitantly over to Nancy, "you know it's not like that."

Sondra looked in bewilderment from Ned's face to Nancy's. "You mean you two are going out?" she asked. "Is *he* a spy, too? Is that how he got this job?"

"We *were* going out!" Nancy said. "But I guess he has other plans." She whirled around and dashed out of the police station. Halting on the steps, she fought back the tears stinging her eyes. "I'm not going to cry," she whispered through gritted teeth.

But Nancy wasn't left alone with her tumultuous thoughts for long. Her father followed her out of the precinct and wrapped a consoling arm around her shoulder.

Nancy threw herself into her father's embrace. "Oh, Dad, how could he do this to me?"

"People sometimes do things they don't mean," Mr. Drew said. "We both know Ned is a fine young man, sensitive and considerate. I think he'll come to his senses, Nancy. Just give him time." But there was really nothing Mr. Drew could say to make his daughter feel better.

"I hate him," Nancy sobbed. "I don't ever want to see him again!"

When Nancy had calmed down, she and her father got into Mr. Drew's silver Cadillac and drove back to River Heights.

For the first half of the ride, Nancy obsessed over the thought of Ned and Sondra together. He's probably taking her out for a fancy dinner right now, Nancy thought. And then they'll go dancing at some nightclub.

But after a while Nancy couldn't stand imagining those things. She was only making herself more miserable. I've got to stop thinking about them, she decided. I've got to, or I'm going to lose my mind!

It was then that Mick's hysterical words in the police station came back to Nancy. *You think I'm a murderer? Me? But I didn't do it, I swear. That gun isn't mine! Someone planted it!* Mick had sounded so surprised at what was happening to him.

With all the evidence against the art director, it seemed as though the case were over, clean and simple. But something was simmering in the back of Nancy's mind.

When Nancy had taken Yvonne's pulse in her office that day, the publisher's heart had been racing. That shouldn't have happened if she had really fainted.

But why would Yvonne fake passing out? Was it possible that she had, in fact, seen the mysterious gunman? Was it someone she wanted to cover for? But why would she cover for someone who was trying to kill her?

Whatever the answer, Nancy was becoming more and more sure that Yvonne was hiding something. Hadn't she had that feeling since her very first day on the case?

Nancy went over that first day in her mind. There'd been that horrible scene with Mick in Yvonne's office and the practical joke with the severed head. After that, Nancy remembered, she'd spent the day looking at shots of Danielle for Mick. And she also recalled being surprised at the thoughtful note the art director had written to her about being careful of staring at the computer for too long.

Suddenly Nancy caught her breath. Mick's spelling had been worse than a fourth-grader's. He'd confused *your* with *you're* and *their* with *they're*. But in the threatening letters to Yvonne, those words had been spelled correctly. Nancy bit her lip. Mick didn't write those letters, she told herself, suddenly sure. But who did?

Nancy decided to take the train into Chicago the next day and do a little investigating on her own. On a Saturday, no one would be around to get in the way.

Nancy spent a leisurely Saturday morning at home with her father. Ned called once, but Nancy told Hannah Gruen to tell him she wasn't home. She'd tried not to cry then, but a few tears escaped nonetheless.

Nancy caught the eleven-fifteen train into Chicago and was in the lobby of the *Flash* building a few minutes before one. A security guard who looked more asleep than awake asked her to sign a visitor's book. She wrote her name and her time of arrival.

Nancy flipped back a couple of pages and noticed Yvonne's name in the book, too. She'd been up to the office late Thursday night. What a workaholic, Nancy thought.

Once Nancy had signed the book, the guard motioned her toward the elevators. It bothered her that he hadn't asked for her I.D. Security certainly was lax.

Nancy rode up to the *Flash* offices. She had made a point of watching Scott activate and deactivate the security system a few times, so she knew just how it worked. All she had to do was push the right coded numbers and the alarm was deactivated. Then Nancy used her credit card to pick the lock. In less than five minutes she had the *Flash* offices completely to herself.

Nancy decided to begin her search in Mick's office. She picked the lock on his door and stepped inside. It looked the same as always, except that Mick's camera was sitting on his desk. Nancy remembered that he'd left it there Friday afternoon, just before she'd come in and clobbered him.

Nancy picked up the expensive Nikon camera. Well, she thought, I might as well see what it has to show. She found the cord to the camera in the top drawer of his desk and hurried down the hall to an empty office with a computer. She knew she was taking a big liberty in uploading Mick's shots without his knowledge, but since she was only doing it in order to clear him of a crime, she figured she was justified.

Nancy plugged the cameras in and let the photos load. Once they all appeared, she printed each shot.

Nancy sat down with the prints and began scrutinizing them for clues. Most of the shots were pretty arty, contrasting light and shadow or picking up odd mixtures of people in the same shot. The work was very different from the commercial portraits Mick took for *Flash*. He was clearly talented at both types of photography.

Still, none of the pictures helped Nancy much. But they *have* to! Nancy thought in frustration. *I've got nothing else to go on.* She redoubled her efforts, checking each photo even more closely.

Thoughtfully, Nancy picked up a picture showing a newspaper stand. There was no doubt that Mick had a special touch with a camera. The newsstand looked so clear. Nancy could actually see Friday's date on the front of one of the papers, and the words on the nearby street sign. Even the shadows were clear.

Suddenly Nancy realized that the photo might be the clue she was looking for! It could be just the thing needed to establish an alibi for Mick. Nancy checked every detail of the picture. It was all there—the street signs to indicate place, the newspapers to show the date. Now if she could just establish the time the picture had been taken, Mick would have an airtight alibi!

Mick had said he'd been shooting the film at the same time that Yvonne had been attacked. If so, the shadows would prove it—since shadows change length according to how high in the sky the sun is. A two o'clock shadow was the same length on Friday as it was on Saturday.

Nancy glanced at her wristwatch. It showed a quarter of two, a little before the time the gunman had invaded the *Flash* studio on Friday. If she hopped into a taxi, she could be at the newsstand in twenty minutes. Nancy grabbed the picture and dashed out of the office, being careful to reset the alarm before she left.

It wasn't hard to find the newsstand. It was the only one at the intersection shown on the street sign. Nancy pulled the photo from her bag as she got out of the taxi and slammed the door. She checked the time again. Five after two. Perfect! Nancy had heard Yvonne scream at ten after.

The photo showed that the shadow of the signpost just reached the edge of the newsstand. The picture was so clear there could be no mistake. Nancy took a careful look at the real street sign and newsstand. Sure enough, the shadows matched.

Nancy let out a triumphant cry. She'd cleared Mick! He'd been far from *Flash* at two o'clock Friday afternoon. He couldn't possibly have taken the photo, then rushed back to shoot Yvonne. Besides, Mick had never tried to use the picture as an alibi. That meant there was no reason for it to be a fake.

So, Nancy told herself, the case isn't over after all. But what did the new development mean? Obviously, the culprit was trying to frame Mick by planting the gun in his desk, but who *was* the culprit? David? Someone else working for MediaCorp? Or just a person who hated Yvonne and Mick?

Nancy knew that she was facing what was the least favorite part of a mystery for her—waiting for the criminal's next move. Meanwhile, a potential killer was on the loose. And when it became known that Nancy had cleared Mick, the criminal just might turn his wrath upon Nancy herself.

CHAPTER TWELVE

Nancy, when are you going to stop dragging into Chicago on these commuter trains and start driving your gorgeous blue Mustang again?" Bess Marvin demanded. "It's such a bummer having to take this smelly old train."

"When they turn the Willis Tower into the world's tallest garage," Nancy said with a smile. "Really, you wouldn't believe how hard it is to find parking in the city."

"Oh," Bess said dreamily, "but there's nothing like cruising down the parkway in that Mustang of yours, the wind blowing through our hair, the sun shining . . ."

"Please, Bess," George said sarcastically. "You sound like a car commercial!" Nancy giggled.

"Aha," George cried, "did I detect a laugh coming from our sad and serious Ms. Drew? I knew your funnybone wasn't broken."

Nancy flashed her friends an apologetic smile. "I'm sorry, you guys. I know I'm not being much fun. But this thing with Ned—"

"Stop right there. Don't say another word," George told Nancy. "We know you're miserable, and we know you probably need a little moral support from your best friends. Why do you think we decided to go into town today? It wasn't because Bess *really* needs that black suede dress."

"I do too need it," Bess protested, "and that store wouldn't take my credit card!"

Nancy smiled again. "It doesn't matter. I'm just glad to have you two around."

Nancy leaned back in her seat and listened to the rhythmic clatter of the train. She was dreading going in to *Flash*. Things were bound to be volatile, for a number of reasons. For starters, Mick would be back at work. Nancy had gone down to the police station with the newsstand photograph on Saturday and explained everything to Detective Graham. Mick had been out of jail within fifteen minutes. But how would the rest of the staff react to him? How would Yvonne behave? Not normally, that was certain.

Also, everyone at *Flash* knew Nancy was a detective, and probably thought she was Yvonne's spy. Nancy was sure she'd be getting the cold shoulder from a lot of people she'd thought were her friends.

Nancy was going to have to see Ned and Sondra, too. She'd managed to avoid Ned's calls all weekend, but he'd left a message for her on Sunday. He'd thanked her for getting Mick out of prison and said that he intended to go back to *Flash* on Monday as an intern. After all, Brenda hadn't blown *his* cover, except with Sondra. He promised to let Nancy know about anything strange that he saw. He'd also said he wanted to see her and hoped they could work things out.

Fat chance, Nancy said to herself.

Nancy was definitely not thrilled about the day's prospects. But having Bess and George to talk to on the train made it all a little better. "I don't know what I'm going to do," Nancy told her friends. "I think I'm going to melt into the ground when I see Ned. Either that or punch him out."

"He's really acting like a creep," Bess agreed.

"But how come?" George wondered. "I mean, Ned's always been totally in love with you. He's never so much as *looked* at another girl. So why now?"

Nancy sighed. "I think I might be partly to blame. Ned was feeling unappreciated. He said I was always busy working and never had time for him. I did treat our vacation pretty lightly. But Ned's been my boyfriend for *years*. And—and I miss him." Suddenly Nancy felt as if she were about to cry.

"Hey, it's okay," George said softly. "Look, either Ned will regain his senses and come back to you, or he's a real jerk and not worth the tears."

"Right," Bess said.

Nancy stared morosely at the dirty train floor. It was a no-win situation. Either she pretended she hated Ned and felt awful or admitted she loved him and felt even worse!

When they reached the city, Nancy kissed her friends good-bye. "Do you want to meet at the end of the day and go back to River Heights together?" Bess asked.

"I wish I could," Nancy said, "but I have no idea when I'm going to be done at *Flash*, so I'll have to pass. I'll see you at home."

"Okay. Good luck," Bess said, giving Nancy an extra hug.

"And be careful today," George advised.

Wow, Nancy thought as she caught the downtown subway, I've got some really great friends—no matter how awful my boyfriend is.

But as Nancy neared the *Flash* building she found her fears about Ned gradually being replaced by worries about the case. Someone in that office was a potential killer. The murderer might even be after *her* now. And she was sure no one at *Flash* was going to be too eager to help her find more information at that point.

Nancy felt like a first-time parachuter. She was about to step into a huge void, and she had no idea what to expect. All she could do was take the leap and hope the parachute worked.

Nancy could feel the change in atmosphere at *Flash* as soon as she stepped into the reception area. Two reporters who were walking by stopped to stare rudely at her. Nancy sighed. Then, trying to make everything seem as normal as possible, she put a smile on her face and called, "Hey, Scott, how's it going?" as she'd done each morning.

"What are you doing here?" Scott replied shortly.

"I—" Scott's coldness stopped Nancy short. She hadn't expected that from *him*. She steeled herself. "I work here. I'm investigating an attempted murder, trying to make sure Yvonne doesn't get killed." Then she added more gently, "Is that so bad?"

Scott stared at his blank computer screen in embarrassment.

Finally he mumbled, "That's not the problem. The problem is what you've been reporting to Yvonne. Some of the things I've said about her haven't been too flattering—and I don't want to lose my job."

Nancy sighed. "I haven't been betraying the people who work here, Scott. That's not what I was hired to do."

"I wish I could believe that," Scott answered. He glanced at Nancy, and in that instant she detected an unmistakable look of fear. Wow, he is really scared, Nancy thought. Then she began to wonder how the others would react. She wanted to wring Brenda Carlton's neck! Once again, she'd ruined everything.

"Mick wants to see you," Scott told Nancy. "He's in the studio doing a shoot. Yvonne wants to see you, too, in her office."

"Thanks," Nancy said, turning to leave.

"Oh, and Sondra left you this." Scott handed Nancy a small, folded piece of paper.

Nancy stepped away from the reception desk, frowning. What does she want? she wondered. She unfolded the paper and read the note:

Dear Nancy,
How can I ever thank you for what you've done
for Mick? I feel really bad about the horrible
things I said to you. Do you think we can
straighten things out?
> *Your friend (I hope), Sondra*

Nancy looked at the note angrily, then crumpled it up and threw it in a nearby wastepaper basket. Sondra hadn't said a single word about Ned.

Nancy walked slowly toward the studio. She knew a lot of the staff would be at the shoot—and judging by Scott's reaction to her, they probably wouldn't be too friendly. Well, she would have to face them at some point. It might as well be now.

When Nancy stepped into the studio she immediately saw Sondra and Ned and purposely avoided making eye contact with either of them. As for the others, no one so much as said hello to Nancy until Mick spotted her.

"Nancy!" he cried. He left his camera and ran over to her, throwing his arms around her in a huge, friendly hug.

Mick's reaction was as uncomfortable for Nancy as the lack of reaction from everyone else. After all, Nancy and Mick hadn't exactly been big buddies before she'd sprung him from jail. Suddenly everything at *Flash* was topsy-turvy. Nancy's friends had deserted her. And the people she hadn't really trusted, like Mick and Sondra, were the only ones being civil to her.

"Nancy," Mick was saying as he casually draped his arm around her shoulder, "I asked you to come here so I could thank you for clearing me. I certainly didn't do anything to deserve your help. I'm really grateful."

Nancy smiled. "Well, I couldn't let an innocent man sit in jail, could I?"

"I'm going to make it up to you somehow," Mick said intently. "I'm not sure how right now, but I will."

"I don't expect any kind of reward," Nancy said. But she had to admit, after all the flak she was getting from other people in the office, that it did feel good to have at least one full-fledged fan.

"You're a good kid," Mick said. He planted a brotherly kiss on Nancy's cheek. "I've got to get back to work now, but we'll talk later, okay?"

"Okay," Nancy said, heading for the door. She shot a glance at Ned before she left. He was gazing at her soulfully. But Nancy wasn't about to give him a break. She tossed her head haughtily and stepped out of the studio.

Forcing a brave smile onto her face, Nancy walked to Yvonne's office.

I wonder how Yvonne's reacting to all this, Nancy thought. She knocked on her door.

"Who's there?"

"It's me, Nancy."

"Door's open. Come in."

"Hi," Nancy said, opening the door and stepping into the publisher's office. She gave Yvonne a friendly smile and closed the door behind her.

But Yvonne wasn't smiling. In fact, her expression was decidedly angry. "Just exactly what are you trying to do?" she burst out.

"I—I don't understand," Nancy said, confused.

"Oh, you don't?" the publisher said sarcastically. "Then let me spell it out for you. I hired you to stop the person who's trying to kill me—"

"And that's just what I'm trying to do," Nancy said, attempting another smile. Yvonne hadn't asked her to sit down, and she felt awkward standing in front of her.

But Yvonne wasn't taking any peace offerings. "Mick's trying to kill me," she practically screamed, "and the detective I hired gets him out of jail so he can finish the job!"

"Yvonne, you've got it all wrong," Nancy cried. "It's not Mick! I have proof of that." She paused. "I don't know how to tell you this, but I think it might be David."

"David!" Yvonne snorted. "What a ridiculous idea. David loves me—and Mick owns the murder weapon."

"No, he doesn't," Nancy said. "That gun was planted in Mick's desk. I know for certain that he wasn't anywhere near the *Flash* building when that shot was fired. Someone's trying to frame him, and I think it might be David. Don't you know that he works for MediaCorp? They've sent him checks!"

For a moment, Yvonne just stared at Nancy. Then she said, "If this is a joke, it's a very bad one. I really don't know what to say except—Nancy Drew, you're fired."

CHAPTER THIRTEEN

Wow, I feel like someone in one of your magazine articles," Nancy exclaimed to Mick. She spread the skirt of her gold silk dress across the seat of the limousine and leaned back against the plush leather cushion.

"Do you want something to drink?" Mick asked, motioning to the car bar. "Sprite, Coke?"

"I'll take a Coke, thanks," Nancy said, feeling very luxurious. "I'm so excited. The Maggie Awards! I've heard about them for years, and watched them on TV, but now I'm actually going to *be* there to see it all happen!"

"Imagine how *I* feel," Mick said, handing Nancy her soda and taking a sip of his own drink. "I've known about the Maggies for years, too. Who would have guessed that my magazine would eventually be nominated for one?"

"Actually, my friend Bess would have," Nancy said with a laugh. "She's been saying *Flash* should win the best teen magazine award for months now." Nancy stared out the window as the limo cruised through the streets of Chicago from Mick's fancy apartment to the Palace nightclub, where the Maggie ceremony would be held.

"Well, we haven't won yet," Mick said, trying to check his excitement. "We've only been nominated. We've got to beat out four other magazines to get the award." He turned to Nancy and smiled. "By the way, you look great."

Nancy's flowing, full-length gold silk dress with long split sleeves showed off her arms beautifully. It was the perfect color to complement her shiny reddish blond hair. She'd completed the outfit with simple gold jewelry, gold sandals, and a gold clutch. She knew she looked good. And she needed to. Mick had told her Ned was going to be at the ceremony, too—with Sondra.

"Thank you, Mick," Nancy said, "but there's no way I could compare with you!" She looked at the art director and smiled. He was wearing beautifully cut tails with a white silk shirt and a black bow tie. Since it was impossible for Mick to wear anything traditional, the tails were made of soft black leather.

Mick smiled, then bit his lip. "Got to look my best, just in case Flash does win and I have to go up there in front of the hottest people in the business to accept the award." He shot a worried glance at Nancy. "Anyway," he went on, "no matter what happens tonight, I'm glad I could share the evening with you. You've done so much for me."

"I know," Nancy said, giggling. "You definitely were not too thrilled about spending time in jail. Hey, I'm thankful for your invitation to the Maggies. I've been feeling a little like a social outcast these days."

"It's kind of unbelievable the way everyone at the office turned against you," Mick said sympathetically. "I guess they're all a little scared of Yvonne. When they found out you were working for her—well, they just wanted to stay away from you."

"As of one week ago, I'm *not* working for her," Nancy said, tapping her fingers on the armrest. "I just don't understand. How could Yvonne fire me when I'm only trying to protect her? And how can she ignore the facts? It's weird."

"Well, I'm glad you're still working on it," Mick said. "I need to find out who tried to frame me."

"It's not really me—it's Ned," Nancy said. "He might make me furious at him, but he is a good detective. And since only you, Sondra, and Yvonne know who he really is . . ."

"You know, Yvonne tried to fire him, too. But I told her I liked his work." Mick grinned. "I just didn't tell her it was his detective work I liked."

Nancy finished her soda. "One way or another, we're going to get concrete proof against whoever's behind these threats, and I'm going to make sure Yvonne stays alive long enough to see that I'm right."

Mick laughed. "You're a fighter, Nancy. You're the most determined person I've ever met." He glanced out the window. "Here we are."

The limo pulled up in front of what in the daytime probably looked like an old abandoned theater. But at the moment, it was bustling with activity. As Nancy and Mick got out of the car, cameras started clicking in a blinding series of flashes. "That's Mick Swanson," Nancy heard someone saying, "but who's the gorgeous woman he's with?"

Nancy beamed. She felt like a real celebrity. She and Mick were ushered quickly into the club. The inside was nothing at all like its unkempt outside. A long red carpet welcomed the guests as if they were royalty, and the Palace glittered with lights. Huge vases of flowers lined the wide hallway leading to the main room. A tall woman in a floor-length gown whisked their coats away.

Nancy walked with Mick into the award room feeling as though she owned the place. But her confidence sank down to the hem of her silk dress as soon as she saw Ned and Sondra standing cozily together in a spot she and Mick would have to pass to find seats.

Sondra wore a stunning green off-the-shoulder evening gown. And Ned looked so handsome that Nancy could barely stand it. He always looked great in a formal suit.

Nancy felt like running off to the bathroom and stalling for time, but she knew that would be silly. Steeling herself, she walked right up to Ned and Sondra, Mick following closely behind. "Hi," she said, trying to sound pleasant, but not too pleasant. It was hard to smile when your heart felt as if it had been split open with a meat cleaver.

"Nancy!" Sondra cried. "I'm so glad you're here. You look fabulous."

"Thanks," Nancy replied tightly.

"Hello, Nancy," Ned said, giving her an intense look. "I've been trying to call you recently but you're never home."

"Yes, I've been busy," Nancy said coolly. "I think I'm going to be busy for a long time."

Meanwhile, Mick had given his sister a hug and a kiss. "Hey, Ned," he said. The two young men shook hands. After that, the foursome stood around uncomfortably for a moment. Finally Mick said, "Well, Nancy, should we go find seats?"

"Sure," Nancy agreed. There was nothing she wanted more than to get away from Ned and Sondra.

"We'll see you at the party after the awards," Sondra told them.

Nancy and Mick found seats in the middle of the audience. "That wasn't so bad, was it?" Mick asked Nancy sympathetically.

"No, but I'm hoping the rest of the evening will be better," Nancy answered, smiling at Mick.

"We should talk about that sometime," Mick told Nancy.

"What's to say?" Nancy asked.

"*Lots*," Mick replied emphatically. "I'm not sure you really understand what's going on between those two."

"The less I know, the better," Nancy said.

"Not necessarily," Mick returned. "Anyway, this is not the time or the place to go into a heavy discussion, so we'll have to do it later."

"Okay, that's fine," Nancy said.

She turned away and looked around the audience to see if she knew anyone. She recognized a few models and other celebrities, all wearing their glitziest. Yvonne, she saw, was sitting in front, close to the stage. She was wearing a classic black gown, and her hair was pulled softly away from her face. What do you know? Nancy thought. Yvonne actually wore something other than a business suit.

David was sitting next to Yvonne, looking as cold and untrustworthy as ever. Nancy just couldn't understand what Yvonne saw in him.

Nancy and Mick settled into their seats and soon the Maggie ceremony began. Nancy found all the preliminary awards very boring, since she didn't know anything about the magazine business. But there was still plenty for her to look at—the great clothes, for instance.

Finally, the master of ceremonies announced the best teen magazine award. "Here goes," Nancy whispered. "I'm crossing all my fingers and all my toes for you."

"Me too," Mick whispered back.

"The competition's been tough this year," the M.C. said, "but our judges came to a unanimous decision despite that. The envelope, please . . ." Nancy held her breath as the M.C. took the envelope and ripped it open. "And the winner is . . . *Flash* magazine. Congratulations, Yvonne Verdi and Mick Swanson!"

"We did it!" Mick cried excitedly to Nancy. "We actually did it!" He gave Nancy a big bear hug.

Nancy hugged Mick back. "Fantastic! You and *Flash* deserve it."

Mick squeezed his way to the end of their row and walked up to the stage. Nancy could tell he was trying to look suave, but his happiness came through clearly in the bounciness of his stride.

Mick met Yvonne at the steps to the stage, and they walked

up together and crossed the stage. When they reached the podium, Mick turned and smiled happily at Yvonne.

At that moment, there was a terrific splintering sound. One of the heavy lights hanging from the ceiling broke loose and came crashing down—headed straight for Mick and Yvonne.

CHAPTER FOURTEEN

Hey, Mick, I brought you something," Nancy told the bandaged and unmoving figure in the bed.

"Not more flowers, I hope," Mick said. "People have given me so many I'm beginning to think I'm in a funeral home instead of a hospital."

"Well, a beautiful spring Thursday would probably be a nice day to be buried on," Nancy joked. "Anyway, thank goodness you aren't going to be." She dropped into a little chair by Mick's bedside. "That light could have finished you off with no trouble. If it had hit you squarely instead of just grazing you, that would have been the end. Thank goodness Yvonne jumped out of the way in time."

"Yeah, I guess I was lucky," Mick said with a laugh. "All I got was a dislocated shoulder, a broken leg, five stitches in my arm, and assorted cuts and bruises. That's the kind of luck you wish on your worst enemy!"

"Speaking of enemies," Nancy said casually, "do you have any, Mick?"

Mick adjusted himself uncomfortably in the bed. "Hey,

what kind of a question is that? And what happened to the present you brought me?"

"Okay," Nancy said, laughing. "Present first. Questions later. Deal?"

"Deal."

Nancy took a silver-wrapped box from her shoulder bag and handed it to Mick. "Get well soon," she said. "Your cameras miss you."

"Uh, do you think you could open that for me? I'm kind of incapacitated here."

"Of course." Nancy tore away the silver foil and took the top off the box. Inside was a remote control dune buggy, perfect for Mick since it was painted with zebra stripes. "It reminded me of those shoes you have," Nancy told him, "so I just had to buy it."

"I *love* it," Mick said. "It's going to be the prize of my collection when I get back to the office. Put it on the floor."

Nancy set the dune buggy down beside Mick and handed him the remote control. Mick had a great time making it do tricks for a few minutes. Pressing the buttons was about the only activity he could do easily, because of his bandages and casts.

"So, Nancy, why the question about enemies?" he asked finally, dropping the remote control onto the bed.

Nancy sighed. "I hate to tell you this, but the police found out that the light didn't fall by accident. The wire holding it in place had been cut—and by a very ingenious device. An ax had been rigged up to a remote control—"

"Oh no," Mick groaned. "Another murder attempt against Yvonne. You don't still suspect me, do you?"

"No. That photo of the newsstand clears you. Besides, half the *Flash* staff saw the stunt you pulled on me and the other half heard about it. Anyone could have used the same trick at the Maggies."

"Whew," Mick said. "I'm glad the killer didn't get Yvonne. She's not as bad as I sometimes make her out to be."

"Yes, the killer messed up again," Nancy told Mick, "but maybe the murderer wasn't as far off the mark as we think! You see, everyone assumes the 'accident' was meant for Yvonne and not you because there have already been two other attempts on her life. But what if that light was meant to get you both?"

"But, Nancy," said Mick with a gasp, "why?"

Nancy leaned forward and rested her hand on Mick's good arm. "Here's what I think. Those other attempts were meant to kill Yvonne and discredit you at the same time. So our killer is out to get you, too."

"That's true," Mick said slowly.

"Well," Nancy continued, "once I cleared you, the creep could no longer do that. So now he has to kill you *and* Yvonne in order to get you both out of the way."

Mick was silent for a moment. "That's really frightening," he said at last. "But who's doing it, Nancy? And why?"

"I'm not sure," Nancy said thoughtfully, "but I have a few good ideas. It's highly possible that MediaCorp's behind the whole thing. By getting rid of *Flash*'s owners, they'd be able to buy the magazine cheaply and without any trouble."

"Incredible!" Mick cried.

"If it *is* MediaCorp, I'd lay bets that David's doing the dirty work. He's on their payroll, you know. I found the evidence in his office. At this point, it's all just speculation," Nancy said more realistically, "but it's a theory I want to investigate further."

"It's a great theory!" Mick exclaimed. "Because other than MediaCorp, I don't think I have any enemies. At least none who hates me enough to try to kill me!"

"Then you think MediaCorp would actually go as far as murder to get something they want?"

"I'm not sure, but it's possible. I told Yvonne that MediaCorp would never give her the price she was asking for *Flash*. Even if I agreed to sell."

"But, Mick," Nancy said, "Yvonne told me she's not planning to sell at *any* price."

"That's what she *says*. Believe me, Nancy, she has her price. Why would I lie to you?"

"Why would *Yvonne* lie?" she said.

"I can't answer that," Mick said.

"Neither can I. Anyway, I'm hoping you'll be able to give me a few leads on what happened at the Maggies. Did you see anything odd? Anyone suspicious in the audience?"

Mick thought for a moment. "I can't remember anything unusual. But to tell you the truth, I was too excited to notice very much that night. It was like a fantasy come true—and who looks for flaws in the middle of a living fantasy?" Mick sighed, remembering the evening. "And to think I never got to accept my award. Now that is a real tragedy."

Nancy laughed. "Well, you certainly made the biggest splash in the history of the Maggie ceremonies! I'm just glad you're all right." Nancy decided to let the questioning go. Clearly, Mick wasn't going to be able to help her much.

"How are you keeping yourself occupied?" she asked.

"Doing a lot of reading," Mick told her. "Yvonne was really sweet. She brought over a whole bunch of mystery novels for me." He pointed to a stack of paperbacks piled on his night table.

"That was thoughtful of her," Nancy mused.

"Yeah. This accident has actually made her want to be civil—even nice—to me."

"Are any of the books any good? Yvonne didn't seem very interested in mysteries when I first met her. I wouldn't suppose she'd know the best writers."

"Are you kidding?" Mick said incredulously. "Yvonne's the biggest mystery fanatic south of Alaska. She probably knows more about them than you or I do! She even *wrote* a few after she got out of college. I've read them. Real thrillers."

Nancy gasped. "And I bet I can guess her pen name. She's not, by any chance, Ivan Green, is she?"

"Brilliant deduction, Detective Drew," Mick said with a laugh. "Ivan, which sounds like Yvonne, and Green, which is English for the Italian word *verdi*, her last name."

Nancy suddenly glanced at her watch. "Oh, look, it's almost

five o'clock!" she exclaimed with fake surprise. "I promised my father I'd meet him for dinner at quarter after, so I'd better be running." Nancy leaned down to kiss Mick's cheek.

"Well, thanks for coming, Nancy. You've definitely broken the monotony of hospital life. And I love the dune buggy. It's kind of like a pet puppy."

"I'm glad. I'll come visit you again soon." Nancy grinned at Mick, but her smile disappeared the moment she stepped out of his room. She was thinking hard. She had a lot of work ahead of her, and she knew she wouldn't be able to do it all alone. But who could she ask for help? Usually she called Bess or George, but they were in River Heights. Too far away. Ned? After everything that had happened between them, could she still call him?

Nancy gave an exasperated sigh. I'll have to, she decided, no matter how much pride is at stake.

Nancy hurried to the hospital cafeteria and found a telephone. Not stopping for a moment, she pushed seven numbers.

The phone rang once before Scott's voice said, "Hello, *Flash* magazine."

"Yes, I'd like to speak to Ned Nickerson," Nancy said, trying not to sound like herself.

"Hold one moment," Scott said. He hadn't recognized her voice.

The next voice Nancy heard was Ned's. "Hello?" he said.

"Hi, Ned, this is Nancy. Are you alone?"

"Oh, wow, I'm so glad you finally called." Ned exclaimed

happily. "I've missed you so much. When can we get together and talk this thing out?"

"Hold on. I'm not calling to make up, and I don't want to hear the sordid details of your relationship with Sondra."

"What sordid details?" Ned cried. "All we did was—"

"I don't care." Nancy cut Ned off. "I need to talk to you about something much more important."

"More important than us, Nancy? I don't think that exists."

"Great. Butter me up, Ned Nickerson. It still doesn't excuse what you've done to me—to us!"

Ned sighed. "Please, let's not fight again."

"Right. I don't have time for it. We've got to meet. Stay at *Flash*. I'll be over there as fast as it takes me to catch a taxi downtown."

"What's up?" Ned asked.

"I've solved the mystery!" Nancy announced. Suddenly she was full of energy and excitement again.

"And you need my help to catch the person who's responsible, right?"

"Not person—people," Nancy told Ned.

"You mean there's more than one?" Ned said, incredulous.

"Yup, there are two! And you'll never guess who!"

CHAPTER FIFTEEN

Two, Nancy? Who?" asked Ned.

"Well, one of them's David Bowers."

"That's no big surprise," Ned said. "What about the second?"

Nancy took a deep breath. "You're not going to believe this, but—Yvonne Verdi!"

"*Yvonne?* Nancy, that's impossible. Yvonne's the one they're trying to kill."

"Nope, Yvonne's the one they're trying to make it *seem* as though they're trying to kill. But really, Mick's been the target of this scheme all along. I'll explain the whole thing later. Just be at *Flash* when I get there."

"Okay, Nancy. I love—" But she had already hung up.

Nancy dashed out of the hospital. She found a taxi right away and within seconds was shooting downtown, the driver dodging bikers and pedestrians. I hope Yvonne and David haven't gone home yet. I hope I haven't missed them! she thought.

The ride to *Flash* took only fifteen minutes, but it felt like hours to Nancy. Wrapping up a mystery and catching the criminals was always hard, but this time an extra complication was going to make it even tougher.

Oh, Ned, Nancy cried to herself, why did you have to leave me? Then her anger flared. How dare you! And how am I ever going to keep my mind on my plan when I feel like this? Nancy nibbled nervously on the nail of her index finger.

Nancy forced herself to think of the plan she was about to carry out—a plan which, if it worked, was going to nab her two attempted murderers. She'd have to play it cool and time things perfectly with Ned. Otherwise there was a good chance *she* would be the next victim.

Suddenly Nancy called to the taxi driver, "Hey, stop here, in front of this store. Keep the meter running. I'll be back in two minutes, okay?"

"Fine with me," the driver said, pulling up in front of the store.

Nancy jumped out of the car and hurried into the store. She spent less than five minutes inside. When she ran back out she was clutching a small brown paper bag. "I think I just broke the shopper's speed record," she commented to the driver as she jumped into the taxi. As he peeled away from the curb, she stuffed the package into her shoulder bag.

It didn't take long to reach the *Flash* building. Nancy paid the driver and tumbled out of the car. Once again she rode the elevator upstairs. She glanced at her watch. It was just after five-thirty. Good, she thought. She was sure that at least one of the crooks was still there and the rest of the staff was probably gone, so they wouldn't mess anything up.

The elevator doors opened on the sixteenth floor, and Nancy stepped out. There was Ned—but he wasn't alone. A yellow-haired figure stood next to him.

Nancy marched angrily over to Ned. She was seething but she hid her feelings as best she could. "Hello," she said evenly.

"Sondra insisted on coming," Ned told Nancy.

"I want to help," Sondra explained. "It's the least I can do for the girl who saved my brother." She gave Nancy a smile full of warmth and hope.

Nancy was silent.

"Nancy," Ned said, moving closer to her, "I told you, it's not the way you think it is. You're supposed to be a detective. Please don't jump to conclusions before you have all the facts."

Suddenly Sondra cut in. "Hold it, you two. You both sound ridiculous. Why don't you try to communicate for real? First thing, Ned, is that you have to be more understanding of Nancy. She probably has good reason to feel a little jealous. But, Nancy, you haven't let Ned explain a word! How's he supposed to get through to you? I'm going to have to take charge here, or we'll never catch the people we came for."

Sondra looked from Nancy to Ned and back.

"Good. Now that you've both shut up long enough to listen, I'm going to set you two straight. Nancy, I didn't steal your boyfriend, no matter what you think. I'll admit at first I was really attracted to Ned. But that was before I found out you two'd been going out for so long. Ned's really helped me recently, at a time when everything seemed to be going wrong. I appreciate it," Sondra said simply. "He's been a good friend to me, a close friend—and that's all.

"But, Ned," Sondra continued, "I think you used me to get back at Nancy a little. You were mad at her for not spending enough time with you, and the fact that she got so jealous did wonders for your ego. Come on, you know it's true."

"I refuse to admit a thing," Ned said, but a tiny smile played at the corners of his lips.

"It's clear to me that you two love each other. But to tell you the truth, I don't care about any of this," Sondra said, "at least not right now. Because we've got some serious detective work to do. The three of us are just going to have to make up. Got it?"

Nancy glanced at Sondra out of the corner of her eye. She had to admit Sondra knew how to get things done. If it had been up to me and Ned, the culprits would have gotten half-way to Acapulco before we even stopped fighting, Nancy said to herself. Nancy couldn't help but admire Sondra. She'd really be okay—if only she'd stay away from Ned.

"All right," Nancy said at last. "Are Yvonne and David still here?"

"Yvonne is," Ned answered. "David went home an hour ago."

"That's fine. Once we've gotten a confession out of Yvonne, David will be easy to nab."

"So where do we start?" Sondra wanted to know.

"In the room, across from Yvonne's office. You two stay there. I'll be with Yvonne. Give me fifteen minutes, then come out and make sure I'm okay." Nancy reached into her shoulder bag. "Here, Ned, I have something to give you." Then she pulled out a small pistol. She was holding it by the barrel.

"Nancy!" Ned exclaimed. "What are you doing with that thing? Get rid of it!"

Nancy giggled. "Good, I'm glad it's so convincing. Ned, it's a water gun, and one of the most realistic I've ever seen. I bought it at Woolworth's on the way over here. If I really do get in trouble with Yvonne, running into her office and yelling 'Boo' isn't going to help. But a gun—or what she thinks is a gun—will!"

Sondra laughed. "Catching a criminal with a toy gun! My brother would really appreciate this!"

Ned frowned, but pocketed the water gun. "Nancy," he said, "you're reaching here."

"It's called improvising," Nancy said with a smile. "You guys ready?"

"Sure, I've got my plastic gun, haven't I?" Ned joked. Then his expression changed to one of concern. "Nancy, be careful."

"I will. Don't worry. Now come on."

Nancy, Ned, and Sondra sneaked quietly down the corridor to the darkroom off of Mick's office. "How are we going to get in? It's locked," Sondra whispered.

Nancy pulled out her credit card and gave Sondra a grin. In half a minute the door was open. "Okay, you two. Remember, fifteen minutes, just long enough for me to get the confession on tape. You're my life insurance!"

Ned and Sondra stepped into the darkroom and Nancy closed the door gently. Then she reached into her shoulder bag and pushed the record button on her tiny portable tape deck. Walking across the hallway, she knocked softly on Yvonne's office door. There was no answer, even after she knocked a second time.

Finally Nancy pushed open the door. The publisher wasn't there. Well, I'll just have to wait for her, Nancy decided. She knew Yvonne hadn't left for the day because her door was unlocked.

Nancy closed the door and leaned thoughtfully against the leather couch. So Yvonne had turned out to be just as selfish and egotistical as she'd seemed to Nancy that first day. However, she also had an evil streak that Nancy hadn't counted on. She hadn't really cared about the magazine at all, just her own success and her wallet. She'd even been willing to kill off Mick, an old friend, when he'd gotten in the way.

Nancy started pacing the room. Where was Yvonne, anyway? Nancy had told Ned and Sondra to appear in fifteen minutes. If Yvonne didn't show up soon, the timing of the plan was going to be thrown off!

All at once the door flew open and Nancy found herself

face-to-face with the publisher. "Nancy!" Yvonne exclaimed. "What are you doing here?" She gave her a sugar-coated smile.

Nancy smiled, too, just as falsely as Yvonne had. "I have great news," she said. "I've discovered who's to blame for the murder attempts."

"Oh, how wonderful," Yvonne said. Nancy could tell from the tone of her voice that Yvonne didn't think she'd been found out. "Sit down." She ushered Nancy onto the black couch. "Tell me all about it." Yvonne took her customary seat behind her desk.

Nancy sat down coolly on the couch. "It was an interesting case," she began, "very cleverly planned in the criminal's mind. I almost didn't crack it. But in the end I was able to, thanks to my partners—Agatha Christie, Sir Arthur Conan Doyle, and all the other fabulous mystery writers whose books I've read over the years."

A strange expression crossed Yvonne's face. It took Nancy a moment to realize that the publisher was scared. And that's the proof, Nancy decided. She knows I know the truth and she's frightened.

Nancy hurried on. "Yes," she said, "I've gotten tons of ideas from books. And I've found that criminals sometimes get ideas from books, too."

Yvonne pursed her lips. "What does all this have to do with the problems at *Flash*?"

Nancy wasn't about to answer the publisher's question—at least not yet. She smiled and asked, "What mystery writers do you like to read, Yvonne? I've just discovered a new one who's very interesting to me. Ivan Green. Ever heard of him?"

But Nancy hadn't counted on what happened next. Suddenly she was staring into the gleaming barrel of a hand revolver—and Yvonne was smiling evilly at her from behind it.

CHAPTER SIXTEEN

Don't make a sound," Yvonne said smoothly, not lowering the polished revolver, "or your face is going to be such a mess even plastic surgery won't help."

"I won't make a peep," Nancy replied. She hoped Yvonne wasn't trigger-happy. Otherwise she was going to be a memory before Ned and Sondra even had a chance to try the toy gun trick.

"You're smart, Nancy Drew," Yvonne was saying. "Smarter than I counted on. I didn't think you'd catch on to my little game. Well, it doesn't make much difference now because, my young detective, you're not careful enough!"

Nancy glanced anxiously over her shoulder at the door. Where were Ned and Sondra? They should have been there already, plastic pistol blazing.

"By the way," Yvonne added cruelly, "someone left the office across the hall open. I made sure it was locked from the outside before I came in here."

Nancy sucked in her breath. Uh-oh. She was on her own. "What are you going to do with me?" she asked calmly.

"In just a moment, I'm going to let you join your friends,"

Yvonne told her gleefully. "Then I will simply dispose of you all. But before I do, I'd like to know how you guessed my secret. I thought I'd created the perfect crime."

"Even the best-planned crimes have flaws," Nancy said. "Yours had a few. The most important one was that you lied to me."

"That's only a flaw if I did it badly," Yvonne cut in, "and I obviously did, since you found out the truth. Which lie are you talking about?" she asked.

"The first day I met you," Nancy continued, stalling for time, "you made a big deal about putting down mystery novels. Then Mick happened to mention that you loved them and had even written a few. I asked myself why you would lie about that to me. What did you have to hide? Then I remembered the copy of *Deadly Potion, Deadly Bite* that I'd seen in Mick's office just after the tarantula appeared in your desk."

"You were *supposed* to remember it," Yvonne commented sourly. "I planted it there to make Mick look guilty to you. I even stole one of his buttons, to make it absolutely clear."

"Right, but I realized later that the author, Ivan Green, was *you.*"

"I see," Yvonne said. "Then it wasn't a flaw in my planning. It was just a silly coincidence—Mick mentioning that I wrote mysteries."

"Silly coincidences are a detective's best friends," Nancy said seriously. "I've rarely solved a mystery without one. But you did make one mistake. When I felt your pulse after you 'fainted' the day the gunman 'broke into' *Flash*, it was racing. So your body tipped me off to another lie—you weren't really unconscious."

"You're thorough," Yvonne said disdainfully, "but clearly not thorough enough." She glanced down at her gun with a satisfied smile.

She's so sure of herself, Nancy thought. She studied Yvonne's face. I've got to get a full confession, she told herself. She needed undeniable evidence—just in case she managed to get out of this situation alive. The tape was running inside her bag. All she had to do was get Yvonne talking.

"I have a few questions, too," Nancy said after a moment. "How did you pull off the 'shooting' in your office? There's no way you could have shot the gun, planted it in Mick's office, and gotten back to your own office in the few seconds it took for us to run to your aid."

"It *was* a rather ingenious scheme, if I do say so myself," Yvonne bragged. "I shot the bullet into the wall on Thursday, the night before the incident."

"That's right," Nancy said, suddenly understanding. "I saw your signature in the security guard's book when I came in to *Flash* on Saturday. That explains why the bullet was so far off the mark. You weren't aiming at any specific target! I figured no one was such a bad shot."

"Very good," Yvonne said condescendingly. "Anyway, as you can guess, I also planted a gun in Mick's desk that night. Then on Friday, I used a second gun to get everyone's attention. I just shot out the window. Then I took it home with me since I knew you'd search my office. And I counted on your searching Mick's, too."

"Well, things almost turned out just the way you wanted," Nancy responded. "And now I've got one more question. Where does David fit into all this?"

"David?" Yvonne smirked. "That wimp? He's too stupid to pull off something like this. I was just using him to get to the top people at MediaCorp. I did it all, Nancy Drew, with no help from anyone."

Well, I've got the confession, Nancy thought. Now if I can just get it and myself out of here. . . . But Yvonne was already standing up, holding a length of rope she'd obviously stashed in one of her desk drawers. Grinning nastily, she walked toward Nancy. Without taking either her eyes or her gun off the girl, she reached into Nancy's shoulder bag and removed the tape recorder.

"An old trick," Yvonne said, triumphantly flicking off the record button and ejecting the cassette. "This one's been used by mystery writers for a long time, too. Oh well. I don't care if the confession's on tape—as long as *I've* got the tape."

Nancy swallowed hard. She hated being outsmarted.

Yvonne pocketed the tape and nudged Nancy's cheek with the gun. "Get moving, Detective. You've got a hot date—very hot, believe me."

Nancy didn't know what Yvonne was talking about, but she stood up and allowed Yvonne to direct her across the hall. Then the publisher reached into her pocket and handed Nancy the keys to the door. "Open it," she said. Nancy unlocked the door and Yvonne shoved her inside.

"Nancy!" Ned and Sondra shouted at once.

"Hi, guys. I think we messed up," Nancy said.

"Are you all right?" Ned cried. "If she's hurt you—"

"I'm fine," Nancy assured him. "Besides, there's nothing you can do to her, so you might as well not make idle threats."

"Smart girl," Yvonne said, obviously enjoying her power. "Okay, Nancy, you're about to become my assistant. I want you to tie up your friends. This gun will be trained on you while you work, so no funny stuff. If the knots aren't good and strong, the gun goes off. Got it?"

"Yes," Nancy muttered.

Yvonne handed Nancy the rope, and the young detective got to work tying Ned's hands behind his back. Yvonne watched over her shoulder, giving her directions and ordering her to pull tighter at every step. Nancy did her best to put a little slack into the knot, but when she was finished she had to admit that the knot wouldn't be easy to untie.

Nancy was forced to tie Ned's feet and Sondra's hands and feet in the same way. After that, Yvonne tied Nancy's herself. "Well," she said, once she was finished, "I hate to spoil the party, so I'll leave. But first . . ."

Yvonne walked over to the shelves where files were stored and pulled them all out, creating a large pile of paper on the floor.

"With all the faulty wiring in these office buildings," Yvonne said nonchalantly, "fires start so easily." She shoved the papers, leaving a large stack in front of the door. "This stuff should light up like desert brush in the dry season."

Yvonne took the tape with her confession on it and deftly deposited it on the worktable. "I can't think of anything nicer to do with this than start a bonfire," she said. She produced a book of matches from her pocket and lit one.

Yvonne walked to the door and stepped just outside it. Then she pitched the match into the room. With a tentative crackle at first, the papers went up in flame. Yvonne slammed the door shut, and Nancy heard her lock it from the outside. The fire began to spread quickly.

Nancy tugged at the ropes that bound her hands. No use— Yvonne had done a professional job. "Ned, Sondra," she cried, "can either of you pull free of your ropes? It's our only chance."

"You kidding me?" Ned asked. "Houdini couldn't get out of these."

"Or these," Sondra called.

"Then that's it," Nancy said finally. "We're trapped."

CHAPTER SEVENTEEN

What are we going to *do*?" Sondra cried, dangerously close to hysteria.

"Not sit here and burn up, that's for sure," Nancy replied. But as if to taunt her, the flames licked her toes. Nancy pulled her legs up to her chest.

"Calm down," Ned told Sondra. "Nancy's gotten out of worse situations than this."

"Well, what *are* you going to do?" Sondra whispered fearfully.

But Nancy didn't answer. She was too busy thinking. She knew that somehow she had to get free of the ropes that tied her hands and feet. Otherwise, all three of them were going to be burned crisper than a batch of overdone French fries. But how?

Ned had mentioned Houdini, the great escape artist. He'd been able to get out of complicated knots, metal chains, locked chests—sometimes while submerged in a tank of water. Of course, legend had it that Houdini had been killed when one of his tricks had failed—but that was after thousands of successful escapes. Come on, Houdini, help us out! Nancy prayed.

Suddenly Nancy realized the answer! Houdini had sometimes untied ropes with his teeth. Nancy had never done it before, but she was about to try!

"Sondra, Ned," Nancy shouted, "I've got it! Sondra, twist around so that your hands are facing me." Sondra did so, while Nancy scooted toward her. Meanwhile, the darkroom was growing hotter by the millisecond.

Nancy was so close to Sondra that she could smell her perfume over the smoke. With one more push, she had reached her, her face shoved up against the stylist's bound hands.

Immediately Nancy began to chew the knots with her teeth.

"Ow," Sondra shrieked.

Nancy spit the rope out of her mouth. "Did I bite you? I'm sorry."

"No," Sondra said, terrified. "It's the flames—they're getting closer!"

"Hurry, Nancy," Ned cried. "I'm about to pass out from the smoke!"

Nancy redoubled her efforts. Suddenly she felt the ropes loosen.

"Nancy," Sondra screamed, "they're coming undone! We're going to get out of here!"

Nancy gave one last jerk at the ropes which held Sondra. "Shake your arms," she cried. "Shake hard! Get those ropes off before the fire reaches us!"

Sondra pumped her hands frantically up and down, maneuvering as best she could with her arms pinned awkwardly behind her back. And then, all at once, she was free.

She turned to Nancy, and in a few moments Nancy felt the ropes falling off her hands.

"Sondra, work on your feet!" exclaimed Nancy. "I'll get Ned's hands!" Nancy crawled over to her boyfriend. In just a few more minutes the three teenagers were on their feet.

Sondra stared dismally around the room. The puddles of chemicals were burning brightly. Here and there stacks of photos and paper had caught on fire. "Now what?" she said. Flames danced in front of the door.

"Nancy," Ned cried, "the only exit is blocked! There aren't any windows."

"I'm not sure how we're going to get out of here," she said, "but I do know how we can stall for time!"

Nancy ran to the sink and filled a plastic bucket. She dashed the water against one flaming wall. But by the time she'd refilled the bucket, the fire was raging once again.

Suddenly Sondra sank to the floor in a dead faint.

"It's the smoke!" Nancy cried. "It can kill you faster than the flames themselves."

At that moment one of the walls collapsed in a shower of sparkling embers. Nancy could see something shining in the room beyond.

"That's it!" Nancy cried. "Look, Ned! It's an escape route, made by the fire."

Ned looked at the flaming opening in the wall. "Uh, one small problem, Nancy," he said. "I don't see how we're going to get through that hole alive!"

"Start bailing, Nickerson," Nancy ordered, tossing Ned a bucket. Together they dumped water on the fiery wall at a frantic pace. They managed to lessen the intensity of the flames, but not to put them out completely.

"This is the best we're going to do," Nancy told Ned. "Get Sondra and yourself out of here!"

"What about you, Nancy?"

"I've got to find that tape with Yvonne's confession. Without it, we're just three careless teenagers in a darkroom, playing with chemicals we don't know anything about. No jury in the world would take our word about this 'accident' against Yvonne's, believe me." Nancy gave her boyfriend a push. "Go on. I'm not intending to let myself go up in a puff of smoke!"

Ned planted a kiss on Nancy's soot-smudged cheek. "I love you," he said. Then he picked Sondra up and ran with her across the charred floor. Soon he and Sondra had disappeared through the glowing wall.

Meanwhile, Nancy was scouring the worktable for the tape. When she saw it, it was inches away from the fire, about to turn into a burnt memory itself. She grabbed it. If the heat hadn't damaged it too much, it meant she had Yvonne right where she wanted her, and ready for a good long jail term.

Nancy turned back to her escape route. She took a deep breath. Then, braving the flames that still licked at the charred hole, she scrambled through.

As Nancy emerged from the flaming room, Ned ran to her and hugged her to him. "Thank heavens you're safe," he said, breathing heavily. "I've already called the fire department. Oh, Nancy, I don't know what I would have done if I'd lost you."

All at once the tension and terror of the past few hours hit Nancy. She felt weak. All she wanted was a pair of strong arms around her, holding her. The anger and pain she'd been holding inside for the last few days dissolved into nothing. She sank gratefully against Ned's chest. "It's over," she said at last. Then she pulled away, looking frantically around the room. "Is Sondra all right?"

"She's fine," Ned whispered. "We're all fine, thanks to you."

Nancy smiled into Ned's dark, tender eyes.

"Thank you, too, Ned. You kept a cool head in there." She sighed. "Um, Ned, I'd love to stay with you like this, but the office is on fire, you know."

Ned laughed. "I think maybe we'd better get out of here."

"I think maybe you're right!"

The two teenagers hurried out of the office, their arms wrapped around each other tenderly. They found Sondra in the lobby, waiting nervously by the elevators. As they stepped into the cool Chicago evening, they heard the musical wail of fire engines.

CHAPTER EIGHTEEN

"Mmm," Nancy purred with satisfaction as she soaked up the rays of the early spring sun. "There's nothing like a long weekend at the beach." She smiled happily and gazed across the serene blue waters of Fox Lake.

Ned laughed and reached out to squeeze Nancy's hand. "You know, that whole ridiculous fight never would have happened if you'd only been this enthusiastic about the vacation from the beginning."

"What can I say?" Nancy asked. "I'm a workaholic when it comes to solving mysteries. I know it's a little intense, but, as the saying goes, either love me or leave me."

Ned inched closer to Nancy and slipped his arm around her shoulders. "No way! Now that I've got you back, I'm hanging on to you. Even if I have to put up with your obsession with detective work."

Nancy laughed. She knew it was partly her passion for adventure and her desire to pursue a challenge that made Ned love her, in spite of the difficulties.

Ned stared seriously into Nancy's eyes. "I swear," he said,

"leaving you behind in that burning darkroom was the hardest thing I've done in my life."

"Harder than being tackled by those huge defensive linemen from Notre Dame during that last game?" Nancy teased.

"Much!" Ned said seriously, then added, "I always knew I loved you, Nancy, but now I really know how much."

"Well, I certainly learned *my* lesson," Nancy said. "If I want you to understand how much *I* love *you*, I've got to show it." She leaned over and brushed her lips lightly against Ned's. "Like this," she said softly. "And there's no time like the present to start."

Ned laughed. "Hey, make sure my parents don't see us. They'll get embarrassed."

Nancy giggled. "I will, too."

"Anyway," Ned said, returning Nancy's kiss, "I'm just glad we're finally here together and that everything's back to normal at *Flash* — or back to whatever passes for normal there." He stared up at the high blue sky.

"Yeah, they are kind of an eccentric bunch," Nancy agreed. "But you know, I actually ended up getting kind of fond of them."

"Yeah, me too," Ned said, lazily rubbing his hand up and down Nancy's arm.

"I'll say!" Nancy exclaimed. "You got a little carried away with one of them."

"Oh no, we don't have to go through the thing about Sondra again, do we?" Ned asked with a laugh. "I told you, we only kissed each other once."

SMILE AND SAY MURDER

"And that was one time too many! What was it like, any-way?"

"Weird, actually," Ned said, "to be kissing anyone other than you."

"Did she kiss better than I do?" Nancy asked.

"I'm not sure," Ned teased. "Pucker up and I'll do a comparison test."

Nancy laughed and pulled Ned into a playful embrace, meeting his tender lips with her own. It felt good to be close to him, sharing jokes and sharing love. She'd missed that so much over the past two weeks.

Finally, the couple broke apart. "You're better," Ned told Nancy. "Much better."

"Smart answer, Ned," Nancy teased. She really couldn't be too mad at Ned about Sondra. Nothing much had happened, as it turned out. She figured that both she and Ned had learned a lot from the experience. For one thing, they had learned how much they belonged together. And for another, they'd learned that even though a little fling wasn't the most horrible thing in the world, it was best kept short and sweet.

"So what do you think will happen to all those people over at *Flash*?" Ned asked. He ran his hand gently through Nancy's silky hair.

"Well, I figure that Yvonne will get a good long jail sentence. After all, she did try to kill Mick at the Maggie Awards, and there were several thousand witnesses, plus nationwide television coverage!"

"I've got to hand it to Yvonne—when she does something, she does it in a big way."

"Yeah, well, that's Yvonne. She likes to make a splash," Nancy commented. "She'll probably have half the prison eating out of her hand by her second week there. Of course, she's blown her career. She's going to have to sell her part of *Flash* to Mick, and I'm sure no one will ever hire her again."

"But she'll have plenty of time to write while she's in jail," Ned said thoughtfully, "which is what she really enjoyed doing anyway."

"And the market for true crime stories is getting bigger and bigger," Nancy said with a smile. "I can just see her writing a best seller called *I Made a Killing in the Magazine Business*."

"Well, she certainly has an imagination," Ned agreed. "It'll probably be a great book!"

"Anyway, I'm glad Mick's going to get the chance to run *Flash* his own way. He's already given MediaCorp a definite buzz-off signal and he told me he's going to try and make the magazine a more pleasant place to work."

"Getting rid of Yvonne will do wonders as far as that's concerned," Ned commented.

"And I hear that David sent in his resignation," Nancy told Ned. "I think he was just working at *Flash* because Yvonne was there."

"Yeah," Ned agreed. "He may have acted like a big slug around everyone else, but I think he actually loved Yvonne."

"It must have been terrible for him to find out she was only interested in him for his connections with MediaCorp," Nancy said.

"Is he going back to the *Law Review?*" Ned asked.

"Yup. It's a good job. And Mick will get an editor in chief who's easier to work with. He deserves that. He's dedicated to *Flash*, and he's got a lot of creative ideas. With the Maggie award behind him, he's going to be a fabulous success."

"Creative ideas, huh?" Ned said. "For instance, a cover story on America's hottest girl detective?"

Nancy sighed, drawing patterns in the sand with her foot. "That's my one regret—that I had to turn down the article Mick wanted to do about me. But if I'd accepted, half the country would have found out who I was. It would have made it impossible to find a believable cover for any future cases."

"Right," Ned said. "Fame and sleuthing mix like oil and vinegar. Or like Mick and Yvonne!"

"Anyhow," Nancy continued, resting her head on Ned's shoulder, "I wasn't about to blow my whole career as a detective for one week in the spotlight."

She and Ned sat silently for a moment, absorbing the peace of the lake and the warmth of each other's company. The trees around the glistening water swayed in the kiss-soft breeze.

"Anyway, I went back to *Flash* after it was all over, and things had already changed," Nancy commented. "Suddenly everyone was crazy about me."

"I'm sure it felt good to straighten things out with the *Flash* staff, right?"

"Sure," Nancy said, smiling happily at Ned. "Lots of those guys were really nice. I guess I can't blame them for being suspicious of me."

"I hear the damage to the offices wasn't too bad," Ned said.

"Yeah, only the room where the fire was and one wall of Mick's office were badly damaged. Once they air the place out, make a few repairs, and find a new editor, *Flash* is going to be better than ever."

"That's good," Ned said, sliding his arm around Nancy's waist.

"Hey," Nancy said suddenly, "you know, I'm supposed to meet Sondra for dinner next Wednesday. She's taking me to her favorite Italian restaurant."

"You're kidding!" Ned exclaimed. "I thought she made you want to commit murder every time you saw her."

Nancy laughed. "I guess she did at first, but it didn't have anything to do with Sondra herself. Now that I know a little more about her, I think we're going to be friends. At the beginning, I was just jealous."

"Then you admit it!"

"Sure," Nancy said. "And I'm not proud of it. But I think I have that under control now. Being stuck in that burning room with her definitely brought us closer. She was pretty brave, and I have to respect her for that. I mean, most people would have flipped out in that situation."

"Except for you," Ned pointed out.

"Yeah, but I've been stuck in dangerous places before,"

Nancy said with a giggle, "so I've had some practice."

Ned slipped his other arm around her and gave her a gentle hug. "Well, try not to do too much more practicing. I love you. I don't want you getting hurt, or even cutting it as close as you did in that room." He kissed her on each cheek before finding her lips.

"Okay," Nancy murmured, "I'll try to stay out of trouble, because I love you, too, Ned."

But the young detective had crossed her fingers behind her boyfriend's back. I'll try, she thought, until the next mystery comes along.

HIT AND RUN HOLIDAY

CHAPTER ONE

We made it!" Nancy Drew said with a grin. "Fort Lauderdale, here we are!"

Gripping the wheel in eager anticipation, Nancy turned the rental car onto Route A1A, a coastal highway lined with tall, swaying palm trees. To the left was a seemingly endless string of hotels and motels, fast-food places, restaurants, and clubs. To the right, shimmering in the late morning sun, was a broad beach of nearly white sand, and beyond that, the sparkling blue-green waters of the Atlantic Ocean.

Beside Nancy, George Fayne gazed out the window at the beach. "I can't wait to get into that water," she said. "I may never come out except to eat."

"Who cares about the water?" Bess Marvin, George's cousin, said with a giggle. "Just look at all those boys out there! I've already counted nine that I could fall in love with." As their car passed a group of boys crossing the street, Bess turned around and looked out the back window. "Make that twelve," she said excitedly.

Nancy glanced into the rearview mirror and laughed. "Help

me find our hotel first," she suggested. *"Then* you can check out the boys."

Early that morning, the three friends had left the cold March sleets of River Heights and flown to the south of Florida, joining thousands of other young people on spring break who poured into Fort Lauderdale in search of sun, sand, fun, and romance.

Actually, Bess was the only one who was looking to fall in love. George was still attached to Jon Berntsen, a boy she'd met on a ski trip, and Nancy's relationship with Ned Nickerson was in good shape at the moment. Nancy knew that Bess, with her blond hair and bubbly personality, would probably have a date in fifteen minutes flat; while athletic, dark-haired George was sure to set some kind of swimming, volleyball, or surfing record. As for herself, Nancy was looking just to have fun and go home with a great tan.

In her last case, *Smile and Say Murder*, she'd discovered that the world of publishing could be deadly, when she'd exposed a clever plot that included murder. So a Florida vacation seemed the perfect way to unwind.

"There it is," she said, pointing to a gleaming white stucco building. "The Surfside Inn. They were right—every room has a window facing the ocean."

"And the boys," Bess said with a sigh.

"Let's hurry and change so we can hit the beach," Nancy suggested, as she pulled the car into a tight parking space on a side street next to the hotel.

"What do you mean, 'we'?" George asked with a laugh. "You've got a case to solve, remember?"

Nancy laughed, too. "It's not a case," claimed the young detective. "I'm just checking up on Kim. It'll take me all of five minutes."

Kim Baylor, a friend of all three girls, had been in Fort Lauderdale for ten days. Just before Nancy left River Heights, Kim's mother had called and told her that Kim had decided to stay on an extra week. Mrs. Baylor wasn't really worried, she said, she simply wanted Nancy to drop by Kim's hotel and see that everything was all right. She'd felt that Kim had sounded odd over the phone, but thought she was probably just being an overprotective parent.

"I bet I can solve your mystery for you without even talking to Kim," Bess told Nancy as they piled out of the car. "It's simple—Kim met a fabulous guy and she's staying on because she's madly in love." Bess tugged two canvas bags from the back of the car, then stared across the street at a tall, well-muscled boy running toward the ocean. "Just look at him," she said dreamily. "What couldn't *I* do with an extra week down here!"

"Stop drooling and help us carry the bags inside," George joked. "The sooner we get changed, the sooner you can start looking for Mr. Right."

The hotel room wasn't large or luxurious, but it had everything the girls needed, and besides, none of them planned to spend much time in it. In ten minutes, they had changed out of their travel clothes and into their swimsuits. Bess had brought six, and for her first trip to the sun and sand, she put on a blazing pink bikini.

George, who was wearing a blue-and-white-striped tank suit cut very high on the legs, gave Bess a wry smile. "Nobody's going to have any trouble seeing you," she commented. "Not in that color."

"That's the whole point," Bess replied seriously. Then she sighed as she looked at Nancy, whose blue-green bikini was the perfect color for her reddish blond hair.

"Well, I'm not here for the guys," Nancy said. "And it will be about half an hour before I show up on the beach."

Bess grabbed a large beach towel. "Why?"

"I've decided to drop by Kim's hotel first," Nancy explained. She found her beach bag and tossed in everything she could possibly need on the beach: sunglasses, suntan lotion, a book, and even an extra bikini. Then she threw on a short cover-up made of soft white cotton. She started toward the door. "I thought I'd solve my 'case' first," she said with a grin. "But after that—look out, Lauderdale!"

Kim's hotel, the Vistamar, turned out to be just three blocks away from the Surfside, and it should have taken Nancy about two minutes to reach it. Instead, it took closer to ten. The sidewalks were jammed with kids heading for the beach or just strolling along, stopping to strike up a conversation with anyone who caught their eye.

Everyone was checking each other out, and Nancy lost

count of how many surfing, swimming, and dancing dates she turned down. She saw plenty of great-looking guys she wouldn't have minded spending time with, but because of Ned, she wasn't really tempted. Still, it was fun just being in the middle of it all, and as she spotted Kim's hotel, she thought that Bess was probably right—Kim must have met somebody special, and she wanted to be with him for as long as possible.

The Vistamar was on a narrow side street just off the main road. It was lime green, five stories high, and when Nancy went in, she just missed the elevator. However, since Kim's room was on the second floor, she climbed the stairs. She found room 207 easily and was just about to knock when she heard Kim's voice through the partially open door.

"Don't blame me, Ricardo!" Kim cried urgently. "I don't know how they found out, but they did!"

There was a pause, and when she didn't hear Ricardo answer, Nancy figured Kim must be talking on the phone. She tried not to eavesdrop, but Kim sounded so frantic it was hard not to hear her.

"I told her not to leave!" Kim went on. "She knew she wasn't supposed to, but . . . I don't know, Ricardo, maybe she got cabin fever or something. What difference does it make? She's gone!"

Nancy wasn't even trying not to listen anymore. Who was gone? she wondered. Kim hadn't come down with a girlfriend.

Nancy knew that. But even if she'd taken on a roommate, what was the business about not leaving the room?

Kim lowered her voice, and Nancy leaned closer to the door. That was when she noticed it—not only was the door ajar, but the lock had obviously been broken. It hadn't been a very smooth job, either. The metal looked as if it had been gouged with a screwdriver, and the wood around it was splintered. Whoever had broken it must have wanted to get inside in a hurry.

Nancy didn't have a clue as to what was going on, and she waited impatiently for Kim to finish talking so she could find out.

"Don't say that, you're scaring me," Kim protested. She waited, then sighed. "All right, okay. I'll meet you at your perch in ten minutes."

Perch? Nancy almost smiled. Was Ricardo a boy or a bird? When she heard Kim say goodbye, she started to knock again. But the door was flung open before she had a chance, and a very startled Kim Baylor was staring at her.

"Nancy!" Kim's brown eyes widened in surprise. "What are you doing here?"

"I told you I might come down, remember?" Nancy said. "Besides, your—"

"Oh, that's right," Kim interrupted. "So much has been going on, I guess I forgot." She was already out the door and hurrying down the hall toward the elevator. "Listen, I can't talk now, I'm in a rush. But I really do want to see you. Maybe when I—"

"Hey, where's the fire?" Nancy joked as Kim kept jabbing at the elevator button. "Let's take the stairs, and then I'll walk you wherever you're going. We can talk on the way." She hurried to keep up with her friend, who was already at the stairs. "Kim, what's going on? You look freaked, to say the least."

Kim hurried down the stairs, her rubber beach sandals slapping on the cement. "I *am* freaked," she called over her shoulder. "You just won't believe what's been happening!"

"Try me," Nancy suggested.

"I will, I will, but, Nancy, it's just too complicated to get into right now. I've got something really important to do, but I promise I'll tell you everything as soon as I can."

Frustrated, Nancy followed Kim through the hotel's small, deserted lobby toward the street door. Kim dashed outside. Nancy ran after her, but her sandal chose that moment to slip off her foot. She bent over, put it back on, and hurried after her friend.

Kim was standing impatiently on the curb, her long brown hair blowing in the sea breeze. She reached up, pulled a strand of hair out of her eyes, and stepped into the street.

Nancy was just leaving the hotel when she heard the sound of a car's engine firing and the squeal of tires as the car peeled away. She saw that Kim had reached the middle of the street. Nancy started after her, but it was at that second that she noticed the dark blue car racing toward Kim.

Nancy yelled but it was too late. The car was barreling down the street at a high speed. Kim opened her mouth to scream, but her voice was drowned out by the sound of the impact.

The car never slowed down. Its tires squealed again as it sped around the corner and out of sight.

CHAPTER TWO

In a second, Nancy was at Kim's side. It was impossible to tell how badly her friend was hurt. All Nancy could see were cuts and scrapes, but she didn't dare move her. She wasn't even going to take the chance of putting her friend's head in her lap. She knelt down, took Kim's hand, and leaned close to her.

"Kim?" Nancy tried to keep her voice from shaking. "It's going to be okay. Just don't move."

Gripping Nancy's hand, Kim licked her lips and tried to say something. Her voice was so weak that Nancy could barely hear her.

"Rosita," Kim whispered. ". . . Rosita." She took another breath and started to say something more, but then her eyelids fluttered closed and she was silent.

Nancy looked up and was surprised to see that a crowd of ten or fifteen people had gathered. She'd been concentrating so hard on Kim that she hadn't even noticed them.

"Could someone call an ambulance, please?" Nancy asked.

An elderly man nodded his head. "Of course," he said, and hurried away.

A voice close to Nancy asked, "Is she dead?"

The person who'd asked about Kim was a young woman, wearing the uniform of a hotel maid.

Nancy swallowed hard and shook her head. "No, she's not dead," she told her. "She's breathing. But she passed out."

The woman nodded and started to leave.

"Wait!" Nancy called. "Did you see what happened?"

"No, I didn't," the woman said. "I was inside. I heard a scream, but that's all. I came out to see, and on the way, I told my boss to call the police. It sounded like a bad accident."

"It was bad," Nancy agreed grimly. "But it wasn't an accident."

"I wouldn't know about that, miss," the woman said, backing away. "I have to go to work now."

In the distance, Nancy could hear the wail of a siren, and she knew help was on the way. Still holding Kim's hand, she glanced up at the other people. "Did anyone see it happen?" she asked. "Did anyone see who was driving the car?"

A few people shook their heads, but no one said anything.

I couldn't have been the only one on the sidewalk, Nancy thought in frustration. Somebody must have seen something.

She knew they couldn't have gotten the license plate number, though. In those few awful seconds before the car hit Kim, Nancy had noticed that it didn't have a front plate, and as it tore off down the street, she realized that the back plate was missing too. But she'd been in such a hurry to get to Kim that she hadn't taken the time to look for anything else.

"How about the make of car or the year?" Nancy asked the

onlookers. "Or whether it had two doors or four doors?"

A few more heads were shaken.

"Anything?" Nancy asked desperately. "This is important. Didn't anyone see *anything*?"

Nancy scanned the crowd, trying to catch a sympathetic eye. At the edge of the group she noticed a young guy, about nineteen or twenty, wearing a black swimsuit. He was one of the handsomest boys Nancy had ever seen, with black hair and eyes and smooth, dark gold skin. But it wasn't his looks that caught her attention—it was the expression in his eyes. He'd been staring at Kim, but as Nancy watched he raised his head and glanced down the street, in the direction the car had gone. His eyes glittered, and his lips curled into a tight smile.

What kind of smile? Nancy wondered. An angry smile? A satisfied one?

But Nancy didn't have time to do more than wonder. Its siren shrill and piercing, a police car rounded the corner, followed by an ambulance. The moment they came into sight, the crowd scattered, leaving Nancy alone with Kim.

"It was a hit and run," she told the officer who hurried over to her. "The car didn't bother to slow down for a second."

The policeman nodded and began firing questions at Nancy. What was Kim's name, where was she staying, where was she from? Nancy answered and then told him all she could about the accident, which wasn't much. "There were a lot of people around," she finished, "but they all split the minute they saw your car."

Closing his pad, the policeman nodded again. "Undocumented, probably," he said. "Afraid to get involved."

Nancy suddenly understood. They'd rather keep their mouths shut than come forward and tell what they saw. Because if they had to testify in court, they'd be discovered.

Nancy looked over at Kim, who was being lifted gently onto a stretcher. "I can't believe this is happening," she said, feeling both sorry for the undocumented immigrants and frustrated no one could relay what happened. "My friend gets run down in front of half a dozen witnesses, but I'm the only one who sees anything."

"Yeah, it's tough," the officer agreed. "There's a lot of ugly business going on down here in paradise."

Kim was being loaded into the ambulance by then. One of the medics jumped in after her.

"What about the car?" Nancy asked. "Do you think you'll find it?"

"There's not much to go on," the officer replied frankly. "But we'll give it our best shot."

"Okay," said Nancy. She climbed into the back of the ambulance and settled herself next to Kim. The medic closed the doors, and the ambulance pulled away, its siren going full blast.

Nancy thought about what the officer had meant—that if the car ever did turn up, it would probably be weeks later, in a junkyard somewhere. If they were lucky.

But Nancy wasn't going to put her trust in luck. She might return to River Heights with her skin as winter-pale as when she left, but she was going to find out why her friend was deliberately run over on a bright, sunny day in the middle of paradise.

It was two o'clock by the time Nancy left the hospital. Kim was still unconscious, but the doctors were almost certain she'd be okay—the worst they could find were a bad concussion and a broken wrist. Nancy had called Kim's mother, and Mrs. Baylor had said she'd be down later that afternoon if she had to hijack a plane to get there.

As Nancy walked down the street, she suddenly realized she was famished. She bought a hot dog from a stand on a street corner and wolfed it down while she headed toward Kim's hotel. What she really wanted to do was jump in the ocean and swim until her nerves stopped jangling. But she couldn't relax, not then. There was too much to find out. What kind of dangerous business had Kim gotten mixed up in? Why had the lock on her door been broken? Who was Ricardo? Who was Rosita?

Nancy knew that Kim's room just might hold some of the answers to those questions, so she tried to ignore the gorgeous beach only yards away from her. She also tried to ignore the gorgeous boys around her, but it wasn't easy.

"Hey," one of them said, "you look frazzled. Wanna chill?"

"Hey, you're going to look like a lobster soon if you're not careful," another one told her. "I'll be glad to rub in your suntan lotion personally!"

Nancy turned them down, worried about Kim. Bess must be in absolute heaven, she thought. She glanced over at the crowded beach and realized that Bess and George didn't even know about Kim yet. I'll tell them later, she thought. First I've got to get a look at that hotel room. Remembering the broken lock, she figured it wouldn't be too hard.

Nancy bounded up the stairs again instead of waiting for the elevator. Quietly she pushed open the door and stepped into the hall. Good. It was empty.

Nancy kept her fingers crossed that it would stay that way. The last thing she wanted was to be seen nosing around Kim's room. She didn't have any idea yet whom she was up against, and until she found out, she couldn't trust a soul.

When Nancy reached room 207, she checked to make sure she was still alone, then put her hand on the doorknob, expecting it to turn easily.

The knob didn't turn at all. The door was locked.

Great, Nancy thought, just what I don't need—an efficient hotel. She didn't have her credit cards with her, so she couldn't force the lock that way. She rummaged through her beach bag, trying to find something thin and made out of metal.

No luck. The only hardware she had was the small hook in the top of her extra bikini.

Well, why not? she thought. It took five minutes, but finally Nancy had the metal hook free of the cloth. She spent another minute unbending it, and at last she held a thin metal probe about as long as her little finger. If this works, she told herself, you will have set some sort of record for ingenuity.

Grinning, Nancy gently slid the "pick" into the keyhole.

Suddenly the knob turned, and the door started to open. Nancy was about to congratulate herself when she realized that she didn't have anything to do with it. Someone—who probably didn't belong there—was inside Kim's room. And Nancy and the intruder were about to come face-to-face.

CHAPTER THREE

Quickly Nancy dropped her pick into her beach bag, stepped away from the door, and put on a confused expression, as if she were having trouble finding her room.

The door opened a little more, and a young man stuck his head out. In his left hand he held a very long pointed screwdriver. When he saw Nancy, his jaw hardened and his blue eyes turned icy. Nancy considered asking him what he was doing in the room, but his look stopped her. He might be involved in Kim's "accident," and if he was, Nancy didn't want him suspicious of her.

"Oh, hi!" she said casually. "Can you tell me where room three-twelve is?"

Opening the door just wide enough to let himself out, the guy gave Nancy a long, cold look, then finally raised his chin and glanced at the ceiling.

Nancy looked up too, pretending she didn't understand what he was trying to tell her. She noticed that he was wearing dark green pants and a matching shirt, the kind of uniform maintenance people wear. He must work for the hotel, Nancy thought, which was why he'd been in Kim's room. He'd probably just fixed the lock.

"Oh!" she said, as if the light had finally dawned on her. "I'm on the wrong floor, huh?"

Nodding briefly, the guy pulled the door shut behind him, and then stood there, obviously waiting for her to leave.

Nancy heard the lock click and was glad she'd been prepared. Smiling brightly, she said, "No wonder I couldn't find three-twelve! Thanks!"

"Mr. Friendly" glared at her again and finally headed for the stairs, so Nancy stood in front of the elevator, pretending to push the button. When she heard the last echo of his footsteps, she rushed back to room 207, fished out her pick, and went to work.

In just a couple of minutes, Nancy was inside Kim's room.

It was a total disaster. Clothes were everywhere—hanging out of drawers, strewn across the floor, even spilling from the wastepaper basket. Postcards, paperbacks, makeup, and skin lotion were ripped, scattered, or overturned. The sheets were on the floor, and the mattress was half off the bed.

It was not the mess made by someone who was having too good a vacation to bother picking things up. It wasn't even the mess made by a slob, Nancy thought. It was the kind of mess made by somebody who was looking for something.

Nancy didn't have to wonder who had searched the room. It must have been handsome "Mr. Friendly," the stone-faced maintenance man. No wonder he'd given her such a dirty look when he found her lurking outside the room. Obviously he didn't work for the hotel, but just who did he work for? Ricardo? Rosita?

For a moment, Nancy was tempted to go after him, but then

she decided it would be a waste of time. People who trashed hotel rooms didn't wait around to answer questions. Mr. Friendly was long gone. She hoped.

The thing to do was figure out what he'd been looking for.

Afraid that somebody might be watching the hotel room, Nancy left the shades down and the lights off. The fluorescent bulb in the bathroom was enough to see by. Not even sure where to begin, she started wading through the piles of clothes and paperbacks on the floor. A piece of newspaper caught in her sandal; as she picked it up she noticed the headline of a story about undocumented immigrants.

The story had been circled in red ink, and Nancy figured Kim had done it. Kim was like that. If I keep my eyes peeled, Nancy thought with a smile, I'll probably find a letter she wrote to the editor, saying what a rotten situation people are in.

But Nancy wasn't getting anywhere. She tossed the paper toward the wastebasket and headed for the bathroom. Medicine cabinets were such obvious hiding places, maybe Mr. Friendly hadn't bothered to look there.

No luck. The "maintenance" man had pulled out every jar, bottle, and tube, and left them piled in the sink. Even the toothbrushes were out of their holders, lying like two pickup sticks on the fake marble vanity top.

Nancy was halfway out the bathroom when it hit her—*two* toothbrushes. She walked back in and took another look. Right, two of them—one blue and obviously well used; the other red, without a single bent bristle.

Kim didn't have a roommate, she reminded herself. Or did she? Nancy looked more carefully at the countertop. One bottle each of shampoo and conditioner. One tube of toothpaste, one can of deodorant. Two hairbrushes, one full of light brown strands, the other with several strands of long black hair caught in it.

Okay, Nancy thought. Kim might have bought a second toothbrush, but there was no way she could have used that other hairbrush. And if she hadn't come to Florida with a roommate, then she'd invited some girl to stay with her once she got there.

Nancy walked back into the main room, looking for more evidence of that roommate, and she found it in the wastepaper basket. A skirt and blouse—cotton, homemade, no labels, muddy, and wrinkled. They must have been pretty once, but Nancy knew they didn't belong to Kim. For one thing, they weren't her style. For another, Kim hated sewing; she'd wait until every last button had fallen off a blouse before picking up a needle and thread.

Nancy was frowning at the skirt and blouse when she heard footsteps in the hall. When they stopped outside the door, she sank down behind the bed as quietly as possible, listening. Was it the maintenance man? Had he gotten suspicious of her and come back? The footsteps shuffled around, then faded away.

As Nancy let her breath out, her head dropped, and she found herself staring at a strip of photo-booth snapshots lying on the rug at her feet. Picking it up gingerly, as if it might suddenly disintegrate, Nancy studied the strip of photos. The first was of Kim alone, mugging for the camera; the second was of Kim and another girl. All the rest were of the second girl, who was very pretty, with long black hair, but who never smiled and who looked into the camera with dark eyes. "Rosita," Nancy whispered to herself. "She has to be Rosita."

Nancy examined the photographs intently, as if by staring hard enough she could bring Rosita to life and ask her all the questions that were spinning through her mind. How did you meet Kim? Why did Kim share her room with you? Who's Ricardo? Who was that phony maintenance man? Just exactly what did Kim mean when she lay in the street and whispered, "Rosita"?

Frustrated, Nancy stood up and began pacing the hotel room, still holding the strip of photos. Where was she going to find the answers to those questions? Who was she going to ask? Kim was still unconscious, and the only other person she thought might be involved was Mr. Friendly. She could hardly ask him, if she ever saw him again.

Well, at least she had something to go on, she thought, looking at the photographs. If she had to, she'd wander up and down the beach, asking anybody and everybody if they'd seen that girl. I'll find you, Rosita, Nancy thought. And when I do, you'd better have some good answers.

Dropping the strip of photos into her beach bag, Nancy took one last look around the torn-up room and then headed for the door. Her hand was on the knob when she heard footsteps in the hall again.

Nancy dropped her hand, figuring she'd rather not be seen, no matter who was out there. The footsteps came closer and then stopped right outside room 207. Nancy stepped backward, her eyes on the door. It could be somebody who really does work for the hotel, she told herself. A maid, maybe, coming to clean up the room. The doorknob jiggled. Then Nancy heard the sound of a key sliding slowly into the lock. No maid would unlock a door like that, Nancy thought. Besides, a maid would knock first. Whoever was unlocking that door was probably looking up and down the hall, making sure no one was watching. Whoever was out there didn't want to be seen.

The doorknob turned. In three quick strides, Nancy was across the room and in the closet, hiding behind the few clothes that were left hanging there. Just as the outer door swung open, Nancy pulled the closet door closed, leaving a half-inch crack to see through.

Because the room was so dim, all Nancy could glimpse at first was a tall, shadowy figure silhouetted against the pale wall. It stood there for a few seconds, obviously sizing up the situation. Then, slowly, it moved away from the door and into the center of the room. Nancy held her breath as it passed the closet and walked cautiously toward the bathroom.

Whoever it was didn't turn on any lights, and Nancy knew she'd been right—the person didn't work for the hotel, even though he or she had a key, and definitely didn't want to be discovered.

For an instant, the figure was framed in the bathroom light, and Nancy saw it from the back: It was the figure of a dark-haired boy, wearing a black bathing suit and a T-shirt, and carrying what looked like a small canvas bag. Nancy opened the closet door a little wider, hoping to get a better look, but by then, the boy was out of the light. In that instant, though, Nancy decided that he looked uncomfortably familiar. Something about his build and the way he held his head reminded her of the handsome boy at the scene of the hit and run, the one who'd smiled so mysteriously and then disappeared.

Was the intruder really the same boy? Nancy wondered. Then she realized that it didn't matter, not at the moment. What mattered was that the boy, who had walked all around the room, and had been in and out of the bathroom, was headed for the closet in which Nancy was hiding. His hand was outstretched, reaching for the doorknob.

CHAPTER FOUR

Nancy stayed absolutely still, not even daring to breathe. At the last second, the boy shook his head, apparently changing his mind about the closet, and returned to the bathroom.

Nancy exhaled a long, shaky, silent breath. She had gathered one more important piece of information. The intruder was definitely the same handsome boy she had seen after Kim's accident.

Nancy could hear him rummaging around in the bathroom, picking things up and putting them down again. Were he and the maintenance man working together? Had the maintenance man seen Nancy enter Kim's room and told the boy to follow her?

Silently Nancy eased back into the darkness of the closet. She couldn't let herself get caught, and she wished her heart would stop beating so hard.

The boy left the bathroom, dropping a few things into the canvas bag. They clattered against each other as they landed, and Nancy thought they must be jars. Makeup? Lotion? What would he want with Kim's makeup and hand lotion?

Again the intruder stepped toward the closet. Nancy took

her hand off the knob, afraid she might shake the door, and held her breath again. What would he do if he found her? What would *she* do?

The boy stopped in front of the closet, and Nancy gripped the strap of her beach bag, figuring she could swing it at his face and make a run for it if she had to. Her hand was sweaty and a muscle in her leg started jumping. She wished he'd do whatever he was going to do so she could move. Anything was better than waiting.

Finally he did move. But not to the closet. Nancy heard a strange shuffling sound, and she peered through the opening.

The boy was bending over, grabbing a few pieces of scattered clothing and stuffing them into his bag. As Nancy watched, he straightened up, his back still to her, and then swiftly walked to the door, opened it, and stepped outside.

Nancy forced herself to count slowly to five. She wanted to give him enough time to reach the stairs or the elevator and think he was safe. Then she'd follow him and try to find out who he was and what he was doing in Kim's room.

At the count of five, she let herself out of the stuffy closet, crossed the room, and opened the door. The hall was empty. The elevator was stopped on the third floor. Nancy raced for the stairs and paused, listening. Two flights below, she heard a door open. Noises from the lobby drifted up to her before it closed again.

That's him, Nancy thought, rushing down the stairs. He

won't be any farther than the street door by the time I get there. On the ground floor, she shoved open the door, nearly collided with a bellboy, and dashed across the lobby and out to the sidewalk.

The street looked almost the same as it had earlier that day, bright with sunlight and busy with vacationers heading for the ocean. Nancy glanced quickly in both directions, thought she saw the black-suited intruder turn onto the main avenue that ran along the beach, and swiftly made her way through the happy, suntanned crowds.

At the corner, Nancy stopped short, looking wildly in every direction. The main street was packed, the beach was packed. She counted at least fifteen guys in black bathing suits and was standing there wondering which one to go after first, when someone called her name.

"Nancy! Nancy, over here!"

Nancy looked across the street and saw Bess and George waving to her from the edge of the beach. Only a few hours had gone by since they'd all been together, changing into their swimsuits, but it seemed like days. She took another look at the crowded beach. Suddenly it seemed as if every boy was wearing a black bathing suit. Shaking her head, Nancy crossed the street and joined her friends.

"I thought you said you'd solve your 'case' in ten minutes," George teased. "What happened, couldn't you find Kim?"

"I found her," Nancy said. "Kim's—"

"Well, it's about time you got here!" Bess broke in. "We thought you'd decided to spend your entire vacation indoors. Nancy," she went on with a big smile, "meet Dirk Bowman. He owns a boat, and he's promised to take us all along on a midnight cruise. Doesn't that sound fantastic?"

Nancy turned and smiled distractedly at Dirk. She hadn't noticed him at first, but she should have guessed that Bess would have found someone by then.

"I don't actually own the boat, I just work for the lady who does," Dirk explained as he smiled back at Nancy. He was a fabulous-looking guy—sandy blond hair, deep blue eyes, and a perfect tan. "But the invitation for the cruise is good. You have my word."

"It sounds great," Nancy told him. "But I don't think I'll be able—"

"Oh, come on, Nan," Bess protested. "We came down here to have fun, right? What could be more fun than a midnight cruise?"

"Really, it sounds great," Nancy said again, "but—"

"What is it, Nancy?" George asked. "You hardly look like somebody who's having a terrific time."

Nancy brushed her hair back and took a deep breath. "You're right. I'm not having a terrific time," she said. "But I'm afraid Kim's having a worse one." She glanced at the three of them and then went on to tell what had happened to their friend that morning.

"Oh, how awful!" Bess said in a horrified voice. "What kind of creep would run over somebody and keep on going?"

"I don't know," Nancy replied. "But I plan to find out. I don't think it was just some jerk who hit Kim and then panicked. I think it was deliberate. I think Kim got mixed up in something dangerous down here and she nearly paid for it with her life."

"What could she have gotten mixed up in?" George asked.

"I don't know yet," Nancy admitted. "But I plan to soon. Some very strange things have been going on." She told them about Kim's hotel room and the mess it was in, about the phony maintenance man, the snapshots of the pretty girl, and the guy who'd broken into the room and taken some clothes.

As she talked, Nancy noticed that Dirk Bowman was becoming extremely interested in what she was saying.

"Sounds like your vacation's not exactly turning out the way you expected," he commented when Nancy finished.

"Not exactly," Nancy agreed.

"Well, from what Bess and George have told me about you," he went on, "I'd bet you're not going to give up until you have all the answers." He smiled at Bess, and Nancy noticed that he had a dimple just to the left of his mouth. Bess looked enchanted. "Don't worry," Dirk went on, "they didn't talk about you that much. They just said that you're a detective, and you don't give up without a fight."

"I guess I don't," Nancy said. "And I sure won't give up on

this case, not when one of my friends is lying in a hospital."
She turned to Bess and George. "Kim's mother is flying down
later today. I think we ought to be at the hospital when she gets
there, don't you?"

"Absolutely," George said, and Bess nodded and sighed.
"Poor Kim," she exclaimed. "I just can't believe it!"

"Listen," Dirk said to Nancy, "if there's anything I can do, I
wish you'd let me know." He put a hand on Nancy's shoulder
and flashed his dimple at her. "I know my way around Fort Lauderdale pretty well. Besides," he added, "I'm sort of a mystery
buff. I'd really like to help you."

"Well, thanks." Nancy was aware that Dirk still had his hand
on her shoulder, and she tried to shrug it off, but it stayed put.

"Listen," said Dirk, "that midnight cruise is probably out for
you tonight, Nancy. I know you've got to be with your friend.
But maybe you and I could get together tomorrow sometime
and talk about this. I'd really like to help."

"I . . . I'm not sure," Nancy said, suddenly uncomfortable. "I
don't know what I'll be doing tomorrow."

"I understand," Dirk replied with another charming, sympathetic smile. "But I'd really like to talk to you about all this."

"Well, I'll have to see." Nancy frowned.

Dirk seemed to have forgotten about Bess. It wasn't exactly
cool, she thought, to dump somebody so fast.

Bess obviously didn't think it was too cool, either. Her eyes
were flashing as she looked angrily at Dirk. Fortunately, George
caught the look and decided that Bess better leave before she

exploded. "Come on," she said, "let's get back to the hotel and change so we can go to the hospital."

"All right," Bess agreed.

"Hey, I'm free all morning tomorrow," Dirk said softly to Nancy. "Why don't I give you a call?"

Nancy felt more and more uncomfortable. She was just about to give Dirk a real brush-off, when he pulled her around to face him.

"I do know my way around Lauderdale," he said seriously, and Nancy noticed his sexy smile was gone. "If we can get together—privately—I think I might be able to give you a few tips about this mystery. You want to help your friend, don't you?"

"Of course I do!" Nancy said. "But right now, you're the one who's being mysterious. If you know something, why don't you just tell me?"

Dirk shook his head. "I would, believe me, but it's just not the right time or place. Besides, first I have to know everything you know." Glancing past Nancy, Dirk seemed to see someone he recognized. He raised his arm in a greeting, then brought his hand down so that it was resting on the back of Nancy's neck. It was like a caress, Nancy thought, but there was nothing romantic about the look in his eyes. "Tomorrow, right?" he asked intently.

Nancy wasn't sure if Dirk was making a pass at her or if he really did know something about Kim. But she had to find out. "Okay," she finally agreed. "Tomorrow."

"Good." Dirk's smile returned, and giving Nancy's neck a gentle squeeze, he sauntered off to meet whomever it was he'd waved to.

Nancy watched him for a second, then turned to catch up with George and Bess. George was almost at the street, but Bess hadn't moved. She'd obviously been watching the whole thing, because she gave Nancy a confused look. Then she strode across the beach, completely ignoring the dozens of boys who tried to get her attention.

Nancy sighed and slipped off her sandals. She jogged across the warm sand toward Bess, trying to decide how to tell her that she didn't like—or trust—Dirk Bowman one bit.

Nancy was only a few yards from Bess when she suddenly stopped short, completely forgetting about Bess and Dirk for the moment. In front of her was a lifeguard's chair, and sitting in that chair was a handsome, bronze-skinned, dark-haired boy in a black bathing suit. Nancy knew he was the guy she'd seen at the hit and run and rummaging around Kim's hotel room not half an hour earlier.

Nancy hoped nobody was drowning at the moment, because the guy sure wouldn't be any help—he couldn't take his eyes off her.

The only place he's seen you is at the hit-and-run scene, she reminded herself. He doesn't know you were in that hotel room, watching him.

Tossing her hair back, Nancy curved her lips in a slow smile and walked over to the lifeguard's chair.

"Hi, there," the lifeguard said when she reached him.

"Hello." Nancy noticed a small canvas beach bag at the foot of the chair. She would have given anything to see what was inside it. Still smiling, she said, "This is my first day in Lauderdale. Got any suggestions about how I should spend my time?"

The lifeguard raised his eyebrows. "Most people come here for the sun and the water," he said, in a slight Hispanic accent. "Isn't that what you came for?"

"Well, sure," Nancy told him. "Sun, surf, and . . . new friends, right?"

"Maybe." He gave her a teasing grin. "If you're lucky."

"Speaking of luck," Nancy went on, "one of my friends ran into a bad streak of it this morning. Or rather, it ran into her."

"Oh?"

"Yes. She was hit by a car, right in front of the Vistamar." Nancy kept her smile in place, trying not to sound too serious. "A lot of people were around. Maybe I'm wrong, but I thought I saw you there."

The lifeguard shifted in his chair, glanced out at the water, and then back at Nancy. His smile was gone, and his dark eyes were hard. "You're right," he said coldly. "You *are* wrong."

"Oh well," Nancy said with a shrug. "My mistake."

The lifeguard didn't answer. He just stared at her a moment longer, then shifted his gaze back to the water.

He was lying, Nancy was sure. But there was no way she could prove it. Not yet. Figuring she'd only make him suspicious if she asked any more questions, she decided to drop the subject for the time being. She hitched her beach bag onto her shoulder and turned to leave.

Nancy was only about three feet away from the lifeguard's chair when she felt it—a sharp, burning pain in her left foot, as if she'd stepped on a red-hot needle. Gasping, she jerked her foot away and fell onto the sand. As she fell, she glanced up at the lifeguard. He was watching her, and his smile was back.

CHAPTER FIVE

Biting her lip to keep from crying out, Nancy grabbed her foot and looked around to see what she'd stepped on. A few inches away she saw a large, bluish, slimy object partly covered by sand. It was a jellyfish, obviously, and as Nancy rubbed her foot, she wondered what kind it was and whether its poison was going to do any more damage than it already had.

A boy who'd seen her fall trotted over and prodded the jellyfish with a stick. "Portuguese man-of-war," he told her. "Ugly looking, huh?"

Nancy nodded. "What's going to happen now?" she asked. "Is my foot going to shrivel up and fall off?" She was trying to joke, but the pain she felt was anything but funny.

The boy didn't look too amused either. "Well, I don't want to scare you," he said, "but I think you ought to hotfoot it to a doctor, excuse the pun."

Nancy suddenly remembered some stories about things like shock and unconsciousness. It's a good thing I'm on my way to the hospital, she thought. The boy offered her a hand, and she got to her feet, wincing. "Thanks."

"Any time," he told her. Glancing up at the lifeguard, he

cupped his hands and called out, "Hey, Ricardo! You're falling down on the job, man. Why didn't you warn her these things are all over the beach today?"

Stunned, Nancy looked at the lifeguard too. So he was Ricardo. And his chair was the "perch" Kim had mentioned. No wonder he'd clammed up when she mentioned seeing him at the hit-and-run site. She wondered what he would have done if she'd told him about overhearing Kim's phone conversation with him, or seeing him sneaking around Kim's hotel room. Instead of letting me step on a jellyfish, he'd probably have tried to feed me to the sharks, she thought with a shudder.

At least she knew who the enemy was. All she had to do was find out why he was the enemy. Looking at Ricardo, who had made no apology and no move to help her, Nancy realized that deliberately letting her step on the man-of-war was his way of telling her to keep her nose out of his business.

You blew it, Ricardo, Nancy thought. Scaring me off doesn't work. And if you hadn't tried it, I might not have learned your name, and then I wouldn't come after you. But I will now.

Nancy started to walk away, stumbled, and nearly fell again. Her foot was beginning to go numb.

"Hey, you okay?" asked the boy who'd helped her up.

"No, but I'm sure I will be," Nancy told him. Then she raised her voice so that Ricardo could hear her. "I'll be fine. I'll be back, too. You can count on it."

As quickly as she could, Nancy made her way up the beach to her hotel. Bess and George had already changed, and when

Nancy told them what had happened, they helped her change, then hustled her into the car and rushed her to the hospital emergency room as fast as possible. By the time they got there, the bottom of Nancy's foot was red and swollen, and the pain went clear up to her knee. But after checking her over, the doctor on duty said she'd be fine.

"You're lucky," she told her, as she rubbed some salve on Nancy's foot. "You must have stepped on just one of its tentacles. If you'd been badly stung, your friends might have had to carry you in here."

Nancy smiled in relief as the medicine started to ease the stinging. The doctor gave her the tube of salve, and after thanking her, Nancy, Bess, and George took the elevator to Kim's room. Kim's mother had just arrived, and she greeted the three girls with tears in her eyes.

"I just don't understand how this could have happened!" Mrs. Baylor pulled a fresh tissue from the box on Kim's bedside table and wiped her eyes. "I was against this trip in the first place. I should never have let her come!"

Nancy reached out to touch Mrs. Baylor's arm. "You can't blame yourself," she said gently.

"Oh, I know." Mrs. Baylor smoothed back her hair and blew her nose. "I'm just so worried. The police don't seem to be very hopeful about finding the driver or the car. They were nice, but I can tell they're not going to spend a lot of time on this. Meanwhile, my daughter's lying here unconscious!"

Nancy, Bess, and George stared at Kim, not knowing what to

say. The doctors had told them that Kim was stable, that things looked very promising for her. But she still hadn't wakened, and it was hard to sit and just watch her. It made them feel helpless, and *that* made them feel edgy.

Nancy was especially edgy. First of all, Kim's mother couldn't seem to stop crying. Not that Nancy blamed her. Her daughter had been run down; she had every right to cry. But all the sniffing and nose-blowing and sobbing made it hard to think. And Nancy needed to think. She was still in the dark about what was going on, despite the fact that she had two good leads—the picture of the girl and Ricardo. He was obviously mixed up in it, but how? And exactly what was he mixed up in? Maybe Dirk Bowman knew. His not-so-subtle hint made Nancy very curious, and she wished she could be with him at that very moment.

But one glance at Bess told Nancy that she'd better keep that wish to herself. Between the man-of-war sting and visiting Kim at the hospital, Nancy hadn't had a chance to explain things to her. Not that she had much explaining to do. She hadn't come on to the guy; he'd come on to her. Bess would realize that.

Actually, when Nancy thought about it, Dirk had started coming on to her as soon as she had mentioned what had happened to Kim. Perhaps he had more than just information for her. Nancy couldn't pass up a chance to learn something. She'd talk to Bess as soon as she could.

About the only thing not annoying Nancy was her foot. It was feeling better by the minute, so she knew she could make good on her promise to Ricardo—she'd be back. That was what was really making her edgy—she wanted to get out of the hospital and back on the trail.

"Oh, how lovely!" Mrs. Baylor exclaimed suddenly. Nancy glanced up and saw that a good-looking guy had just entered Kim's room carrying a big arrangement of flowers. He was wearing a brown uniform, so he must have been from a flower shop. He set the basket on the table, gave Kim a close look, then quickly left the room.

"That was so nice of you girls," Mrs. Baylor said tearfully.

George looked embarrassed. "Don't thank us," she said. "I'm afraid we didn't send them."

"Then who did?" mused Kim's mother.

Nancy reached over and carefully pushed aside the daisies and carnations, but she could find no card. Strange, she thought. Why would somebody send flowers without a card? And just who had sent them?

Kim's mother started to cry again. "This is like a nightmare," she sobbed. "Who on earth would want to hurt my daughter?"

"I don't know, Mrs. Baylor," Nancy told her. "But I promise you, I'm going to find out."

When Dirk Bowman arrived at the Surfside Inn the next morning to pick her up, Nancy was sure of one thing—Bess was no longer upset with her. She understood what Nancy had to do. However, she was still hurt, and she was furious with Dirk for dumping her so rudely.

Nancy dressed casually in light cotton pants and a cotton shirt with a wild island print over her bikini. She wished she could wear her new sandals, but she put on her sneakers instead, since she wasn't sure what Dirk would end up showing her.

At precisely eleven o'clock, Dirk, lean and tan, showed up. Nancy greeted him, then stepped out with him into the fresh morning air.

"Ever been windsurfing?" Dirk asked, taking her hand and leading her toward a red sports car parked at the curb.

"No," Nancy told him. "I've surfed and I've sailed, but never at the same time." She liked his car, and she couldn't help admitting that she also liked the feel of his hand. Bess has great taste, she thought.

"Well, then, you'll probably catch on quickly," Dirk said with a dimpled smile. He put the car in gear and drove quickly down the street. "It's really terrific once you get the hang of it." For the next ten minutes, he kept up a steady, one-sided conversation about the joys of windsurfing.

It was all very interesting, Nancy thought, but it wasn't the information she was after. If Dirk really wanted to turn Nancy on, he'd tell her what he knew about Kim.

"Listen," she said, finally interrupting him. "I don't want to be rude, but you said you might be able to help me out on this case, that you might have some information for me."

"That's right," Dirk answered with an easy smile. "I might. But I told you, I need to know everything you know first."

Nancy was trying to decide what to tell him when Dirk parked the car, got out, and led her to a dock where an outboard boat loaded with two surfboards was tied. They jumped on, Dirk started the engine, and as they sped away, Nancy glanced back at the dock. Ricardo was standing there, watching them. Nancy felt a chill as she watched his figure grow smaller and smaller. What was Ricardo doing there, anyway? Had he followed her and Dirk? Were he and Dirk connected in some way?

It was impossible to talk over the buzz of the motor and the thumping of the waves as the boat plowed through the ocean, but Nancy did manage to ask Dirk where they were going. When he answered her—telling her they were headed for a small island—he leaned so close she could smell his aftershave. He reminded her of Daryl Gray, a guy she'd almost fallen for. In fact, there was a lot about Dirk that reminded her of Daryl. He was gorgeous and friendly and would be easy to fall for too, but Nancy wasn't about to do that. She was after information, not involvement.

After twenty minutes, Dirk cut the motor and let the boat drift gently toward a sandy island dotted with palm trees. It shimmered in the sun, like a beautiful mirage.

"This is where we bring all the partygoers," he explained. "We drop them off around midnight and pick them up a few hours later. It's wild, sort of a big bash in the middle of nowhere."

Nancy nodded, remembering that he worked for some kind of excursion boat. As they beached the motorboat, she asked if he liked the job.

"It's great," he said. "And my boss, Lila Templeton, is one

fun lady. Running these parties to nowhere isn't a job for her—she doesn't need one. Her boat is just a big toy. Ever eat a Templeton orange?"

"Probably," Nancy said.

"Well, every time you do, you're putting money in Lila's pocket. Her family owns half the citrus and sugarcane farms in Florida."

Nancy looked around. The island really is in the middle of nowhere, she thought. "Where does the party boat go after you drop everybody off?" she asked.

"Oh, it just cruises around." Dirk took Nancy's hand again and smiled at her. "I'm really glad you came out with me, you know. I wanted to be alone with you the minute I laid eyes on you, Detective."

Again Nancy noticed the warmth of his hand and the dimple alongside his mouth. Dirk Bowman was a real charmer, all right, but charm wasn't what she was after. "You called me 'Detective,'" she pointed out, "so let's do some detecting, okay?"

With a laugh, Dirk agreed, so while they stripped down to their bathing suits, unloaded the surfboards, and unfurled the brightly colored sails, Nancy told him what had gone on the day before without giving away any important details. By the time she finished, they were on the boards, paddling away from the shore. "It's your turn," she said. "Tell me what *you* know."

Dirk sighed and shook his head. "Sorry, Detective. I'm afraid I came up with a great big zero."

Stunned, Nancy sat up, straddling the board. He never knew anything in the first place, she told herself furiously. It was just a line to get you out here, and you fell for it!

As if he read her mind, Dirk reached out and touched her knee. "Aw, come on, Detective. Don't be mad. I did ask around, but nobody knew anything. If I'd told you that this morning, you wouldn't have come with me, right?"

"Right," Nancy agreed instantly.

But Dirk didn't look insulted. Instead, he laughed. "Look at it this way. You're already in the water, so why not relax and let me teach you how to windsurf? It's the least I can do."

His laugh was hard for Nancy to resist, even with the thoughts of Ricardo and Kim and Rosita whirling through her mind. But she managed to keep a straight face. "One lesson, one ride," she said seriously. "That's it. Then we go back."

"You got it, Detective," Dirk promised. He went on to give her instructions about how to handle the board, how to pull up the sail, when to turn the boom, and how to bail out. "Always bail out backward, right onto your backside," he said. "That way the board won't break your skull."

Soon, Nancy was on her own, in deep water. Carefully she eased up from her stomach to her knees, reached into the water, and pulled up the sail. Keeping a tight grip on the boom, she got to her feet, found her balance, and stood up straight.

Wind filled the sail, and suddenly Nancy felt as if she were flying over the water. She heard Dirk shouting encouragement and found herself laughing out loud as the board slapped over the waves. For just a moment, she forgot about everything but the sun and the wind and the salt spray.

Just when Nancy thought she was going as fast as it was possible to go, the board picked up speed. She wasn't sure if she could handle it, so she turned the boom, hoping to slow down. But she must have turned it the wrong way, because the sail was so full it looked ready to rip. Nancy decided to try one more time to slow down. If that didn't work, then she'd bail out.

Nancy turned the boom. Instantly, the pole fell over as if it had been snapped in two. The board tipped, pushing Nancy forward, and before she had time to react, she found herself hitting the water. Behind her, the heavy surfboard rose up like a sailfish leaping from the ocean. Then it started to fall—heading straight for Nancy's head.

CHAPTER SIX

Nancy tossed her head back and desperately gulped in a mouthful of air. The board was falling fast; in a few seconds it would be on top of her. Nancy flipped sideways, kicked up with her legs, and felt the lethal board graze her thigh as she pulled herself deep under the water.

The current was strong; it somersaulted her over and over until she couldn't tell which way was up. Her lungs felt ready to burst, and for a second, she almost panicked. She'd escaped the surfboard, she realized frantically, but she was in danger of drowning.

Just as she thought she might never make it, Nancy caught sight of the sky above her. The undercurrent tried to spin her over again, but she fought it and pulled herself up through the water until her head broke the surface. Gratefully Nancy filled her lungs with air, pushed her streaming hair out of her face, and looked around. Just a few feet away, her surfboard bobbed peacefully on the waves. Nancy swam over to it and climbed on, then spotted her sail. It was spread out on the water like a giant magenta scarf, and Nancy remembered that awful snap she'd felt when she'd turned the boom. What had happened?

Those poles had to be sturdy, they couldn't just snap in two when the wind got strong. Or could they?

Off in the distance, Dirk Bowman was stretched out on his board, pulling himself against the current to reach Nancy. She waved to let him know she was okay, then caught hold of her sail and dragged it from the water. Hand over hand, she pulled the pole up. When she saw the end of it, where it had snapped, she shivered in spite of the hot sun beating down on her back.

There was a clean slice three quarters of the way through the pole and then a ragged edge where the wind had done the rest of the job. Someone had sawed partway through it, and Nancy shivered again, remembering Ricardo standing at the dock that morning, watching her climb into the boat.

Nancy raised her head and looked at Dirk, who was still bucking the waves to get to her. Maybe he and Ricardo knew each other. Why not? Their jobs brought them to the same beach every day, and maybe Dirk had mentioned that he was taking her windsurfing, so Ricardo had decided to try to get rid of her, making it look like an accident. Just like Kim, Nancy thought.

First the man-of-war, then the windsurfing incident. Ricardo wasn't exactly subtle with the messages he was sending her, and Nancy wondered how many more "accidents" she'd have to survive before she found out what he was involved in.

She was still staring at the pole, fingering the ragged edge, when she heard the buzz of a motor close by. Looking up, she saw a sleek raspberry-and-turquoise speedboat heading toward her. It zipped past, making choppy waves so that Nancy had to drop the pole and clutch the board with both hands. The driver made a sharp turn and then sped back, cutting the twin engines at the last possible second.

"Hi there!" the driver called out. She was a beautiful woman just a couple of years older than Nancy, with golden skin, silky blond hair, and a smile in her wide green eyes. "Need a lift?" she asked.

"It looks that way, doesn't it?" Nancy said, laughing. "I'm not really stranded, though." She pointed to Dirk. "But thanks for the offer."

The woman pulled her dark glasses down from the top of her head and peered through them at Dirk. "Oh, are you with him? Well, let me tell you, he's cute, but he's a klutz, if you know what I mean. I should know—I'm his boss." With a delightful smile, she stuck her hand over the side of the boat. "I'm Lila Templeton."

So she was the fun lady Dirk had mentioned. Shaking Lila's outstretched hand, Nancy glanced over her shoulder at Dirk, who was closer but still struggling with the waves. He lied to get me out here, she thought, and now it's time to pay him back. Laughing again, she hauled herself into Lila's boat. "I think I'll take you up on that offer after all," she said, "if you don't mind stopping at the island a moment so I can get my things."

Grinning, Lila Templeton started the engines, and the boat took off with a roar. As they passed Dirk, Lila slowed long enough to shout, "I want to talk to you the minute you get back!" She and Nancy made a fast stop at the island. Then Lila put the boat into high gear and sped off, leaving Dirk Bowman floundering in its wake.

As they sped back to the mainland, Lila kept up a steady stream of chatter about where Nancy should go and what she should do while she was in Florida. Mostly, though, she gave a sales pitch for her party to nowhere. "It's absolutely the wildest party you'll ever go to," she shouted. "You ought to try it while you're down here. You won't forget it, I promise you that!"

Nancy started to say that Dirk had already invited her, but she changed her mind. Lila seemed genuinely friendly, and Nancy didn't want to disappoint her. She was pretty sure she wouldn't have time for any wild island parties. She had other things to do, she thought grimly, and other people to see. Beginning with Ricardo.

"So what brings you to Lauderdale?" Lila asked, as they approached the docks. "Let me guess—spring break, right?"

"Right," Nancy said. She didn't like lying, but even though Lila seemed harmless, Nancy decided she shouldn't trust anyone. She'd talked to Dirk and look what had happened. Dirk had probably mentioned her to Ricardo, and it was just luck that her surfboard hadn't cracked open her skull half an hour ago.

When Lila docked the boat, Nancy thanked her for the ride

and climbed out. "Don't forget the party, Nancy!" Lila called after her, and Nancy said she wouldn't. But she knew that that night she wouldn't be at any party.

Twenty minutes later, Nancy had grabbed a bite to eat and was back on Fort Lauderdale Beach, looking for Ricardo. She had a strong urge to use one of George's most painful judo moves on him, but she knew that instead she would simply have to be patient. She would have to watch him, see where he went, whom he talked to. If she was careful, he just might lead her to Rosita.

The first place Nancy checked was Ricardo's lifeguard chair, but he wasn't in it. She strolled along the beach, keeping one eye out for Ricardo and the other out for stray men-of-war. Two of a kind, she thought with a grim smile.

Finally Nancy spotted the lifeguard standing ankle-deep in the surf. Beside him, holding his hand, was a blond girl in a red string bikini. It was Bess.

Nancy stopped, trying to figure out what to do. If Ricardo found out she and Bess were friends, he might decide that Bess should be the victim of a few accidents too. But if he thought that Bess was just another pretty girl out for a good time, he might relax with her. And Bess might learn something important about him. Nancy dropped back, trying to blend in with a group of sunbathers.

"Well, hi there, how's your foot?" a voice shouted. "I see you survived your encounter with the deadly man-of-war!"

Wishing he'd keep his voice down, Nancy smiled at the boy

who'd helped her up the day before. "Yes, I'm fine," she said softly.

"Great! I gotta hand it to you, you said you'd be back and here you are!" The boy didn't lower his voice a notch.

"Right," Nancy replied, watching as Ricardo turned his head and looked straight at her. Without a word to Bess, he dropped her hand and trotted down the beach, through the mass of sunbathing bodies, and out of sight. Here I am and there he goes, Nancy thought.

Bess looked at Nancy, her expression puzzled. Nancy waved goodbye to the boy and went to join Bess.

"Gosh," said Bess. "That was weird. That guy took one look at you and left."

Nancy started to explain that his name was Ricardo, and that he was the one she'd seen snooping around Kim's hotel room. But Bess was off on another subject.

"You're back awfully soon," she remarked. "Didn't your date with Dirk work out?"

"As a matter of fact, it was a real washout," Nancy admitted. "I shouldn't have gone with him. He didn't know a thing about the case."

"So now I guess he's through with you, right?" Bess said sarcastically. "Gee, maybe I still have a chance."

"Come on, Bess." Nancy sighed. "I'm sorry things got messed up for you, but you know I'm trying to find out what happened to Kim."

"Oh, and speaking of Kim," Bess said, "she still hasn't come to. While you were off with Dirk I was at the hospital. George is there now, but she has to leave in about an hour." Bess waded out of the water and onto the hard-packed sand. "Maybe you should go visit her. . . . So this Ricardo is really the same guy you saw in Kim's hotel room?"

Nancy nodded. "Don't take this the wrong way, Bess, but be careful around him, okay?"

"Okay," replied Bess, wide-eyed.

"All right. I'll see you around. I've got more investigating to do."

For a while, Nancy wandered along the beach, hoping she'd see Ricardo. But after an hour had gone by, she realized she was wasting her time. He probably wasn't on duty that day, and she knew he wouldn't put in an appearance unless he had to, not if he thought she was hanging around.

Nancy gave up and decided to go to the hospital. Maybe Kim would be awake by then. That would solve everything, she thought hopefully.

When she got to the hospital, Nancy saw Mrs. Baylor standing outside Kim's room, and for a moment, Nancy really was hopeful—Mrs. Baylor wasn't crying.

Keeping her fingers crossed, Nancy rushed down the hall. But as she got closer to Kim's mother she realized that if Mrs. Baylor wasn't crying, it was only because she was too shocked and frightened for tears.

"Mrs. Baylor?" Nancy was breathless, afraid of what she might hear. "Is Kim . . . is she . . . ?"

"She's worse," Mrs. Baylor whispered. "She's growing weaker, and the doctors are worried she might slip into a coma or . . ."

Or die, Nancy thought. And if that happens, then you'll be trying to solve more than a hit and run. It will be murder.

CHAPTER SEVEN

It was early evening when Nancy let herself into her room at the Surfside Inn. She felt slightly guilty about leaving the hospital, but Mrs. Baylor had insisted. "You'll help Kim more by finding out why this happened to her," she'd said. And Nancy knew she was right; what she didn't know yet was how to solve the case. She had two leads—Ricardo and Rosita—and so far, she hadn't been able to follow either of them.

Maybe a shower will help clear your head, she thought, as she flicked on the lights. She stepped into the bathroom and was peeling off her clothes when she noticed the note stuck in the mirror.

> *Nan—I promised Bess I'd go with her on the
> party-to-nowhere boat, so that's where we are—
> nowhere! Bess still likes Dirk, which is why she
> insisted on going. She's also still ticked off at
> him for brushing her off and going out with you
> instead. But I know she understands that you
> have to do everything possible to solve the case.*
>   *George*

Sighing, Nancy turned the shower on full blast and stepped into the warm spray. If all she had to worry about was Bess being mad at her, things would be great. Instead, things were about as rotten as they could be. She'd fallen for Dirk's line and spent an entire morning following a phony lead. And she'd really goofed with Ricardo. She should never have even hinted to him that she knew who he was. She'd probably be a lot closer to solving the case if she'd just kept her eyes open and her mouth shut.

With another sigh, Nancy stepped out of the shower and wrapped a towel around herself. She left the bathroom and stood in front of the window, staring out at the beach. Already, campfires were blazing here and there as groups of kids gathered for the next round of all-night parties. Nancy couldn't help thinking that she'd much rather be out there having fun than holed up alone in her hotel room. Then it hit her—if *she'd* rather be out somewhere, maybe Ricardo and Rosita would too. If not that night, then surely they'd been out on other nights.

She had Rosita's picture. And of the hundreds of kids on the beach and in the clubs, there had to be at least one who'd seen her. It's worth a try, Nancy thought, as she put on a flashy sundress and her new sandals. After all, you said yesterday that if you had to, you'd walk up and down the beach asking anyone and everyone if they'd seen this girl. Well, now, it looks as if you have to.

It was eight o'clock by the time Nancy set out on her search. She was already on the beach when she realized she hadn't eaten anything since noon. There were plenty of fast-food places around. She could grab some food and ask a few questions at the same time.

Asking questions turned out to be easier than she'd anticipated. Halfway through a slice of pepperoni pizza, Nancy noticed that a cute boy in the next booth was paying more attention to her than to his pizza, which was getting cold, fast.

Nancy swallowed a bite of cheese, wiped her mouth, and raised her can of soda. That was all it took. In two seconds, the boy was sitting next to her. "Hi there," he said with a grin. "How you doing?"

"I'm not sure," Nancy replied, trying to look confused.

"What's the problem?"

"Oh, well, this is going to sound weird, but I was supposed to meet a friend of a friend when I got to Lauderdale," Nancy explained, making it up as she went along. "But I get here and what happens? I can't find her! She's not at the hotel, she's not on the beach, she's not anywhere."

"So?" The boy moved over in the booth and casually slid his arm across the back of it. "My name's Mike, by the way, and I don't think your story's weird at all. Your friend's friend is probably having a blast and just forgot about you. My advice is to enjoy yourself and forget about *her*."

"Well, I would, except for one thing." Nancy noticed that Mike's hand was now resting on her bare shoulder. "I was supposed to give her something . . . some money. And I just know I can't have a good time until I find her and get that cash off my hands."

"Well, a good time's definitely what it's all about," Mike said, tightening his fingers on her shoulder. "Why don't you let me help you?"

"I was hoping you'd say that." Nancy reached into her straw shoulder bag and took out the photo. "Here she is. Her name's Rosita."

"Pretty," Mike said, barely glancing at the picture. "But not as pretty as you."

"Thanks," Nancy replied, "but have you seen her?"

"Afraid not. Now, what are you and I going to do for fun tonight?" Mike scooted even closer to Nancy and bent his head down as if he were going to kiss her.

At the last second, Nancy ducked under his arms and left him sitting alone in the booth. Her plans for the night just didn't include Mike. "Until I find Rosita," she told him, "I'm afraid I won't have any fun at all."

Abandoning her pizza, Nancy went out into the warm, breezy night, Mike frowning after her. From now on, she told herself, no more warm-up conversations. Just show the picture and ask the question. If you get stuck with any more Mikes, this search will take forever.

Unfortunately, Fort Lauderdale was full of Mikes, looking to have fun. Some were nice, some came on a little too strong, a few actually took her questions seriously. All of them were interested in Nancy, and none of them had seen Rosita.

By ten-thirty, Nancy was starting to feel discouraged. She'd hit every fast-food place on the strip and turned down invitations to dance in at least half the clubs—and still no Rosita.

What was the girl, anyway, a phantom? Somebody has to have seen her, Nancy thought.

By that time, the beach parties were going strong. Campfires were blazing, and music was blasting up and down the shoreline. Carrying her sandals, Nancy strolled along the soft, cool sand, stopping at every gathering to ask if anyone had seen the girl in the picture.

One girl thought she looked just like a girl from her dorm. "But she didn't come to Lauderdale, so it couldn't be the same one, could it?"

No, Nancy agreed, it couldn't. She was getting so many "sorrys," and "never saw hers," and "forget about her, stick with mes," that when she finally heard the words, "Oh, sure," she thought she'd imagined them.

"What did you say?" she asked the boy who'd spoken.

"I said, sure, I saw her about twenty minutes ago." He took a closer look at the photograph. "Yeah, that's the one. She was with one of the lifeguards. Ricardo, I think his name is."

Suddenly Nancy wasn't tired anymore. Her luck was changing. "Where were they?" she asked.

"Over that way," the boy said, pointing down the beach. "They were leaning against some trees, talking." He smiled and gave Nancy a long look. "Hey, if you don't find them, come on back, why don't you? I plan to be here all night long."

"Thanks," Nancy replied, smiling, "but I don't." She trotted down the beach, keeping her fingers crossed that Ricardo and Rosita would still be there.

As Nancy approached a grove of palm trees she saw two shadowy figures emerge and begin walking along the wet sand, close to the water, toward the docks where Dirk had taken her that morning. The tide was still out, and the moon was full. Nancy could see clearly that one of the figures was Ricardo. The other one—shorter and with long, dark hair—had to be Rosita.

Nancy followed them, keeping a safe distance, sticking to the trees wherever there were any. Ricardo and Rosita seemed to be having a very intense conversation, and Nancy was sure they had no idea she was behind them. She was looking ahead, not really watching where she was going, when she stepped into another grove of palms, tripped over two reclining bodies and went sprawling headfirst into the sand.

A girl gave a piercing shriek and a boy grumbled, "Hey, give us a break, huh? Things were just getting romantic here!"

"Sorry, sorry," Nancy said, trying not to laugh. It would have been funny, but she was worried. Had Ricardo and Rosita heard the shriek? Not wanting to lose sight of them—or ruin the little love scene—Nancy stepped out of the trees and into the bright moonlight.

Ricardo and Rosita had stopped. They were looking in Nancy's direction. As soon as Ricardo saw her, he grabbed Rosita's hand, and the two of them took off running.

Nancy tore after them, not bothering to hide anymore. All she wanted was to catch up with them. Running on the wet, hard-packed sand, she saw them round a bend in the shoreline, and pushed herself even harder, not wanting to lose them. The music from the beach parties was growing fainter; as Nancy rounded the bend, she realized she'd left the crowds behind. She stopped suddenly and looked around, panting from her dash along the beach.

In front of her were the docks. She saw a few boats tied up and heard soft thuds as they bumped against the pilings. But that was all. Nancy was alone.

Still breathing hard, Nancy kicked at the sand in frustration. Then she headed for the docks, thinking that Ricardo and Rosita might be hiding in one of the boats. Of course, the way her luck was running, they'd probably doubled back. They could be sitting around a campfire at that very minute, she told herself, roasting hot dogs and having a good laugh.

Nancy had dropped her sandals somewhere along the way, and as she stepped onto the wooden pier, she reminded herself to be careful of splinters. But before she'd taken two steps, she gasped — not because she felt a splinter sliding into her foot, but because a hand, reaching out from the shadows, was closing tightly on her arm.

CHAPTER EIGHT

Nancy whirled around, ready to fight as hard as she had to, and found herself facing the pretty, black-haired girl whose photograph she'd been carrying with her for the past four hours. Nancy glanced around nervously. No Ricardo in sight, but she figured he was lurking somewhere close by, watching.

Still on edge, Nancy looked at the girl again and was surprised to see that she was nervous too. Her eyes were wide with fear. She'd dropped Nancy's arm and was clenching her hands together tightly.

"Rosita," Nancy said. "You're Rosita, aren't you?"

The name turned the girl's fear to terror. She backed away and shook her head vehemently. "Maria," she stammered. "Maria."

Nancy was confused. For one thing, the girl whom she'd thought was her enemy was hardly acting like an enemy—one loud "boo" from Nancy and she'd probably collapse. Furthermore, her name wasn't Rosita.

"Okay," Nancy said. "You're Maria. My name's Nancy Drew.

Now that the introduction's out of the way, why don't you tell me what you and Ricardo and Rosita are up to? Whatever you got Kim involved in just might have killed her, and . . ."

The girl was shaking her head again, looking pained at the mention of Kim and her accident. She held out her hand for Nancy to stop talking. In Spanish, she said that she could explain everything, but that she spoke very little English.

Nancy nodded. She replied that she knew some Spanish, and she asked Maria to go ahead and explain.

Maria breathed a sigh of relief and began to talk.

Nancy *did* know Spanish, but after two sentences, she realized she didn't know Maria's Spanish. Still frightened, Maria was talking away a mile a minute, and she was speaking in a dialect that Nancy could hardly follow.

Nancy followed Maria's story as best she could, though, and did manage to learn that Maria was undocumented. Kim had been hiding her in her hotel room. She said something about the "evil people" she'd paid to bring her to Florida. They didn't let her go, as they'd promised; they were going to make her work for them for nothing. She was running from them, and Kim had helped her.

Maria said something about Ricardo, but Nancy didn't understand. She decided to let Maria finish talking; then she'd ask questions.

Kim had made Maria promise to stay in the hotel room, but after many days, Maria had had to get out. She was followed and ran back to the hotel; someone broke in later while she was in the room, but she escaped.

That's how they found out about Kim, Nancy thought. But who were "they"? Kim definitely had been talking to Ricardo that morning on the phone, but why? He had to be one of the "evil people," and Kim just didn't know it. She'd trusted him for some reason, and he'd double-crossed her.

Nancy asked about Ricardo.

Maria said a lot of things, none of which Nancy understood except that Ricardo had a bad temper. Nancy didn't need to be told that.

Maria stopped in midsentence, her eyes widening in terror. "Oh no!" she cried, pointing behind Nancy. "No!"

Nancy heard a scuffling sound in back of her and started to turn, but it was too late. Something hard—a rock? a club?— came crashing down on her head. She heard Maria scream, but it sounded muffled and distant. Then she saw the wooden slats of the dock as she fell. They were fuzzy because a dark mist was rising in front of her eyes. She blinked, but the mist kept rising; she tried to listen, but her ears were filled with a low roar, like highway traffic heard from far away. Finally the mist closed over her completely, and she couldn't see or hear anything at all.

When Nancy came to, the first thing she felt was pain. She hurt all over, but her head was the worst. She started to open her eyes, then shut them tightly, gasping at the pain. If only she could move her hand to the back of her head to rub it and ease some of the throbbing.

Something was stopping her, though; she wasn't sure what. She must have been lying on her arms, because they were tingling as if they'd been asleep. She tried to stretch one arm, then the other, to make the needles go away, but all she could move were her fingers.

Suddenly she became aware of another sensation—water. Her feet and legs were wet, and every few seconds, water splashed against her thighs. Had she fallen asleep on the beach?

Then she remembered.

She'd been talking to Rosita. No, not Rosita. Maria. Maria had screamed, and then everything had gone black. Nancy hadn't fallen asleep, she'd been knocked out. And whoever had done it—she'd put her money on Ricardo—had dragged her onto the beach and left her there with the waves lapping at her legs. Funny, she'd always thought the sand would make a nice soft bed. So why did she feel as if she were lying on cement?

Time to get up, Nancy, she told herself. Forget the pain, just get up and go after him.

She tried to stretch her arms again and suddenly realized that they were above her head. And she wasn't lying on soft sand, either. In fact, she wasn't lying at all. She was leaning against something very hard, something that had absolutely no give to it.

Nancy forced her eyes open and waited for her vision to clear. It was still night—pitch-black—but if she craned her neck back, she could see the moon up above.

She could also see where her hands were. They were up above her too, tied over her head. No wonder her arms ached.

Nancy turned her head, scraping her cheek against something rough and cold. Then she felt the water wash against her thighs again, and realized that her feet were tied too. She peered down, trying to see where she was.

The night breeze was warm, but Nancy started shivering violently when she realized that she'd been tied, hand and foot, to one of the pier pilings, a rough, wooden pillar shooting straight out of the water. She was somewhere in the middle of it; if she tilted her head back far enough, she could just see the lip of the pier. But what made her shiver, what made her want to scream, was that she could also see the waterline on the piling. It was a foot above her head. Already the water was lapping against her thighs. Soon it would be at her waist, then at her shoulders. The tide was coming in, and Nancy was trapped in its path.

She heard a low, moaning sound and realized it was coming from her. Scream, she told herself. You got hit on the head, not in the throat. She tried to take a deep breath, and that's when she felt the gag in her mouth and the tape on her cheek. There was no way she could scream; the only sound she could make was a soft moan nobody would hear. She'd been tied, gagged, and left to drown.

CHAPTER NINE

Nancy fought to keep from panicking, but she lost the battle. She'd never been so trapped; the feelings of terror and helplessness were overwhelming. She was at the end of the pier, which was far enough out in the water to give her a tantalizing view of the bonfires around the bend in the beach. She could even see the shadows of the people around those bonfires, and every once in a while she heard shouts of laughter.

Frantically Nancy pulled and twisted against the ties that held her to the pier. She didn't know how long she kept it up, but when she finally stopped, she was limp with exhaustion and her skin was burning from being scraped against the piling. If she could have screamed, her throat would have been raw.

If they wanted to kill you, she thought tiredly, why didn't they just dump you in the middle of the ocean while you were still unconscious? Why put you through this kind of torture? They'd even tied her hands with the sash of her sundress. An extra-evil touch.

Evil. That's what Maria had called them, and she'd been right. For a moment, Nancy wondered what had happened to the frightened girl. Ricardo must have gotten her, she thought.

Then, as the water washed up, hitting the middle of her back, Nancy began struggling and twisting again. But she was too tired and too sore to keep it up for very long. Sagging against the piling, she rubbed her forehead on the back of her wrist and closed her eyes.

Breathless, half-covered with water, Nancy thought of how she must look—like a huge barnacle in a dress. The thought made her want to laugh. You're getting hysterical, she warned herself. Her head was throbbing violently, and when she opened her eyes, she saw that the dark mist was closing in. If she passed out, she knew she'd never make it.

Nancy closed her eyes again, and that's when she heard the footsteps on the pier. Looking up, she saw two faces bending over the edge, staring down at her. Nancy blinked, fighting back the mist, and realized that she recognized the faces. One belonged to the handsome "maintenance" man from Kim's hotel room; the other was the guy who'd delivered the flowers to the hospital. Not bothering to wonder what they were doing there, Nancy moaned as loudly as she could, begging them with her eyes to help her. The two faces lingered above her for a moment, then faded away like ghosts into the darkness.

Ghosts, Nancy thought. That's what they were. You're so far gone, you're hallucinating. She let her head drop and felt a wave splash high on her back, hitting her shoulder blades.

Then Nancy felt something else, something that made the dark mist evaporate—her feet were loose. Whatever they were tied with had stretched, and Nancy was almost able to uncross her ankles. If she could do that, she could get her feet free. What she'd do then, she wasn't sure, but she didn't care. One thing at a time, she told herself, and started to wiggle her feet, ignoring the scrapes on her knees and the ache in her arms.

It seemed to take forever, but finally Nancy did it. Her feet were side by side and she was able to slip one and then the other out of the binding. Her arms felt as if they were going to rip out at the shoulders, and she managed to wrap her legs around the piling. Then what?

The water lapped at her neck, and Nancy instinctively gripped the piling with her knees and tried to push herself up. The sash binding her hands moved up too, just a fraction. That's it, Nancy told herself. You've climbed enough trees, now shinny up this pole.

Inch by inch, Nancy pushed herself up the piling. The tide kept coming in, and she must have swallowed half the ocean, but finally her head was above the waterline, and even though she was still trapped, she knew she was going to make it.

She couldn't use her teeth on the sash, but when she saw that the cloth wasn't completely soaked, Nancy began to scrape it up and down on a corner of the piling. At last she felt the cloth begin to give. With a final burst of strength, Nancy pulled her hands free, shinnied the rest of the way up the piling, and hauled herself onto the pier.

The first thing she did was rip the gag from her mouth. Then she lay still, gasping and listening to the water swirl below her.

She told herself to get moving, but her body wouldn't budge. Her mind was working, though, and when she thought of Maria, she was finally able to sit up. For all Nancy knew, Maria was dead. No, Maria had said something about being made to work like a slave. Whoever wanted her, wanted her alive, and Ricardo must have taken her to that person.

Ricardo. Nancy had to find him, not just for Maria's sake, but for her own. She had a personal score to settle with him. But she wasn't going to do it on her own, not again. She wanted the police backing her up the next time. It was safer, and besides, she'd need them to keep her from setting fire to Ricardo's chair while he was in it.

Nancy felt the adrenaline pumping as she pushed herself to her feet and stumbled away from the pier. She even managed to trot a little as she rounded the bend in the beach and came within sight of the all-night partiers. The bonfires were still glowing, but not so brightly, and the music was turned down low. It was getting late. No, it was getting early, Nancy reminded herself; morning couldn't be far away.

As soon as she reached the main beach, Nancy headed for the street, looking for a phone. She'd thought of calling from her hotel and then cleaning up while she waited for the police, but she wanted them to see her first. She knew she looked like the survivor of a shipwreck, and if the police saw what Ricardo had done, they'd work that much harder.

When she was halfway down the beach, she spotted a tiki bar that was still open. The adrenaline wasn't pumping so hard by then, and she felt exhausted, as if she were trekking across a desert, and the business was her oasis.

Nancy had almost reached it when a scream rang out. At first she took it to be a good-natured, party-type scream, but then she heard other screams and saw people running toward the water. The tide had washed something ashore. What was it? A shark? A jellyfish?

"It's a body!" a boy shouted, rushing by Nancy. "It's a *body*!"

Maria, Nancy thought instantly. Maria put up too big a fight, and Ricardo or whoever he worked with killed her. Forgetting about the police for the moment, Nancy joined the rest of the crowd heading toward the water. She didn't want to see a dead body, but she had to find out if it was Maria.

There must have been a hundred people gathered around, and Nancy had to push through them until she was able to see. Someone had thrown a large beach towel over the body. Nancy broke free of the crowd and moved quickly to the towel, wanting to get it over with.

"Poor guy," a voice said, and Nancy stopped.

"Yeah," someone else said. "Drowning—what a way for a lifeguard to go, huh?"

"Lifeguard?" Nancy asked.

"Yeah." A boy nodded grimly. "What was his name? Ricardo, that's it. Ricardo."

CHAPTER TEN

Nancy stepped back from the towel-draped body. "Are you sure it's Ricardo?" she asked.

"Hey, I helped pull him out of the water," the boy replied. "And I've talked to him every day since I've been here. I know what he looks like." The boy paused. "Hey, you look sick. Were you a friend of his?" he asked.

Nancy shook her head. "No, but I knew who he was."

"Yeah, well, it's too bad, huh? And you want to know something? He didn't drown—he was shot." The boy held up his hand. "And, yes, I'm sure. I pulled him out of the water, remember?"

Stunned, Nancy pushed her way through the crowd and stumbled back up the beach, trying to figure out what had happened. Why had Ricardo been shot? Had he lost Maria, and had the people he worked with killed him for it?

When she reached the street, Nancy heard the wail of a siren in the distance. The police, coming to investigate Ricardo's murder. She knew she should talk to them, but what would she say? The last time she saw him, he was with a girl named Maria, but she had no idea where Maria was. She had no idea who

Ricardo worked for or who killed him. You don't really know anything at all, Nancy told herself. Your main suspect is dead, and you're back to square one.

The Surfside Inn was just across the street, and Nancy decided to go there first, to shower and change. Then she'd return to the beach and talk to the police. But after she got the key from the desk and let herself into the room, Nancy realized she was too tired to take a shower. She was so wiped out, she was actually staggering. Her eyes were playing tricks on her, too. Instead of two single beds, she saw four, then two, then four again. Stumbling across the room, she bumped into the cot that Bess used, fell onto it, and was asleep before her head hit the pillow.

"Look at this!" a voice was saying. "There's a body on my cot!"

Nancy burrowed her face deeper into the crook of her elbow. "Go away," she mumbled.

Another voice said, "Look, she didn't even bother to change. How's that for lazy?"

"Please," Nancy groaned, "not so loud." She yawned and tried to slip back into sleep, but someone sat down on the cot, making it jiggle back and forth.

"Hey, Nan," Bess said, laughing, "I don't mind if you sleep here, but don't you think you'd be more comfortable without my makeup kit poking you in the neck?"

Nancy moaned and shook her head, but it was too late—she was awake. She opened one eye and peered up through her tangled hair. Bess and George were staring down at her, looking extremely amused. "What's happening?" she asked.

"Why don't *you* tell *us*?" George suggested.

"Yeah," Bess said, grinning. "We thought *we* had a wild night, but it looks like yours was wilder. Couldn't even bother to take off your clothes before you fell asleep, huh?"

"Wild night?" Nancy croaked. Her throat was bone-dry, and her tongue felt too big for her mouth. Swallowing, she pushed herself up on her elbows and turned onto her back. "It was wild, all right."

When Bess and George saw how scratched and bruised she was, their teasing grins disappeared and their mouths dropped open.

"Nan, what *happened* to you?" Bess cried in horror.

"That must have been some battle," George said. "Are you okay?"

"I will be, once I shower and eat and drink about a gallon of water." Nancy sat up slowly and rubbed her neck. "You're right, George," she remarked, "it was some battle."

"Well, tell us!" Bess demanded.

George went to the vending machine in the hall and brought back a soda and a package of peanut butter crackers. Nancy ate first, then told them everything that had happened the night before.

"We heard about Ricardo when we got in," Bess told her. "That's all anybody's talking about on the beach."

"It looks like he wasn't a bad guy after all," George said.

"What do you mean?"

"Well, he was undocumented himself."

Hmm, thought Nancy. Just like Maria.

"Yeah," Bess said, "the police tried to check up on him and found out he'd been working with a fake green card ever since he reached Florida. And it seems that a lot of people around here knew about it."

George nodded. "One of the other lifeguards told me that Ricardo tried to help others—you know, get them cards and find them work, stuff like that."

"So he must have been helping Maria all along," Nancy said. That explained why he'd smiled when Kim got hit, she thought. It was a smile of anger—he'd been challenged and he was ready to fight. "But why did he have it in for me?" she wondered aloud, remembering the satisfied look on his face when she'd stepped on the man-of-war.

"Why shouldn't he? He didn't know who you were," Bess pointed out. "Kim didn't know you were coming down, and she probably never even mentioned you. He probably thought you were going to turn him in or something."

"Right," Nancy agreed. "He didn't trust anyone." She ran her fingers through her hair and sighed. "Boy, I'm really stuck now. I don't have the vaguest idea what to do next."

Bess took Nancy's hand and pulled her off the bed. "Take a shower and then put something in your stomach besides soda and crackers," she told her. "Once you feel human again, you'll be able to think."

Nancy couldn't help noticing that Bess was back to her old friendly self. Dirk must have made all the right moves, she thought. Then she thought of something else. "Kim!" she cried. "I completely forgot!" She quickly told Bess and George about Kim's condition while she dialed the hospital room. The line was busy.

Ten minutes and three calls later, it was still busy.

"Look," George said, "go shower. We'll keep trying the hospital. Anyway, who knows? Kim might have recovered."

"Let's hope so," Nancy said, and headed for the shower. Even though the sharp spray stung every cut and scratch, the water felt wonderful, and Nancy thought she might never come out. She was soaping her hair for the second time when Bess walked in.

"Nan?" she called. "I just wanted to apologize for the way I acted about Dirk. I was really mad at him, not at you. I hope you know that."

"It's okay," Nancy called back, over the hiss of the water. Then she poked her head out of the shower curtain and grinned. "I take it you two got together again last night?"

"We sure did!" Bess ran a brush through her hair and laughed. "He's absolutely incredible!"

"Well, I'm glad somebody had fun," Nancy joked. "Did you meet Lila Templeton?"

Bess nodded. "She was really nice. She asked why you weren't there, but I just said something had come up."

"That's for sure!" Nancy ducked back in the shower and started rinsing her hair.

"I wouldn't mind being in Lila's shoes," Bess went on with a giggle. "Everybody who works for her is tan, male, and gorgeous! And when they drop the partiers off at the island, she gets to take off in that boat with ten beautiful men!"

Nancy laughed and poured some conditioner on her hair. "Sounds great!"

"It is," Bess agreed, "but I'm starting to feel a little guilty."

"Guilty? What for?"

"Well, I mean, there we were, cruising along in the *Rosita*, having a terrific time, while you were tied to that piling, fighting for your life, and—"

"The what?" Nancy turned the water off and stuck her head out again. "What did you say?"

"I said I was feeling a little guilty about having such a good time when—"

"I heard that part," Nancy interrupted. "You said you were cruising along in the . . . the what?"

"The boat," Bess said, looking confused. "Lila Templeton's boat—the *Rosita*."

CHAPTER ELEVEN

I missed it!" Nancy said. "I completely missed it!" She stepped into her new yellow drawstring shorts, pulled on a stretchy, yellow-striped tank top, and reached for the blow-dryer. "Kim said 'Rosita' after the car hit her. I kept thinking she meant a girl, and all the time she meant a boat!"

"You really think Lila Templeton brings people in illegally?" Bess asked.

"I think she does more than that," Nancy said over the whine of the blow-dryer. "I think she brings them in, takes their money, and then ships them off to work for her family for nothing."

"Cheap labor," George remarked.

"The cheapest," Nancy agreed. "No wonder she's got so much money. No wonder the *Rosita* is just a big water toy to her. Except it isn't really a toy," she added. "It's a perfect front for what she's doing."

"You mean while everybody's partying on the island," Bess said, "Lila takes the boat, picks up immigrants, and hides them somewhere on the boat until she gets back to Fort Lauderdale?"

"Why not?" George asked. "The *Rosita*'s big enough."

Nancy turned off the dryer. "I don't think it's just Lila, though," she said. "Remember the guys I told you about—the 'maintenance' man and the one who dropped off the flowers at the hospital? When I was out on that pier, I thought I'd imagined them. But now I'm positive they were there."

"You think they work for Lila," George said.

"Right. It makes sense, doesn't it?" Nancy asked. "That maintenance guy was as phony as a three-dollar bill; I just didn't know what he was doing there. But he was probably checking the room to make sure there wasn't any evidence against Lila. And the florist guy must have been checking to make sure Kim wasn't spilling the beans."

"I'll bet they followed you around last night," George told her. "And you led them right to Maria and Ricardo."

Nancy nodded. "Lila's got a whole fleet of men doing her dirty work." Her feet still sore, she limped over to the cot and, wincing, slipped on a pair of flip-flops. The sandals she'd worn the night before were lost forever on the beach. "And, Bess," she said, "remember what happened when you first introduced me to Dirk?"

"How could I forget? He practically tripped over his own feet to stand next to you." Bess rolled her eyes and shook her head. "The minute he met you, it was like I didn't exist."

"Not the minute he met me," Nancy reminded her. "It was the minute I started talking about Kim."

"That's right," George said. "He said he was 'sort of a mystery buff' and he'd like to help you."

Bess shook her head again. "What a line!"

"Yeah, but he wasn't using that line because he was interested in me," Nancy said. "The only one he was interested in was Kim, and that's because—"

"Because he works for Lila Templeton," Bess finished with a groan. "How come I always fall for the wrong guy?" she asked, plopping down on one of the beds. "This time I really, really thought I'd found somebody special, and he turns out to be a creep, *the* creep!"

Nancy couldn't help laughing. "Don't feel too bad, Bess. I fell for him, too." Grinning, she told them about the broken pole on her windsurfing sail. "I mean I really fell for him!"

"Well, now that we've got it all figured out," George said, "what are we going to do about it?"

"Good question," Bess remarked. "The only one who can prove anything is Maria, and who knows where she is?"

"Kim could prove it," Nancy said, "if she's still . . ." Instead of finishing the awful thought, Nancy reached for the phone and dialed Kim's hospital room. "Now there's no answer at all," she reported.

"What could that mean?" Bess asked.

"I don't know." Nancy suddenly jumped up and headed for the door. "Come on, let's get to the hospital and find out."

• • •

Half an hour later, Nancy, Bess, and George were standing nervously outside the door to Kim's hospital room. They looked at each other for a moment; then Nancy took a deep breath and pushed it open.

Kim was gone.

The bed was empty and freshly made, ready for a new patient. The only reminders of Kim were two flower arrangements—one was dried and drooping, but the second looked as if it had just been delivered.

Bess's eyes filled with tears. "We're too late," she whispered.

George bit her lip. "I can't believe she's—"

"Wait a minute," Nancy broke in. "This doesn't have to mean she's dead. Maybe they moved her to a different room or took her for tests or X-rays or something. Come on!"

The three friends dashed out of the room and headed down the hall. As they turned a corner they heard a loud commotion at the nurses' station.

"I never authorized any such thing!" a voice cried. "How could you possibly think I would?"

It was Kim's mother, but she didn't look grief-stricken. She looked furious.

"Mrs. Baylor?" Nancy rushed up to her. "What's going on?"

"I'd like to know myself!" Mrs. Baylor exclaimed. "I leave my daughter's room for all of twenty minutes to get a cup of coffee in the cafeteria and what do I find when I come back? An empty bed, that's what I find. With no daughter in it!"

"I'm sorry, Mrs. Baylor," the nurse said nervously. "But the doctor who signed her out said you wanted her taken back to River Heights as soon as possible."

"That's ridiculous! Why would I have her moved at such a crucial time?"

"You mean Kim had gotten even worse?" Nancy asked.

"No, she was getting better! Just a couple of hours ago, she actually woke up," Mrs. Baylor explained. "She didn't say anything, of course, she was too weak. But she knew who I was—she smiled at me before she went back to sleep. The doctors said it would be just a matter of days before she'd be back on her feet." She turned to the nurse again. "They also told me it was very important to keep her quiet and calm," she said accusingly. "It would be the most ridiculous thing in the world for me to take her back to River Heights right now!"

The nurse started to say something, but Mrs. Baylor didn't give her a chance. "I'm going to see your supervisor right this minute," she told her. "And you'd better hope she has some answers for me. If she doesn't, heads are going to roll around here!" Without a backward glance, Mrs. Baylor strode to the elevator and furiously punched the button.

When she was gone, the red-faced nurse puffed out about a gallon of air. "This is definitely not my day," she complained. "I'm new here and all I did was follow a doctor's orders, and now my job's on the line."

Nancy barely heard her. "If we'd just gotten here an hour ago, this whole thing would never have happened," she muttered.

"What are you talking about?" Bess asked.

"Those flowers," Nancy said, pacing back and forth in front of the desk.

"What flowers?"

"In Kim's room, remember? One of the bouquets was drooping and the other was fresh. I'll bet you that they were both sent by the same person."

"Lila?" George asked.

"Lila." Nancy stopped pacing and shook her head. "Lila Templeton has been one step ahead of me ever since I got here. That tan hunk who works for her probably delivered those flowers so he could find out what shape Kim was in. When he realized she was recovering, he called Lila. That's why the phone was busy. And Lila decided that Kim better disappear."

Nancy thought for a moment, then suddenly turned to the nurse. "That doctor," she said, "the one who signed Kim Baylor out. Who was he?"

"It wasn't a he, honey," the nurse replied. "That doctor was a she, and she had two of the cutest orderlies with her that I ever saw in my life."

"Lila Templeton," Nancy said again. "The doctor had blond hair, right?" she asked.

"Blond hair and big green eyes," the nurse replied. "She was real friendly, smiled a lot."

"A great bedside manner, huh?" Nancy asked with a wry smile. Without waiting for an answer, she looked at Bess and George. "We've got to get going," she said.

"Where?" Bess wanted to know.

"To the *Rosita*."

"You think Lila has Kim on her boat?" George asked.

"Kim *and* Maria," Nancy said. "It makes sense, doesn't it? They're the only two people who can point a finger at Lila. She knows she has to get rid of them, and the *Rosita* is a perfect way to do it."

Bess's face turned pale under its tan. "You mean she'll kill them and dump them in the ocean?"

Nancy nodded. "Don't forget Ricardo," she said. "Lila Templeton has killed before, and unless we stop her, she's going to kill again."

CHAPTER TWELVE

At seven-thirty that night, the *Rosita* sat peacefully at the dock, swaying slightly in the breeze. It was a beautiful boat, sleek and trim, but with enough deck space for close to fifty people to dance on. Its rails were strung with brightly colored lights, and from somewhere on board, powerful speakers blasted rock music into the evening air. It was scheduled to leave at eight o'clock, and already the decks were filling with laughing, joking people, eager to party the night away.

As Nancy, Bess, and George joined a crowd of kids heading for the gangplank, Nancy raised her eyes and scanned the crew on the small upper deck. "I just spotted my friend the maintenance man," she whispered. "The florist is up there, too."

"And there's Dirk the Jerk," Bess hissed. "Is it my imagination, or does he look nervous?"

Dirk Bowman, wearing white cotton shorts and a muscle-hugging T-shirt, was standing at the rail, his eyes roving over the approaching partiers.

"I'd be nervous too," George said, "if I had Kim and Maria hidden away in the hold somewhere."

"Lila probably ordered them all to keep an eye out for me," Nancy said.

"But she thinks you're dead," Bess reminded her.

"She can't be sure," Nancy told her. "If she sent one of her goons to check, all he would have found is the sash from my sundress. Until she hears about my body being washed ashore, she can't take any chances."

"*We're* the ones taking a chance right now," George remarked. "If Dirk spots the three of us together, he's going to see right through our 'disguises.'"

Nancy nodded. She wished they really could have disguised themselves, but after all, they had to wear clothes that were right for a party to nowhere. George had on a long striped caftan with a hood that covered her hair and shadowed her face. Bess, whose figure was a dead giveaway, especially to Dirk, had reluctantly decided on a pair of baggy cotton pants, rolled to the knees and topped with an oversized shirt patterned with gaudy palm trees. "I look like a tourist," she'd complained, tucking her blond hair under a wide-brimmed straw hat.

Nancy was wearing a caftan too, but it didn't have a hood. She'd wrapped her hair in a bright paisley scarf, and put on so much makeup that her face itched and her eyelids felt weighted down. She knew she and her friends looked completely different, but she also knew they had to be careful. "You're right," she said to George, "we'd better split up. As soon as the *Rosita* gets going, we can meet somewhere—how about the bow?—and start looking for Kim and Maria."

The minute the three friends parted, Nancy felt a hand on her arm. "Hey," a voice said in her ear, "want some company?"

Nancy turned and found herself looking into the brown eyes of a boy wearing a fishnet shirt, a gold neck chain, and a self-satisfied grin that didn't attract her at all, but she smiled at him anyway. "I sure do," she said softly. "I don't know anybody at all, and I was starting to feel a little lonely."

"Well, now you don't have to, because you know me. And I have a feeling that before the night's over, we'll be real close friends." He squeezed her hand and grinned again.

Nancy forced herself to laugh, and as they walked up the gangplank she glanced over her shoulder. George, tall and mysterious-looking in her hooded caftan, was in deep conversation with two guys, and Bess had attached herself to a group of giggling, dateless girls. She must be miserable, Nancy thought, smiling to herself.

"Welcome!" a sultry voice called out. "Welcome aboard the *Rosita*."

It was Lila Templeton, dressed in a long robe of shimmering sea green silk that opened in the front to reveal an extremely small bikini. Her honey blond hair spilled over her bare shoulders, and she was flashing her toothpaste-ad smile to everyone coming up the gangplank. "If there's anything my boys or I can do for you, just let us know," she called out, "because we want each and every one of you to have the most fantastic night of your lives!"

Each and every one of us except two, Nancy said to herself, thinking of Kim and Maria. Turning to her "date," she flashed a smile of her own, ducking her head and pretending to be fascinated with whatever he was babbling about. That got her safely past Lila, but she knew she'd still have to be careful of Lila's "boys," who were patrolling the deck like sentries.

Fortunately, the party to nowhere was booked solid, and Nancy soon found herself on the jam-packed deck, trying to dance and make conversation with her new friend, whose name she still didn't know. She was hot and sweaty, and she'd lost sight of Bess and George, but at least she was inconspicuous.

At eight o'clock, a cheer went up as the *Rosita* pulled smoothly away from the dock. In twenty minutes, they'd left the lights of Fort Lauderdale behind and were moving swiftly through the water under a starlit sky. Nancy decided she'd better start exploring. It wouldn't take long to reach the island, and she knew she had to find Kim and Maria before then, or it might be too late.

"Listen," she said when there was a break in the music, "I'm going to collapse if I don't get some breathing space. I think I'll just wander around a little bit, okay?"

"Aww, come on," her date said, "the party's just getting started." Grabbing her hand, he pulled Nancy close to him as a slow number began playing. "I thought you and I were going to spend the whole night together," he whispered in her ear.

"You thought wrong," Nancy whispered back. She slipped down out of the circle of his arms and turned him around until he was facing another girl. "But I'm sure you won't have any trouble finding a partner."

Obviously not heartbroken, the boy immediately asked the other girl if she wanted to dance, and Nancy left them together, threading her way quickly through the crowd until she reached the deck rail. Then she craned her neck around, trying to find Bess and George.

She spotted George standing near the entrance to the galley, which was roped off, sipping a can of soda and watching the dancers. Bess was still attached to the group of unattached girls, tapping her foot to the music and looking frustrated. Lila was nowhere to be seen, but her boys were all over the place, carrying trays of drinks, mingling with the crowd, and keeping their eyes wide open, Nancy noticed.

Casually Nancy raised her hands above her head, as if she were stretching. Bess and George both caught the movement, and just as casually, started making their way toward the *Rosita*'s bow. Nancy lowered her hands, pretending to be adjusting her turban, but instead of the silk of the scarf, her hands came down on her hair.

What had happened to her scarf? Nancy's reddish blond locks were a big clue to her identity. With her hair swirling around her shoulders and her thick makeup dissolving in sweat, Nancy knew she'd be recognized by anyone who'd spent even five minutes with her. And that includes Lila, Dirk, and at least two more of Lila's boys, she thought frantically.

Nancy realized it was too late to go searching for her scarf.

It must have come loose when she broke free from her date's arms, and had probably already been trampled by at least eighty feet. She grabbed her hair in both hands and swept it back, tying it in a loose knot that she knew wouldn't hold for long, but it was the best she could do. Hoping to get lost in the crowd, she moved into the mass of dancing bodies, and that's when she saw Lila's "maintenance" man.

He was heading straight toward Nancy, one hand in his pocket and both eyes on her face.

Whirling around, Nancy grabbed the hands of the nearest boy, not caring if he was with anyone else or not, and started dancing with him. When she sensed that the maintenance man was drawing close to her, she spun around again so that her back was to him. By that time, she'd lost her dance partner, but it didn't matter. What mattered was that the maintenance man had recognized her. She was sure of it. Just keep dancing, she told herself; at least it's a dance mix and you can move fast.

With a few quick dance steps, Nancy reached the other side of the *Rosita*. Only then did she dare look back. She expected to spot the maintenance man somewhere in the crowd, but she found that was impossible. There were too many people bouncing, clapping, and swirling around the deck.

Nancy took a deep breath, tightened the knot in her hair, and headed toward the bow. The water was becoming rougher, and she clung to the rail, bumping into a few romantic couples on the way, but finally she reached the bow.

The deck was narrow there, and in spite of the lights on the rail, it was dark. Nancy stepped into the shadows, expecting to find Bess and George waiting for her.

No one was there. Nancy edged her way around the bow, toward the other side of the boat, but before she reached it, a voice—throaty and sultry—called out, "Looking for someone, Miss Drew?"

CHAPTER THIRTEEN

Turning slowly, Nancy found herself face-to-face with Lila Templeton, her silk robe billowing gently in the breeze, her green eyes glittering as brightly as the barrel of the gun she held in her hand.

"I said," Lila repeated, "are you looking for someone?"

Nancy didn't bother to answer. "I have a question too," she said, keeping her eyes on the gun. "Is that the same gun that killed Ricardo?"

Lila laughed softly. "I'm afraid I don't know what you're talking about, but I suggest that you be careful, or it just might kill *you*. I also suggest that you be cooperative," she went on. "I want you to turn around and walk slowly and calmly back to the main deck."

"Then what?" Nancy asked.

"I guess you don't understand," Lila told her, stepping so close to Nancy that she felt the gun barrel pressing against her stomach. "I'm in charge. You don't ask questions, you don't make comments. You just do what I tell you. Now move!"

Nancy turned, raised her hands above her head and started walking. Behind her, Lila hissed, "Put your hands down!" and when Nancy felt the gun prodding her in the back, she decided not to push Lila any further. She lowered her arms and walked slowly around the bow, heading back to the main deck.

The music and laughter were still going strong, and for a second Nancy was tempted to break away and try to lose herself in the dancing crowd. But then what? she wondered. It wouldn't get her any closer to Kim and Maria, or to Bess and George, wherever they were. If she let Lila call the shots for a while, she might learn something. Besides, with a gun at her back, she figured she didn't have much choice.

"The galley," Lila ordered.

"I thought it would be off limits," Nancy quipped, figuring that that might be where Kim and Maria were hidden.

Lila laughed again. "Not for you, Miss Drew. Consider the *Rosita* your home. The last home you'll ever have."

With the gun barrel nestled between her shoulder blades, Nancy went down the steps and into the narrow galley. But Lila didn't stop there. She urged Nancy through it and past some bunk beds. At last Nancy stopped, thinking there was nowhere else to go.

But Lila shoved her roughly aside and, still aiming the gun at Nancy, dropped to her knees, took hold of a brass ring on the floor, and pulled up a section of the floor. Looking down, Nancy saw a steep metal staircase leading to the bottom of the boat.

"After you," Lila said.

Nancy lowered herself through the hole, found her footing, and stepped backward down the staircase. When she reached the bottom, she looked up, hoping that Lila would back down too, so she could grab her ankle and get the gun. But Lila came down facing forward, holding the gun in front of her, aimed at Nancy's chest.

They were in a very narrow, dimly lit passageway, with two doors on each side. Obviously not first-class accommodations, Nancy thought. "Look, I know all about your operation," she said to Lila. "I know you bring people here, and then force them to work on your family's farms. They don't have any ID, not even fake ID, and they don't have any money, because you charged them so much to bring them into the country. If they escape you, they get caught by ICE. They're trapped."

"That's right," Lila agreed. "They're trapped, and so are you."

"Then you admit it?" Nancy asked.

Lila shrugged. "Why not? You're not going to tell anyone. In a few hours, you'll be food for the fish." Reaching into her pocket, she pulled out a key and slid it into the lock on one of the doors.

"One of my boys will be down soon to take care of you," she said, opening the right-hand door. "Until then, I suggest you and your friends enjoy the time you have left."

My friends? Nancy barely had time to wonder whether she meant Kim and Maria or Bess and George, before Lila shoved her inside and slammed the door shut.

"Nan!" Bess raced across the small, stuffy room and hugged her friend. "Thank goodness you're okay!" She pulled Nancy farther into the room. "Come on, join the party!"

Nancy looked around the dim room and couldn't help smiling. *All* her friends were there. George, Kim, and Maria were sitting on storage crates, a single can of soda on the floor in front of them. With a slight grin, George pointed to it. "We've been passing it around," she said. "Help yourself."

Nancy shook her head. "Some party," she joked.

Everyone laughed, and the tension was broken for a moment. Then Nancy crossed the room and looked closely at Kim, who was wearing Bess's baggy pants and print shirt. Bess, she noticed, looked much more comfortable since she had stripped down to the bikini she'd brought along—for fun on the island. "Are you all right?" Nancy asked Kim gently.

"Physically, I'm okay, except for this," Kim replied quietly, holding up her plaster-casted arm. "Mentally, I'm terrified."

"That makes two of us," Nancy admitted. The room was incredibly hot, so she slipped out of her caftan, and instructed George to do the same. If they ended up in the water, Nancy didn't want them bogged down by unnecessary clothing. Feeling slightly cooler in her bikini, she sat down on a crate and took a sip of the soda. "Kim, why didn't you tell me what was going on when I came to your room the other day?"

"I didn't think there was time," Kim said. "I was freaking out—Maria was gone, and Ricardo was yelling at me to meet him. I just panicked."

Nancy nodded. "Did George and Bess tell you what happened to Ricardo?"

Kim took a deep breath and lowered her eyes. "Yes," she said softly. "I still can't believe it. I feel terrible about it. We weren't in love," she admitted with a sigh, "but he was special."

"How did you get involved in all this?" Bess asked.

"By the time Maria escaped from Lila, Ricardo and I were good friends," Kim explained. "He'd told me all about himself—how he tried to help undocumented immigrants—and he knew I was sympathetic. So when Maria needed a place to stay, I was the obvious one to ask."

"How come you didn't go to the police?" George asked.

"I wanted to," Kim told her. "I knew Ricardo couldn't because he was undocumented too, but there was nothing to stop me. He didn't trust the police, though. He asked me to wait, and I did. But I should have gone anyway."

Maria, who had been quiet until then, brushed her long hair back from her face and spoke rapidly in Spanish.

Kim nodded. "Maria wants me to tell you that she'd tried to get Ricardo to talk to you. I'd told Maria about you when she was hiding out in my hotel room. I guess I said something about having a friend who was a detective and wishing you were here," Kim said with a smile. "But Ricardo wouldn't listen to her. He just didn't trust anyone. He didn't let her talk to you until last night."

"We really can't blame him for that," Nancy said softly.

"I don't think we should be talking about blame at all," Bess pointed out. "I think we should be talking about how to get out of here."

Nancy laughed. "You're right. It's a good thing the five of us are here, too, because we need all the brainpower we can get to figure this one out."

Springing to her feet, Nancy started exploring the room, which took her all of two minutes. "There's not even a closet to hide in," she remarked. "Not that hiding would do us any good."

"How about the crates?" George said. "Is there something we could do with them—hide in them, block the door with them?"

"I was thinking the same thing," Nancy said.

"They'd find us anyway," Bess told her. "I mean, nobody but Lila and her crew knows we're in here. So what if we blocked the door? They'd just wait until everybody's partying on the island and then break it down. We're trapped!"

Nancy knew that Bess was right. Hiding or blocking the door would only postpone whatever was going to happen. It was a stopgap, and they needed an escape hatch. But Lila had made certain they didn't have one. She'd backed them into a corner, and she was closing in fast.

Suddenly Nancy felt a change in the rhythm of the *Rosita*; it seemed to slow down. The five girls steadied themselves as the boat began rocking from side to side.

"What's happening?" Kim asked.

"We've almost reached the island," George said. "The *Rosita*'s too big to go all the way to shore, so they take everybody in on little speedboats. We'll be stopping any minute."

"And after everybody's ashore, the *Rosita* sails away," Bess continued. "With us on it."

"Yeah," Nancy said with a grim smile. "Then Lila's private party begins."

The girls looked at each other fearfully; they knew what was going to happen, but they didn't know how to stop it. At that moment, the door handle clicked. Everyone jumped, and then Bess gasped.

Standing in the open doorway was Dirk Bowman, a dimpled smile on his face and a shiny revolver in his hand.

CHAPTER FOURTEEN

In a flash, Bess darted across the room, stopping just a couple of feet in front of Dirk.

"Listen to me, Dirk! Please listen!" she cried. "I know what you think, but it's not true, it's really not! I don't know what's going on here. I don't know *anything*, and even if I did I wouldn't tell. You have to believe me!"

"Wait a minute," Dirk said, frowning. "I—"

"There's no time to wait!" Bess interrupted frantically. "I know what Lila plans to do with us, and you have to get me out of here. Please, Dirk, I'll do anything you want, I'll say anything you want, if you'll just let me go!"

As the other four listened in amazement, Bess kept on pleading with Dirk Bowman to save her. Kim and Maria stared at her in horror; obviously, they thought she was so panicked that she was willing to say anything to save her own neck.

Nancy was amazed too, but for a different reason: She knew that Bess was acting—and it was working. Dirk couldn't get a word in edgewise; he'd try to say something, but Bess would immediately interrupt him, pleading, whining, shouting, whispering, doing anything to distract him. From the look on George's face, Nancy could tell that she hadn't been fooled either. If the situation hadn't been so serious, the two of them might have started clapping. It was a beautiful performance, and it was up to Nancy to take advantage of it.

Slowly but smoothly, Nancy moved closer to Dirk Bowman. Bess was saying something about how she and Dirk could spend the rest of their lives together. "It'll be fantastic, just the two of us, I promise you!" she pleaded, her voice almost cracking. Dirk was completely distracted. He didn't notice anything but the near-hysterical girl in front of him.

Nancy was less than a foot away from him; it was time to make her move. Without warning, she pivoted into a powerful spinning back kick, her heel hitting Dirk's hand. The gun went flying upward, and Nancy moved in, slamming her shoulder into Dirk's stomach, pushing him across the room and into a stack of storage crates.

"Somebody get the gun!" Nancy shouted, scrambling off of Dirk.

"Got it!" George called triumphantly, holding the revolver up. "Nice work, Nancy."

"You taught me that move, remember?" Nancy said. Turning to Bess, she grinned. "I think you missed your calling. You should go on the stage."

Bess laughed. "I just hope I don't have to give any encores. I've never been so scared in my life!"

Kim and Maria were standing over Dirk. "He's out cold," Kim reported. She put an arm around Maria and hugged her. "We're free," she said.

"Yeah, but now what?" George asked.

"What do you mean?" Bess said. "Now we split!"

"No, wait." Nancy thought a minute. "It's not such a great idea for all of us to go trooping up on deck together. I think I'd better scout around first and see what's happening. Maybe I can figure out a way to get us off this boat."

"What about him?" George asked, pointing to Dirk.

"Sit on him if you have to," Nancy replied. "And don't forget, if anybody comes knocking, you've got the gun."

Nancy drew in a deep breath and pushed the door open. She checked the hall, then gave the others a thumbs-up signal and slipped into the empty corridor. She ran silently up the metal stairs.

The *Rosita* had come to a complete stop. Nancy could feel it. She hoped that meant that everybody was gathered on one side of the deck, waiting to be taken to the island. If someone was in the galley, Nancy knew she'd be a sitting duck when she raised that trapdoor, but there was no way to tell. She'd just have to take her chances.

Cautiously Nancy pushed the door up about half an inch and waited. Nothing. She pushed some more until the opening was big enough for her head. From a distance, she heard the laughter and shouts of people waiting for the launches, but she didn't see anyone in the galley.

It's now or never, she thought, and pushed the door up until the opening was wide enough for her to crawl through. She lowered the door as quietly as possible and then crouched on the floor, waiting.

Nancy didn't know how long the galley would remain empty. She had to get moving or she'd be trapped again. She crept forward, until she could peer around the edge of the entrance.

The partiers were gathered at the railing, milling around, joking. Nancy didn't see Lila or any of her boys and figured that they were either directing traffic or driving the launches.

Suddenly Nancy realized that a launch was her answer. If she could just get her hands on one of those speedboats, then the five of them might have a chance of breaking free for good.

For a second, Nancy was tempted to join the crowd and lower herself over the side of the *Rosita*. But then she saw one of Lila's boys—the guy who had delivered the flowers—making his way through the partygoers. He moved slowly and casually, smiling at everyone, but his eyes darted swiftly over the faces of the crowd, and Nancy knew that Lila had posted him as a lookout. If Nancy tried to lose herself in the group, he'd spot her. She could just see herself halfway down the rope ladder, trapped in the glare of a powerful flashlight, like an animal paralyzed by the headlights of a car.

But a launch was the only way off the *Rosita*, and Nancy knew she had to get her hands on one. She was trying to figure how when she saw the "florist" making his way toward the galley.

He was fifteen feet away, and Nancy knew there was no going back. In one quick move, she stepped through the galley entrance and slid around to the far side of the deck. Then she waited, heart pounding, listening for a shout, for rapid footsteps that meant he had seen her and was coming after her.

Nothing. Nancy slumped against the outer wall of the galley, knowing she was safe—for the moment. But she couldn't hang around much longer. She had to find a way to get herself and four other people off the boat, or that fancy move she had used to flatten Dirk would turn out to be a total waste.

The noise of the crowd was dying down; it wouldn't be long before everyone was off the boat and on the island. Suddenly, over the sound of the fading laughter, Nancy heard footsteps approaching the galley.

Move! she told herself, and slipped quickly along the rail, glancing over her shoulder every step of the way. She had to find someplace to hide, fast, or she might as well go back down and join the others.

It was as she neared the bow that Nancy saw the metal ladder leading to the top deck. She raced for it, her bare feet almost silent on the deck, and scampered up. She reached the top rung, glanced back, and saw the florist rounding the galley. Nancy gripped the ladder and willed him not to look up.

But apparently Lila's florist was just looking for stray partiers and only glanced carelessly down the passageway before disappearing. Nancy let her breath out and climbed onto the top deck, immediately flattening herself out on her stomach.

The deck was deserted, but Nancy wasn't taking any chances. Still on her stomach, she elbowed her way to the other side and peered over the rail toward the island. Several bonfires had already been started on the beach, and in the glow, Nancy could see a single speedboat heading for the shore. Two others were already tied up just off the beach. The one she was watching must be the last, and she knew it wouldn't be long before the *Rosita* would take off with its human cargo. She had to get her hands on one of those launches, and that meant she had to get to the island—unseen.

Nancy heard a cough, and looking down, saw the florist pacing the deck below. She scrambled back to the far rail and waited to see if he was going to patrol the other side too. As she looked out over the water, it suddenly occurred to her that she could *swim* to the island. It wasn't too far away, and once she got there, she could steal one of the speedboats and zip back to the *Rosita*. She wished she could tell the others to be ready and waiting for her, but she couldn't take the chance of going back down to the hold. She told herself that if the *Rosita* took off before she got back to it, she'd head for Fort Lauderdale and get the police. But she didn't think she'd have to do that. Nancy figured that Lila would need at least half an hour to make sure the island party was going strong before she returned to the *Rosita*.

You can do it, Nancy thought. You have to do it, so don't waste any more time. She got to her knees and looked over the rail, checking to make sure the lower deck was clear. No one was in sight, so Nancy stood up and put her foot on the top rail, gripping it with her toes. She brought her other foot up, found her balance, and slowly straightened to her full height. The water was at least twenty feet below her. Don't think about it, she told herself, just do it.

Nancy raised her arms above her head and pushed out and off the rail, diving headfirst into the dark waters of the Atlantic.

The ocean hit her like a cold slap in the face, and it seemed as if she sank forever before she was able to start pulling herself up. Finally, though, she broke the surface. Gasping, she tossed her hair out of her face and then pulled herself toward the *Rosita*'s stern with strong, steady strokes.

When Nancy reached it, she stopped, treading water. The rail lights and the glow from the bonfires sent a faint path of light along the water, and in that path, about fifteen feet away, Nancy saw a dark triangular shape gliding smoothly through the waves. She wiped her eyes again and blinked, trying to tell herself that she was seeing things.

But she wasn't. The black triangle was a shark's fin, and as Nancy watched, frozen, she saw it swerve sharply and begin to slice through the water, heading straight for her.

CHAPTER FIFTEEN

Nancy felt panic wash over her, colder than the water lapping at her throat. She'd done her share of detective work, but she'd never had to deal with a shark before, and she didn't want to start then.

The shark was swimming closer. Nancy clamped her lips together, forcing back the scream that was threatening to break loose. It would surely attract attention, either the shark's or Lila's, and Nancy wasn't sure which would be worse.

For several minutes, Nancy treaded water, deciding to wait until the shark did whatever it was going to do. But she had no idea what it was going to do, and it probably didn't either, so what was the point? Besides, waiting was just too scary. She had to move or that scream was going to escape her lips.

Not wanting to make any waves, Nancy used just her arms to pull herself smoothly toward the shore. After a moment, she realized she didn't know where the shark was anymore—in front of her, behind her, or below her. Somehow, not knowing was more frightening than knowing, and for a while she kept looking around, trying to locate the telltale fin. But after a few minutes, she simply concentrated on getting ashore. The shark's got the whole ocean to fish in, she kept telling herself. Why should it pick on you?

Avoiding the paths of light cast by the bonfires, Nancy swam in a wide arc, heading for a deserted part of the beach. She thought that once she got there, she could find a subtle way to join the crowd, pretending she'd always been part of it. *If you get there*, she reminded herself, and looked over her shoulder again. She didn't see the shark, but that didn't mean it wasn't lurking somewhere, biding its time.

But Nancy couldn't afford to bide her time. She realized she couldn't keep up the slow pace. She was taking forever to reach the island, and she didn't want to risk letting the *Rosita* get away. Sure, she could send the police after it eventually, but by then it might be too late for the four friends she'd left behind.

Forcing herself to forget every shark movie ever made, Nancy put her head down, started a strong, steady kick with her legs, and shot through the water like an Olympic swimmer going for the gold. She didn't stop until she felt sand grazing her thighs, and even then she didn't stand up. Instead, she crawled out of the water, her stomach brushing the sand, and then flopped down, hoping no one had seen her emerging from the ocean.

When she raised her head and looked toward the party, Nancy realized her fear of being seen was ridiculous. Absolutely nobody was looking her way. They were all too involved in dancing, eating, flirting, and splashing in the water. It would be simple to join them, and since the speedboats were beached close to the party, Nancy knew that was what she had to do.

Confident that no one was watching, Nancy stood up, brushed the sand from her body and picked the seaweed out of her hair. Then she began a slow saunter toward the bonfires, trying to look like she'd been for a solitary stroll along the beach and had decided to rejoin the party.

It was simple, just as she'd thought it would be. The party to nowhere was nothing more than a fancier version of the parties on the Fort Lauderdale beach. The food was a lot better than hot dogs and potato chips, but other than that, it was really just a bunch of people having too good a time to pay any attention to a single girl striding along the sand.

When Nancy reached the thick of the crowd, she put on a smile and started dancing with no one in particular. As she spun to her left, she spotted three of Lila's boys. One was wrapping ears of corn to be roasted in the coals, one was stationed at a table, serving drinks, and the third one—handsome "Mr. Friendly," the maintenance man—was leaning against one of the speedboats, his eyes roving over the crowd. There was no sign of Lila, and Nancy wondered suddenly if she was still on the *Rosita*.

Spinning again so that her back was to the maintenance man, Nancy realized that she had to do something, fast. If Lila was still on the *Rosita*, then the boat might be taking off sooner than Nancy had anticipated. Nancy knew she had to get her hands on one of those launches, but there was no way she could slip past the watchful eye of Mr. Friendly. Somehow, she had to make him leave his post.

Suddenly the group she was with began moving toward the

water, and Nancy found herself swept along with them until she was knee-deep in the surf. Splashing each other and laughing as they tried to dance on the shifting sand beneath their feet, they kept moving into deeper water. They were getting farther from the shore and farther, Nancy noticed, from the light cast by the bonfires.

No one was trying to dance anymore; they were all diving under the waves, or swimming lazily. That was when Nancy got her idea. She needed a major distraction, something to get that maintenance man away from the speedboats, and she was going to create it herself.

A wave was rolling in, and Nancy dived under it, surfacing about ten feet from the rest of her group. She checked to make sure no one was paying any attention to her, and then she let out a high-pitched, bloodcurdling scream. "Shark!" she shrieked at the top of her lungs, "I see a shark!"

In seconds, everyone had taken up the cry. It didn't seem to matter whether there really was a shark, all that mattered was getting out of the water.

Screaming and shouting, Nancy's group started swimming frantically for the island, while the people on shore raced to the water's edge, yelling for everyone to hurry. When the two groups met on the sand, they all stared out over the dark water, still screaming in fear and excitement.

"I think I see it!" a girl called out. "Look—is that it?"

"It must be!" Nancy answered, not bothering to look. "My gosh, it's huge!"

While everyone stared at the water, Nancy was checking out the launches, and she saw exactly what she'd hoped to see—no maintenance man, no florist, none of Lila's boys. The entire party to nowhere was gathered at the shore, craning their necks for a glimpse of a shark.

This is your chance, Nancy told herself, and it might be the only one you'll get. "There it is!" she shouted, and waited until everyone was looking the other way. Then she turned and raced along the beach toward the speedboats.

When she reached the first one, Nancy ducked behind it and glanced back. The crowd was still at the edge of the water, but no one was screaming anymore, and she knew it would only be a minute or two before they lost interest and started partying again. Two minutes, she thought, that's all you've got.

Her heart pounding, Nancy straightened up and looked into the speedboat. In the glow of the bonfires, she saw something glittering just to the right of the wheel, and let out her breath in a sigh of relief. It was the key. She hadn't even thought about the key, but there it was, thank goodness, ready to ignite the engine.

Keeping low on the sand, Nancy crept to the front of the boat and started pushing. It didn't budge. She shoved harder and when it still didn't move, she realized she'd have to stand up straight if she wanted to shove as hard as she could. She knew she'd be in the full glow of the firelight, and if anyone looked over, they couldn't miss seeing her, but she didn't have a choice. She had to push the boat into the water and get going.

Nancy straightened up and shoved against the boat as hard as she could. It slid two feet forward. Nancy rubbed her palms together and got ready to push again.

Suddenly someone was shouting, and before Nancy had a chance to move, the shout rang out again, loud and clear and furious. It was Lila, standing on the deck of the *Rosita* and pointing straight at Nancy.

"Stop her!" Lila screamed. "She's got a boat! Stop her!"

Nancy spun around to face the crowd of partiers. They were still milling around at the water's edge. All but one. That one— the maintenance man—had broken away from the group and was loping across the sand toward Nancy.

Nancy knew there was no longer any sense in trying to get the boat in the water. She'd never make it. She'd been caught, and as she watched the maintenance man closing the gap between them, she wondered if she'd been caught for good.

For a split second, Nancy stood rooted to the spot and ready to give up. But when she actually heard the sharp, steady breathing of the man, she snapped to attention. Come on, she told herself. You can probably outrun that creep. And if not, you can certainly outthink him!

In a flash, Nancy was off, her heels sending out sprays of sand as she headed away from the boats and the bonfires toward the dark center of the island. She had no idea what she'd find there, but it couldn't be any more dangerous than what she was leaving behind.

Nancy kept running, plunging through the sand until finally

the broad, empty stretch of beach gave way to palm trees and undergrowth. It was suddenly very dark, which was good, but she couldn't see a thing, and the tangled vines and bushes made it impossible to run quietly, which wasn't so good. She knew she sounded like a scared deer crashing through a forest. She also knew that if Mr. Friendly couldn't see her, he could hear her, since she could certainly hear him, crashing along right behind her, and he was much too close for comfort.

After a few minutes, the clumps of trees started to thin out, and Nancy realized she was heading uphill. She forced herself to keep going, thinking that at least Lila wouldn't take off. She couldn't take that chance, not as long as Nancy was on the run.

Nancy ran until she was no longer under the safe cover of the trees. She burst out into an open space, under a bright moon, and looked around wildly. If she didn't find someplace to hide soon, the maintenance man could just bide his time until she collapsed.

He might already be doing that, Nancy thought. She couldn't hear him anymore, but she knew he couldn't be far behind.

Struggling to keep her balance, Nancy scrambled up a steep incline, and then she stopped, gasping more from fear than from exhaustion. She was on some kind of cliff, and below her—in a sheer, thirty-foot drop—was a smooth stretch of sand, sparkling in the moonlight. Unless she managed to turn herself into a mountain goat, there was no way she could get down.

And at that moment, Nancy heard heavy gasping sounds. The maintenance man. He was closing in fast, and she knew she was too tired to go through another chase scene with him. She would have to face him. Glancing frantically around, she saw three large rocks grouped together. As the breathing grew louder, Nancy rushed over and hid herself behind them.

In seconds, the maintenance man was on the cliff. As Nancy watched, peering between two of the rocks, he stopped to get his breath, then turned and began walking slowly in Nancy's direction, looking everywhere for signs of the girl he'd been chasing.

Her heart pounding, Nancy made herself wait until he was so close to her hiding place that she could reach out and touch him. Then, in one swift move, her leg shot out, sweeping his feet out from under him, sending him sprawling on the ground.

The maintenance man was caught completely by surprise, and Nancy was just trying to decide what to do with him when she heard a shout. She looked up, and there, on the edge of the cliff in the bright moonlight, stood Dirk Bowman.

CHAPTER SIXTEEN

The moment Nancy paused, the maintenance man took action, throwing her aside in one strong movement. Nancy was outnumbered, but she wasn't about to give up.

She and the maintenance man faced each other, squaring off like boxers in the ring. Out of the corner of her eye, Nancy saw Dirk Bowman rushing toward them. Lashing out at the maintenance man with a kick, she spun around to face Dirk.

But Dirk Bowman ignored Nancy. Instead, he caught the maintenance man with his left hand, and, swinging his right arm up from somewhere around his knees, crashed his fist squarely into the man's jaw. Lila's boy gasped, sank to his knees, then pitched forward onto his face. He wouldn't be chasing anybody for quite a while.

Stunned, Nancy looked at Dirk, who was rubbing his knuckles and grinning at her. "I've been wanting to do that for a long time," he said.

"Who are you?" Nancy asked warily. "How did you get away? And what happened to my friends?"

"Your friends helped me get away," Dirk told her. "And they're safe. They're waiting for us right now, in the launch we

251

stole. Now come on," he said, reaching for her hand, "let's get going. I'd love to take a nice romantic stroll in the moonlight, but we just don't have time."

Nancy pulled her hand away. "I'm not going anywhere until you tell me who you are."

"I'm a police detective," Dirk said calmly. "I've been working undercover for two months, trying to get enough evidence against Lila to stop her operation for good." He started walking again. "Why don't you walk behind me?" he suggested, grinning at her over his shoulder. "If you think I'm leading you into a trap, you can always jump me again, the way you did on the *Rosita*."

Nancy didn't think she had enough energy left to jump anybody. She really wanted to believe Dirk, but she was still suspicious of him, so she followed his advice and stayed about five feet behind him. "Why didn't you tell me who you were when we first met?" she called out.

"I couldn't risk it," he said. "If my cover had been blown, there would have been no way to stop Lila. Besides, the lady would probably have killed me."

"But you knew what was going on," Nancy reminded him. "Wasn't that enough evidence?"

"We suspected, we didn't know for sure. We needed witnesses," he explained. "And even after I started working for Lila, it was a long time before she trusted me with her little secret. In fact," he said with a laugh, "you and your friends were my first assignment."

"Me and my friends?" Nancy asked. "What about before that? What about my windsurfing accident? You didn't have anything to do with that?"

"Nope. My guess is that one of Lila's boys saw us together and reported it to her, and she told him to take care of you," Dirk said. "She still didn't trust me then. But I put on a pretty convincing act, and finally she decided I was okay."

"So tonight, when you came down to the hold, you were supposed to kill us, right?" Nancy asked.

"Right." Dirk stopped and turned, looking at Nancy. "I wasn't going to follow Lila's orders, of course. But Bess never gave me a chance to tell you that, and when I came to, you'd already taken off for the island. How did you get here, anyway?"

"I swam!" Quickly Nancy told him everything that had happened since she'd escaped from the *Rosita*.

As Dirk listened his eyes lit up in admiration, and when she finished he gave a low whistle. "You're really something, Detective." He held out his hand, and Nancy shook it.

"But just think," he went on, his eyes twinkling mischievously, "if you hadn't knocked me out, you could have saved yourself that swim."

Nancy started to argue, but when she caught the look in his eyes, she found herself laughing instead. He grabbed her other hand, and the two of them began running together.

Soon they were back in the trees, and it wasn't long before Nancy heard the distant strains of music and laughter from the party to nowhere. Halfway back to the shore, Dirk started heading to the right. "The launch is around a curve in the beach," he told Nancy. "We'll use the trees for cover."

"How did you get it there without anyone hearing the motor?" Nancy asked.

"Kim navigated and the rest of us paddled," Dirk replied with a laugh. "We made a great team. The only thing we really had to worry about was Lila spotting us from the *Rosita*. But I guess she was too busy making sure you were brought back to notice us."

"She must be wondering what's taking that guy so long," Nancy said. "She's probably getting very antsy."

Dirk laughed again. "Wait'll I come after her with four or five other cops. Then she'll know what antsy really is!"

Nancy began to forget about sore feet and sore muscles. She forgot about everything but leaving the island, and when they finally caught sight of the sleek little speedboat waiting a few feet from the shoreline, she grabbed Dirk's hand again and pulled him along behind her as she broke into a run.

"Finally!" Bess's voice cried out. "We've been sitting in this boat so long I was beginning to grow barnacles."

Nancy laughed and splashed into the water. "You think *you've* had it bad," she joked as she reached the boat. "Wait'll you hear what *I've* been through!"

There was no time to exchange stories, though. In spite of what Dirk had said, he and Nancy knew that Lila wouldn't wait forever. If she discovered that they'd escaped, she might just take off, maybe for another country. That would leave the police with no one to arrest but her troop of handsome boys. Dirk didn't want that, and neither did Nancy. They both wanted Lila Templeton caught.

Quickly Nancy, Dirk, and George pushed the speedboat far enough out so they could lower the engine into the water. When they climbed in, Dirk slid into the driver's seat and turned the key. The engine caught with a roar, and as the boat pulled smoothly away from the island, the six passengers laughed with relief.

"I never thought I'd say it," Bess admitted, "but I'll actually be glad to get back to River Heights."

"But you haven't fallen in love yet," George teased. "Are you sure you don't want to stick around?"

"No thanks!" Bess said. "There are plenty of guys at home."

"Hey, what about me?" Dirk joked. "I thought you said you'd spend the rest of your life with me if I just got you off the *Rosita*."

Bess giggled, and leaning forward, planted a kiss on his cheek. "You're fantastic, Dirk," she told him, "but I'm afraid that was a promise I just can't keep."

Everyone laughed again, but Nancy stopped suddenly as she became aware of another sound. Even over the whine of the speedboat, she could hear it—a heavy throbbing, almost a rumbling, like a powerful motor. She glanced around. Maria was staring out the back of the boat, her eyes wide with fear.

"Maria?" Nancy said. "What is it? What do you see?"

"Look," Maria said, pointing. "She's found us!"

Straining to see, Nancy could just make out a large, dark shape looming behind them. It didn't stay dark for long, though. As Nancy watched, the deck and rail lights of the *Rosita* flashed on.

The *Rosita* was only about a hundred feet away, its powerful engines louder than ever as Lila Templeton aimed it straight at the tiny speedboat.

Bess stood halfway up and let out a scream. "She's going to ram us!"

"I'm afraid that's exactly what she has in mind," Dirk agreed. "And if she gets close enough, she'll probably take a few shots at us, too. The lady is definitely desperate."

"I thought the party was over," George said grimly, "but it looks like it's just getting started."

The speedboat was fast, but so was the *Rosita*, and as the six of them watched, Lila's powerful boat surged through the water, shortening the gap between them.

"Can't we go any faster?" Nancy called to Dirk.

"Not much," he told her. Slipping an arm around her shoulder, he pulled her head close to his lips, speaking quietly so the others wouldn't hear. "We're low on gas," he said, "and I'm not sure how long we'll last if she decides to chase us all over the Atlantic."

Shivering with tension, Nancy stared at the gas gauge. The arrow was hovering around the one-quarter mark. It might be enough to get them back to Fort Lauderdale, but only if they made a beeline for it. If they had to do many fancy maneuvers to get away from Lila, they'd never make it.

At that moment, Nancy heard a faint popping sound, something like a firecracker. She turned and saw one of Lila's boys on the top deck of the *Rosita*. He was braced against the rail like a sharpshooter, aiming a long-barreled rifle at the six people in the speedboat.

"Everybody, down!" Nancy shouted.

"If they get much closer, he'll be able to pick us off one by one!" Bess cried out, as she huddled in the bottom of the boat.

"Us or the engine!" George exclaimed. "And if he hits the engine, there won't be anything left of us to pick off!"

Dirk fumbled around on the floor and pulled up the revolver that Nancy had kicked out of his hand a few hours before. "It's hardly a rifle," he commented wryly, "but it's better than nothing!"

Nancy nodded and reached for his hand, pulling him up. "You deal with Lila," she suggested, "and leave the driving to me."

Dirk nodded and crawled to the back of the boat, while Nancy slid into the driver's seat. The fuel gauge was just under the quarter mark by then, and she knew she didn't have much time. Glancing back, she saw that the *Rosita* hadn't gained on them, but she also saw that Lila wasn't directly behind them anymore. She'd pulled the *Rosita* out, so that it was between the speedboat and the mainland.

Wiping the spray from her face, Nancy pushed the stick up a notch, giving the boat more power. It slapped over the water like a roller-coaster car, but Nancy could still hear the throbbing of the *Rosita*'s engines, and she knew that Lila was keeping up with her.

"I could go around behind them!" she shouted to Dirk. "The *Rosita* can't turn as fast as we can!"

"Try it!" he called back. "Just be careful of sandbars. They're all over the place!"

Now he tells me, Nancy thought. She checked the fuel again and decided to risk the extra mileage. Getting a good grip on the wheel, she cut it sharply, turning the boat so that it was heading back toward the *Rosita*. As they passed the *Rosita*'s bow, Nancy saw Lila's boy leave his post and scramble toward the stern, rifle in hand.

Suddenly the *Rosita* began to turn toward the mainland. She knows what I'm trying to do, Nancy thought. She's going to cut me off if she can!

Nancy turned the wheel again and felt the boat begin to bounce wildly as it cut across the *Rosita*'s wake. Both boats were heading for the mainland, but Lila's had a slight lead, and she'd angled it toward the speedboat. If she managed to get much farther ahead, she *would* be able to cut them off, and Nancy knew they didn't have enough gas left to try any more tricks.

The spray was practically blinding her, and her hands were so wet they kept slipping off the wheel, but Nancy wiped her face and eyes and tried frantically to see exactly what was ahead of her. All she had to light her way were the moon and the dim glow from the *Rosita*.

Suddenly, though, they were all Nancy needed. Ahead of

her, stretching across the water like a pale ribbon, was one of the sandbars Dirk had warned her about. It seemed to go on forever, and Nancy knew that if she tried to zip around it, she'd crash into the *Rosita* going one way, or run out of gas going the other.

Bess had crawled up beside her, and Nancy could tell from the look on her face that she'd seen the sandbar too. Her teeth chattering with fear, Bess tried to smile. "Wouldn't it be nice if this boat had wings?" she asked.

"That's it!" Nancy cried out.

"What's it?"

"Wings!" Nancy grinned and pushed Bess back down. "Hang on, everybody," she shouted, "we're going to fly!"

Nancy gripped the wheel and eased the stick up to full speed. As the little boat shot forward with all the power its engine could give it, Nancy gritted her teeth and aimed it straight for the sandbar.

CHAPTER SEVENTEEN

The front of the speedboat hit the sand with a bone-jarring thump. Then, its blade stirring the air, it sailed up and over the sandbar, splashed down hard on the other side, and sped on toward the lights of Fort Lauderdale.

As soon as they caught their breath, everyone turned to look behind them, and what they saw made them cheer out loud. Lila was trying to avoid the sandbar, but she was moving too fast, and as the six people in the speedboat looked on, the *Rosita* plowed straight into it. Its engines grinding uselessly, Lila's boat came to a dead stop. Lila was trapped, and her party was finally over.

"Nancy, you did it!" George shouted.

"That was one nice piece of driving, Detective," Dirk said with a grin.

Nancy laughed. "Thanks. Just don't ask me to do it again!"

"Being stuck out there serves Lila right," Bess said. "I just hope there's no way she can escape."

"Uh-oh, I just thought of something," Nancy said. "I'll bet the *Rosita* has lifeboats. That means Lila *does* have a way to escape. And you can bet she'll use it."

"She couldn't get very far, but you're right, Nancy," Dirk agreed, "she's not the kind to give up until every last door's been slammed in her face."

"I don't think even that would make her give up," George commented. "Not when she's as desperate as she is right now."

There was no time to waste. As soon as they were safely back to shore, Dirk made sure his backup team was on the way to help capture Lila and her crew. Nancy and the others hopped into their rental car and rushed Kim back to the hospital.

"I wanted to stick around and see them bring Lila in," Kim protested on the way. "Honestly, I'm perfectly fine!"

"*You* might be fine," Nancy told her, "but your mother's probably having a nervous breakdown by now."

"That's right," Bess said. "She wasn't even with us when we left the hospital before, so she's still completely in the dark. She must be frantic!"

Bess was right. When they got to the hospital, they found Mrs. Baylor still frantic with worry, and the entire staff in an uproar over the missing patient. As soon as Kim appeared, the doctors whisked her away to check on her condition, and finally her mother calmed down enough to listen to what had happened.

When Nancy finished telling the story, Mrs. Baylor sighed in relief. "Thank goodness you were here, Nancy, and that it's over!"

"That's exactly what I was thinking," Bess said with a yawn.

"Well, it's not quite over," Nancy reminded them. "We'll all have to give statements to the police. And if there's a trial, Kim and Maria will probably have to testify."

"I will be very happy to do that," Maria said. "Even if it means that I can't stay here. I want to see Lila Templeton get . . ." She searched for the right words.

"Get what's coming to her!" Bess finished with a laugh.

"You're very brave, Maria," Nancy said. "I hope things work out for you so you can stay in the U.S. if you want to."

One of the doctors came in then and gave them the good news—Kim was weak and worn out, but otherwise she seemed to be fine. They just wanted to keep her in the hospital for a couple of days to make sure.

Leaving Maria at the hospital with Kim's mother, Nancy, Bess, and George sped back to the docks just in time to see the police patrol boat arrive. A very happy looking Dirk Bowman waved to them from the deck, then pointed to a small group of people—it was Lila Templeton and her handsome, deadly crew, looking very *un*happy.

The sun was just coming up as Nancy, Bess, and George let themselves into their room at the Surfside Inn. They took turns in the shower, and then George and Nancy started packing. But Bess wrapped a towel around her wet head and flopped down on the cot.

"I've never been so exhausted in my entire life," she yawned. "Nobody wake me for at least twelve hours."

"Sorry," George told her, "but our plane leaves in four hours. You don't want to miss it, do you?"

"I don't know," Bess said. "Now that everything's over, I wouldn't mind sticking around for a couple of days. There *are* a lot of cute guys around and I'd hate to miss out."

Nancy laughed. "I thought you said there were plenty of guys back home," she teased.

"That was when I thought I was going to die," Bess protested. "But now that Lila and her crew are behind bars, I figure I might as well enjoy the rest of spring break."

"I would have given anything to see the look on Lila's face when the police came to 'rescue' her," George said. "I wonder if she tried to lie her way out of it."

"If she did, it didn't do her any good," Nancy said. "Not with Kim and Maria and Dirk as witnesses against her."

"Speaking of Dirk," George said, peering out the window, "he just pulled up in that fancy red car of his, and it looks like he's heading this way."

Nancy opened the door and smiled as she watched Dirk Bowman come down the hall. "I thought you'd at least take the rest of the day off," she said.

"The day? I'm taking a week off," he replied with a grin. "But I knew you were leaving, and I had a couple of things I wanted to tell you. How about a quick walk?"

Nancy slipped on a pair of sandals, and together she and Dirk strolled down the sidewalk in the early morning sun.

"First," Dirk said, reaching for Nancy's hand, "I've got some good news. Maria can stay in the U.S. in exchange for testifying, and Kim's mother got her a job with some friends here in Fort Lauderdale. She says she's going to start college as soon as she can. She wants to be an engineer."

"That's great," Nancy said with relief. "I was worried that she'd be deported." She stifled a yawn. "Sorry. I'm completely wiped out."

"Well, that's the second thing I wanted to talk to you about," Dirk said. He stopped walking and put his hands on her shoulders. "I wanted to thank you, Detective. You were fantastic. And if you ever come back to Fort Lauderdale, let me know. Thanks to you, Lila Templeton won't be throwing any more parties."

For a moment, Nancy leaned her head against his shoulder, smiling. Then, with a gasp, she suddenly pulled away.

"What's wrong?" Dirk asked.

"I just remembered," Nancy said, trying not to laugh. "The party. The party to nowhere! All those people are still stranded out there on that island!"

Dirk's blue eyes widened in shock, and he shook his head. "I guess I'll start my vacation this afternoon," he said. He raced off to his car. "See what I mean?" he called back over his shoulder. "I could use you down here, Detective!"

Laughing, Nancy watched the red car speed down the palm-lined street. Then she headed back to her hotel. It was time to go home.

WHITE WATER TERROR

CHAPTER ONE

Y ou've got to be kidding," Bess Marvin said. She looked up from her seat in Nancy Drew's bedroom, where she was polishing her long, delicate nails. "I'm not going on any wilderness trip!"

"But, Bess, you'll love it," countered her cousin George Fayne.

Sitting cross-legged on her bed, Nancy Drew was engrossed in a puzzle and trying to block out the sound of her best friends' voices. The more difficult the puzzle, the better Nancy liked it. Thinking hard kept her mind limbered up for her more challenging work as a detective.

"Really, Bess, you *will* love it," George said again, seeing her cousin roll her eyes. "Lost River, the mountains, the trees, the birds—they're all yours, just for sitting comfortably in a rubber raft for a couple of days. You probably won't even have to paddle. The river will do all the work."

"I'll loathe it!" Bess exclaimed with a shudder. "Nancy," she implored, "please help me shut this down."

Nancy put down her puzzle and looked at her friends. George, who had just come from her regular three-mile afternoon jog, was wearing a blue-and-green running suit that emphasized her athletic wiriness and made her look ready for anything. White water rafting was exactly the kind of thing that would turn George on. She loved any challenge. That was what made her so valuable to Nancy.

At the same time, rafting was exactly the kind of thing that would turn Bess *off*. At the moment, for instance, she was wearing a pair of tight purple stirrup pants and an enormous gauzy shirt, cinched with a thin gold belt. Her long, straw-colored hair curled loosely around her shoulders. It wasn't that Bess was afraid of adventure, and it wasn't that she was terribly lazy. She was just . . . well, Bess liked to do things the *easy* way. Maybe she *was* a bit timid, but she always enjoyed being where things were happening—and things always happened with Nancy around.

Nancy folded her arms and looked from one friend to the other with a grin. "Okay, George, start from the beginning," she said. "Tell us just how you managed to get *four* places on this rafting expedition. And where *is* Lost River, anyway?"

"I *told* you," said George, her dark eyes gleaming with excitement, "I don't even remember entering the contest. Maybe I did it when I bought those jogging shoes at the sporting goods store a couple of months ago. I vaguely remember filling out an entry blank for some sort of contest. Anyway, I got this letter yesterday from somebody named Paula Hancock, who owns White Water Rafting, notifying me that I'd won the grand prize in this national contest. Four places on a white water raft trip down Lost River, in the mountains of northwest Montana. They're even offering free plane tickets to Great Falls—the nearest city."

"Did the letter say anything about the kind of trip it might be?" Nancy asked. "I mean, there are rivers and then there are *rivers*."

"According to the letter, Lost River is the ultimate white water challenge, full of rapids and falls. What a terrific vacation—and free, too. Anyway, we need a vacation," George said emphatically. "We've been working too hard."

Bess put the cap on her nail polish and shook her head. "George, come on," she said. "Going rafting down some wild mountain river is no vacation—it's sheer torture!"

Nancy thought back to her last case, *Hit and Run Holiday*, a Florida "vacation" that had nearly gotten her killed. She had come to realize the importance of spending relaxed time with her friends. "We *do* need a break," she said.

"Yes," Bess said, brightening. "You're absolutely right, Nancy. But what we need is a break, not a breakdown. I vote for a long weekend at the beach. I know we were just in Fort Lauderdale, but what happened there certainly wasn't a vacation. I want to do nothing but lie in the sun and baste ourselves with tanning lotion. And when we're tired of the beach, we can go shopping." She threw Nancy a hopeful glance.

"Shopping!" George hooted, springing to her feet. "All you *ever* want to do is go shopping, Bess Marvin. Don't you have a larger purpose in life?"

Bess looked at George calmly. "Of course I do," she said

with a twinkle in her eye. "Going out with a good-looking boy, for one. Or eating," she added.

George shook her head. "Funny. Ha, ha," she replied.

Nancy climbed off the bed and went to the window, where she stood looking out at the soft summer drizzle that was falling. A river trip might be fun, but she could see Bess's point. A beach vacation, a *real* one, would be relaxing, and baking under the hot sun on the shores of Fox Lake might be just the thing to take her mind off the detective business. But there was something else to think about. "You say you won a trip for four people?" she asked George again.

George nodded.

"Well, then, how about inviting Ned to go along?" Ned Nickerson was Nancy's longtime boyfriend. He was away at summer school just then, at Emerson College, and Nancy missed him. She had the feeling that her friendship with Ned could be the most important relationship in her life—if she could just make a little more time for it. But Ned, who had always been the most understanding guy on earth, seemed to be getting a little impatient with her. Nancy couldn't forget that during their case at *Flash* magazine, Ned had become involved with another girl. That hadn't lasted long, but . . .

The raft trip might be exactly the kind of thing to give the two of them plenty of relaxed, fun time together.

Nancy turned away from the window and continued thinking out loud. "Didn't Ned go on a couple of white water trips with his uncle a few years ago? He'd probably be a big help in case of an emergency or something."

"Emergency?" Bess went pale. "Like—like the raft tipping over?"

George looked at her scornfully. "Rafts don't 'tip over.' They *capsize.*"

Bess turned a shade paler.

"Rafts don't capsize, either," Nancy said, patting Bess comfortingly on the shoulder. "They're too stable." She stretched and yawned. "Listen, Bess, if you want a vacation at the beach, go for it. But I've never been white water rafting, and it sounds like fun to me—if Ned can come along." She turned to George.

"Sure," George said enthusiastically. "Yeah. Ask Ned. We'll have a great time with him." She cast a sideways glance at Bess. "And with all the other boys."

"What other boys?" Bess asked.

"Are you kidding?" George replied. "The letter said there are six other kids coming along on the trip. Probably boys." She paused. "Rugged, masculine, plaid-shirted boys with broad shoulders and . . ."

"Well . . ." Bess said indecisively.

"Oh, come on," Nancy said. "It'll be great."

"Boys," George teased.

"Okay," Bess agreed. "I'll come."

"Bess Marvin has agreed to go white water rafting with you and George?" Ned said incredulously. He propped his feet up on Carson Drew's favorite ottoman.

Nancy's father was an internationally known criminal lawyer.

He had taught Nancy a great deal of what she knew about detective work. At the moment, he was on one of his frequent trips, this one to the Middle East. Nancy missed him, but she wasn't alone. She had Hannah Gruen, the Drews' longtime housekeeper, who had been like a second mother to Nancy since the death of Nancy's real mother.

Nancy glanced at Ned. He was home for the weekend, and she was glad to see him. She was enjoying their cozy evening in the den watching TV.

"How'd you ever talk Bess into it?" Ned asked. "Lost River must be hundreds of miles from the nearest Neiman-Marcus."

Nancy dipped into a bowl of popcorn that Hannah had made for them before she'd gone to bed. "It wasn't easy," she admitted. She looked at Ned. He was wearing his light brown hair a little longer than usual and his face was darkly tanned. She wondered if he had been spending time at the college swimming pool—and if so, whether he'd been alone or . . .

She put her hand on his arm. "How about you?" she asked softly. "Could I talk you into a white water trip?"

"Me?"

"Yeah, you. As in you and me. And George and Bess, too, of course."

Ned pretended to look stunned. "I—I hardly know what to say. This is all so sudden. I . . ." Grinning, he ducked the pillow that Nancy tossed at him. "Yeah, sure, I'll go, Nan. Summer school will be over next week, and I won't have anything else to do."

"Well, I must say you don't sound all that wild about it."

Ned's grin faded. "I guess I'm just surprised," he said quietly. "Let's face it, Nancy. We've seen each other only two or three times in the last couple of months, and even then I was taking you away from your detective work—from something I felt you'd rather be doing. In fact, during a couple of your recent cases, I've gotten the idea that I wasn't a very important part of your life. We've patched things up, but who can tell whether the patch is going to be permanent? After all, maybe you've changed in the way you feel about me."

Nancy swallowed painfully, remembering how she had felt during the *Flash* case when she had seen Ned holding Sondra in his arms, when they had learned that Sondra's brother Mick was in trouble. "I guess that's a logical conclusion," she said, "but it's not the *right* one. I know I've been awfully busy, but that doesn't mean you're not important to me, Ned." She leaned back against the sofa pillows and clasped her hands behind her head. "You're so important to me that I can sort of relax knowing you'll be around, without having to worry about it a whole lot."

Ned leaned toward her and touched her cheek with the tip of his finger. There was a slight smile on his lips. "What you're saying is that you've been taking me for granted. Is that it?"

Nancy nodded regretfully. "I guess so. Maybe that's why I was so ready to accept George's offer of the raft trip. I think we need time together so you can help me figure out all over again just why it is I love you so much."

"We don't have to wait until we get to Montana for me to

start working on that assignment," Ned said softly. He leaned closer and put his arms around her. "Let me give you a couple of reminders." He kissed her tenderly, then kissed her again. "Got it figured out yet, Detective Drew?"

Nancy relaxed into his arms. "No, not yet," she said. "Why don't you try again? When it comes to love, I'm a very slow learner."

At that moment, the phone rang. Nancy sighed. "Somebody's got awfully poor timing," she said as she answered.

"Nancy Drew?" The voice on the other end of the line was low and muffled.

"Yes?" Nancy said slowly, sensing that something was wrong.

The next words struck her with an icy coldness. Her stomach twisted into a frigid knot. "The trip your friend won is no prize," the voice said ominously. "If you know what's good for you, you'll stay home—and stay alive!"

CHAPTER TWO

W hat's still not clear to me," Nancy told George and Bess the next day, leaning across the table at Bennie's Ice Cream Parlor, "is whether the phone call I got last night was a warning or a threat. I mean, I couldn't tell from the tone of voice whether the caller meant to threaten me with harm or keep me from getting hurt." She chewed her lip, puzzled. "I couldn't even tell whether the voice was female or male."

George dug into her favorite chocolate-mint ice-cream sundae. "Why in the world would anybody want to keep you from going on the trip?" she demanded. After a moment's hesitation, she turned to Bess. "That phone call . . . it wasn't *you*, was it?" she asked suspiciously.

Bess looked hurt. "I went to a concert last night and didn't get back until after midnight. Anyway, you know I wouldn't do something that ridiculous. If I wanted to keep you or Nancy from going on the trip, I'd try to convince you in person."

George sighed. "I know. Sorry."

Nancy took the last bite of her banana split, watching George intently. "Are you sure you've told us absolutely everything you know about the contest?"

"All I know is what's in that letter from Paula Hancock. I've tried and tried to remember exactly when I entered the contest, but I can't."

Bess smiled mischievously. "Well, then, maybe it would be better if we didn't go." She pushed her half-finished drink away. "The beach is awfully nice at this time of year."

Nancy looked at George. In the back of her mind was the growing conviction that there was something not right about the contest. But the phone call and George's inability to recall entering it were her only clues.

"I don't suppose you'd reconsider your decision to go?" Nancy asked half hopefully. "Maybe we could find another white water rafting trip, if you've got your heart set on that. There must be others that would be just as exciting."

"Yes, but this is a *free* trip," George reminded.

Nancy and Bess exchanged long looks. "What about it, Bess?" Nancy asked.

"Well," Bess said reluctantly, "I'm not exactly thrilled by the idea of spending two whole days hanging on to a raft, getting drenched by icy water, and bouncing from one rock to another. But I hate to think of you out there on the river with some person who makes weird phone calls." She shrugged. "You can count me in, I guess."

"That settles it, then," Nancy said with a grin, laying her spoon beside her empty dish. She felt good remembering that the three of them had always stuck together, even in tough times. Whatever happened, they weren't going to let George face the

trip alone. Besides, it was already shaping up to be a very interesting vacation. "Lost River, here we come!" she exclaimed.

"Where in the world do you suppose we are?" Bess asked from
the backseat of the rental car that Ned was driving. She leaned
over and took the hand-drawn map out of George's hands.
"Here, let *me* have a look at that map. Maybe I can find us."

Nancy leaned precariously over the front seat. "The road
just made another left turn back there," she said, pointing to the
small map that Bess was holding.

"Well, what do you think, Bess?" Ned asked, braking suddenly and twisting the wheel to avoid a granite boulder that had
tumbled off a cliff and lay in fragments in the road. "Are we
taking the right route?"

"It looks like we are," Bess said, grabbing frantically for the
armrest as the car lurched sideways and threatened to go into a
skid. "But who cares? The map doesn't have any route numbers
or anything. If this is all we have to go on, Lost River is likely to
stay lost." She thrust the map back at George. "You know, it's
almost as if whoever drew this map *wants* us to spend the whole
morning wandering around in the mountains."

"I hate to admit it, but Bess may have something there,"
George said, staring at the map with a puzzled frown. "And
another thing. I can't figure out why nobody met us at the airport yesterday, the way the letter promised. You'd think that a
company big enough to run a national contest would arrange to
meet the grand-prize winner when she got off the plane."

Nancy nodded. "I wondered about that myself. What a start for a vacation!"

Actually, Nancy thought as she settled back into the car seat, it hadn't even begun to feel like a vacation yet. The four of them had rushed to the airport but waited several hours for a flight from Denver that was so bumpy it would have made an eagle airsick. In Great Falls, there was nobody to meet them— only an envelope containing a hand-drawn map. Scrawled on the bottom were unsigned instructions to pick up a rental car and drive to Lost River Junction that night.

But by the time a car was available, it was late. They had spent the night at the only place they could find—a motel next door to the airport, where jets seemed to plow through the bedrooms every hour on the hour. Dragging themselves out of bed, they were on the road by five o'clock—anxious to get to Lost River Junction before the rafts left at nine.

"Well," Ned said, rolling down the window and taking a deep breath, "now that we're here, I'm glad. Smell those pine trees. What a wilderness this is!"

It *was* a wilderness, Nancy thought. They hadn't seen a sign of civilization for miles. For the last half hour, the narrow two-lane asphalt road had twisted and turned upward into the mountains like a mountain-goat trail. At the moment it was zigzagging precariously across the face of a vertical rock cliff.

Above the cliff and on the other side of the creek, huge pine and spruce trees reached toward the clear blue Montana sky.

Even though it was the middle of July, the breeze was cool

and brisk and invigorating, not at all like the steamy, oven-hot summer weather they had left back home.

Nancy stretched and filled her lungs with the clean air. In spite of everything, she was glad they had come. She glanced at Ned's calm profile and his sturdy, capable hands on the steering wheel. She was glad to be with him. With Ned along to help her laugh, the trip hadn't seemed nearly so bad.

Bess looked out the window. "I suppose there are wild animals out there," she said in a worried tone.

"Right," agreed Ned. "Plenty of them." He grinned at Bess in the rearview mirror. "Black bears and cougars and mountain lions and rattlesnakes."

With a little moan, Bess shut her eyes tight and hunched down in the seat.

"You know, I'm really getting worried about how late we are," George said, glancing at her watch. "It's after eight o'clock, and we're scheduled to leave at nine. You don't suppose they'd start the trip without us, do you?"

"I don't think they'd leave without their grand-prize winner," Nancy consoled her. "They wouldn't dare. After all, you *are* the reason for this trip." She hesitated. If George were the reason for the trip, why had *Nancy* received the mysterious phone call?

"Anyway, I'm just as glad things got screwed up with the rental car and that we didn't have to drive this road last night," Ned said. "With all these twists and turns, it's dangerous enough in broad daylight. I don't think we—"

"Ned!" Nancy yelled. "Stop!"

Just a few yards ahead of the front bumper, the road vanished into thin air.

Bess gasped.

Ned jammed his foot on the pedal, making the brakes squeal. "Oh no!" George screamed. "We're going over!"

CHAPTER THREE

The rental car screeched around in a circle before skidding erratically to a halt. The four friends sat for a moment in stunned silence, once again staring at the sheer emptiness ahead. The road was completely gone, carried down the cliff and into the ravine by a massive rockslide.

"Ned!" Nancy exclaimed, her horror mixed with limp relief. "If you hadn't stopped when you did . . ."

"We're just lucky it was daylight," Ned said soberly.

Shuddering, Nancy peered down into the ravine where the slide had loosened enormous boulders and huge gray slabs of asphalt. "We would have been killed if we'd dropped down there!" She looked around. "Is everybody okay?"

Bess rubbed her head. A bump was beginning to appear where she had hit her head against the car window. "I think so," she said in a dazed voice. "Good thing we were wearing seat belts."

"But why isn't there a barricade across the road?" George asked, jumping out of the car and stepping cautiously to the edge of the drop-off.

"Maybe the slide just happened," Ned suggested.

Nancy got out and looked around. "I don't think so," she said. "There are signs of erosion down there, and even a few weeds in the rubble. I'd say this road has been out of commission for weeks, at least."

Bess came to stand beside Nancy. "What's that?" she asked, pointing to something orange half-hidden behind a pile of brush a dozen yards below. "Isn't that a barricade?"

George scrambled partway down the slope. "It *is* a barricade," she called. "It looks as if somebody tried to hide it!"

"You mean somebody tried to *kill* us?" Bess asked.

Nancy frowned. "I don't think we can draw that conclusion from the evidence," she said slowly. "All we know is that the road is out and the barricade is missing."

"That barricade was deliberately hidden," George corrected her breathlessly, climbing back up to the road. "There's no way it could have *accidentally* gotten covered up under all that brush." She shivered. "You know, Nancy, as Ned was saying a few minutes ago, if we'd driven up here last night after dark—the way we were supposed to—we wouldn't have stood a chance."

"That's true," Nancy said. "But we don't know that the barricade was removed just for *our* benefit. A road crew might have come to inspect the slide and forgotten to put it back up."

"Well, maybe you're right," Bess said, looking pale and shaken. "But I don't know. Between this and your phone call, Nancy, the whole thing looks really suspicious."

"You're right," Nancy agreed. "I'd say that we have to be on our guard."

"In fact," Bess said hopefully, "maybe we ought to reconsider." She turned to George. "Haven't we already had enough excitement for one trip?"

Ned had managed to turn the car around, and the girls got back in. "Well, what now?" he asked.

Nancy looked at the others. "Do you want to go back to Great Falls and take the next plane home? Or do we keep trying to find Lost River?"

"I want to get to the bottom of this thing," said George. "And I'm stubborn. I don't want to give up my prize." She looked around. "But just because I'm determined, doesn't mean you all have to stay. I'll understand if anybody decides to go back home."

Bess heaved a sigh of resignation. "If George is staying, I guess I will, too."

Ned reached over and ruffled Nancy's hair. "I'm in this as long as you are, Nan," he said.

"In that case," Nancy said briskly, "we'd better find an alternative route. This road isn't going anywhere but down." She pulled a state highway map out of the glove compartment and began to compare it to the map they had been given. "I think I see how to get there," she reported after several minutes. "Let's go back to the last fork in the road and take a left. Then it looks like we take two more left turns—we'll be there in thirty or forty minutes."

"You're the detective," Ned replied cheerfully, and drove back down the mountain.

Thirty minutes later, they pulled up at Lost River Junction, a small cluster of weathered, tired-looking wooden sheds huddled under tall pine trees beside the road. As Nancy got out of the car, she saw that one of the sheds sported a crude sign that said White Water Rafting in crooked letters. The sign looked new, she noticed, in contrast to the old building. Down the hill, behind the building, she glimpsed a group of people standing on the bank of a river, next to two big rubber rafts.

"Looks like we've made it—finally," Ned announced, turning off the ignition.

"Fantastic!" George exclaimed. She got out of the car, her concern about the trip momentarily forgotten. "Listen to that river!"

"I hate to tell you guys this," Bess remarked, "but I hear roaring. *Loud* roaring."

"Right," Ned said, opening the trunk and beginning to pull out their gear. "Sounds like a pretty big falls not far away." Grinning, he handed Bess her duffel bag. "That's what white water rafting is all about, you know, Bess. Water falling over the rocks. It always makes a noise."

Bess took the bag, shaking her head.

Nancy slung her backpack over her shoulder and followed George to the river. She was wearing khaki-colored safari shorts and a red knit polo shirt, a sweatshirt tied around her neck. The sun felt warm on her shoulders.

"Hi!" George said, hailing a tall, thin-faced young woman who was standing beside one of the rafts. "I'm George Fayne. Can you tell me where to find Paula Hancock? She runs White Water Rafting."

The young woman looked up. Nancy couldn't tell whether she was surprised to see them. "I'm Paula," the woman said. She was in her early twenties, Nancy judged, wiry-thin and tense, like a nervous animal. "You're late. We expected you last night."

George bristled. "Yeah. Well, you might say that we've been victims of circumstance. That map you left for us at the airport took us on a wild-goose chase, and then we—"

Nancy stepped in. "Then we got lost," she interrupted smoothly, leaning her backpack against a tree. She threw George a warning glance. There wasn't any point in alerting Paula Hancock to their suspicions. If she had anything to do with the warning phone call or the missing barricade, Nancy didn't want to put her on her guard. "I'm Nancy Drew," she said, holding out her hand and studying Paula. "George invited me to come along."

"Glad to have you," Paula replied brusquely. She ignored Nancy's hand. She had odd amber eyes, Nancy noticed, cold and remote.

Nancy shivered as though somebody had dropped an ice cube down her neck. "Have we . . . have we met?" she asked hesitantly. Those eyes—where had she seen them?

Paula straightened up. "I don't think so," she said more casually. "Not unless you've been up here before."

"No," Nancy said. "This is my first trip to Montana." She was sure she had never met Paula, but she couldn't shake the feeling that she knew those eyes.

Paula turned to a dark, good-looking young man in a faded blue denim work shirt and jeans, who was loading a radio into one of the rafts. "Max, come and meet our grand-prize winner, Georgia Fayne. Max is an expert river-rafter," she said, turning back to George and Nancy. "He'll handle one of our rafts. I'm taking the other."

"It's not Georgia, it's *George*," George said, shaking Max's hand. "This is my friend Nancy. And Bess," she added as the others came up, "and Ned. We're really looking forward to the trip. Ned's been on a raft trip before, but the rest of us are novices."

"Glad to meet you," Max said. A long, hairline scar cut across the corner of his square jaw, giving him a lopsided look. He smiled at Bess as he shook her hand, his dark eyes glinting appreciatively. "Real glad."

Nancy looked at Max closely. The voice on the phone could just as easily have been a man's voice as a woman's. In her experience, it was better to consider everybody a candidate for suspicion. And Max looked like a likely one. But then, so did Paula. Since she was the owner of White Water Rafting, she must have been responsible for the contest—and for that killer map. Nancy decided to watch both of them closely.

Paula glanced at the sleeping bags and packs that Ned was carrying. "Go ahead and stow your gear in Max's raft," she commanded. "The sooner we get started, the better." She frowned at Max. "Did you check the batteries before you loaded the emergency radio?"

Max nodded. "Sure thing," he said carelessly. "Can't be out on the river with a radio we don't trust, can we?"

"Hi! Let me show you where to put those." A pretty girl walked over to Ned and took one of the sleeping bags from him. She was petite and willowy, and her ash-blond hair swept softly over her shoulders. "I'm Samantha," she told him in a soft southern drawl. "But my friends call me Sammy."

"Well . . . sure," Ned said, with a shrug and a quick glance at Nancy. He followed Sammy to the raft. Paula went along, too, calling out instructions for stowing the gear.

Nancy looked at George. "Maybe we should meet some of the others," she suggested, pointing to a group of kids standing beside one of the rafts.

"Okay," George said. "I'm looking forward to —"

George didn't get to finish her sentence. Suddenly the air around them exploded in a series of sharp, staccato sounds, like gunshots fired in rapid succession. Somebody was shooting at them.

CHAPTER FOUR

G et down!" Nancy yelled, pulling George with her in a wild dash for the shelter of a nearby tree. The gunshots continued, echoing through the trees. Crouching low, Nancy waved frantically at several other kids who were still standing beside the rafts, out in the open. "Get down!" she yelled. "Somebody's shooting!"

"Oh, come on," one of the girls called back. "That's not a gun. It's just Tod and Mike shooting their firecrackers." The explosions stopped suddenly and there was absolute quiet, except for the sound of the falls.

"What?" Nancy stood up and looked around. "Tod and Mike? Firecrackers?"

"Those two clowns love practical jokes," the girl explained, coming over to them with a smile. "Firecrackers under a trash can. They've been at it all morning." The girl was short, thin, and dark-haired, and she had a nervous intensity that reminded Nancy of Paula.

Nancy let out the breath she'd been holding. She felt her pulse slow down to its normal rate.

"Hah! We sure scored one on you, didn't we?" The boy who

came running to Nancy and George looked very pleased with himself. He was short and stocky and wore a pair of faded cut-offs and a plaid flannel shirt with the sleeves rolled up. "I'm Tod. And this is Mike." He pointed to the boy who had followed him over. The accomplice was tall and thin, his legs looking like pipestems in his frayed cutoffs.

"Listen, you guys, I don't think it was funny at all," George protested, coming out from behind the tree. "You scared us to death!"

But Nancy just said mildly, "Yeah, you sure scored one. We *were* pretty scared." Were Tod and Mike really immature enough to think it was *funny* to frighten people like that?

"Well, I've got to say this," Mike observed, looking at Nancy appraisingly. "You sure think fast and act fast." He grinned and shuffled his feet. Maybe, thought Nancy, he was shy.

The dark-haired girl spoke up. "I'm Mercedes." She pointed to two others who had come up behind her. "This is Linda and this is Ralph. I guess you've already met Sammy," she added, looking toward the raft, where Sammy was standing close to Ned, talking animatedly with him.

Nancy followed her glance. "Yes," she said wryly, wondering if Sammy was going to be another Sondra—or worse. "We've already met Sammy. She seems very . . . friendly. And helpful."

"Yeah, that's Sammy, all right." Tod nudged Mike. "*Very* friendly. And *very* helpful."

Linda was a delicate, fragile-looking girl with a narrow, pointed face that reminded Nancy of a princess in a fairy-tale book. Ralph, slender with intense black eyes, was probably the scholarly type. He seemed a little out of place next to Tod and Mike, both of whom looked as if they'd grown up in the woods. Nancy listened carefully to them as Mercedes introduced them, trying to detect any trace of the voice that had made the phone call. But the week-old memory of a muffled voice wasn't much to go on.

However, after a few minutes of conversation, Nancy had found out some essential details about their companions. Except for Nancy, Ned, Bess, and George, everyone seemed to be from the area, which struck Nancy as a little odd. Hadn't George said that the contest was *national*? If that was true, why weren't there any winners from other parts of the country? Mercedes turned out to be Paula's cousin, a fact which didn't surprise Nancy, given the nervous energy they seemed to share. Linda and Ralph were both from Great Falls and appeared to be close friends—also not surprising, Nancy thought, since they, too, seemed alike, both quiet and shy. Tod and Mike came from a nearby small town and, according to them, were experienced rafters.

"There's not much about Lost River that we don't know," Tod bragged. "We've made half a dozen trips down it in the past couple of years. We could handle these rafts ourselves, without any trouble—and all the gear, too. Like the radio, for instance. Isn't it a beauty?" He jerked his thumb toward Mike. "Mike here is the expert on this baby. Right, Mike?"

Mike nodded. "Yeah, I guess so," he said. "Radios are my hobby."

"Is rafting dangerous?" George asked excitedly. She sounded as if she wished it were, but she wasn't sure she should. She cocked an ear. "It *sounds* dangerous," she said, listening to the thundering of the falls.

Mike shrugged. "Not if you know what you're doing." He cast a meaningful glance at Max, who had just joined the group and was busily talking to Bess. "Of course, if you're careless, somebody's going to get hurt—or worse." Nancy thought that Mike sounded as if he were challenging Max's raft-handling ability. She wondered if he knew something about Max that the others didn't.

Max turned to Mike. "Lost River is *always* dangerous," he said flatly. "It doesn't matter how much skill you have. The worst thing you can do is take it for granted."

Linda and Bess looked frightened. "You mean the rafts aren't safe?" Linda said haltingly.

"A raft is always safe as long as it is right-side-up and everybody stays on it," Mike replied, with another challenging look at Max.

"Do they capsize often?" Bess asked, glancing at George and putting special emphasis on the word *capsize*. Nancy hid a smile. Bess was learning the vocabulary.

"Hardly ever." Max tipped his cap toward the back of his head.

"As long as you don't get careless," Tod put in. "If you do . . ."

"Right," Max said, avoiding Mike's eyes. He put his hand casually on Bess's arm. "Listen, Bess, if you're scared, ride along with me, and I'll show you what to watch out for. That way, you'll understand what's going on."

A happy smile lit Bess's face. "Sure," she said. "I'd love to."

Nancy and George exchanged worried looks. Why did Bess have to give away her heart on a moment's notice? They'd have to talk with her first chance they got and warn her.

For the time being, Nancy just wanted some answers to the questions that had been bothering her all along. How much did the others know about the contest? George couldn't remember entering it—could they? She turned to Linda. "So," she said, "another lucky winner. Tell me how *you* won the contest."

Linda shook her head. "You know, it's funny," she replied timidly. "When the letter from Paula Hancock came, I was completely surprised. I couldn't even remember *entering* a contest."

"Me, neither," Ralph volunteered. "Linda and I have talked about it, and neither one of us can figure out exactly how we got here."

Nancy looked at Mike and Tod. "What about you?" she asked.

Tod shrugged. "Who knows? I don't remember entering, but I might have. You know how it goes. When you see a contest at a store or something, you always put your name in the box. I figure that's what happened here. I probably entered it at the sporting goods store."

"Yeah," Mike put in. "When we got the letters we couldn't remember exactly." He glanced around with a slightly puzzled look on his face. "In fact, neither of us could remember ever hearing about White Water Rafting, which is kind of funny, since we live so close by. It must be a new company."

"What does it matter how any of us got here?" Mercedes interrupted quickly, stepping forward. "We're all going to have the time of our lives—and White Water Rafting is paying for the whole thing! What's the point of asking all these questions?"

Before Nancy could answer, Paula hurried over to them, followed by Ned and Sammy. Nancy noticed that Sammy was casting very interested glances at Ned—and that Ned didn't seem at all reluctant. In fact, he was laughing at something Sammy had said.

Nancy gave an inward sigh. This was supposed to be a time when she and Ned could get reacquainted with each other. But with all the distracting questions and frightening events, it was beginning to look more like a case than a vacation. And Sammy was giving her something else to worry about.

"Okay, everybody. The rafts are loaded," Paula announced. "Now, I'm going to give you a few important instructions." She pointed toward the rafts, big rubber boats eighteen or twenty feet long and five or six feet wide. One was pulled up on the shore, the other was in the river, moored with a line.

"See those wooden platforms toward the stern, where the oars are? Max and I sit on them. Everybody else sits down inside the raft—no standing up, no clowning around. Wear your life vest all the time, no matter how uncomfortable it gets. Pick a buddy—if anything happens, keep your eye on your buddy and be responsible for each other." She looked around the group. "Any questions?"

When nobody answered, she said, "Okay, then, let's get going. The first major falls is only about fifty yards downstream. It's too dangerous to raft over, so we'll take the sluice to the left to avoid the worst of it. It's a sort of natural waterslide along the left shore, and it's much tamer than the falls. We know what we're doing, but it'll be rough going for a few minutes, so hang on." She eyed Nancy. "I'm assigning you to the raft on the right, Nancy. Climb aboard. There are some life vests stowed under the platform."

The raft was moored to the shore with a line tied to a stake stuck in the mud. Nancy pulled it toward her and clambered aboard, scrambling awkwardly over a small heap of supplies and equipment stowed in the middle of the raft. The raft bobbed violently under her weight, and she grabbed for a handhold. She could feel the current tugging against the mooring line as if it were trying to tear the raft free.

Suddenly the line gave, jolting her to her knees as the raft swept away. The turbulent current of Lost River was pulling Nancy directly toward the falls.

CHAPTER FIVE

Nancy! Hang on!" she heard Ned shout.

The roar of the falls was growing louder. Grabbing for the oars, Nancy figured she had only fifty yards or so before she went over, and Paula had said that the falls were too dangerous for the raft to negotiate.

So, Nancy told herself, she'd have to hurry—do *something* so she wouldn't be dashed to death on the rocks.

Glancing up, she saw Ned racing along the riverbank. Max and George were running hard behind him. Ned carried a coil of rope. "Row!" he called. "You've got to get out of the current!"

Nancy swallowed nervously. The ten-foot oars felt heavy and awkward, and her knuckles were white from gripping them so hard.

"Swing the raft toward the left!" Max yelled, coming up behind Ned. "Push on the right oar and pull on the left!"

Bracing her feet, Nancy followed Max's instructions. The oars cut into the water. After a moment, the raft swung left, responding like a huge, sluggish whale. She began to row forward, toward the bank. But the current was much too strong.

"She'll never make it!" Bess yelled.

"Maybe we can get a line to you," Ned shouted. "Row to the left. The current's not so bad closer to the shore."

Mustering all her strength, Nancy pulled hard on both oars, trying to keep the bow of the boat moving left. She frantically looked for a life vest, but couldn't see one on the raft. If she fell in the water, she couldn't fight the current.

"Closer!" Ned ran along the bank to keep up with the raft. "The rope's too short. I can't reach you!"

Then Nancy remembered the sluice. Hadn't Paula said something about avoiding the falls by taking it? She peered downriver. There, near the left shore, was the natural waterslide, funneling the river along safely in a milky white froth, neatly avoiding the falls. "I'm heading for the sluice!" Nancy shouted to Ned. She was still rowing energetically, but her endurance was fading.

Despite her aching shoulders, Nancy held on. She focused every ounce of will on getting away from the pull of the falls.

Finally, the swifter current seemed to yield to her power. Almost magically, the raft swung toward the sluice, and now, at least, she had a chance.

On shore, Ned vaulted over a fallen tree, still trying to keep pace. "There's a sandbar ahead," he called. "Beach the raft on it!"

For an instant the raft was balanced on the lip of the long slide. Nancy raised the oars and lay far back, icy water spraying her face. With a giant *whoosh!* the raft dropped over the edge. Nancy squeezed her eyes shut and prayed. It was like being on the giant waterslide at the amusement park—but without any guarantee of safety.

The raft was completely out of control. It hit the turbulent water at the foot of the sluice with a giant splash, completely drenching Nancy. Then it bobbed along more quietly as she grabbed for the oars again and began to steer toward the sandbar. There was Ned, with George and Bess. He still had the rope in his hand.

"Here," he shouted, tossing the end of the rope to her. She grabbed it and let him pull her ashore.

When the raft was safely beached, Nancy stumbled out. Ned caught her in his arms and held her for a minute, shivering.

"Well," Max said with a grin as he caught up to them, "that wasn't exactly the way we planned to get started. But now you know what rafting is all about."

"We've got to get you some dry clothes, Nancy," Bess added.

"Forget it," Paula said, joining them. "Before the day is over, *everybody* will be wet." She frowned at Nancy. "Where was your life vest? How come you didn't put it on?"

"Life vest?" Nancy asked. "There weren't any in the raft!"

Paula shrugged. "I guess they hadn't been loaded yet." She looked around at the rest of the group that had gathered. "So now you know. Accidents are a matter of routine on the river. You've got to be prepared for the worst."

Accident? Nancy wasn't convinced. She bent over the raft to examine the mooring closely. The stake was still attached to the line.

"What do you think?" Ned whispered to her. "Was it done deliberately?"

Nancy straightened up just in time to catch Paula's intense gaze. Had she heard Ned's question?

"I can't be sure," she replied in a low voice. She took Ned's arm and walked casually away. "The mooring line hadn't been cut or damaged. It looks like the stake just pulled out of the mud. So maybe it *was* an accident."

"The other raft was pulled up partway on the shore," George pointed out, hurrying to them. "That looks like a safer way to load people. And after the missing barricade . . ."

"Yeah, I know," Nancy said grimly. "It's beginning to look like we're awfully accident-prone."

Half of the group, including Linda and Ralph, went back upstream to board Max's raft. Linda seemed very frightened and kept saying that she wanted to back out, but Ralph put his arm around her comfortingly, and after a few minutes she calmed down. Nancy could hear Bess talking to Max. "Are you sure the raft is safe?" she was asking anxiously.

"Couldn't be safer," Max assured her confidently. "There are only two things that can destroy one of these rafts. One is to hang it up on a sharp rock. The other is to take a knife to it." He laughed. "We're going to make sure the first thing doesn't happen. And I can't imagine anybody being foolish enough to do the second. Can you?"

Nancy and George, Ned, Tod, and Sammy stayed behind on the sandbar to board Paula's raft. As they got on, Sammy managed to settle down cozily in the bow next to Ned.

"Paula said to choose 'buddies,'" she reminded him, edging closer to Ned. "I choose you!"

Ned cast a quick glance at Nancy, who was sitting farther back in the raft. Nancy shrugged. She wasn't thrilled about the idea of Sammy being Ned's "buddy," but she wasn't going to make a big thing about it.

"Well, okay," Ned said. He seemed flattered. "For now, anyway."

"Oh, that's just wonderful!" Sammy exclaimed happily. She pulled her life vest over her head. "Will you show me how to buckle this, Ned?"

Nancy turned away. The last thing she needed was giggly Samantha making a play for Ned.

"Don't worry," George whispered, squeezing Nancy's hand. "Ned's not going to be taken in by her."

"I don't know," Nancy said doubtfully. Ned looked as if he were enjoying himself, bent close to Sammy, fastening the straps of the life vest around her slender waist. "She *is* awfully pretty."

At that moment, Max's raft came over the sluice, everyone screaming at the top of their lungs. It bounced into the pool with a giant splash. "Okay, here we go," Paula said to Nancy's group. She and Tod gave the raft a push off the sand and into the current. "Everybody hang on!"

With Paula seated on the platform and rowing strongly, the raft swung slowly out into the current and then picked up speed, following Max's raft. Since it was nearly ten o'clock, the sun was high overhead, but the air was still cool. Nancy settled back comfortably. This stretch of Lost River was broader and deeper, and for the next half hour or so, the rafts rode smoothly and easily. Pines and spruce trees crowded both banks. High against the blue sky a hawk soared powerfully, and somewhere deep in the woods a woodpecker drummed a staccato beat.

"Isn't this terrific?" George sighed. She was wearing her binoculars around her neck and suddenly raised them to her eyes. "I think that's a bald eagle in that tree!" she said, awed.

"I wouldn't be surprised," Tod said casually from his spot next to Nancy.

"I thought they were rare," Nancy said.

Tod shrugged. "To the rest of the country, maybe. Not around here." He grinned. "One of my buddies had one for a while."

George's eyes got round. "A bald eagle? You mean as a pet?"

"Yeah, a little one. For a while. He had a coon, too, but it got to be a pest." He grinned broadly, and Nancy noticed that he was missing a tooth. "Made a nice cap."

"A cap?" Nancy asked in disgust. "He skinned it?"

"Naw." Tod grinned. "*I* skinned it." He pulled a six-inch switchblade out of his pocket and began flicking the blade in and out. "Butchered and skinned it, all with this knife." A flick of his hand brought the blade out again. "Sharp as a razor." He grabbed Nancy's arm and turned it over. "Bet I could kill a bear with this knife," he boasted, touching the sharp-honed blade to the blue veins of her wrist.

Nancy jerked her arm away, staring at Tod. His eyes looked innocent, but she had seen plenty of criminals who looked that way. She would have to keep a watch on him.

But at the same time, she had the feeling that several people were keeping a watch on *her*. She could feel Paula's amber eyes constantly on her. And from the other raft, both Mercedes and Max seemed to be watching her, too. Why?

After another hour and a half, Paula began to paddle the raft out of the current, toward shore. "Lunch break," she called. She beached the raft on the sandy bank, where a small creek came gurgling out of a narrow canyon to join the larger river.

Paula pointed. "There's a huckleberry patch a little way up that creek, under those willows. If you've never eaten wild huckleberries, why don't you go try some while Max and I fix lunch?" She handed over a bucket for the berries.

"I'm ready for some huckleberries," George said enthusiastically. "It's been a long time since breakfast back at that motel."

"Oh, Ned, this sounds like such fun!" Sammy exclaimed, clutching Ned's arm.

Ned cast a look at Nancy, but Nancy glanced stubbornly away. If he was going to fall for Sammy's ridiculous little game, let him. She watched him follow Sammy up the creek. Then she and the others trailed behind. The huckleberry patch was fragrant. Most of the kids feasted while they picked, and their faces and hands were stained with purple huckleberry juice.

Bess sighed contentedly, bending over the dense bushes next to Nancy.

"Almost as good as the beach?" Nancy teased.

"Well, not quite," Bess admitted. "Still . . ."

Suddenly she was startled by the crackling twigs and the loud rustle of leaves nearby. Bess looked up in alarm. She clapped her hand to her mouth. Then she gave a loud, shrill shriek.

"What is it?" cried Nancy.

Bess gasped.

Nancy whirled around, and there, rising up before her on its hind paws, its teeth bared in a fierce snarl, was a huge black bear.

CHAPTER SIX

Nancy's heart nearly stopped beating as she looked, terrified, into the ferocious mouth of the bear, its teeth gleaming yellow against the darkness of its throat. For a moment, like a slow-motion scene in a horror movie, the bear seemed to tower over them, claws outstretched, mouth open, roaring.

Ned and Sammy were a dozen paces away, picking berries. Ned looked up, horror in his eyes. "Get back, Nancy!" he shouted.

"Ned!" Sammy cried as Ned crept toward Nancy. "Don't leave me!" She lunged for him, and they both fell sideways into the berry bushes.

"Scat! Shoo! Beat it! Get out of here, bear!" Suddenly Max was in front of Nancy and Bess, between them and the bear, clapping his hands and shouting. He snatched off his cap and flapped it under the bear's astonished nose. "Scram! Shoo! Go!"

For a moment, the bear hesitated. Then its surprise turned to panic and it wheeled, dropped to all fours, and loped off into the bushes without a backward look.

"Wow!" Bess sank down weakly onto a nearby boulder and

mopped her forehead with the tail of her blouse. Her face was white. "I have never been so scared in all my life!"

Nancy let out the breath she had been holding. "Me, nei-ther!" she said.

"Are you all right?" George rushed up, looking anxious.

"Max saved us," Bess whispered, gazing at him adoringly: "He scared a grizzly bear away just by yelling at it."

"That wasn't any grizzly," Max said as Tod dashed up, pant-ing. "And it wasn't very big, either. When you're scared, things have a way of seeming bigger than they are. It was just an ordinary black bear, probably no more than a yearling, taking a morning sunbath and a berry break at the same time." He laughed. "When it comes right down to it, *we're* the ones who are trespassing. This is *his* berry patch, you know."

"I wish I'd been there," Tod said. He glanced at Max. "That ol' bear wouldn't have been able to walk away when I got through with him."

"Don't be ridiculous," Max snapped. "You don't want to go messing around with bears—not with that toy knife of yours."

Nancy stepped between them. "We're just glad this is all over," she said, interrupting Tod. "And that nobody got hurt."

Tod threw them a baleful look and turned angrily away. "You think you're so smart," Nancy heard him say under his breath as he stormed past her.

She stared after him, puzzled. Was his remark aimed at her or at Max?

Bess looked around. "Where's Ned?" she exclaimed. "I

heard him shouting just a moment ago, but I haven't seen him since before the bear attacked."

"Here I am," Ned said. He limped up to them, covered with scratches. Sammy was still sitting in the berry bushes with a sullen look on her face. "I tried to help, but I didn't quite make it." He threw a disgusted look over his shoulder at Sammy. "I'm sorry," he said.

Nancy couldn't help chuckling. "By the looks of you, you'd have been better off meeting up with the bear."

Ned flashed a weak smile, then grew red-faced. Nancy knew he was embarrassed about Sammy, and that it was time to help him feel better about what had happened.

"That's okay," she said comfortingly. "It's the thought that counts. I know you would have helped if you could have."

Ned came closer. "Forgiven?" he asked softly.

"Nothing to forgive," Nancy replied, and Ned's face broke into a wide grin. Sammy scrambled to her feet and walked away without a word, her face stormy. Nancy looked after her. She didn't think Sammy was the kind to bear a grudge, but it might not be a bad idea to keep an eye on her.

Max called for attention. "Listen, kids, when you're out in the woods, make a lot of noise to let the bears and other big animals know that you're not trying to sneak up on them. If you happen to surprise a mama bear when she's out for a stroll with her cub, or if you manage to get between a mama and her cub, you're asking to have a tremendous bite taken out of you."

"Is that how you got that scar on your face?" Bess asked curiously. "A bear?"

Max ran his hand across his jaw. "No," he said brusquely. "I got it in a rafting accident." He picked his cap up off the ground and jammed it on his head. "Got to go see how lunch is coming along," he said, and left.

Bess looked longingly after him. "I wonder what kind of accident it was," she said with a sigh. "I'll bet he rescued somebody, or something like that."

"Well, it's obviously something he doesn't want to talk about," Nancy said. It concerned her that Bess was developing a giant crush on Max—the kind of crush that could easily blind her to the real person.

Apprehensively, Nancy remembered how Mike and Tod had implied that there might be something wrong with Max's raft-handling abilities.

"Listen, Bess," Nancy said, as they started together down the path to the river. "I need to say something to you about Max."

"Isn't he wonderful?" Bess asked with a dreamy look in her eyes, her words bubbling over. "You know, I wasn't sold on this trip in the beginning. But *now*, well, you should see Max handle the oars on that raft, Nan. He knows exactly what he's doing. And those muscles—wow!"

Nancy gave her a cautioning look. "You know, Bess, maybe it isn't a good idea to let yourself fall head over heels for this guy. There are some pretty weird things going on on this trip, and Max could be involved in them."

"He isn't that kind of person," Bess said flatly. "He saved us from the bear, remember? I mean, he could have let the bear attack us, and that would have taken care of us for good."

Nancy flung up her hands in confusion. "I don't know. Maybe the bear wasn't part of the plan, and he just reacted spontaneously. Or maybe I'm entirely wrong and he's not involved at all. But there's something awfully strange here, and I don't want you to get hurt, that's all."

They reached the end of the trail, where it opened out onto the sandy beach. "Well, I appreciate your concern for my feelings," Bess said huffily, "but I'm a big girl now. I think I can be trusted to know what's good for me and what isn't. I—"

Nancy put a hand on Bess's arm. "Shh," she said. The rafts had been pulled up on the deserted beach about ten yards ahead. Everybody else was off picking berries or making lunch farther down the beach, or walking in the woods. Everyone except Mercedes. She was bent over the pile of gear stowed in the middle of Paula's raft.

"What's she doing there?" Bess wondered. "Hey! She's going through someone's pack."

But Nancy was already on the beach, marching forward. "That's not anybody's pack," she said grimly. "She's going through mine!"

CHAPTER SEVEN

Nancy walked toward the raft, Bess following her closely. "Can I help you, Mercedes?" she asked pleasantly.

Mercedes straightened up and jumped back. "Help me?" she stammered. "No, I . . . I was just looking . . . in Paula's pack. For—for some sunscreen."

Nancy pointed. "The pack you're looking in just happens to be mine."

"Yours?" Mercedes looked down. She gave a nervous little laugh. "How silly of me. Of course it's yours. It even has your name on it. I don't know what I was thinking. I'm so sorry. I hope you don't think that I—"

"Well, as a matter of fact—" Bess began hotly.

"No, of course not," Nancy interrupted, overriding her friend. "I'm sure it must be easy to make a mistake like that."

Nodding, Mercedes backed away, then turned and hurried up the beach.

"Now, what was that all about?" Bess asked, turning to Nancy. "Mercedes *knew* what she was doing."

Nancy looked quickly through her pack. "Nothing's missing," she said. "But you know, in a funny way this doesn't surprise me. I've had the feeling all morning that Mercedes has been watching me."

"Could she have anything to do with the mooring line?" Bess asked.

"I suppose so. But so could almost anybody else—especially Paula and Max."

"Now, wait a minute," Bess said. "I still don't think that Max—"

Nancy held up her hand. "Finding a criminal is different from defending him in the courtroom, Bess. Out here, everybody is guilty until we know beyond the shadow of a doubt that they're innocent. No exceptions."

Bess sighed. "Well, I still don't think he did it," she muttered.

Fifteen yards down the beach, everybody was beginning to gather around the fire that Paula had built. She and Max had spread sandwiches on a towel, along with apples and bananas and bags of chips. George and Ned were there, helping themselves, when Nancy and Bess arrived. The four friends sat down on the sand with their lunches, a little apart from the others.

". . . and then she just walked away," Nancy said in a low voice as she finished telling George and Ned how she and Bess had caught Mercedes rifling her pack. On the other side of the fire, Sammy and Mercedes were deep in conversation. Nancy wished she could hear what they were saying.

"Mercedes is Paula's cousin, isn't she?" George asked quietly. "Do you think it's possible that Paula or Max asked her to look through your pack?"

"At this point, there's no way to know—she might even have done it on her own," Nancy said, ignoring the look Bess gave George. "You know, this is really an odd situation. Usually when I'm working on a case, I know what kind of crime we're dealing with—and the clues usually make some sort of sense."

"Yeah," Ned agreed. He trailed his fingers idly up and down her spine. "But this time, there are just these unexplainable things that keep happening. Since there's no real crime, it's hard to know whether any of the things are tied together."

"It's all so bizarre," Nancy said, moving a little closer to Ned. The touch of his fingers tingled through her. At that moment, Sammy looked up and saw what Ned was doing. She glared at him and then turned back to Mercedes.

George pushed a brown curl out of her eyes. "You know, I'm beginning to think that maybe the most bizarre thing of all was my winning the contest in the first place."

Nancy nodded. "None of the other kids can remember entering the contest, either. It's as though this whole thing were invented." A shadow fell across her shoulder and George's cautioning glance made Nancy stop talking.

"So you've had your first taste of rafting," Max said, squatting down next to Bess. "Did you like it?" His voice was friendly, but his eyes were watchful. From the way Max had reacted when Bess asked about his scar, Nancy knew she would have to be cautious questioning him.

"Yeah, we're having a good time," Nancy said casually. "And

we're getting curious about the rafting business. Are there many rafting companies on Lost River?"

Max picked up a stick and turned it in his fingers. "Maybe a half-dozen or so. Most of them are headquartered up at the Junction."

"Have you and Paula worked together often?" Nancy asked.

"Nope," Max said, shaking his head.

Nancy waited, hoping he would say something else. "We're sort of curious about her company, White Water Rafting," she went on. "The sign on the building looked new. Has she been in business long?"

"I don't think so."

"And the contest," Nancy pressed. "What do you know about the contest?"

"Nothing," Max replied. "Paula just hired me to run the raft for this trip. She didn't even tell me there was a contest. I heard that from one of the kids after I got here. It seemed a little weird to me."

"Weird?"

"Oh, you know—I mean, what was she running a contest *for*, anyway? But what do I know? I'm just a rafter. I don't know anything about the business end." He raised an eyebrow. "You sure are asking a lot of questions."

Nancy shrugged. "Just curious."

"You know, I've got this feeling that I know you," Max said. "Like maybe I've seen your picture somewhere. Have you been on television or something? Are you famous?"

"No, I wouldn't say I'm famous." Nancy decided it wouldn't hurt to tell him who she was. "Actually, I'm a private detective."

"A pretty *famous* private detective," Ned put in proudly. "Internationally famous."

"So maybe you *have* seen her picture," Bess added. "She's been in the newspapers more than once."

"A detective?" Max asked, surprised. "You mean a private eye, like in books and on TV?"

Linda and Ralph wandered over. "A *girl* detective?" Linda asked curiously. At that, Mike and Tod broke away from the fire and joined the others. They listened intently.

"That's right," Nancy said, laughing.

Max gave her a long look, as if he were trying to remember something. "What kind of cases have you worked on?" he asked.

"Oh, all kinds," Nancy said modestly. "Blackmail, sabotage, embezzlement, murder, theft . . . you name it—"

Suddenly Max gave a quick flicker of recognition—and then, just as suddenly, it was as if a shutter had closed down over Max's eyes. He stood up abruptly. "Got to see about a few things," he said. And he walked quickly away.

Bess looked at Nancy anxiously. She got to her feet, too. "I think I'll just make sure Max isn't angry about something."

Nancy watched Bess follow Max as he walked away. Why had he gotten so upset? She could swear that he recognized her—but she couldn't remember meeting him, and he wasn't exactly the kind of person she would forget. Was Max trying to decide whether to tell her something? That was possible—but it was also possible there was something he would go to any lengths to keep her from finding out.

She frowned as Bess caught up with Max a little distance away. She wished that Bess could manage more control over her feelings. It really wasn't a good idea for her to get so involved so quickly.

Linda stepped forward. "Gosh, I've never known a *real* detective," she said with a shy smile.

"Well, I don't know if I count," Nancy said. "I'm a real detective, all right, but I'm on vacation."

"Well, I sure hope we won't need your services," Ralph said cheerfully.

"Okay, everybody," Paula called. "Lunch break's over!"

By the time the rafts were loaded up again, the sun had faded behind a bank of threatening clouds. Mike asked George to trade places with him so he could ride with Tod. Sammy asked Mercedes to trade places with her, probably because she didn't want to be around Ned and Nancy, so Mercedes sat just ahead of Nancy and Ned, with Tod and Mike in the bow together. Secretly, Nancy was glad that Sammy was on the other raft. And she welcomed the chance to talk to Mercedes. But it was difficult to find out anything from her.

"I don't know the first thing about the contest," Mercedes insisted with a nervous glance over her shoulder at Paula. Nancy sensed that Mercedes was afraid of her cousin. "When I heard about the trip, I asked Paula if I could go. That's all." She bit her thumbnail. "I thought it would be fun to get out on the river. I've never been rafting."

"Did you see any advertisements for the contest?" Nancy asked in a low voice. "The others can't remember entering it." Mercedes shrugged and turned away.

Mercedes *was* afraid of her cousin. But why?

The afternoon was uneventful. For the first couple of hours, there was as much drifting as paddling, then Nancy began to notice that the water was moving more rapidly. Her raft was following the other one down a deep, shadowy gorge where the water ran even faster, foaming and curling against the rocks as the channel of the river narrowed and twisted. In the distance Nancy could hear a deeper sound, like faraway drums echoing between the walls of the cliffs.

"What's that?" she asked nervously.

"Dead Man's Falls," Paula replied.

"Do you think we can skip that landmark?" Nancy kidded.

Tod laughed. "The name makes it sound worse than it is," he said. "A couple of guys drowned there last year, but the rafter was at fault. Sloppy handling."

"You don't know that, Tod," Paula said sharply. "Even the best raft-handlers have trouble there in high water, because of the way the rocks line up."

"Is the water high right now?" Ned asked curiously.

Paula shook her head. "Nope. It's only a four-foot drop, anyway. These eighteen-foot rafts are big enough to take it easily when the water's down, the way it is now."

They came around another bend, and at the far end, the riverbed began to step down in a series of small, rough rapids that tossed the raft against rock after rock. Nancy found herself clinging to the side.

"There's the falls!" Tod shouted, pointing. Nancy looked. She could see Max's raft just ahead.

"Okay," Paula shouted. "This'll be just like going down a steep sliding board. Once we're over, the water will suck us down and then force us up again. It'll be like riding a bucking horse, so hang on. Check your life vests to see that they're fastened."

Nancy looked at the other raft. "She's not wearing her life vest!" Nancy gasped, pointing to Bess.

"She probably didn't think it looked pretty enough," Ned said with a laugh. He sobered quickly. "She's not a very strong swimmer, is she?"

Nancy shook her head, cinching her own life jacket a little tighter. "Sometimes Bess doesn't have much sense," she muttered.

The raft gathered speed as the current dragged it toward the falls. A few yards upstream, Max's raft seemed to hang up against a rock. Frantically, Max fought the current with his oars, and Ralph tried to push off.

"Uh-oh!" Paula muttered. "That's real trouble."

Nancy and the others watched helplessly as the raft broke loose from the rock and was captured by the swirling water. It somersaulted broadside over the lip of the falls, heaving its shrieking passengers to almost certain death in the raging torrent.

"Bess!" Nancy screamed into the cold spray, hardly feeling it sting her face. "Answer me! Bess! Where are you?"

CHAPTER EIGHT

Paula leaned on the oars. "Hang on!" she shouted. "We're going over!" And with that the raft poised for a nosedive over the edge of the falls.

The bow hit the water at the foot of the falls with an enormous splash that drenched everyone, dived down, and came up again, riding the crest of a wave. Paula dug in deep with the oars, and in a moment they were out of the worst of the swirling current. They were carried fifty yards below the falls before they could beach the raft on a jutting sandbar.

Everybody abandoned the raft and dashed back upstream. In the gorge, the evening shadows were already falling, but Nancy could see heads bobbing in the frothing water. Linda was clinging desperately to a large rock, Ralph keeping a firm hand around her waist. Max supported Sammy as he swam toward them, towing her. And she could see George's dark head in the water, about twenty feet out, one arm waving frantically. But where was Bess?

"There she is!" Ned shouted as Bess's head emerged from the water. "George has her." He dived into the water.

"Hurry, Ned!" Nancy cried. "She's going down again!"

With powerful strokes, Ned swam toward George and Bess, catching Bess just as she slipped out of George's grasp and disappeared again under the white water. He towed her back to the bank, George just ahead of him.

Nancy and George bent over their friend's limp form as Ned pulled her up on the sand. "Bess! Are you all right?"

Nancy rolled her over on her stomach and lifted her up by the middle. The water emptied out of her. After a minute, Bess spluttered and sat up. "I—I'm okay," she said, shaking the water out of her hair. "What happened?"

"Capsize," Tod said grimly. He had thrown a line to Ralph and Linda, and the two of them were now safely on the bank, holding on to each other. Mike was salvaging some of their gear from the water. Paula and Max had clambered back under the falls to detach the raft from a jagged rock.

Tod turned back to Nancy, scowling darkly. He began to coil the line in his hands. "You saw what happened," he said. "Max let the raft get broadside to the current and dumped everybody. Just like the last time."

"Last time?" Nancy said sharply.

"Yeah, when the two guys drowned."

Bess looked up, her eyes wide. "What are you saying?"

"I'm saying it was Max's fault just like last year's capsize," Tod replied. "Max was the rafter I was talking about earlier. His raft got hung up last year and flipped. Everybody fell out— that's how Max got his scar. Only last year there wasn't another raft standing by, and two people drowned." Tod shook his head angrily and slung the coil of rope over his shoulder. "That's why Mike traded places with George. He wouldn't ride with Max on this part of the trip. Once you lose your nerve at a dangerous spot like this, it's tough to get it back."

"Does Paula know about what happened last year?" Nancy asked, her mind shifting quickly into detective gear.

"Yeah, she knows," Tod said bitterly. "Everybody on the river knows. None of the other rafting companies will hire Max now—she shouldn't have either."

"How many other people on *this* trip know?" Nancy asked.

Tod shrugged. "Mike. And Paula. I guess that's it. Why?"

"No reason." Nancy stood up. Could the anonymous caller have known about Max's past—and wanted to warn her? But why had *she* been the one to get the call?

"We've got a problem, gang," Paula announced soberly when she and Max returned. Mike and Tod had built a roaring fire beside the remaining raft, and everybody was gathered around it, trying to dry off. They shivered in the cool evening breeze that funneled up through the gorge.

"A problem?" Ned asked.

"Yeah," Paula replied, shrugging into her roomy red-and-black plaid jacket. "The raft got pretty badly beaten up by the water. It's ripped in a half-dozen places—totally beyond repair."

George stared. "Beyond repair? But that means . . ."

"That means we'll have to load everybody into one raft," Paula said matter-of-factly. "Either that, or we'll have to leave some of you here while the others go downriver and send help back." She paused and looked around. "That's going to be a problem, too, because most of the gear that was in that raft—sleeping bags, tents, food—has all been washed away."

"Ooh!" Linda wailed. "Ralph, I *told* you we shouldn't have come!"

"What I want to know," Sammy demanded sharply, "is how this happened. What about it, Max? How come we capsized?"

Max spread his hands out over the fire for warmth. "I don't know," he said slowly. "There's this V-shaped rock just upstream of the falls, hidden under the water. The raft can't go over it, and somehow, we got hung up on it and the current shifted us broadside to the falls." He shrugged. "You know the rest."

"Yeah, we know," Sammy said in a low voice, poking the fire viciously. "We're lucky to be alive, that's what we know."

Nancy looked at Tod. For a minute she thought he was going to tell the others what he had told her. When he didn't she breathed a little easier. It would only make things more difficult if the others knew about the first accident.

"Listen, I know you're all upset," Paula said. "But you'll feel better in the morning, when you're not so tired." She glanced at the grove of willows behind them. "It's going to get dark before long. I suggest we gather enough firewood to last the night, fix ourselves some supper, and bed down early. Tomorrow morning we can decide what to do."

"I want to decide right now," Sammy said sullenly.

Ralph spoke up. "I think the girls ought to be the ones to go out tomorrow on the raft. The guys can stay behind and wait."

"I don't think that's fair," Tod said. "I think we ought to draw straws to see who goes out."

"But I thought Paula said we could all go in one raft," Bess pointed out.

Ned turned to Paula. "Is that safe? I don't think we would have made it over those falls if we had been loaded any heavier."

Paula looked grim. "I wouldn't really recommend everybody going in one raft," she admitted. "Of course, if we had to, I suppose we could."

"There's another big rapids about three miles downstream," Max said, looking very tired. "I think we'd be asking for trouble if we all tried to go in one raft."

"How about a vote?" Nancy suggested.

When they raised their hands, it was six to four in favor of splitting the group.

"So, that leaves us with the decision of who to keep and who to throw away," Mike joked.

"We can draw straws—or twigs," Sammy said.

It was decided that George, Nancy, Sammy, Mike, and Ralph would be going downstream in the morning with Max. The others would wait.

"Well, I don't know about the rest of you," Nancy said, "but I'm hungry."

"Food's got *my* vote," Bess said.

"Firewood first, then food," Paula said. "And we'd better check what kind of sleeping gear we have."

An hour later, a huge pile of driftwood was stacked on the

beach, a pot of Mercedes's thick stew with dumplings was simmering on the fire, and a stack of peanut-butter-and-jelly sandwiches sat on a plate nearby. A pot of hot chocolate was perched next to the fire on a flat rock. The gear had been pulled out and inspected: there were four sleeping bags and six blankets. Nancy's and Ned's packs were wet, but otherwise unharmed; George's and Bess's had been swept away in the capsize.

"Well, at least we'll sleep with a full stomach," George said, leaning back against a rock, her feet to the fire. "That stew was great, Mercedes."

"Yes, it *was* good," Nancy added.

"Thanks," Mercedes said, sounding preoccupied. She was sitting on the other side of the fire with a surly Sammy. "I'm glad it wasn't Paula's raft that went over," she went on. "At least tonight's supper didn't get dumped."

"What *is* our food situation?" Mike asked.

"We lost what was in Max's raft, of course," Paula said. She and Max were sitting together. From time to time Paula had looked at Nancy intently, and once Max had seemed to be getting very angry. He had looked over at Nancy at that point too, as if they were talking about *her*. "But we've got enough for one more day, if we're careful. We'll leave most of it with the group that's staying here, since it'll be a day or so before we can get back with another raft."

Tod reached in his pocket for his knife. "We can always

go hunting," he said, flipping the knife open and running his thumb down the edge of the shiny blade. "Last year I got a squirrel with this thing."

"I wish you'd keep that knife in your pocket, Tod," Linda said irritably. "It makes me nervous."

"Everything makes you nervous, little lady," Tod teased, leaning toward her.

Ralph put his hand on Tod's shoulder. "Give me the knife," he said softly, "or I'll take it away from you."

"You and who else?" Tod scrambled to his feet.

Without warning, Ralph stepped forward easily, his open hand ramming Tod in the chest. Tod's arms flew up as he tumbled backward. His knife fell at Ralph's feet.

"Just me," Ralph replied pleasantly, picking up the knife. He turned to Mike, who was sitting openmouthed. "Here. Why don't you keep this for your friend. He's a little careless with it."

"A smooth karate style," Nancy said, staring admiringly at Ralph. "He reminds me of a certain mild-mannered reporter."

Ned laughed. "Yeah, Clark Kent in disguise."

Tod had picked himself off the ground and was brushing himself off. He snatched his knife out of Mike's hand and glared at Ralph. "Next time," he threatened, "it won't be so easy, hotshot."

"Well, I know what's going to be easy for me," Ned said, yawning. "Sleep."

"Good night, Nancy," he whispered tenderly, bending over to kiss her. "And remember, no matter what happens on this wild vacation, at least we're together."

"Right," she said softly. "At least we're together."

Nancy, George, and Bess bedded down close to the fire, huddling under blankets. "I'm beginning to wish I'd listened to Bess," George mumbled.

Bess pulled her blanket up over her chin. "I'm glad you didn't. If we'd gone to the beach, I'd never have met Max."

George sat up. "You can still care about that guy after what he did to us today?"

Bess sat up, too. "How do you know that the capsize wasn't an accident!"

"How do you know it *was*?" George asked, folding her arms.

"I wish you guys would go somewhere else to argue," Nancy said.

In the distance, an owl hooted eerily, and Bess dived under the blanket. Nancy and George laughed, and they all fell into a restless sleep.

There was no moon that night. The faint star-shine hardly penetrated the deep shadows of the gorge. So, when Nancy awakened to the sound of footsteps crunching stealthily on the gravel, her eyes opened to darkness.

Then, an odd ripping noise and a muttered curse. Had a man spoken—or a woman?

Nancy slipped from between George and Bess, who both were sleeping soundly, and headed for the noise. She'd almost reached the river when she saw a figure—little more than a deeper shadow in the darkness—moving in front of her.

"Who is it?" Nancy asked.

The only answer was a blow to her shoulder as the figure rammed past her, to melt into the night and disappear.

CHAPTER NINE

Noiselessly, Nancy tried to follow, but after a few moments, she had to admit that she had lost whomever it was she had seen and had no choice but to crawl back under the blanket and try to get some sleep.

She was awake as soon as the sun touched the lip of the sheer cliff on the other side of the river. Quietly, trying not to disturb Bess and George, she crept out from under the blanket and pulled on her tennis shoes, which were still damp from the day before.

George stirred reluctantly. "What are you doing up at this hour?" she asked sleepily.

"I heard footsteps last night, and a funny noise," Nancy replied, tugging a comb through her tangled hair. "I'm going to look around and see what I can find."

"I'll come with you," George offered, throwing off the blanket. She had slept in the jeans and sweatshirt she had put on after the dunking, but she was still shivering. "It's *cold!*" she exclaimed, rummaging in her duffel bag for her red jacket.

The ashes of the previous night's campfire still glowed in the chilly gray dawn. Beyond, the raft was like the shadowy carcass of a beached whale.

"That's odd," Nancy said, staring. "Doesn't the raft look a little lopsided?"

Nancy and George ran forward, then stopped, gasping in horror. The raft had been slashed from end to end, and its rubber walls were soft and deflated. Even though she didn't know much about rafts, Nancy could tell that the rips were much too large to be repaired.

"Well, *this* was no accident," George said grimly. "Somebody wants to keep us from getting out of here."

"That must have been the noise I heard last night!" Nancy said.

"Remember Tod's threat to get even with Ralph?" George said thoughtfully. "Do you suppose this is how he tried to do it?"

"Boy, you guys sure are up early," Ned said groggily. He appeared behind them, rubbing the sleep out of his eyes and shivering in spite of his heavy down vest. "I hope you were warmer last night than I—" His eyes widened as he saw the damaged raft. He whistled softly between his teeth. "Uh-oh! Now we're *really* up a creek."

"I'll say," Nancy agreed crossly. "And I wish you wouldn't make such awful puns so early in the morning."

"Sorry," Ned said. "But who do you think did it? More important, what do we do *now*?"

Nancy shrugged. She told him what she had heard the night before. "I got up to investigate, but whoever it was made off into the dark before I could catch him."

"Or her," George added. "It could have been a woman's."

She shook her head distractedly. "I can't imagine why anybody would do this. I mean, we're all in this mess together, aren't we? Whoever did it is just as stuck as we are."

"Right," Nancy replied. She got down on her hands and knees and examined the damp sand. It was packed hard, and she couldn't see any footprints. Carefully, she went over the entire raft, looking for clues. "Dead end," she concluded, staring at the disabled raft. "Well, I guess Ned's right. We've got a bigger question than 'Who?' It's 'Now what?' I'm afraid we're down to a matter of survival."

"Who would do such a thing?" Sammy cried angrily a short while later as the group stood looking at the raft. Gradually the horrible truth dawned on her. "Hey, it's got to be one of *us*! One of *us* did this—and whoever it is, he's got to be crazy!"

"Tod's the one with the knife!" Linda said shrilly. "Remember what he said last night about getting even? And look! He's wearing a bandage. I'll bet he cut himself last night when he was cutting up the raft!"

Tod shook his head violently. "You're not pinning this thing on *me*," he protested.

"How did you cut your hand?" Nancy asked him calmly.

Tod looked at the ground. "Mike and I were having a little game of knife-throwing—after everyone went to sleep," he said. "And I—I just got careless, that's all."

"He's right," Mike spoke up quickly. "It happened the way he said. I saw it."

"Yeah, how do we know you're not just covering up for your

friend?" Ralph asked, stepping forward, his fists clenched.

Tod stepped backward, away from Ralph. He licked his lips nervously. "Why would I want to hole the raft?" he said. "I've got to get out of here just like everybody else, don't I?" He jerked his finger toward Max. "If you want to know what I think, I think he did it. He finished off one raft yesterday afternoon under the falls, and he got the other one last night."

"Hey!" Max said angrily. "You've got no right—"

"Yeah, well, you're the guy with the bad record," Mike put in.

"Bad record?" Sammy asked.

"That's right," Tod replied. "Yesterday's 'accident' at the falls wasn't the first time Max has been in trouble. He's responsible for the drownings of two men here last year."

"Yesterday was an accident!" Bess exclaimed heatedly as everybody stared, horror stricken, at Max. "Anyway, whatever happened last summer doesn't have anything to do with last night. Why would Max want to sabotage the raft?"

"Why would anybody want to sabotage the raft?" Mercedes asked quietly. Nancy noticed that her face was very pale, and that her voice sounded flat and hard, as if she were trying to keep it steady.

"Only somebody who's dangerous," Linda answered, her voice going high with terror. She turned to Nancy. "You're a detective. Can you make any sense out of this?"

"Not so far," Nancy replied. She looked around the group. "Did anybody see or hear anything out of the ordinary during the night?"

All the heads shook negatively. "Well, then, did anybody see anyone get up in the middle of the night?" More head shaking. "One more question. Who were you sleeping close to?"

"Well, the four of us were sleeping together," George volunteered. "You, me, Bess under the blanket, and Ned in his sleeping bag."

"And Linda and I slept side by side," Ralph said. Linda blushed.

"I slept next to Tod," Mike volunteered. "And I can guarantee that he didn't get up."

"Right," Sammy muttered. "And I'll bet he says the same for you."

"How about you, Sammy?" Nancy asked.

"I slept next to Mercedes, if you have to know," Sammy said loftily. "And Paula slept on the other side of me."

Nancy turned to Max. "That leaves you, Max," she said.

"Yeah, I know where that leaves me," he replied bitterly. "Under suspicion. I slept by myself."

"Actually, *everybody's* under suspicion," Nancy said, turning back to the group. "Any of us could have gotten up without the others knowing. I'm proof of that."

Paula stepped forward. "Well, now that our internationally famous detective has struck out, we've got some important decisions to make," she said.

Nancy looked closely at Paula. She looked almost satisfied.

"Yeah," Sammy said. "What *do* we do? Do we hike out downriver?"

"No way," Max answered firmly. "This gorge goes on for three or four miles with no banks. There's no way we can walk along the edge of the river."

Ned looked up the cliff wall. At first it had seemed almost vertical, stretching fifty feet or more straight toward the sky, but he could see places for footholds. "It looks like a tough climb out that way," he said, "but we might be able to make it."

"I don't know . . . ," Paula said.

Nancy brightened. "Wait a minute. We've got a radio. Right?"

"Right," Paula answered slowly.

"Then why don't we radio for help? In fact," Nancy asked, looking questioningly at Paula, "why didn't we radio yesterday after the accident?"

"Because," Paula said almost too quickly. "You—that is I— didn't think the signal would reach that far." Her amber eyes blazed at Nancy. "Are you satisfied?"

Nancy wasn't sure, Paula looked so flustered.

"Hey, I'm almost positive the signal would reach," Mike put in confidently. "It broadcasts through the repeater tower at the ranger station."

"Yeah," Max said, "the tower would boost the signal so that it could be received at ranger headquarters."

"Then if we send them a message, they'll come to rescue us?" Linda asked hopefully.

"That's right," Mike said, and he and Max suddenly looked sheepish.

"I don't know what's wrong with me," Max grumbled. "With

everything going on, I didn't think of the most obvious thing." His face reddened. "I forgot we even *had* a radio."

"Me too," Mike admitted. "The way my mind's been working the past day or so, I was thinking it got dumped when the first raft flipped."

"Where *is* the radio?" Bess asked.

Max reached under the platform on the raft. "Right here," he said, pulling out a small, waterproof box.

The radio was a small, handheld model with a pull-out antenna, almost like a walkie-talkie. Max flipped on the power switch. Nancy, watching closely, saw his mouth tighten. He flipped the switch again.

"What's wrong?" she asked.

Max shook his head impatiently. "I don't know," he said, clicking the switch on and off, "but the power won't go on."

"Ohhh," Bess and Linda chorused nervously.

Max raised his shoulders, heaving a sigh. "Well, Ned, I guess your direction is the one we take."

"Direction?" Ned said quizzically. "What direction?"

"Up," Max said grimly, eyeing the steep cliff face. "Straight up."

CHAPTER TEN

Paula grabbed the radio away from Max. "What do you mean, it's not working? Didn't you check the batteries before we left?"

For a moment, Max looked confused. "Yeah," he mumbled. "I even put new ones in. The radio was working just fine."

Paula fiddled with the power switch. "Well, it's not working now," she said disgustedly. "Great. That's all we need, to be stranded out here without an operating radio."

"Here, let *me* see," Mike said, reaching for it. He took the batteries out and then put them back in again—that didn't help. Then he took the back off.

"Check the diode," Nancy said suddenly.

Mike looked up. "You know something about radios?"

"Not much," she admitted. "But I had a case once where a diode was stolen from a radio. Does this one need a diode?"

"A tiny one," Mike said. Intently, he bent over the radio. "Hey! The diode's gone!"

Linda pointed at Max. "You were the one who put the radio in the raft," she said accusingly. "I *saw* you. You were the last one to touch it. *You* must have taken the diode!"

"You have no right to make accusations like that," Bess retorted. "The person who sabotaged the raft could just as easily have removed the diode. Right, Nancy?"

Nancy nodded. "Actually, it could have been taken at any time." She examined the radio case. Even if she had brought her fingerprint kit along, it would have been a hopeless job. The case was made of a roughly grained vinyl that wouldn't hold a print. And there didn't seem to be any other clues.

Mike closed up the radio again. "Well, that's that," he said.

Nancy looked at him. Whoever had done this had to know what the diode was and where to look for it. Maybe Mike had destroyed the radio and Tod had destroyed the raft—all as part of some silly prank.

She shook her head. Surely not. But the whole thing was beginning to seem like a hopeless muddle.

Paula glanced at Nancy. "I don't suppose our girl detective has any ideas about who did it," she remarked sarcastically.

Nancy shook her head. "Afraid not," she replied. Then she noticed that Max was staring at Paula, dumbfounded, as if he had suddenly thought of something but wasn't quite sure whether he ought to believe it.

"So?" Sammy demanded. "Do we just sit here and wait for somebody to raft downriver and spot us?"

"I don't think anybody will be coming down until the middle of next week," Paula said. "I checked the schedule board yesterday, just before we left. The next trip downriver doesn't leave until a week from Wednesday."

"By that time we could starve to death!" Linda exclaimed.

"Well, we *have* got another alternative," Paula said.

Everybody looked at her. "What's that?" George asked.

Paula pointed to the top of the cliff. "We can hike out," she replied. "It's a tough climb, as Ned said, but we *could* make it. Once we get to the top, there's a trail, maybe five or six miles back in the woods, that leads to the ranger station, which is another eight or nine miles away. I think I could find the trail."

"Yes, but that means a fourteen-mile hike!" Sammy exclaimed. She looked at Max. "What do *you* think?"

Max gave an uncertain shrug. "I'm a good woodsman, but I don't know anything about the trails in this particular area. We'll have to rely on Paula."

Paula's amber eyes were narrowed to slits. "Maybe some of you don't want to rely on me," she said, turning to Nancy. "You're not afraid of a little walking, are you, Nancy?"

Nancy caught the unpleasant undertone, but answered quietly, "No, I'm not afraid of walking—as long as we're sure of where we're going. At least on the river, we know where we are. Once we're in the wilderness, we could get lost pretty easily." She sneaked a glance at Max, who was still staring at Paula.

"Well, I can't guarantee anything," Paula said crossly. "But I don't see that we've got any alternative."

"Well, then," Ned spoke up quickly, "maybe we ought to take an inventory and figure out how much food we've got. How long will this hike take us?"

"We'll probably get to the ranger station late tomorrow," Paula said.

"And we've got only enough food for today?" Ned asked.

"Looks like we'll be going on half-rations," George said glumly.

"Yes, but that means we won't have to carry so much," Paula pointed out. "Just our sleeping gear and whatever jackets and sweaters you have. It's going to get pretty cold up there tonight." She looked around. "Ned, will you and Max inventory the food and distribute it among the packs so that we all have an equal load to carry? Max!"

"Huh?" Max seemed to be jerked away from his thoughts. "What did you say?"

Paula put her hands on her hips. "If you'd been listening," she said, "you'd know. I asked you and Ned to inventory the food. Mercedes, there's a tarp in the raft. Better get it out—Tod will give you a hand. The tarp might come in handy if it rains tonight. Ralph, get the flashlight and the lantern." She fished in her pocket. "Bess?"

"Yes?"

"Here's a compass. I'm giving you the job of checking our direction so we don't end up wandering in circles. When we get to the top of the cliff, I'll show you how to read it. Okay?"

"Well, okay," Bess said. "I mean, I'm not very good at things like that, but—"

"You'll do fine," Paula said shortly. She picked up her red-

and-black plaid jacket and slung it over her shoulder. "Okay, everybody. Let's break camp! Take what you need to keep warm and dry, but don't take anything that you don't want to carry for the next two days!"

The cliff wasn't quite as steep as it had looked from below. Bushes and small trees grew in the rocky rubble, and the hikers found plenty of hand- and footholds.

"I want you to climb in front of me, Nancy," Ned said as they got ready. "That way, if you slip, I'm right behind you."

The climb took the group almost two hours. The rocks were soft and crumbling from exposure to the weather, and Nancy had to concentrate on where she put her feet. Above her, Bess and George moved up carefully, pressing close to the steep slope. Nobody said much.

They were almost at the top when Nancy heard a scream from below, then the sound of loose rock sliding and the babble of frantic voices.

"What's happening?" Nancy called to Ned.

"I think it's Linda," he said anxiously, peering down. He pulled a coil of rope from his shoulder. "Hey, down there! Do you need a hand?"

It took three of them—Ralph, Max, and Ned—to hoist Linda to the top. The others were there already, sprawled on the rocky ground, breathless and weary from the climb.

"She's going to be all right. It's only a sprain," Paula said brusquely, probing Linda's ankle with her fingers. "Too bad we don't have any ice for it."

"It hurts," Linda moaned. "I don't think I can walk."

"You'll be okay," Ralph comforted her. "I'll help you."

Ned came out of the woods with a long branch. "We can make a crutch out of this," he said.

After a few minutes, Linda's crutch was ready and the group started out, following Paula. Bess, with the compass, was right behind her.

"We're going northeast," Paula told them, before they started. "Since there's no trail, and the terrain is so rough, we'll be moving slowly. We don't want anybody getting lost."

Nancy nodded, and she and the others set out through the woods. At every step, huge swarms of mosquitoes flew up, and Nancy had to keep swatting them. The sweat poured off her face in little rivers.

"Some vacation," George grunted as she pushed up a vine and tried to crawl under it. "I'll have to call our travel agent when we get home. I think we got into the wrong contest."

"Either that," Nancy said, half chuckling, "or we won the wrong prize."

George swallowed a giggle. "Do you suppose Paula knows where's she's going?" she asked, peering through the tangle of underbrush. "I'd hate to walk through this stuff *twice*."

"Hey!" Ned kidded. "How can you doubt her? After all, she's got Bess right beside her, carrying our one and only compass."

"That's exactly what I'm worried about," George said.

• • •

It was nearly noon by the time they stopped for lunch in a large clearing. The sun filtered through the dense trees, and Bess took off her jacket and tossed it on a nearby rock. She was eating a sandwich, her knees pulled up wearily, her back to a tree, when Nancy sat down beside her.

"Tired?" Nancy asked, taking a bite of her own sandwich. It was the last of the peanut butter, and there was only enough bread for one more meal.

"You know it." Bess sighed. "Paula's in good shape, and keeping up with her in these woods is tough."

"I don't suppose you've found out anything about her," Nancy said, lowering her voice and looking around to be sure she wasn't overheard.

Bess shook her head. "I've tried talking to her, but she won't say a word. I did notice Max watching her in a funny way, though. It's as if he knows something about her that the rest of us don't."

"Yeah, I noticed that, too," Nancy said. She finished her sandwich and stood up, brushing herself off. "And maybe now is a good time to ask him about it." But everybody else was finishing lunch, too, and Nancy didn't have a chance.

"Will you get the compass?" Paula asked Bess just then. "I want to check our direction before we get started again."

"Sure," Bess said, reaching for her jacket, which was spread out on the rock. She felt in the pocket. Then her face went white. Frantically she began to search the other pockets as well.

"What's wrong?" Paula snapped. "Where's the compass?"

"I don't know!" Bess exclaimed, sitting down limply on the rock. "It's not in my pocket and I know it was there before lunch. The compass is gone—now we'll never find our way out of here!"

CHAPTER ELEVEN

Gone?" George gasped. "You lost the compass? I can't believe it. Bess Marvin, you are so *incredibly* careless."

"But I *wasn't* careless!" Bess wailed, holding her jacket like a shield against her. "It *was* here. Somebody must have taken it!"

Nancy glanced at the others. Mike, Tod, and Ralph were staring at Bess, grim faced. It was obvious that they agreed with George: Bess had lost the compass. Sammy, Linda, and Mercedes had their arms around one another, and Linda was sobbing. They seemed to think that George was right, too. But Max was watching Paula, and he wore the same odd look on his face that Nancy had seen earlier.

What was just as interesting was that Paula seemed to be aware of his gaze. She kept her head turned away from him, and her cheeks were flushed.

She looked darkly at Bess. "Without that compass, I don't know if we *will* find the trail," she said. "These woods are really confusing. We could walk around in circles for a week!"

"What's going to happen?" Sammy whispered. "Are we going to *die* here?"

"Nancy Drew is supposed to be the expert in finding things out," Paula said. "Why don't you ask her?"

"Wait a minute!" George shouted. "Nancy doesn't know anything about the woods. *You're* supposed to be *that* expert!"

"Yeah, well, you can't expect me to be much of an expert without a compass," Paula growled.

"Nancy, I have to talk to you," Ned said quietly, coming up behind her. He pulled her into the woods. "Bess didn't lose the compass," he said when they were out of earshot. "I saw who took it!"

Nancy waited expectantly.

"It was *Paula*," said Ned, mystified. "She waited until she thought nobody was watching, and she took it out of Bess's pocket."

"Paula!" Nancy exclaimed. "Why would she do that?"

Ned shook his head. "I don't know. But I wasn't the only one who saw her take it. Max did, too. And it was funny: *I* was surprised, but I don't think Max was. I think he half suspected that Paula might try something."

"I saw him give her a strange look this morning, after we discovered the raft. Maybe he suspected then that she had wrecked it. I think he's been keeping an eye on her all day."

Ned's face was tight. "Well, if that's what he's been doing, Paula knows," he said. "She looked up and saw him watching her take the compass."

"That *really* complicates things," Nancy said.

Ned frowned. "Do you think Paula could have destroyed the raft?"

"It's possible, although for the life of me I can't think of a motive. I can't think of a motive for her taking the compass, either. But I'm still disturbed by it—the broken radio, too. Right now, though, I want to find out what *Max* thinks."

"Are you going to question him?"

Nancy hesitated. "I was going to. But instead, maybe we should keep our eye on the two of them for a while. We might learn more." She laughed a little. "At least we're not as lost as Paula wants us to think we are."

Ned put his arms around Nancy's shoulders. "Listen, Nan," he said, turning her toward him as they walked back to face the group. "We're in a tight spot right now, but whatever happens," he went on, his voice getting tight, "I want you to know how much I love you."

Nancy felt her arms go around his neck. "I love you, too, Ned," she whispered, letting herself forget Paula, forget the river, forget everything but the kiss Ned bent down to give her.

"Nancy!" It was Bess calling. "Nancy, where are you?" Bess appeared behind Nancy and Ned, George right behind her.

"Here I am." Reluctantly Nancy broke away from Ned's arms.

"Nancy, you've got to get George off my back," Bess begged, tears streaking down her dusty face.

"Get off your back?" George exploded. "The way I feel right now I'll be on your back for thirty-five years—if we live that long." George spun Bess around. "I've put up with lost car keys, lost plane tickets, even lost money—but this thing, Bess Marvin . . ."

"Knock it off!" Nancy held her hand up. She turned to George. "Bess didn't lose the compass. Ned saw Paula take it out of Bess's pocket."

George's eyes grew round. "Paula!" she exclaimed.

Bess stared at Nancy, consternation on her face. "Why would Paula do that? Is she *trying* to get us lost?"

"It's beginning to look that way," Nancy admitted. "Max saw her steal the compass, too, and I think he also suspects her of holing the raft."

George put her arms around Bess. "I'm sorry I blew up at you," she said. "Really."

"It's okay, George," Bess replied, patting her cousin on the shoulder. "Everybody is uptight right now. We're in a real mess."

"Bess is right," Ned said soberly. "Some of those kids—Linda and Sammy especially—look as if they might go to pieces at any minute. If George can blow up this way, others are bound to."

"That's what worries me," Nancy said. "We can't tell the others just yet about Paula taking the compass, so they're going to continue to accuse Bess." She turned to her friend. "Can you stick it out for a little while?"

Bess smiled weakly. "As long as I know you guys believe me."

"George, it might be a good idea if you continued to act angry at Bess," Nancy said. "That'll keep Paula from getting suspicious."

"My pleasure," George teased. She gave Bess a friendly poke.

"George!" Bess responded, trying not to laugh.

When Nancy and her friends rejoined the group, they found

them quarreling about which direction to take. Nancy could see that the group spirit was beginning to deteriorate rapidly.

"This is all your fault," Sammy told Bess bitterly as they began to make their way through the woods again. "We're all going to *die* in this wilderness, and *you're* responsible!"

"Sammy's right," George agreed, playing her part. "If you hadn't lost the compass, at least we would know which direction we were heading in!"

Looking unhappy, Bess didn't answer.

Except for the occasional angry quarrels that seemed to break out with greater frequency, the group walked in silence for the next two hours. The terrain became even rougher as they moved away from the river. Walking was very difficult, especially for Linda, who was limping along with her crutch, leaning heavily on Ralph and moaning every few minutes.

Nancy walked within hearing distance of Max and Paula, keeping a careful eye on them.

Suddenly she was aware of the noise of tumbling water. "What's that?" she asked, catching up to Max and Paula. "Is it Lost River? Are we going in circles?"

"I don't think so," Paula said. She had tied the sleeves of her jacket around her waist, but now she pulled the jacket on. "If I'm right," she continued, "that's Little Horn Creek. The trail isn't too far away."

Little Horn Creek was in a deep ravine, full of rocks and tangled trees. The group, which was nearly exhausted, stopped to rest on a rocky ledge, partway up the cliff over the ravine.

"Thank goodness," Sammy said with a sigh, sinking down against the rock. "I can't walk another step."

"You've got to," Tod told her. "It's either that or stay here and starve to death—or die of exposure."

Sammy burst into tears. "Stop saying that! You're just trying to scare me!"

"No," Mike said quietly, "it's the truth."

Max seemed to have made up his mind about something. He looked up at the cliff and then at Paula. "The cliff top looks clear," he said. "The climb is a little rough, Paula, but I think you and I can make it. Let's climb up there and see if we can tell where we are."

Paula considered his suggestion. "Good idea," she said, after a moment. She raised her voice. "The rest of you stay here and rest. Max and I are going to climb to the top. We'll be back in a few minutes." The two of them began to scale the cliff, which rose up vertically behind the ledge.

"I wish we could climb up there and hear what they say," Nancy said fretfully, watching them climb the sheer wall.

"No way, Drew," Ned said, coming up behind her. "Climbing that rock is a job for experts. I have the feeling that Max picked the top of the cliff to talk to Paula because he knew we couldn't follow up there, and he didn't want any uninvited listeners." He pulled Nancy down beside him. "Come on, relax. There's nothing we can do but wait."

They waited. In about fifteen minutes, Nancy began to stir worriedly. At that moment, she heard Paula's voice, although the words were indistinguishable. A few small rocks showered down the cliff ten yards to their right. Then there was the sound of a violent scuffle and a loud, dull thump. "No, Max!" Paula cried clearly. Nancy could hear terror in her voice. "Don't!"

"Max! Paula!" Ned shouted, looking up.

For a minute or two there was silence. Then, in a flash of red and black, a limp body hurtled spread-eagled through the air and down into the depths of the creek!

CHAPTER TWELVE

That was Paula!" Linda screamed.

Mercedes moaned and turned away, covering her eyes. Ashen-faced, Sammy put her arms comfortingly around her.

"Do you think she's dead?" Tod asked, peering over the edge. "Can you see her? Where is she?"

"There," Mike said excitedly, pointing down the ravine. "In the creek." They all watched in incredulous horror as Paula's plaid jacket ballooned up in the deep water of the creek far below, buoying the body along almost like a life jacket. It drifted lazily in the water for a minute or two, then it was sucked into the swift current and swept down over a jumble of rocks and out of sight.

"We've got to get down there!" Mercedes said, struggling hysterically against Sammy's restraining arms.

Ned shook his head. "It's a fifty-foot cliff," he said. "None of us has the experience to climb it, especially without any rock-climbing gear. Anyway, the chances of survival from a fall like that are next to nothing." He gave Mercedes a sympathetic look. "We'll have to send a team back to recover her body—after *we* get out."

"Max!" Bess suddenly exclaimed. She looked up the cliff. "Where *is* he?"

Tod laughed harshly. "If you were Max, would you hang around to shake hands with your audience after you'd murdered somebody?"

"Murdered?" Linda whispered, her mouth dropping open. "You mean Max pushed her?"

"Wait a second. We don't know that Max—" Bess began hesitantly.

George whipped around to confront her. "For Pete's sake, Bess. We heard their fight. We heard Paula scream. And then we saw her go over. It's as simple as one, two, three. Paula's dead and Max killed her!"

Bess sat down and put her face in her hands.

"I'm afraid George may be right, Bess," Nancy said gently, kneeling beside her. "But there is still a chance Max may not have killed Paula. After all, we don't know exactly what happened up there—only what we saw and heard."

"What do you want? A signed confession?" Tod said.

"But why?" asked Ralph. "Did he and Paula sabotage both rafts and the radio just to get us stranded out here?" He shook his head in puzzlement. "It doesn't make sense."

"Maybe Paula found out that Max did all those things," Tod suggested. "And when she confronted him with what she knew, he pushed her over the edge to shut her up."

"Could be," Mike said. "Or maybe she was getting on his case about capsizing the raft. Between that and those drownings last year, he'd be finished on the river. Maybe she said some-thing—"

"Listen, everybody," Nancy broke in. "Before you get too far out on a limb with your theories, I'd better tell you that Paula stole the compass out of Bess's pocket. Ned saw her take it—and so did Max."

"*Paula* took it?" Mercedes exclaimed. "Why?" It seemed to Nancy that there was an odd note in her voice, almost as if *Mercedes* had half suspected that that might happen.

Nancy nodded, convinced Mercedes knew more than she was revealing. Maybe with Paula out of the picture, Mercedes would be willing to talk.

"I think Max believed Paula holed the raft, as well," Nancy continued, "and that he thought he knew what her motive was. I intended to question him about it this afternoon, but now it's too late."

"But *why*?" Sammy demanded. "Ralph's right. It just doesn't make sense. Why would Paula take the compass?"

"Maybe she wanted to keep us lost, for some reason we don't understand," Ned pointed out. "Don't forget, as long as *she* had the compass, *she* wasn't lost. She could find her way out—even if the rest of us couldn't."

"So you're suggesting that *Paula* was up to something," George said thoughtfully.

Nancy nodded. "Yes, but we probably won't know what until we can talk to Max. That's why it's so important that we find him."

Sammy shivered. "Well, *you* can have the pleasure of finding him. If *I* saw him, I'd run as fast as I could in the other direction. He's dangerous!"

"Right now," Nancy said, "we have to concentrate on finding our way out of here. Then we have to find Max—dangerous or not."

They sat for a few more minutes on the ledge, trying to decide which direction they should take.

"Paula seemed to be headed up this creek," Ned pointed out, picking up his pack and adjusting it over his shoulders. "I think we should keep on in that direction. Tod, you and Mike are the ones who are most at home in the woods. I vote that you try to pick out the trail for us."

They set off again with their packs, even more subdued this time, following Tod and Mike. The going got steeper and steeper, and the underbrush seemed to grow more dense with every yard. Just as Nancy had decided that she was too exhausted to climb over one more twig, the terrain flattened out and the forest opened up. Ahead was the dim outline of what looked like an old logging road, leading in both directions into the dense woods.

"Finally," Linda moaned, sitting down in the middle of the trail.

"Thank goodness!" Sammy said, dropping her pack wearily. "I was beginning to think we'd *never* find it!"

"This isn't luck," Tod said, grinning. "It's superior woodsmanship!"

"Whatever it is," Nancy said, "I'm grateful. Which way is the ranger station?" she asked Mike. "Right or left?"

Mike looked blank. "You've got me," he said.

"Do *you* know?" Nancy asked Tod.

Tod frowned. "Not for sure. But I'd say it's probably that way." He jerked his thumb to the right.

"What makes you say that?" Mike asked quickly. "If I had to guess, I'd say it's probably *that* way." He pointed to the left. "Once I saw the ranger station on a map, and I think it's farther south than this."

"But the ranger station has a fire tower," Tod argued. "They always build fire towers high up. And the trail to the right goes *up*."

"I think you're dead wrong," Mike said flatly.

"Hey, you guys," Ned said. "We've got to make a decision."

"We could split up," Ralph suggested tentatively. "Whichever group reaches the ranger station could get help for the others."

"No way!" Sammy said. "With ten of us, we're a big enough group to handle most situations. A smaller group might get into trouble."

Ned nodded vigorously. "I agree. There's safety in numbers."

"Let's vote," George said. "I vote for going uphill."

Nancy counted hands. The majority wanted to go to the right.

"I just don't think I can walk uphill anymore," Linda said, beginning to cry again.

"We don't have any choice," Ralph said, helping her up.

"Come on. The sooner we get going, the sooner we'll be there."

"Well, we can't count on getting there today," Ned reminded them.

"You mean we've got to spend the night in the woods?" Linda asked.

"I mean that Paula told us that the ranger station was seven or eight miles away, once we got on the fire trail," Ned said. "That's a good five-hour hike, at the rate we're going. And it's going to get dark soon. We need to think about finding somewhere to camp."

"Okay, everybody," Tod said. "Let's start keeping our eyes open for a campsite." He shook their only canteen. "And a spring, too. We're almost out of water."

"Out of water?" Mercedes asked faintly. "What about the food?"

Ned shook his head. "We've got some beef jerky and some dried fruit left," he said. "And three packages of instant soup. In other words, there's enough for supper and maybe breakfast, if we're willing to go on short rations tonight." He frowned. "Let's hope we find some ripe berries."

"Remember what happened the last time we found ripe berries," Bess reminded him.

The group gathered themselves together and set out along the trail.

Before long the sun began to drop toward the western horizon. In places, the trail was littered with rocks—some of them very large—and everyone had to pick their way gingerly across the unstable ground, trying not to trigger rock slides.

Nancy was walking a few paces ahead of Ned when suddenly she felt a peculiar prickle between her shoulder blades. She turned around, but there was only Ned behind her. He grinned wearily.

"Everything okay?" he asked. "You've been pulling farther and farther behind."

Nancy wiped the sweat from her face. "I may be wrong, but I think we're being watched—and I want to watch back."

"That's funny. I've been thinking the same thing."

Nancy paused, listening. "Ned!" she exclaimed, looking up. "Someone's—"

Her voice was drowned out by a loud crash, and a rumble that seemed to shake the earth. Nancy stood frozen. A huge boulder had broken loose from its place on the hillside above. It was hurtling straight at her.

CHAPTER THIRTEEN

Nancy! Look out!" Ned shouted. He lunged at her, grabbing her arm and pulling her out of the path of the careening boulder. Nancy could feel the huge rock rumbling the earth beneath her feet as it thundered down the hill. When it reached the bottom, it tore like an out-of-control truck into two pines, splintering them at the base, before it rolled to a shuddering halt in a spruce thicket.

As Ned put his arms around her, Nancy began to tremble uncontrollably. Ned's arms felt so strong and protective, as if they could shield her from anything the world could throw at her. She leaned against him, gazing up the hill, and caught a glimpse of shadowy movement, something darting into the trees. Was it an animal she had seen—or a human?

Suddenly she realized the enormity of what had just happened. If it hadn't been for Ned's quick action, she'd be smashed like those trees. She swayed dizzily and sagged against Ned.

He held her tightly, then lowered her gently onto a rock.

After a few minutes, Nancy pushed her hair out of her eyes. "I'm okay," she said shakily. Then she laughed. "Lucky we let everyone go on ahead. At least they didn't see me playing handball with that boulder."

Ned grinned for a moment, tracing his finger along her cheek. But as he helped Nancy to her feet, he looked down at her, soberly. "I was scared, Nancy," he said hoarsely. "You could have been killed."

"Ned," Nancy said, "I saw something moving up there, after the boulder came down. Do you suppose . . ."

". . . that it was Max?"

Nancy nodded.

"I didn't see what you saw, Nan, but it's entirely possible."

"Max might not have intended to kill Paula, but she's dead. Now he's got to worry about us. If we get out of here alive, he knows we'll go straight to the police!"

"So he's got to kill us?" Ned asked.

"If he's guilty," Nancy answered. "Or he might try to scare us so thoroughly that we keep our mouths shut." Nancy shuddered. "Hey," she said, "will you lend me your jacket for a little while? Thinking about Max out there loose gives me the chills."

Ned wrapped his jacket around her. "We've got to let the others know what happened," he said. "Otherwise I'd keep you warm myself."

Nancy grinned at him. "Control yourself, Nickerson—for the time being anyway," she whispered.

The rest of the group had already chosen a camping spot for the night and had divided up the responsibilities for getting settled.

Mercedes was bent over the fire, her cheeks flushed with the heat. She was stirring soup in a small aluminum pan, balanced carefully on three rocks.

Nancy sat down beside her. "Mmm, that smells good," she said appreciatively. "Vegetable?"

Mercedes nodded. "I wish we had more. I'm afraid this is just going to be enough to whet everyone's appetite."

"Well, maybe we'll get lucky tomorrow and find a berry patch," Nancy replied, laughing. "Minus the bear. Or a creek—then maybe we could catch some fish or something."

Mercedes laughed a little, too. "This *has* been some trip, hasn't it?" she said gravely. She shivered. "I can't believe what happened to Paula. When I get home, I'm going to have to tell her family . . ."

Nancy nodded sympathetically. Then, choosing her words carefully, she said, "Earlier, I asked if you knew about the contest. I was wondering if you remembered anything else about it."

Mercedes shook her head. "I *told* you," she said impatiently. "I don't know a thing. The contest was already set up when I first heard about the trip."

"Well, then, maybe you can tell me something about Paula's business," Nancy went on, "or about her friendship with Max."

Mercedes frowned. "I don't think they were friends at all. Max was just somebody who was available for this trip. Somebody who knew the river."

"Okay, what about her family?" Nancy asked. "Did your families see each other very often?"

Mercedes looked away. "Why do you want to know? There's no point in dragging up the past."

"What past?" Nancy asked sharply.

Mercedes looked flustered. "I—I just meant the things that have happened in the past two days," she said. "We've got to get out of here. What's the point in trying to figure out why things happened the way they did? Especially now that—" She choked. "Now that Paula is dead." Her eyes filled with tears and she turned back to the fire.

"You might be right. But why," Nancy persisted, "weren't you surprised to learn that Paula had taken the compass? Why did you suspect her?" Nancy knew that if Mercedes would open up, she'd have the key to the case.

"I don't want to talk anymore," Mercedes said sullenly. "You can't *make* me talk to you."

"No," Nancy admitted. "But when we get back to civilization, the police can."

"I'll cross that bridge when I come to it," Mercedes said, removing the pot from the fire and standing up. "Who knows? We might not even get back to civilization. We've still got another day to go, at least." She turned away from Nancy. "Okay, everybody," she called, "the soup's ready."

While Nancy was eating the soup and the piece of beef jerky she had been rationed, she thought about what Mercedes had told her: *There's no point in dragging up the past.* Nancy was sure Mercedes *hadn't* meant the events of the last two days. In fact, she was sure Mercedes knew something—

something she wasn't telling. Something she wouldn't tell.

Nancy snuggled into Ned's jacket, glad he wasn't cold and she could keep it around her. Then she frowned, thinking more about the case. Sure, there weren't a lot of clues, but she sensed there were a couple of possibilities right under her nose that she was overlooking. Every once in a while they began to form in her mind, then vanished before she had a chance to focus on them.

Well, she thought resolutely, Mercedes couldn't keep her from finding out the truth. Nothing could, not even the frustration she was feeling. Nancy Drew always got to the bottom of things, and she'd get to the bottom of this case, too—if it *killed* her.

When supper was over, everyone huddled wearily around the fire, scratched and sore from their long hike. There wasn't much conversation. It was a moonless night, and outside the circle of firelight, the dark pressed in ominously.

Then in the near distance, the quiet was shattered by an eerie scream.

"What was that?" Linda cried out, clinging to Ralph.

Tod laughed. "Just a mountain lion," he replied.

"But don't worry," Mike said. "A mountain lion won't attack you unless you corner him. He's a whole lot more fond of rabbits and squirrels than he is of people."

Sammy shivered. "Well, he can keep his rabbits and his squirrels," she said. "I'll settle for a hamburger with fries and onions."

George groaned tragically, rubbing her stomach. "*Please.* Don't talk about real food. You might just as well knock me out—it would be much kinder."

Nancy threw a glance at Ned, who was sitting next to her. Now was the time to tell everyone what had happened before supper that evening. Briefly, she told her story.

"It must have been Max!" Ralph and Linda exclaimed when Nancy had finished.

"Max?" Bess asked, in a half-longing voice.

"Oh, will you stop, Bess," George said impatiently. "Haven't we got enough trouble without—"

"It's trouble, all right," Nancy said. "If Max really is dangerous, he's not going to let us out of here to tell the police what happened."

Bess shook her head stubbornly. "I can't *believe* that."

"You might believe it if you'd been standing on that trail, staring up at that boulder coming down on Nancy," Ned said. "It was as big as a house. And it sounded like a freight train."

Nancy shuddered, remembering how frightened she had been—and how strong and supportive Ned's arms had felt around her when for a minute she had lost her own strength. It was ironic, she thought. She had wanted Ned to come on this trip so that he could feel a little protective about her. Well, he certainly was protecting her.

"Yeah, but you don't *know* that somebody pushed the rock," Bess was insisting. "It might just have come loose. After all, rock slides happen here all the time, even when there's no one around. Anyway," she went on insistently, "you aren't even sure you saw somebody up there. How do you know that it wasn't just your imagination?"

"I don't," Nancy admitted. "Just the same, we can't afford to take any chances. If Max *did* push that boulder down, he's dangerous." She looked around at the group. "We've got to be careful."

"Careful?" Sammy asked, frowning. "And just how do we do that?"

"Well, for one thing," Nancy answered, "we shouldn't go off by ourselves."

"Yeah," Ned said, "and we need to pay attention to what's going on around us, so that Max isn't able to sneak up on us."

"Then it might be a good idea to keep watches tonight," Mike said, stirring the fire.

"Right," Nancy agreed.

"I was afraid of losing sleep tonight," Bess said, making a face, "but I had it figured a little differently. I thought my *hunger* would keep me awake!"

Ned drew the first watch and Nancy the second. "I'll wake you up in an hour," he promised as Nancy crawled under her blanket between Bess and George. He bent over and kissed her.

"Thanks," Nancy said sleepily. "And Ned?"

"Uh-huh?"

"Thanks for being there this afternoon. It feels good to be alive." She smiled. "You know, if we get out of this in one piece, I swear I'll never take another vacation the rest of my life. Detective work is a lot safer."

Ned laughed and gave her another quick kiss.

In an hour, he awakened her and she took her turn beside the fire. At the end of her hour, she woke Mike, who had the third watch, before going back to sleep. But her dreams were full of gigantic boulders that roared down on her.

Nancy woke at dawn, curled up into a tight ball, cold and stiff. The campfire was out and Ralph, who had the last watch, was drowsing beside it.

No wonder I'm cold, Nancy thought. My blanket slipped down. She tugged on the blanket, but the end of it seemed to be caught on something. A rock? She raised her head to look— and froze.

A huge rattlesnake lay coiled on the blanket. At Nancy's movement, its head came up, staring at Nancy with beady amber eyes.

CHAPTER FOURTEEN

The rattler's tail was buzzing like a swarm of angry bees. What could Nancy do? Even though her feet weren't trapped under it, if she moved a muscle—or if George or Bess turned over—the snake was bound to strike.

"Ned," Nancy whispered urgently. "Ned, wake up!"

Ned stirred sleepily on the other side of the fire. "What?" he mumbled.

"Ned," she said again, in a low voice. "There's a huge snake on the foot of my blanket."

"A snake?" Ned exclaimed, throwing off his blanket. "Stay put, Nancy. Don't move!"

"Don't you move too fast, either," she whispered.

"What's going on?" Ralph sat up beside the cold fire, rubbing his eyes. "Is it Max? Where is he?"

"No, it's a snake," Ned replied softly, pulling on his shoes and signaling for Ralph to stay still.

The snake's head began to weave back and forth and its tongue flicked nervously. Beside Nancy, George mumbled something in her sleep. Oh, please, George, Nancy thought, don't turn over! Aloud, she said, "Hurry, Ned! I think it's getting ready to strike!" The buzz of the rattles grew louder.

Noiselessly, Ned circled around behind the snake. He bent down, picked up a large flat rock, and raised it high above his head. Just as the snake coiled itself to strike, Ned brought the rock down hard on its head. For a moment the snake twisted and writhed, and then it lay still.

"Oh, Ned," Nancy said.

"What's going on?" George asked, sitting up. "Who's throwing rocks?"

Bess stirred under the blanket and mumbled something.

George stared unbelievingly at the snake that Ned had stretched out across the foot of the blanket. "Nancy, it's a monster! It's big enough to have eaten both of us for breakfast—in one gulp."

Bess burrowed deeper into the blanket. "A monster?" she quavered. "Not another bear!"

Nancy laughed and yanked the blanket off Bess's head. "No, it's not another bear," she said teasingly, pulling her friend to a sitting position. "It's only a snake. Wake up and see."

"A snake!" Bess covered up her eyes. "I don't *want* to see!" After a minute she peeked between her fingers. "Yikes!" she screeched. "It *is* a snake!"

"Must be about five feet long," Ned said, hoisting the snake up on a stout stick. "And I count seven rattles and a button." He shook his head. "It's a good thing you woke up when you did, Nancy. This snake is packing a lot of venom. It could have killed you, or made you plenty sick."

"It's a good thing you were here to kill it, Ned," George pointed out.

"George is right," Nancy said. She looked up at Ned. "You know, that's twice in two days," she said soberly.

"Twice?" Ned asked.

"Last night you pulled me out of the path of the rock. This morning you killed the snake. That's twice in two days that you've saved my life."

Ned laughed. "Sounds like it's getting to be a habit."

Ned disposed of the snake under a large pile of rocks while the others got up and began to break camp. They shared the last of the dried fruit and beef jerky for breakfast and then made their way to a huckleberry patch that Mike had found near the spring the night before. They were careful to make lots of noise to ward off any bear that might be breakfasting there. Then they washed off the berry juice, filled their canteens at the spring, and gathered back at the campsite.

They were a ragtag bunch, Nancy thought, surveying the group. Linda's ankle was so badly swollen she could barely hobble, even with the help of Ned's crutch. Sammy's arms were breaking out with long, red streaks of something that looked like poison ivy, and she was scratching ferociously. Mercedes was withdrawn and uncommunicative, and Mike and Tod seemed to have quarreled again about the direction they should be taking.

"How far away is the ranger station?" Sammy asked. "How long will it take us to get there?"

Tod shrugged. "I'd guess we walked two or three miles yesterday, after we found the trail. If Paula estimated right, we've got maybe five or six miles to go."

"*If* we're going in the right direction," Mike said sullenly.

"There's no point in going through all of that again," Ned said sharply. "We agreed that we would go in this direction. Let's give ourselves a break and stop quarreling."

They set out, with Tod and Mike in front, followed by George and Bess, Mercedes, Sammy, Ralph and Linda, and Ned and Nancy. The trail was even more difficult than it had been the night before, a switchback that zigzagged up a mountain, through dense woods. The underbrush hung over the faint path like a thick green canopy, shutting out most of the sun, and even in the daylight the shadows seemed ominous. The day before, Nancy had developed a blister on her right heel, and it was rapidly getting worse, making walking even more difficult.

"Did you get a chance to talk to Mercedes last night?" Ned asked Nancy, helping her over a fallen log.

"Well, I tried," Nancy said with a sigh. She bent over to adjust her tennis shoe, trying to relieve the pressure on her blister. "I didn't get anywhere. She really clammed up. But she *did* say something interesting. When I asked her about Paula's family, she said she didn't want to drag up the past."

Ned looked at her. "So she *does* know something."

"Right. But whatever it is, she's not going to tell me."

"Do you suppose she'd tell me?"

"I don't know. It's worth a try."

"I might be able to catch her off guard." He grinned. "Or I might be able to use some of that charm that Sammy seemed to enjoy." He ducked the playful punch Nancy threw at him.

"Listen, Ned," Nancy said, "all joking aside, I think it's a good idea. Why don't you try to catch up to her now and see what you can find out?"

"Okay, I will." Ned put his hand on Nancy's shoulder. "But you've got to promise to catch up with Ralph and Linda and not hang around at the back of the group."

"I promise," Nancy said as Ned began to jog ahead. When he reached the curve in the path, he turned and waved, and Nancy waved back.

She wasn't worried—Ralph and Linda were somewhere ahead, within calling distance. But her blister was really beginning to hurt her. Nancy sat down on a rock and unlaced her shoe. Maybe the blister was getting infected. Sure enough, her whole heel was red and inflamed. She would have to try to catch up to Mike, who was carrying the first-aid kit, and see if he had a bandage.

Nancy was lacing her shoe up when she felt that prickle between her shoulder blades—the prickle that always meant she was being watched. She turned around. No one was in sight—but had she heard a rustling in the dense leaves? She got up and began to hurry down the trail, suddenly feeling very vulnerable and wishing that she hadn't let the others get so far ahead.

"Wait!" a rough voice commanded.

Nancy stopped, then turned, her heart in her mouth. There, lurching clumsily toward her through the thick underbrush, was Max! His shirt was ripped in several places, he wore a two-day stubble of beard, and there was an inch-long gash just above his right eye. He carried a heavy tree branch like a club, and his eyes were wild and staring.

Nancy started to run. She had to get away. Max was dangerous. He would kill her!

"Don't run!" he shouted, stumbling after her. "I have to talk—"

At that moment, Nancy tripped over a tree root and went sprawling. She struggled back to her feet just as Max reached her.

"You can't get away," he said, panting. "I won't let you!" He swung the club around. That was the last thing Nancy saw before the world went black.

CHAPTER FIFTEEN

For a minute Nancy thought the loud chirping in her ears was a noisy bird perched on a branch just over her head. But she soon realized that the sound was coming from inside her head. The side of her head hurt, and she tried to raise her hand to explore the ache with her fingers. But her hands were fastened tightly behind her back!

Without moving a muscle, Nancy opened her eyes cautiously, just enough to see. She was on her side in a clearing. Her back was resting against a granite boulder, and her cheek was pressed against a pillow of pale green moss. The ground was thickly carpeted with pine needles, but whatever Max had used to tie her with was cutting into the circulation at her wrists, and her fingers felt numb.

Max was crouched on the ground five or six feet away, whittling a spearlike point on a long straight stick and coughing intermittently. Nancy closed her eyes and tried to formulate some sort of logical plan of action through the painful throbbing in her head.

She didn't hear any voices. That could either mean the others hadn't yet discovered she was missing or that Max had dragged her so far off the trail that she wasn't able to hear them.

Using her numb fingers, she explored the binding around her wrists. It didn't feel very strong or heavy. Perhaps she could saw through it with a piece of jagged rock. She felt along the boulder at her back. Yes, there was a sharp, protruding seam, where the rock had weathered and split.

Very carefully, she began to push the rope up and down against the seam of the rock, trying not to move her shoulders. She peered surreptitiously through her lashes. Max had raised his head and was listening intently, as if he heard something in the distance. There was a look of fear on his face.

Nancy felt a surge of hope. Maybe Ned and the others were looking for her.

Max got painfully to his feet and picked up his club. When he moved away, out of the line of Nancy's vision, she heard the sound of his footsteps scuffling through the dry leaves and began sawing at the rope frantically.

When her hands came free, Nancy didn't move. Surprise was her only weapon. She had to get Max to come near enough to her so that she could catch him with one unexpected karate blow. But where was he?

In a few minutes, Max returned and leaned over to pick up his crude spear.

"O-oh," Nancy moaned, stirring a little. She could hear Max move toward her. "Nancy?" he said. She moaned again, more faintly this time.

"Nancy?" He bent over her and touched her shoulder. "Are

you okay?" he asked in a worried voice. "I didn't mean to hit you so hard, really. I just wanted to talk . . ."

Suddenly Nancy opened her eyes and leaped up. Taken by surprise, Max stumbled back, off balance, his mouth open. Nancy jumped at him, aiming a quick, hard blow to his solar plexus, and Max fell with a loud "Oomph!" He hit his head against a rock and went limp.

Nancy spun away and began to race through the woods. Her head still hurt, and she felt slightly dizzy and disoriented.

She slowed down to a walk, thinking maybe she shouldn't run until she figured out which direction to go in. A puzzled frown came to her face as she remembered Max's words. What was he talking about when he said that he hadn't meant to hurt her—that he just needed to talk? She stopped, hesitating.

"Nancy! Nancy, where are you!" It was Ned's voice, and he sounded frantic. "Nancy!"

"Here, Ned!" Nancy called. "I'm here!" She ran toward the sound of his voice, still calling his name.

"Oh, Nancy!" Breathlessly, Ned burst through a clearing and enveloped her in a huge hug. Bess and George were with him.

"What happened to you? Where have you been all this time?" Bess asked anxiously.

"We told the others we'd be looking for you—Linda was glad to have the rest," George said.

"But, Nan . . . ," Ned began.

"What?"

"Why did you leave the trail?"

"I didn't *leave* the trail," Nancy said, feeling the knot on the side of her head. "Max came up behind me and hit me over the head. He carried me pretty far into the woods and tied me up, but I managed to get loose and catch him by surprise. I got away just a few minutes ago."

"Oh, I'm so *glad* you're safe," George said, hugging her. She turned to Bess. "See? I keep telling you Max is dangerous."

Nancy waved her hand to interrupt. "Probably. But there's something that bothers me."

"Bothers you?" Ned asked. "I'd be bothered, too, if somebody knocked me out and tied me up in the middle of the woods."

"Yeah, I know." Nancy sighed. "But Max said something odd, just before I got away. He said that he hadn't meant to hit me so hard, that he just wanted to talk."

"But why would he want to *talk* to you?" Ned asked. "Was he trying to keep you from going to the police?"

Nancy shook her head. "I don't know, but I wish I hadn't hit him so quickly."

Ned considered. "You couldn't take that chance. But we could go back and talk to him now," he suggested. "There're four of us and only one of him."

Nancy looked around. "To tell you the truth, Ned," she confessed, "I don't know which direction I ran after I got away from Max."

Ned followed her scuffed track in the leaves. "It looks like you came from over there," he said, pointing. "Let's go that way."

But even though they searched the woods, they couldn't find the clearing where Max had held Nancy captive. Ned glanced down at his watch.

"It's nearly two o'clock," he said reluctantly. "The others are waiting. We'll have to push hard if we're going to reach the ranger station this afternoon."

"*If* the ranger station is in this direction," Nancy reminded him.

"Right." Ned sighed and took her hand as the four of them headed back to the trail. "If."

"Did you manage to talk to Mercedes?" Nancy asked after a few minutes.

"I tried," Ned answered.

"Oh. No luck?"

"Nope. She wouldn't say a word to me." Ned grinned and squeezed Nancy's hand. "Not even when I turned on some charm."

"Now I really *do* wish I'd had the sense to play possum just a few minutes longer," Nancy said unhappily. "If I'd just listened to Max, he might have given us a clue to this whole thing. I wish—"

"I wish you'd shut up, Detective Drew," Ned said. He slipped his arm affectionately around her shoulders. "It's good to have you safe. Even if you didn't get the clue you wanted."

"He kidnapped you!" Linda exclaimed hysterically when Nancy and her friends finally caught up with the rest of the group and told them what had happened. "He's going to kill us all. He'll track us down and isolate us, one at a time, and kill us."

Ralph rubbed her back. "Don't, Linda," he said helplessly.

Mercedes jumped up. "Maybe Max doesn't want to hurt the rest of us," she blurted. "Maybe he's just after Nancy."

"No!" Sammy exclaimed. "He's out to kill all of us. I'll bet he's somewhere nearby right now, spying on us, deciding which one of us will be next."

"What do you mean, maybe he was just out after me?" Nancy asked Mercedes. "Why would you think that?"

Mercedes pressed her lips into a tight line. "I don't know," she said. "I was just trying to make Linda feel better, that's all."

Linda began to cry harder, and Sammy looked as if she were going to burst into tears, too. Mercedes's face was closed and dark.

"Listen, everybody," Tod interrupted. "I know we're all tired and sore, but if we don't keep going, we're not going to get to the ranger station before dark."

The climb to the top of the ridge was one of the longest and most wearying hikes that Nancy had ever been on. Her heel was painful, and in spite of the beauty of the mountain, she kept her eyes on the ground, trying to pick out the easiest path. Ahead of her, Linda seemed to moan with every step, and she could hear Sammy complaining bitterly to Mike that they were going the wrong way.

At last they reached the top of the ridge.

"Oh, it's beautiful!" Bess exclaimed. "What a view!"

"And there's the fire tower!" Tod said triumphantly, pointing along the ridge to the left. "It's only a half-mile or so away!"

"All right!" Ralph let loose a giant whoop.

"Hey, wait a minute," Nancy said, her wide grin fading. "If the tower's deserted, will it still have a radio? We can still get a message out, can't we?"

"Yup," Tod assured her, "and the Forest Service will send a helicopter for us—probably before sunset! Of course, they'll have to send a team in to look for Paula's body."

With the ranger station so close, the group seemed a great deal more relaxed. Even Linda managed a smile when a small brown fawn hopped across the trail in front of them.

"I don't see any signs of life," Ned observed when they reached the station. Beside the trail stood a small cabin with a sign on it reading United States Forest Service, but grass was growing up in front of the door—the cabin seemed to be deserted.

"How do they get people and supplies up here?" Sammy wanted to know. "I don't see any roads."

"There *aren't* roads to some of these backcountry towers," Mike replied. "That's why they use helicopters."

"So that's the tower," Bess said, looking across the yard that separated it from the station. It was a squat, square box built on stilts forty feet in the air, with a stair zigzagging between the stilts. Halfway up was an open platform. "I'll bet there's a good view from up there."

"You're right," Mike told her. "Since these lookout towers

are built so that rangers can watch for fires, they have an unob- structed view of the whole country." He grinned. "Want to take a look? I'm going to go up and get that message out."

"We'll all go," Sammy decided.

"I'm not sure I can climb that high," Linda objected.

"You'll never have another chance like this one," Ralph told her.

"Oh, okay."

"Well, then, let's go," Mike said, and they started toward the tower.

Suddenly George clutched Nancy's sleeve. "Nancy! I saw somebody run behind that building over there!"

Nancy turned to see a blur of movement behind one of the rickety wooden sheds only a few yards away.

Linda gasped. "It's Max!" she cried when the figure stepped out and started toward them. "He's coming to kill us."

CHAPTER SIXTEEN

et's get him!" Tod shouted.

"Watch out," Mike cautioned. "He's got a club."

"That's okay," Tod said, his eyes narrowed to slits. "We can handle that."

"Wait," Ned said. "I think he just wants to talk."

But Tod and Mike ignored Ned and advanced threateningly toward Max.

"Hold on," Max rasped. He kept walking toward them. His shoulders slumped wearily, and he seemed to be dragging one foot. "I don't want to hurt anybody. All I want is to talk to Nancy."

"Then put that club down," Ned said reasonably, stepping forward and holding out both hands to show that they were empty. "Nobody's got any weapons here. Nancy will talk to you if you throw your weapon away."

"Not on your life," Max said with a gesture toward Tod and Mike.

He lifted the stick, and Nancy could see that he had driven a giant, lethal-looking spike into the end of it. "Stay back!" he rasped when Tod moved closer. "Where's Nancy Drew? It's a matter of life and death." A shadow of pain crossed his face, and he began to cough.

"Here I am," Nancy said, stepping forward beside Ned. She could hear Max's harsh, labored breathing. "What do you want?"

For an instant, distracted by Nancy's voice and by his own coughing, Max lowered the stick. Mike and Tod rushed him. Mike tackled him around the knees, bringing him down, and Tod tried to pin his arms behind his back. Max fought back with the strength of a madman, and the three rolled on the dusty ground in a silent, violent tangle. But after a moment, the two were too much for Max, and Tod managed to get astride him. He put his hands around Max's neck, trying to throttle him.

"Ned!" Nancy screamed, running toward them. "Stop him! We've *got* to hear what Max has to say! He may be our key to this mystery!"

Ned jumped in with the skill that made him Emerson's star quarterback. He grabbed Mike by the collar and tossed him several feet away. But as he reached for Tod, Tod jumped up and picked up the club Max had dropped.

"Now I've got you!" Tod shouted down at Max. "You're not going to get away with killing Paula!" He poised to strike, the spike glinting viciously at the end of the stick.

Suddenly Nancy lashed out with a hard, flying kick at the small of Tod's back. As she struck him, the club was knocked out of his hands and he fell to the ground, gasping.

Max had raised himself to his hands and knees, trying painfully to push himself up off the ground. Blood oozed out of the corner of his mouth. The gash over his right eye had opened up again. His other eye was already puffed and swelling where Tod had hit him. Max crouched and fell forward.

Ned took off his canvas belt and bent over Max, hauling him up to a sitting position. "I'm not going to hurt him, I'm just going to make sure he doesn't get away," he told Nancy. He pulled Max's arms behind his back and looped the belt twice around his forearms, before he pushed it through the buckle and cinched it tight.

Helplessly, Max dropped his head between his knees. Nancy leaned over him. It sounded as if he were trying to say something.

"It wasn't me!" he said, sucking in his breath with a hollow, whistling sound. "I didn't . . . I didn't kill Paula!"

"What?" Nancy and Ned said together.

Max coughed again. "It . . . it was the other way around," he gasped, attempting to pull himself up straight. "She . . ." His eyes glazed over, and he fell heavily to his side in the dirt. "Be careful," he whispered to Nancy, his voice fading. "She's after you."

"After me? But why? What are you trying to say, Max?"

"She's trying to kill you. She's not . . . she's not . . ." Max's head fell back limply.

Ned felt for a pulse. "He's passed out," he said grimly.

Nancy stared up at Ned. "Do you suppose he was telling

the truth?" she asked. "That he *didn't* kill Paula?"

"Max!" Bess came running up. She had ripped off the tail of her blouse and soaked it in water from the canteen. She knelt down beside Max and began to wipe the blood off his face. "Is he going to be all right?" she asked fearfully.

Ned stood up after freeing Max's hands. "It's hard to say," he replied, looking down on Max's unconscious face. "He's probably got some internal injuries—maybe some broken ribs, maybe worse." He scowled at Tod and Mike. "The beating didn't help any."

Tod hung his head. "It looked like he was going to try to get away. We were just making sure he didn't." Tod glanced up again. "What did he mean when he said he didn't kill Paula?"

"Maybe there was somebody *else* up there with them?" Mike said. "I don't know—do you suppose somebody else pushed Paula over the cliff?"

"And what about his warning to you?" Ned asked Nancy, with a puzzled look. "When Max said that Paula is out to kill you, he was talking like she's still alive."

"That's impossible," Tod scoffed. "We *saw* her fall from the cliff and into the water."

Nancy shook her head, frowning. "We'll have to wait until Max regains consciousness to be sure that's what happened. Then we can ask him some more questions."

"There's a shed over there," Ned said, pointing toward a group of weathered, ramshackle outbuildings. "And I see a folded-up tarp just inside the door. Let's put Max on the tarp and move him into the shed, where he'll be out of this sun."

It took a few minutes to move Max. The others stood silently, watching, as if they were afraid Max might come to and attack them.

When Max was lying on the floor of the shed, Mike straightened up and dusted off his hands, looking at his watch. "I'm going to go up to the tower and send off that message," he said. "It's nearly three o'clock now. If we don't let the rangers know right away that we're here, they might not be able to get us out before dark."

Nancy, Ned, and Bess decided to stay with Max while the others climbed the tower with Mike. They had been gone for five minutes or so when Max began to stir.

"Max," Nancy said urgently, bending over him. "Can you talk? Who pushed Paula over the cliff? Was somebody else up there with you?"

Max didn't answer. After opening his eyes he just stared, then lapsed into a delirious sleep.

"Oh," Bess moaned, twisting her fingers anxiously. "He looks like he's going to die."

"I'm going to go after Mike and tell him to ask the Forest Service to send a doctor with the helicopter," Nancy said suddenly, scrambling to her feet. She pulled out the tiny notebook and pencil that she always carried and handed it to Ned. "If he says anything you can understand—even if it sounds like nonsense—write it down."

"Okay," Ned promised.

Nancy started across the dusty yard of the ranger station toward the tower. She was deep in thought. Max had said that *he* didn't kill Paula. "It was the other way around," he had said. But that could only mean one thing: That Paula had tried to kill him.

The wind picked up suddenly, moaning around the tower.

Nancy began to climb the stairs. She was partway up when she caught a flash of movement below her. A slight figure dashed out of the dense woods that surrounded the ranger station and ran across the yard toward the tower. Staring unbelievingly at the runner, who had already begun to take the stairs toward her, two at a time, Nancy gripped the steel railing.

"Paula!" she gasped.

CHAPTER SEVENTEEN

Y es, it's me," Paula said, panting and out of breath. She clattered up the stairs toward Nancy. Her long hair was matted and full of twigs and brambles, her cold amber eyes wild and staring. In that instant, Nancy realized that Paula was out for blood.

"What do you want?" She held Paula's eyes with her own as she gingerly backed up the stairs.

"I want you," Paula said over the roar of the wind. "You're the one I've been after all along. I'm going to kill you!"

Nancy sensed that if she could keep Paula talking, she might be able to distract her. At least she could stave off an attack for a few minutes until Paula was in a position where she could be overpowered.

"Why are you trying to kill me?" Nancy said. "I don't even know you."

"Are you sure?" Paula asked, baring her teeth in a smile. Her amber eyes glittered like the eyes of the rattlesnake. She came up another step. "Does the name Peter Hancock mean anything to you?"

"Peter Hancock?" Nancy was genuinely puzzled. "No," she said. "Why should it?" And then she remembered. Suddenly she knew where she had seen those strange amber eyes.

Peter Hancock was the name of an embezzler who had worked as an accountant at a bank in New York. It had been Nancy's careful detective work that had uncovered his fraudulent activities and sent him to prison.

Menacingly, Paula stepped closer. "Peter Hancock was my father. *You* sent him to prison, and now he's dead!" Paula's eyes were gleaming. "He escaped a few months ago. But he died — in this very wilderness. And you're going to die here, too."

"So," Nancy said quickly, "you rigged this whole thing to get me here."

"That's right," Paula replied, brushing a strand of her matted hair out of her eyes. "There wasn't any contest — just like there wasn't any White Water Rafting, Incorporated. Both those tricks were part of a plan to get you on the river, where I could teach you a lesson, once and for all."

"So you picked your winners at random?"

"Yes," Paula bragged.

"Well, that was smart," Nancy said, stalling. If only the group on top of the tower could hear her above the wind. "People are always putting their names into a box for one contest or another. I guess you figured they'd think they'd just forgotten about entering this one."

"You got it, Nancy Drew," Paula sneered. "You're bright, all right. Too bad you're not bright enough to get yourself out of the mess you're in now."

Nancy ignored her. "And you sent the letter to George

because you knew that she'd be enthusiastic about a white water rafting trip," Nancy prompted.

"Of course I knew it. I've been doing my homework. I know all about you and your friends. It was a sure thing that George Fayne would ask you to come on this trip with her."

"The map? The missing barricade?"

"They were easy," Paula said scornfully. "You know, you would have made a lot less trouble for me if you'd sailed off that cliff." She sighed. "But I'm glad those tricks didn't work. It's going to be a lot more fun to watch you die."

"What about the slipped mooring line?" Nancy asked before Paula could make a move. "Was that another one of your clever tricks?"

"I figured it would be interesting to watch the expressions on your friends' faces when we fished your body out from under the falls," Paula explained. She stepped up closer to Nancy. "But I'm getting tired of all this talk."

Nancy retreated a step higher. Just three or four more steps and she'd be on the tower's lower platform. If she could lure Paula up there, she might be able to maneuver her into a more vulnerable position. "Max—" Nancy said, "was he in on your plan?"

Paula gave a disdainful laugh. "Not at all—at least not until he began to figure out what was going on. Of course, I didn't count on his capsizing the raft—"

"I guess that was a stroke of good luck for you," Nancy put in. "It put one of the rafts out of commission. When that happened, you probably thought it would be a better idea to get me off into the woods and kill me there."

"Very impressive brainwork, Detective Drew. When the first raft was destroyed, I had to finish off the other one, too—to keep you from going downriver the next morning. And I nearly did get you in the woods."

"You certainly did. If it hadn't been for Ned—"

"The boulder would have crushed you," Paula finished. She smiled cruelly.

"You know, I've got to admire you," Nancy said, grudgingly. "We actually thought *you* were dead—that Max had killed you and was out to kill us, too. I bet I know how you arranged that," Nancy said.

"I don't care if you know or not," Paula snapped, her face twisting. She lunged for Nancy, surprising her.

Nancy took two steps up and back but couldn't escape Paula's grasp on her arm. They fell together onto the wooden deck of the platform. Nancy felt Paula's elbow dig into her side. She rolled onto her back and raised her feet, catching Paula's shoulders. Then she shoved as hard as she could.

With a howl of rage, Paula launched herself forward from the railing. "I'm going to kill you!" she shouted, but this time Nancy was ready for her. As Paula rushed with full force, Nancy sidestepped adroitly and tripped her.

For an instant, Paula's arms flailed wildly. Then she crashed against the weather-beaten wood. There was a splintering sound as the railing gave way under her weight. She tried to catch herself. Then, in a clumsy slow-motion swan dive, she fell over the edge, screaming.

The scream broke off, and Nancy looked over the splintered railing. Paula was sprawled faceup and motionless on the concrete apron at the foot of the tower, one arm bent under her, eyes staring up at the sky.

The wind had died down. The air was perfectly still.

From the contorted position in which Paula lay, Nancy knew Paula was dead.

"Hey! What's going on down there?"

Nancy looked above her and saw Sammy peering down at Paula's sprawled body. Sammy looked as if she were seeing a ghost. "Is Paula really dead?" Sammy asked.

Bess was kneeling next to the body, feeling for a pulse. "I think so," she called up soberly.

Nancy leaned weakly against the solid part of the railing until Ned streaked up the stairs and pulled her into his arms. After clinging together for a moment or two, they followed the group, who had just raced down from the lookout tower.

"I don't understand," Linda said. "How did Paula survive the fall from the cliff?"

"She never fell off the cliff. Max did—or, rather, he was—"

"Pushed."

It was Max's voice. Nancy looked up. Max was leaning against the doorjamb of the shed.

Ned and Tod hurried over to Max and helped him walk across the yard.

Bess approached him anxiously. "Are you sure you're up to this? The helicopter is bringing a doctor in a little while."

"I'm all right," Max said weakly, but his breathing came in jagged gasps.

"Paula pushed you—is that what you're saying?" Ralph asked in astonishment. "But we heard Paula shout. . . . And we saw . . ." He stopped. "Oh, I see," he said. "Paula faked it—the shout and everything."

Ned's arm had been around Nancy. "You're trembling," he said to her. "Are you cold? Do you want to borrow my jacket again?"

Nancy gave one last nervous shiver. Then all at once she smiled at Ned. "No, thanks," she said, as if she had a secret. She turned to Max. "But that's what Paula did, didn't she, Max—give you her jacket?" Max nodded weakly and tried to talk. "Let me tell it," Nancy said.

"When you got to the top of the cliff, you confronted Paula with what you knew, and then you got into a big argument. She distracted you and knocked you over the head with something—a rock maybe?"

"Yes," Max said, fingering the gash over his eye.

"And when you fell," Nancy went on, "that's when we heard the thump. The jacket—now that was a clever move on Paula's part, since she knew I'd be on my guard against her every second if I thought she'd pushed *you* off the cliff. That's why she had to make believe *she* was the victim.

"And until I remembered that Ned had loaned me his jacket,

she almost had me fooled. It took me a while, but suddenly I realized how easy it would have been for her to put her jacket on you—it was big enough."

Max coughed and spoke. "The trick boomeranged, though. Her jacket is what saved my life. It was so big, air got trapped in it and helped keep me afloat until I could grab on to a limb and pull myself out."

Wincing in pain, he sank to the ground. "But I think I broke a couple of ribs in the fall."

Bess knelt beside him and wiped away the beads of sweat on his forehead.

Sammy looked from Max to Paula's body. "But why did Paula do it? Was she responsible for holing the raft and stealing the diode out of the radio?"

"Paula was responsible for everything," Nancy said. "She invented the contest—"

"Invented the contest?" Mike exclaimed.

"Yes, it was a trick to get *me* here."

"See?" Linda said smugly to Ralph. "I told you the whole thing had to be a joke."

"Some joke," George said bitterly. She turned to Nancy. "But I don't understand why Paula did all this."

"Revenge," Nancy replied simply, and she told everyone the story of Peter Hancock.

"So she didn't care who else got hurt in the process," Tod put in, shaking his head.

"You're right," Max said, sounding the slightest bit stronger.

"On the cliff, she said she was going to kill me because I knew too much. And she told me she'd kill everybody else if she had to—just to get to Nancy Drew." He turned to Nancy with a lopsided grin. "That's what I was trying to tell you when I pulled you into the woods this morning. I didn't mean to knock you out. I just wanted to warn you about Paula."

"I wasn't sure about the mooring line," Max went on, "but I saw her push the boulder down on you yesterday—"

"You did?"

"Yeah, and when I saw you walking by yourself, I figured it would be a good time to let you know about the danger you were in."

Nancy looked at Max curiously. "When did you realize what was going on?" she asked. "Was it before you saw Paula take the compass?"

"I guess it was when I began to suspect that she was the one who holed the raft," Max answered. "You see, when you told me you were a detective, I suddenly remembered I'd seen your picture in the local newspaper after Peter Hancock's trial.

"I realized then that you were the person who'd blown the whistle on Paula's father. And yesterday morning, when Paula made the crack about the 'famous girl detective,' I began to suspect that she had it in for you."

"Hmm," said Nancy. "You didn't suspect Paula till yesterday? Then you couldn't have been the person who made the phone call warning me not to take this trip, could you have, Max?" Nancy turned slowly to Mercedes. Mercedes stepped forward wearily. "You were trying to protect Paula, isn't that right?" Nancy asked her gently.

Mercedes broke into tears. "If you'd known her before her father died, you would understand—" She looked up. "I'm so sorry, Nancy. I never wanted you to get hurt—or anyone else, either. Really."

"How did you know what Paula was planning?" Nancy asked.

"Well, I knew how distraught Paula had been since my uncle Peter died—you know, they found his body only a few miles from here. Anyway, I found your name on the list of 'contest winners' that Paula gave me when she told me about the trip."

Nancy frowned. "Didn't you question her?"

"Sure I did, but she said she just wanted to teach you a little lesson. I called you just in case, I guess. I thought the call might make you bring along some extra protection."

"Ah," Nancy said. "That's why you were snooping around in my pack—you were trying to see if I had a weapon or something, to scare Paula with it if I had to."

Mercedes nodded tearfully. "Sort of. But I don't know what I would have done if I'd found one. I wanted to protect you, but I wanted to protect Paula, and after she was dead, I didn't think there was any point—"

"—in dragging up the past," Nancy finished.

Ned got the tarp out of the shed and covered up Paula's body. "She must have been overwhelmed with grief over her father's death. It just . . . changed her," he said grimly.

"It did," Mercedes said, sobbing heavily. "It did."

• • •

Later that afternoon, they boarded one of the helicopters that came to pick them up.

"Maybe next time you'll listen," Bess said, trying to comb the tangles out of her hair with her fingers. "We could have been sunning ourselves for the last three days." Then she brightened, glancing toward the front of the helicopter where Max was lying on a stretcher. "But I've met Max. So it wasn't a total loss."

Ned settled himself next to Nancy. "It wasn't a romantic holiday," he said softly to her, "but at least I had you in sight the whole time."

Nancy sighed, thinking of how scratched and bitten she must look. "Yes, and *what* a sight."

"Well, you know what they say about love," Ned said, laughing.

"No, what's that?" Nancy asked, raising her voice over the clatter of the helicopter engines.

"Love is blind," Ned shouted into her ear, and leaned over to kiss her.

"It's a good thing!" Nancy exclaimed, and kissed him back.

TO SAVE THE WORLD, YOU NEED AN UNSTOPPABLE GIRL.

EBOOK EDITIONS ALSO AVAILABLE

Simon Pulse simonandschuster.com/teen

RIVETED

BY *simon* teen ♥

BELIEVE IN YOUR SHELF

Visit RivetedLit.com & connect with us on social to:

DISCOVER NEW YA READS

READ BOOKS FOR FREE

DISCUSS YOUR FAVORITES

SHARE YOUR IDEAS

ENTER SWEEPSTAKES FOR THE CHANCE TO WIN BOOKS

Follow @SimonTeen on

to stay up to date with all things Riveted!